THE AMERICAN REVOLUTION, 1776

PHOTOS ©: 150 BOTTOM LEFT: COURTESY OF LAUREN TARSHIS; 150 BOTTOM RIGHT: ROBERT K. CHIN - STOREFRONTS/ALAMY STOCK PHOTO; 151 TOP: COURTESY OF THE WALSH GALLERY AT SETON HALL UNIVERSITY, FIM610; 151 LEFT: GRANDRIVER/GETTY IMAGES; 151 CENTER RIGHT: STUART CAHILL/MEDIANEWS GROUP/BOSTON HERALD/GETTY IMAGES; 151 BOTTOM RIGHT: RICK EGAN/THE SALT LAKE TRIBUNE/AP IMAGES; 152 TOP: HAROLD M. LAMBERT/KEAN COLLECTION/ARCHIVE PHOTOS/GETTY IMAGES; 152 BOTTOM LEFT: STEVE STANKIEWICZ FOR SCHOLASTIC INC.; 152 BOTTOM RIGHT: NATIONAL GALLERIES OF SCOTLAND/GETTY IMAGES; 153 TOP: HULTON ARCHIVE/GETTY IMAGES; 153 BOTTOM: GL ARCHIVE/ALAMY STOCK PHOTO; 154 TOP: PIERCE ARCHIVE LLC/ BUYENLARGE/GETTY IMAGES; 154 CENTER LEFT: B CHRISTOPHER/ALAMY STOCK PHOTO; 154 CENTER RIGHT: NORTH WIND PICTURE ARCHIVES/ALAMY STOCK PHOTO; 154 BOTTOM: NORTH WIND PICTURE ARCHIVES/ALAMY STOCK PHOTO; 155 TOP: KEITH LANCE/GETTY IMAGES; 155 BOTTOM: STANIA KASULA/ALAMY STOCK PHOTO; 156 TOP: GRAPHICAARTIS/GETTY IMAGES; 156 CENTER TOP: WWING/GETTY IMAGES; 156 CENTER BOTTOM: CENTRAL PRESS/GETTY IMAGES; 156 BOTTOM LEFT: FPG/ARCHIVE PHOTOS/GETTY IMAGES; 156 BOTTOM RIGHT: NATIONAL PHOTO/BUYENLARGE/GETTY IMAGES.

SPECIAL THANKS TO BARNET SCHECTER

WHILE INSPIRED BY REAL EVENTS AND HISTORICAL CHARACTERS, THIS IS A WORK OF FICTION AND DOES NOT CLAIM TO BE HISTORICALLY ACCURATE OR TO PORTRAY FACTUAL EVENTS OR RELATIONSHIPS. PLEASE KEEP IN MIND THAT REFERENCES TO ACTUAL PERSONS, LIVING OR DEAD, BUSINESS ESTABLISHMENTS, EVENTS, OR LOCALES MAY NOT BE FACTUALLY ACCURATE, BUT RATHER FICTIONALIZED BY THE AUTHOR.

LIBRARY OF CONGRESS CONTROL NUMBER AVAILABLE
ISBN 978-1-338-82518-3

10 9 8 7 6 5 4 3 2 1 23 24 25 26 27

PRINTED IN THE U.S.A. 40
FIRST EDITION, SEPTEMBER 2023
EDITED BY KATIE WOEHR AND BECKY HERRICK
LETTERING BY JANICE CHIANG
INKS AND COLOR BY LEO TRINIDAD
BOOK DESIGN BY KATIE FITCH AND BECKY JAMES
CREATIVE DIRECTOR: YAFFA JASKOLL

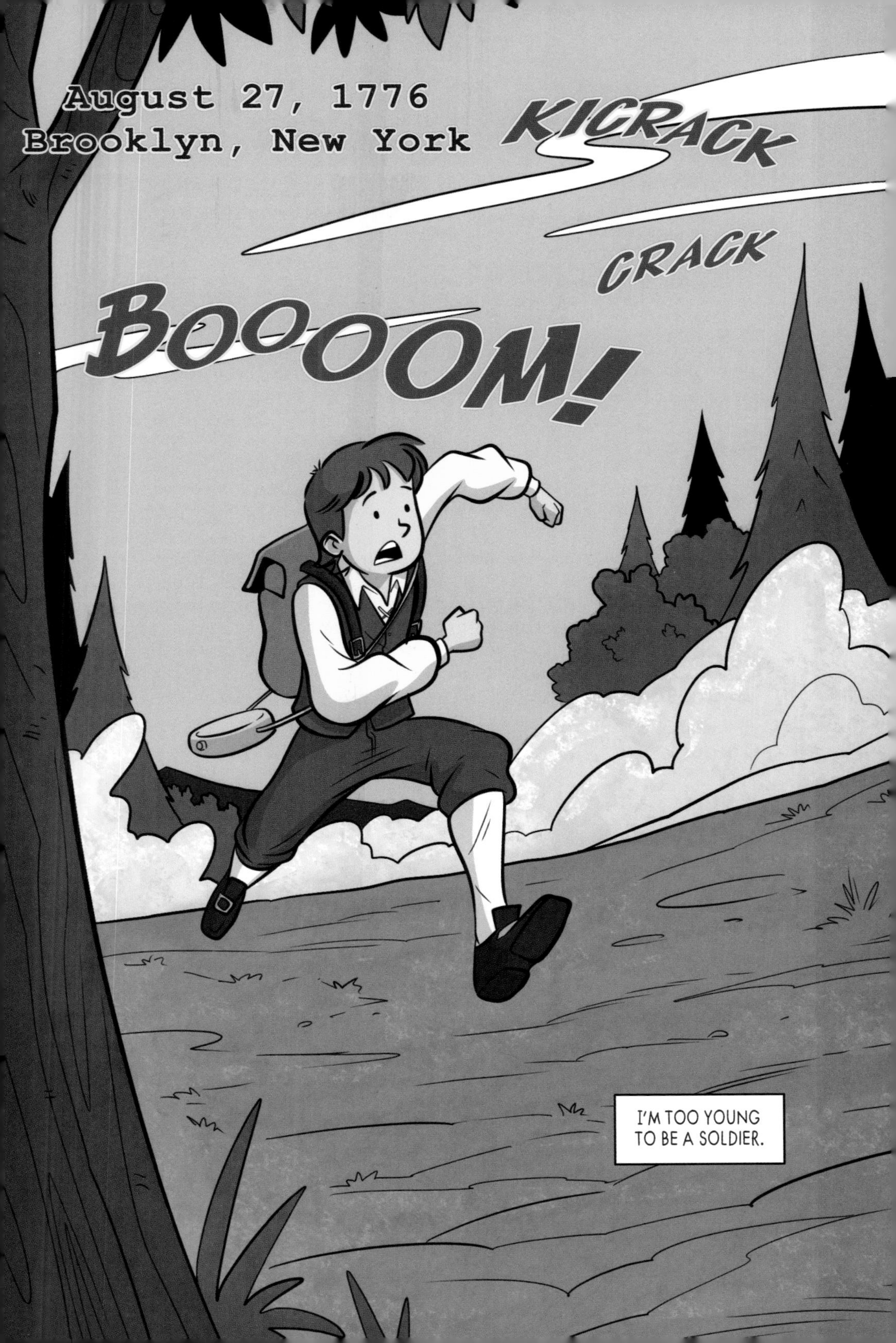
August 27, 1776
Brooklyn, New York
KICRACK
CRACK
BOOOOM!
I'M TOO YOUNG TO BE A SOLDIER.

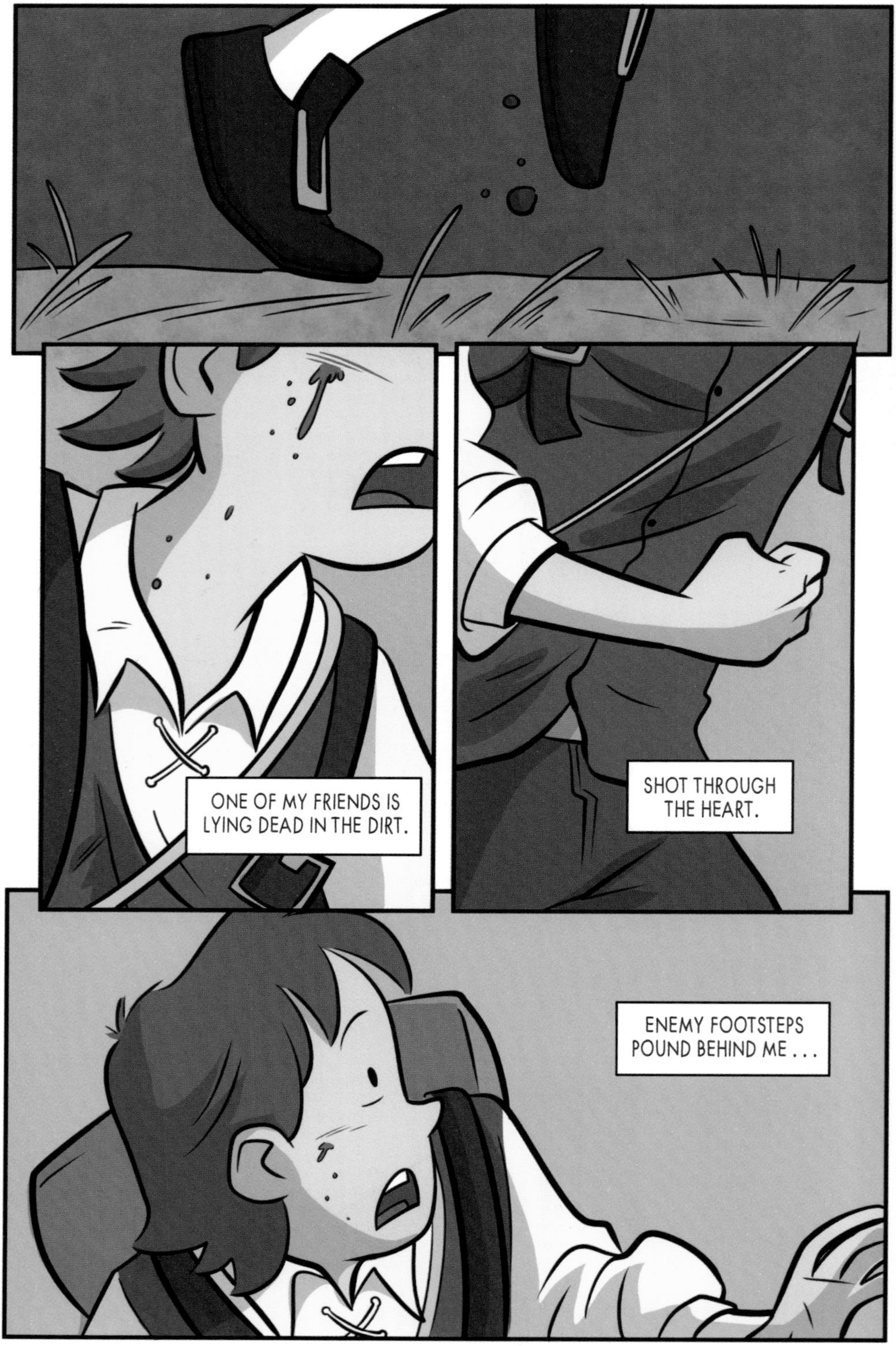
ONE OF MY FRIENDS IS LYING DEAD IN THE DIRT.
SHOT THROUGH THE HEART.
ENEMY FOOTSTEPS POUND BEHIND ME . . .

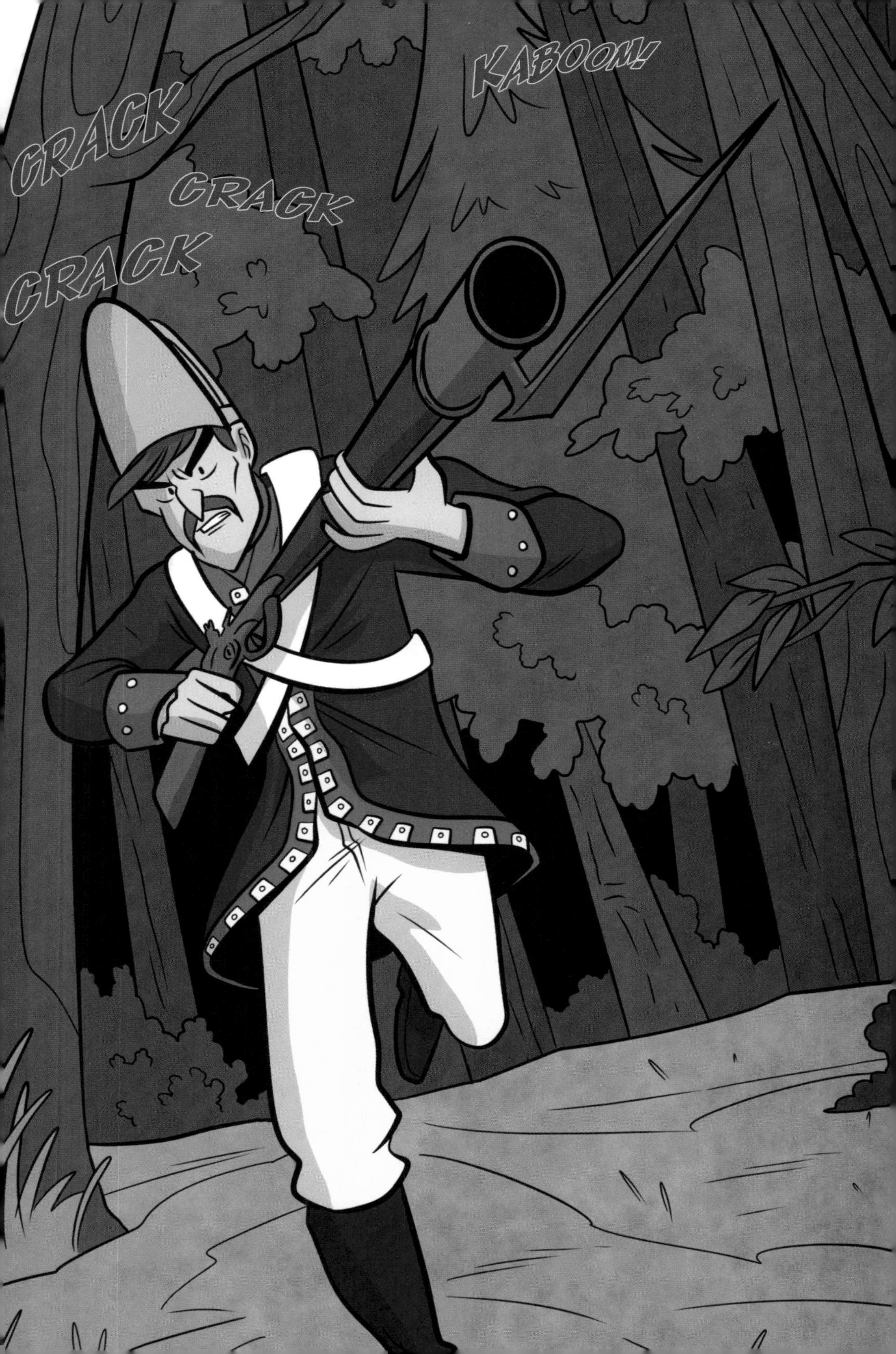
CRACK
CRACK
CRACK
KABOOM!

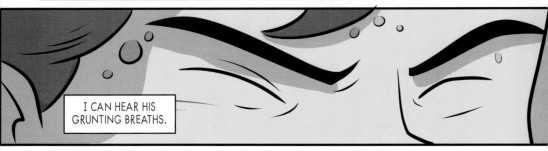

I CAN HEAR HIS GRUNTING BREATHS.

I WANT TO SCREAM—

— I'M NOT A SOLDIER!

I BRACE MYSELF FOR THE END.

A FLASH . . .

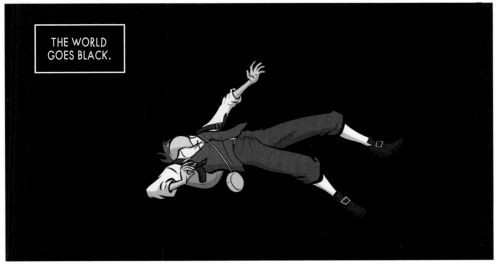

THE WORLD GOES BLACK.

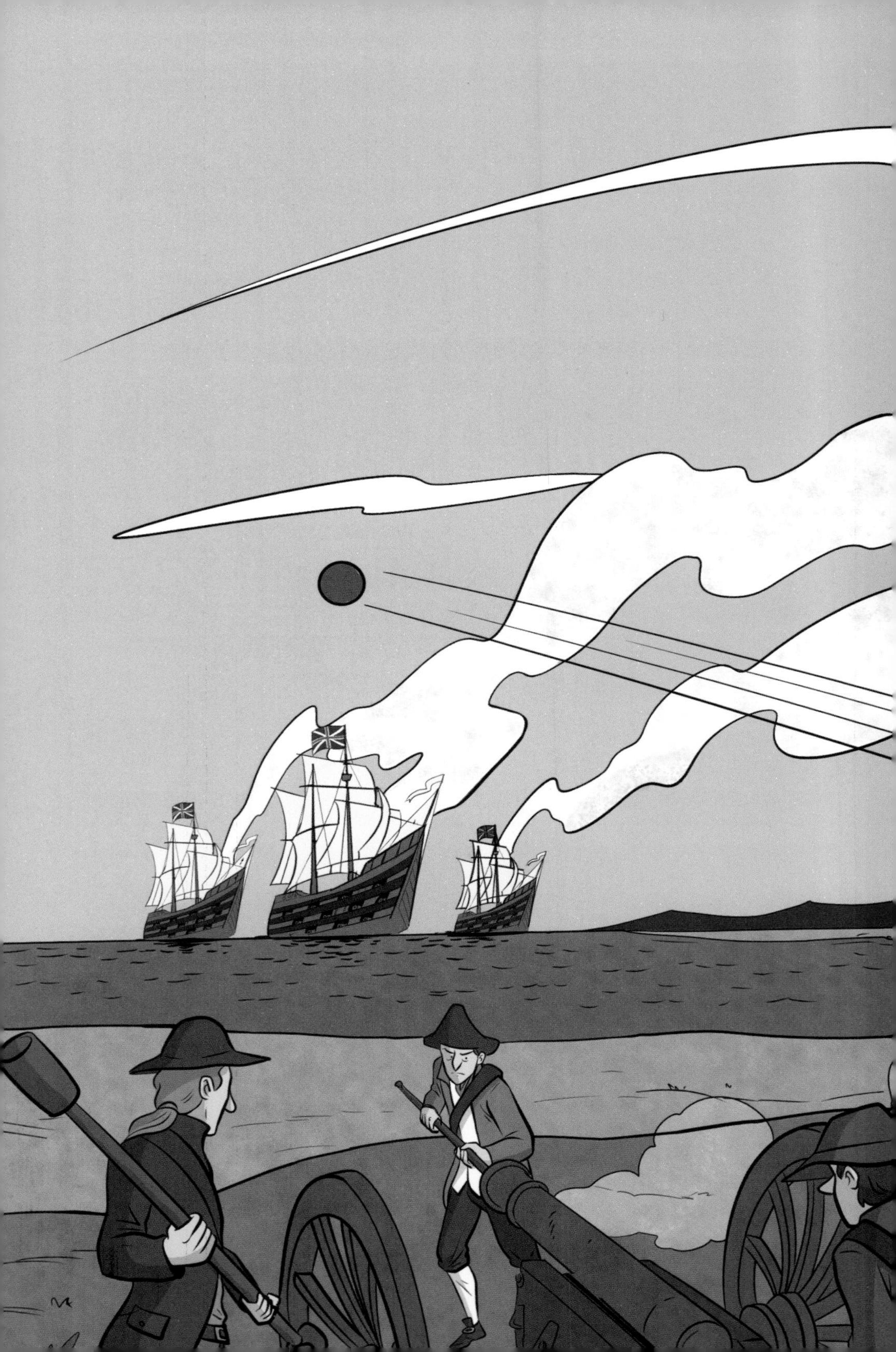

I SURVIVED

THE AMERICAN REVOLUTION, 1776

BASED ON THE NOVEL IN THE *NEW YORK TIMES* BESTSELLING SERIES BY LAUREN TARSHIS

ADAPTED BY GEORGIA BALL
WITH ART BY LEO TRINIDAD

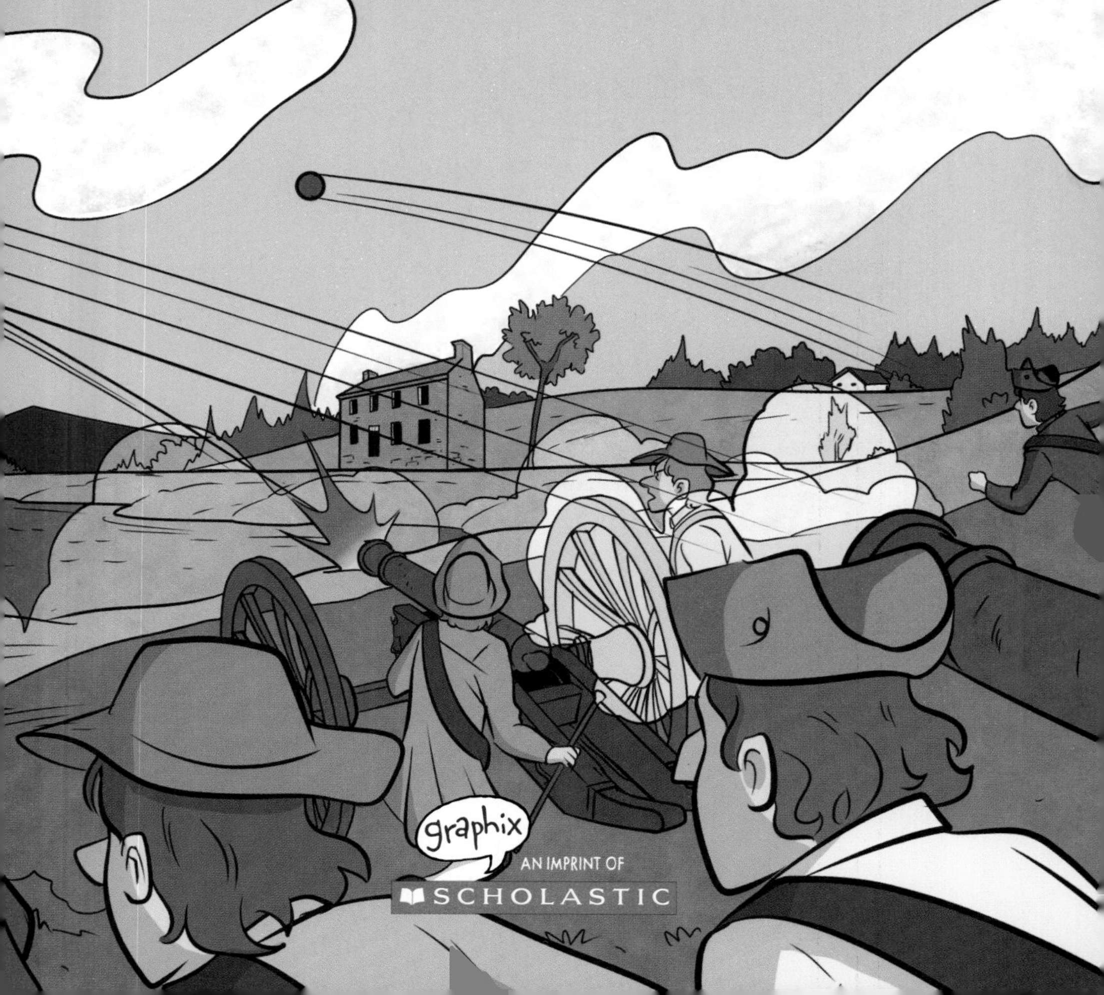

graphix
AN IMPRINT OF
SCHOLASTIC

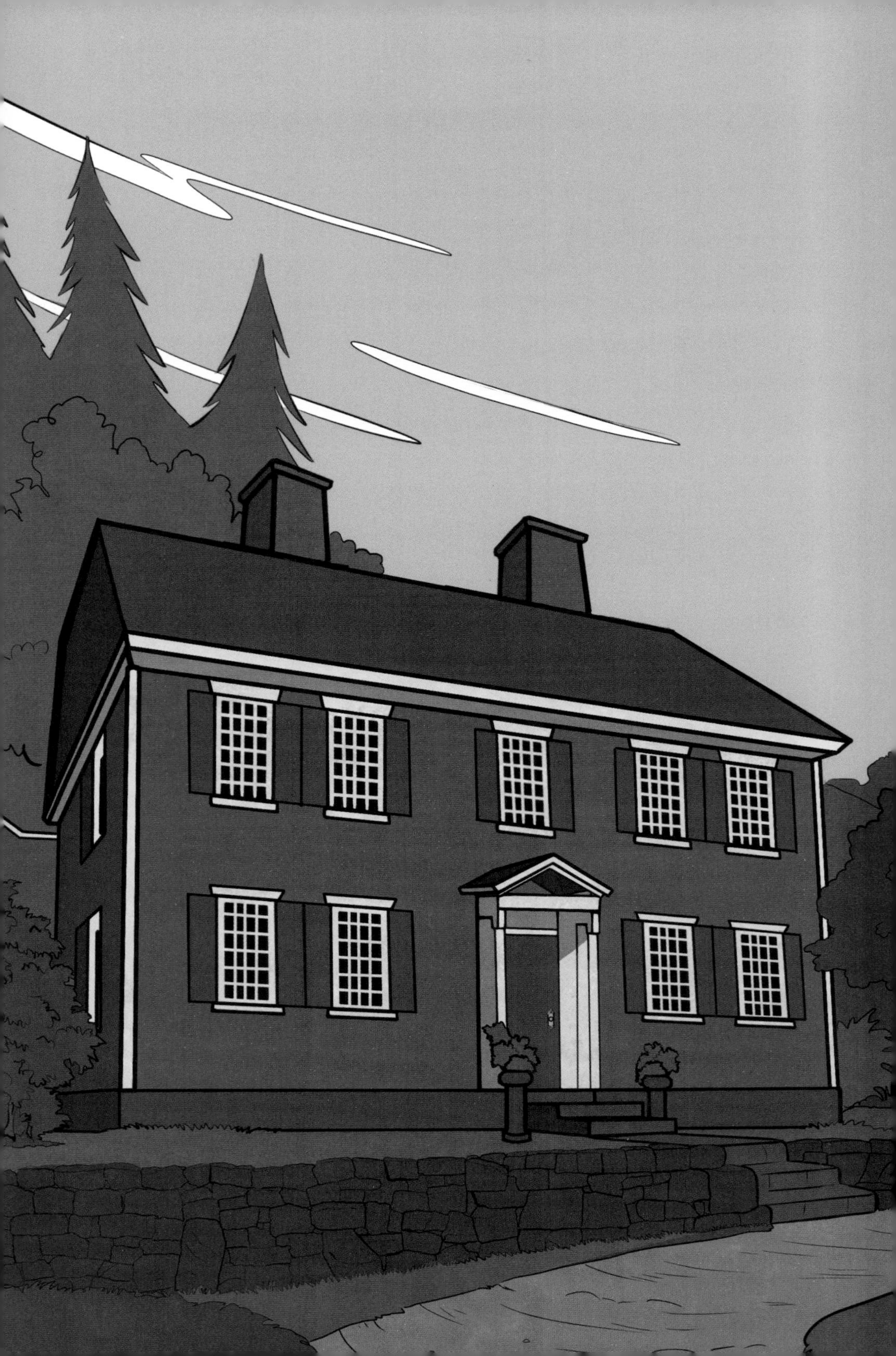

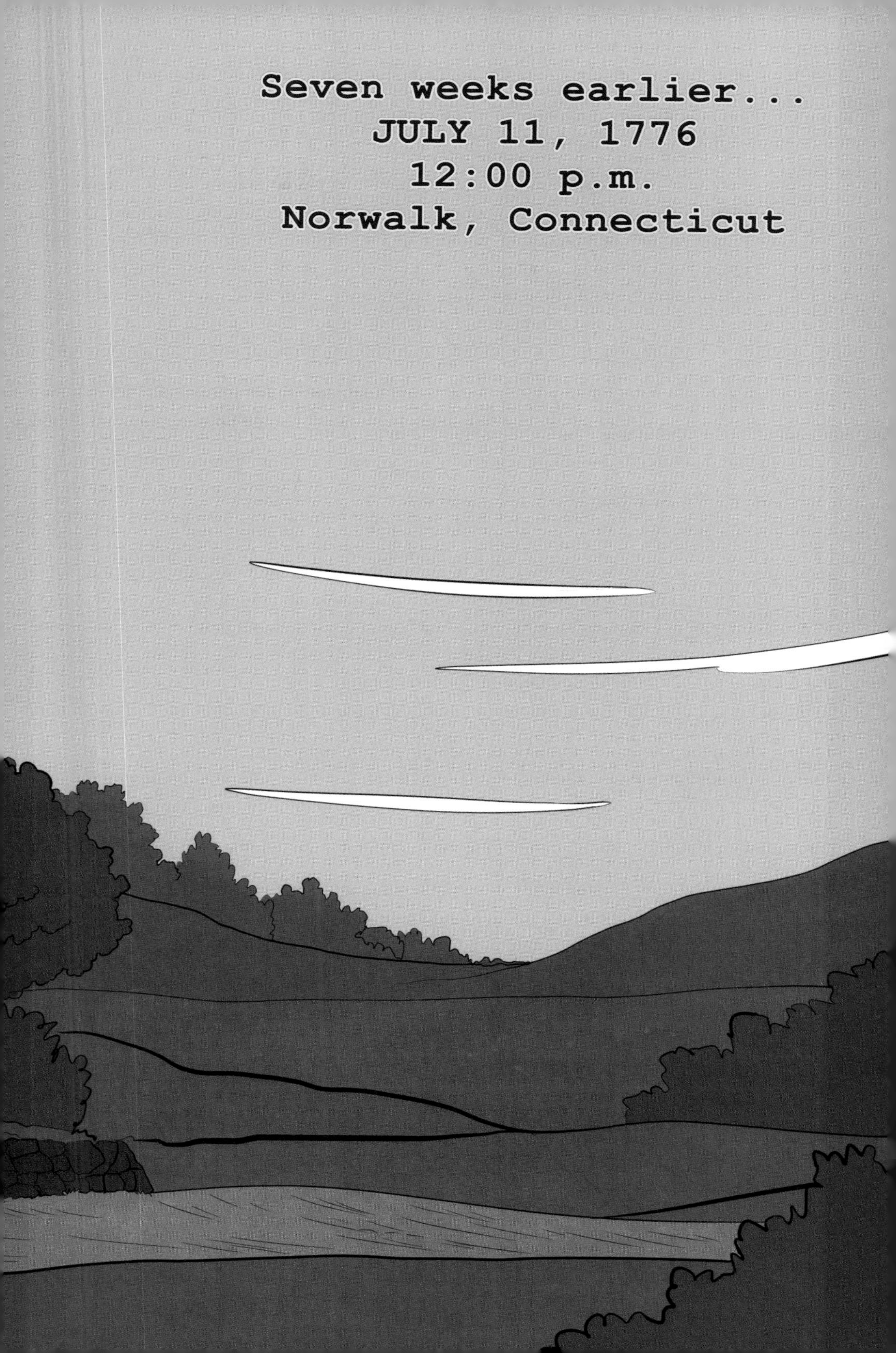
Seven weeks earlier...
JULY 11, 1776
12:00 p.m.
Norwalk, Connecticut

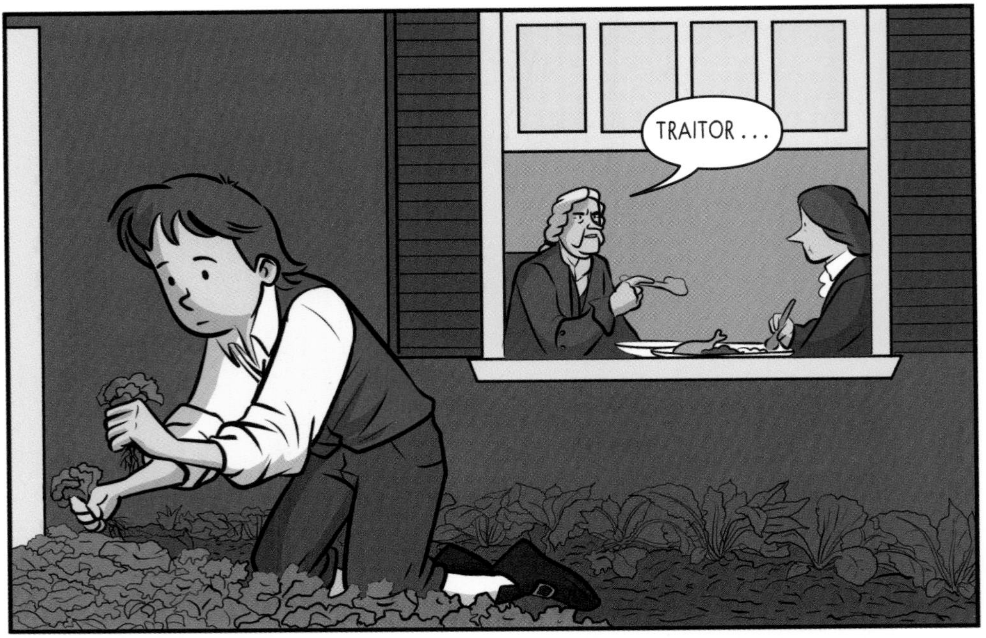
TRAITOR . . .

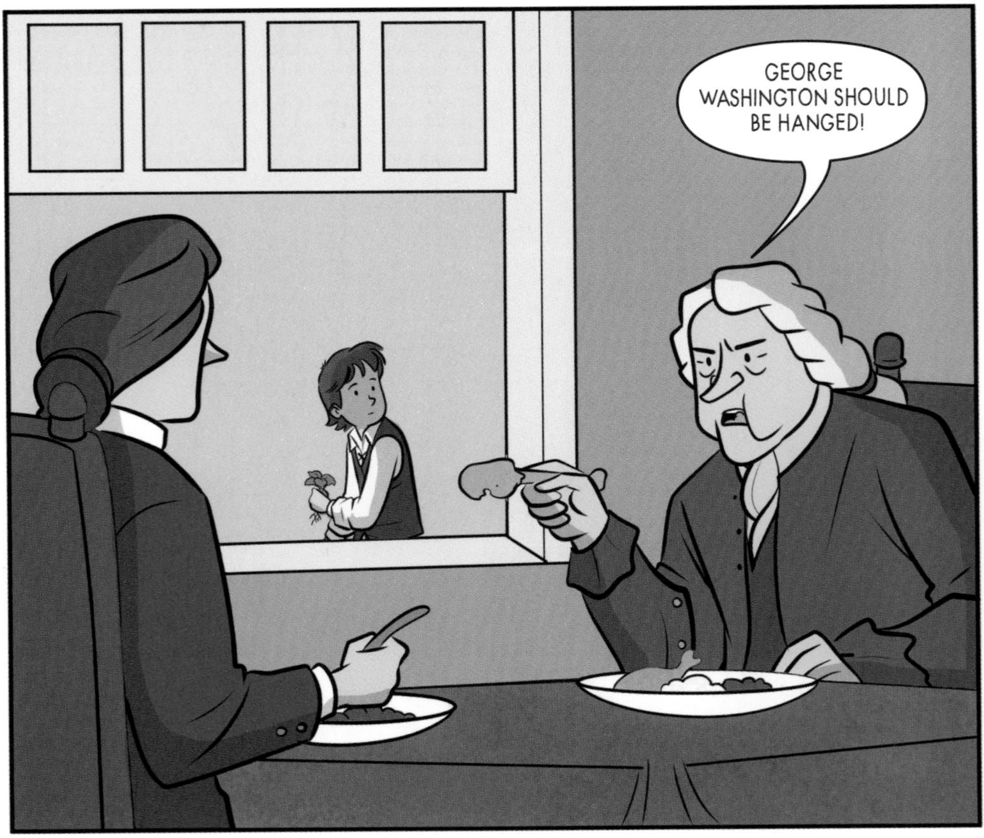
GEORGE WASHINGTON SHOULD BE HANGED!

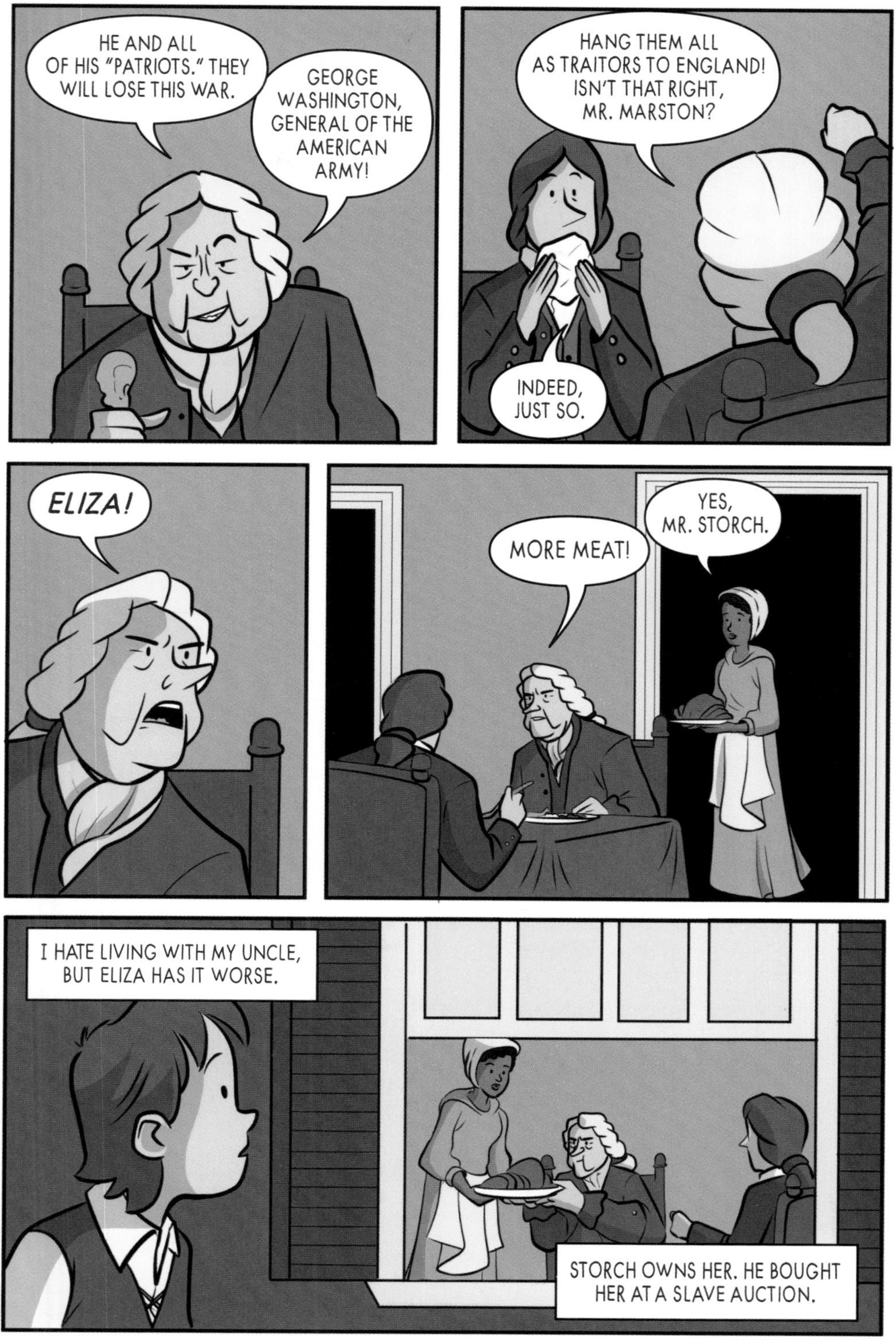
HE AND ALL OF HIS "PATRIOTS." THEY WILL LOSE THIS WAR.
GEORGE WASHINGTON, GENERAL OF THE AMERICAN ARMY!
HANG THEM ALL AS TRAITORS TO ENGLAND! ISN'T THAT RIGHT, MR. MARSTON?
INDEED, JUST SO.
ELIZA!
MORE MEAT!
YES, MR. STORCH.
I HATE LIVING WITH MY UNCLE, BUT ELIZA HAS IT WORSE.
STORCH OWNS HER. HE BOUGHT HER AT A SLAVE AUCTION.

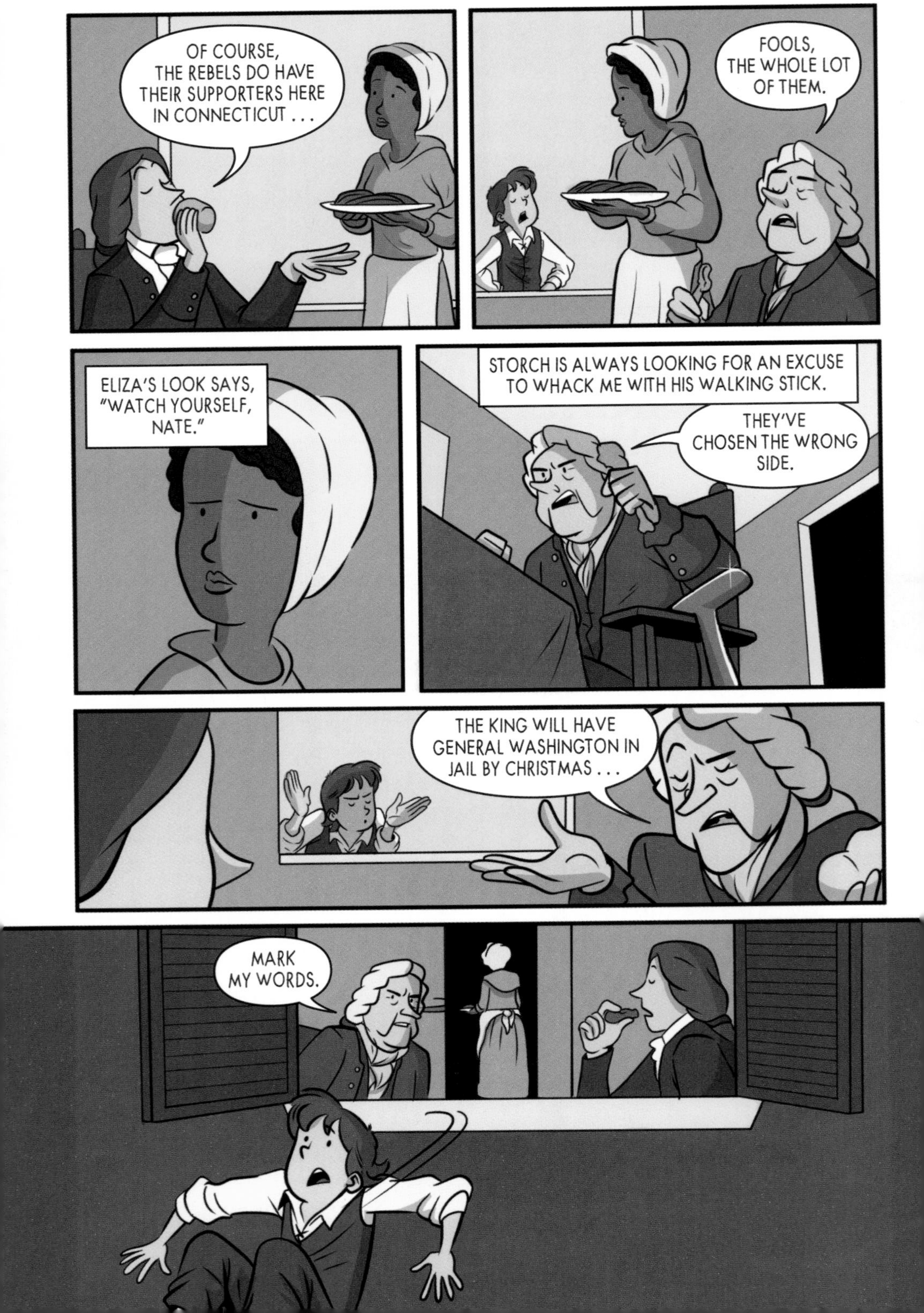
OF COURSE, THE REBELS DO HAVE THEIR SUPPORTERS HERE IN CONNECTICUT . . .
FOOLS, THE WHOLE LOT OF THEM.
ELIZA'S LOOK SAYS, "WATCH YOURSELF, NATE."
STORCH IS ALWAYS LOOKING FOR AN EXCUSE TO WHACK ME WITH HIS WALKING STICK.
THEY'VE CHOSEN THE WRONG SIDE.
THE KING WILL HAVE GENERAL WASHINGTON IN JAIL BY CHRISTMAS . . .
MARK MY WORDS.

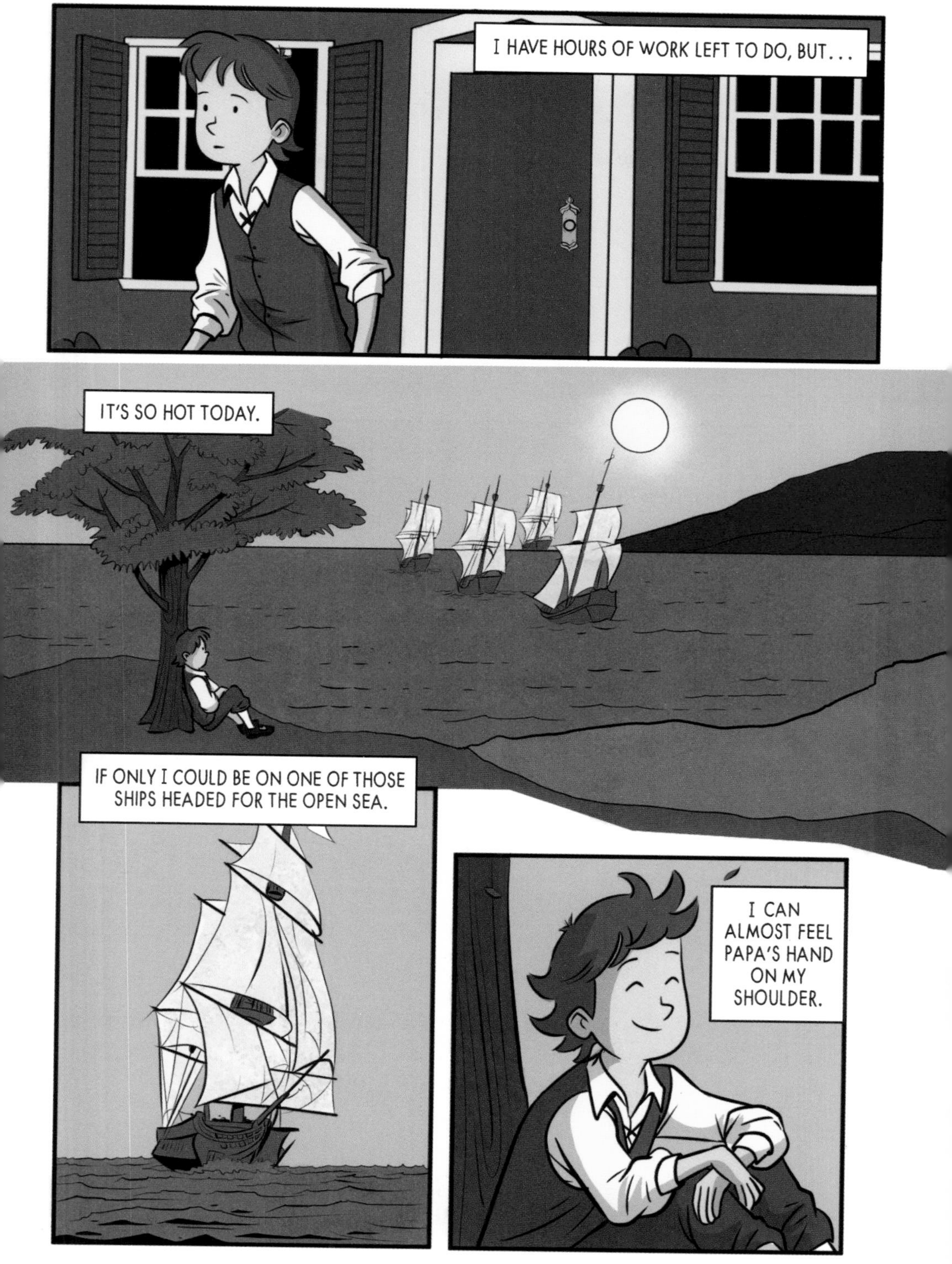
I HAVE HOURS OF WORK LEFT TO DO, BUT...
IT'S SO HOT TODAY.
IF ONLY I COULD BE ON ONE OF THOSE SHIPS HEADED FOR THE OPEN SEA.
I CAN ALMOST FEEL PAPA'S HAND ON MY SHOULDER.

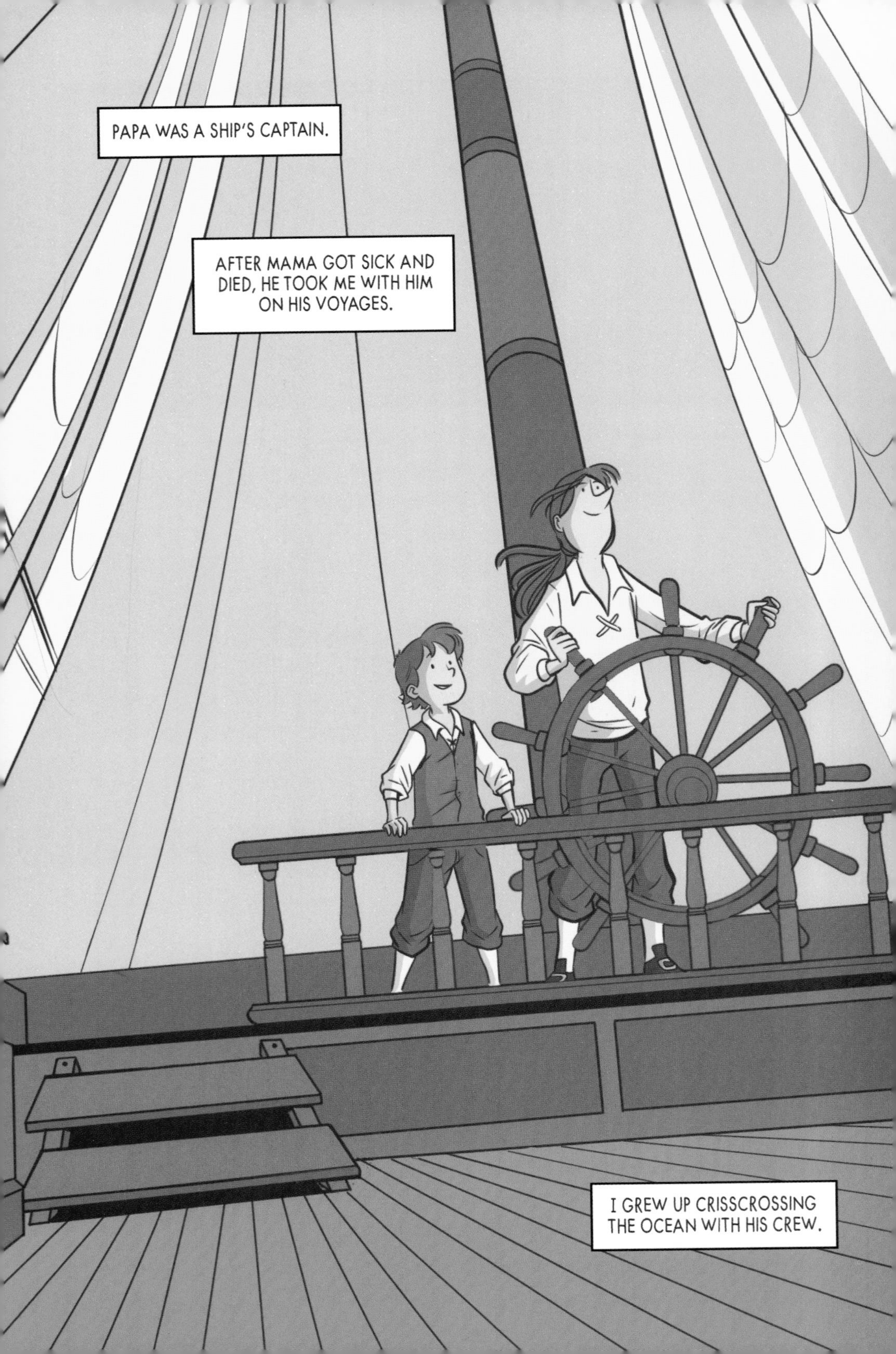
PAPA WAS A SHIP'S CAPTAIN.
AFTER MAMA GOT SICK AND DIED, HE TOOK ME WITH HIM ON HIS VOYAGES.
I GREW UP CRISSCROSSING THE OCEAN WITH HIS CREW.

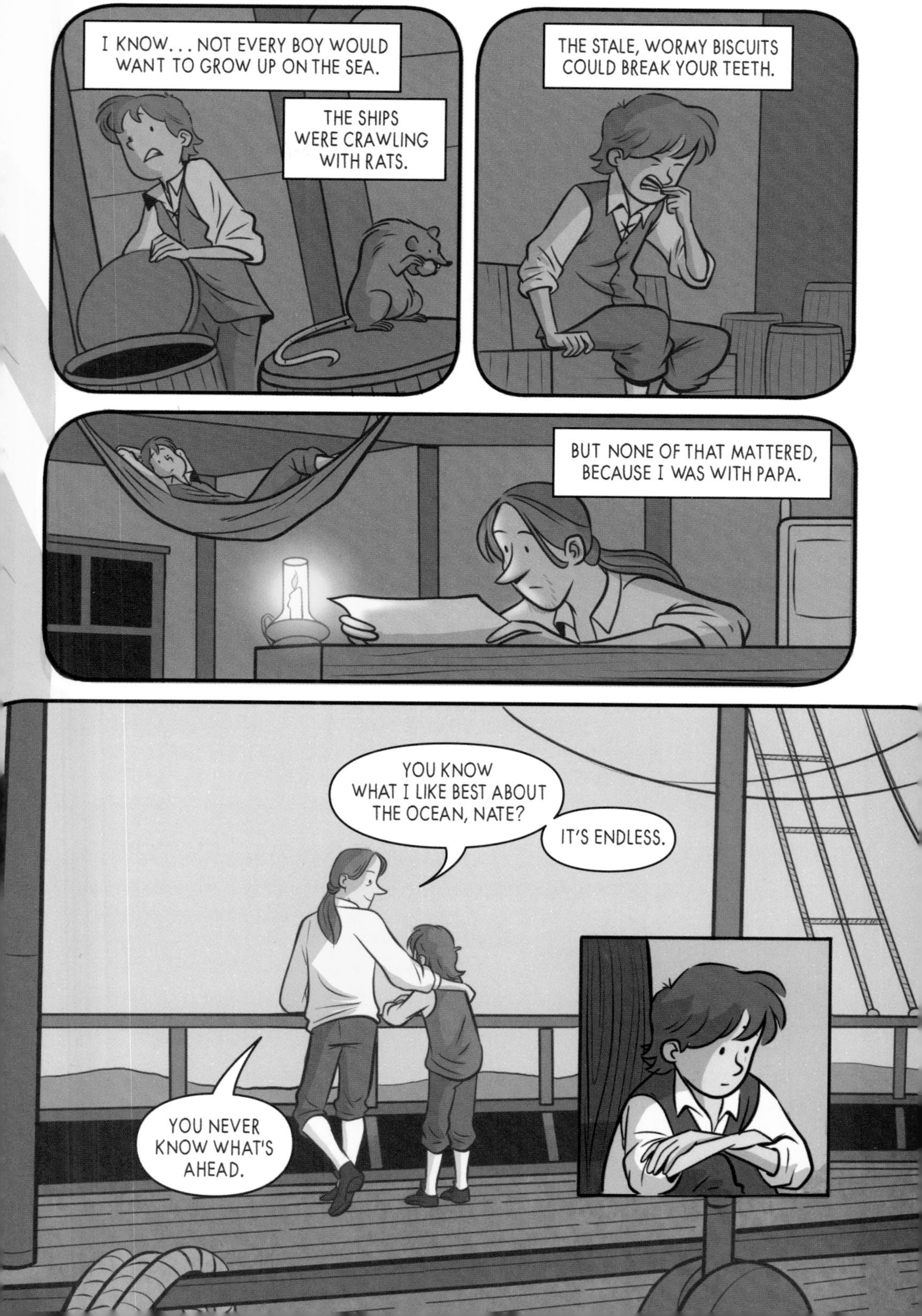
I KNOW. . . NOT EVERY BOY WOULD WANT TO GROW UP ON THE SEA.
THE SHIPS WERE CRAWLING WITH RATS.
THE STALE, WORMY BISCUITS COULD BREAK YOUR TEETH.
BUT NONE OF THAT MATTERED, BECAUSE I WAS WITH PAPA.
YOU KNOW WHAT I LIKE BEST ABOUT THE OCEAN, NATE?
IT'S ENDLESS.
YOU NEVER KNOW WHAT'S AHEAD.

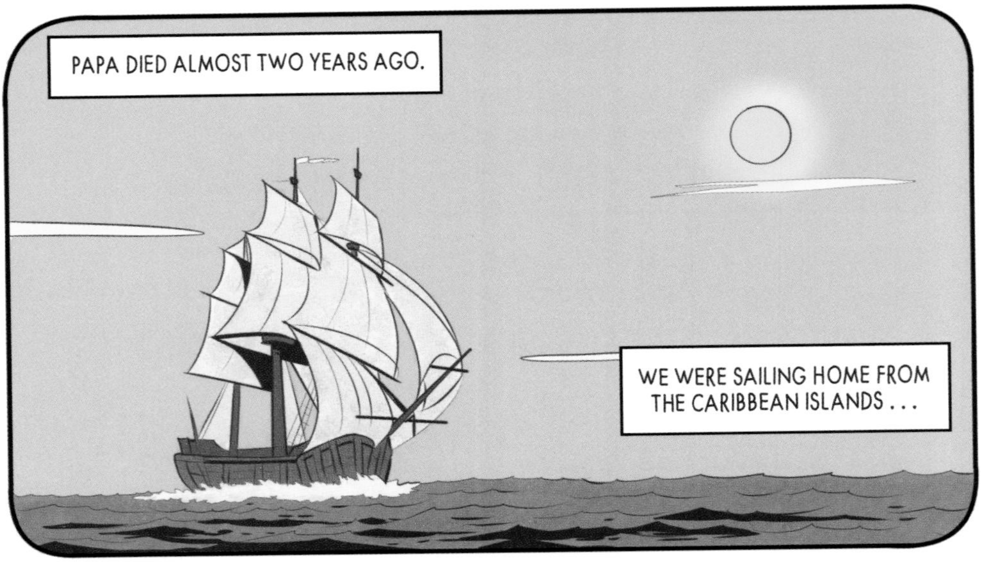
PAPA DIED ALMOST TWO YEARS AGO.
WE WERE SAILING HOME FROM THE CARIBBEAN ISLANDS . . .

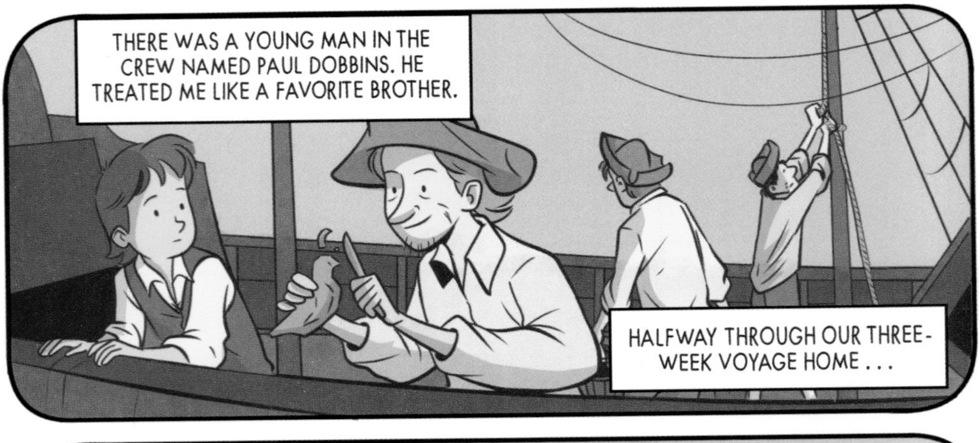
THERE WAS A YOUNG MAN IN THE CREW NAMED PAUL DOBBINS. HE TREATED ME LIKE A FAVORITE BROTHER.
HALFWAY THROUGH OUR THREE-WEEK VOYAGE HOME . . .

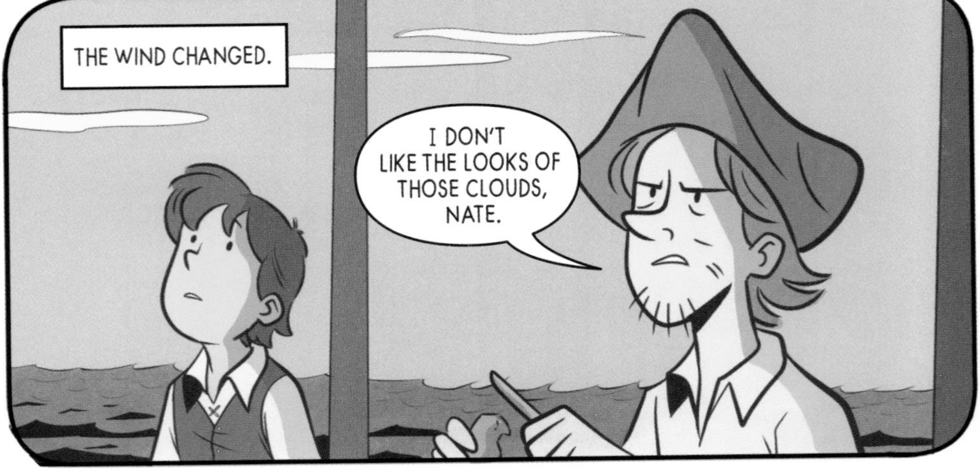
THE WIND CHANGED.
I DON'T LIKE THE LOOKS OF THOSE CLOUDS, NATE.

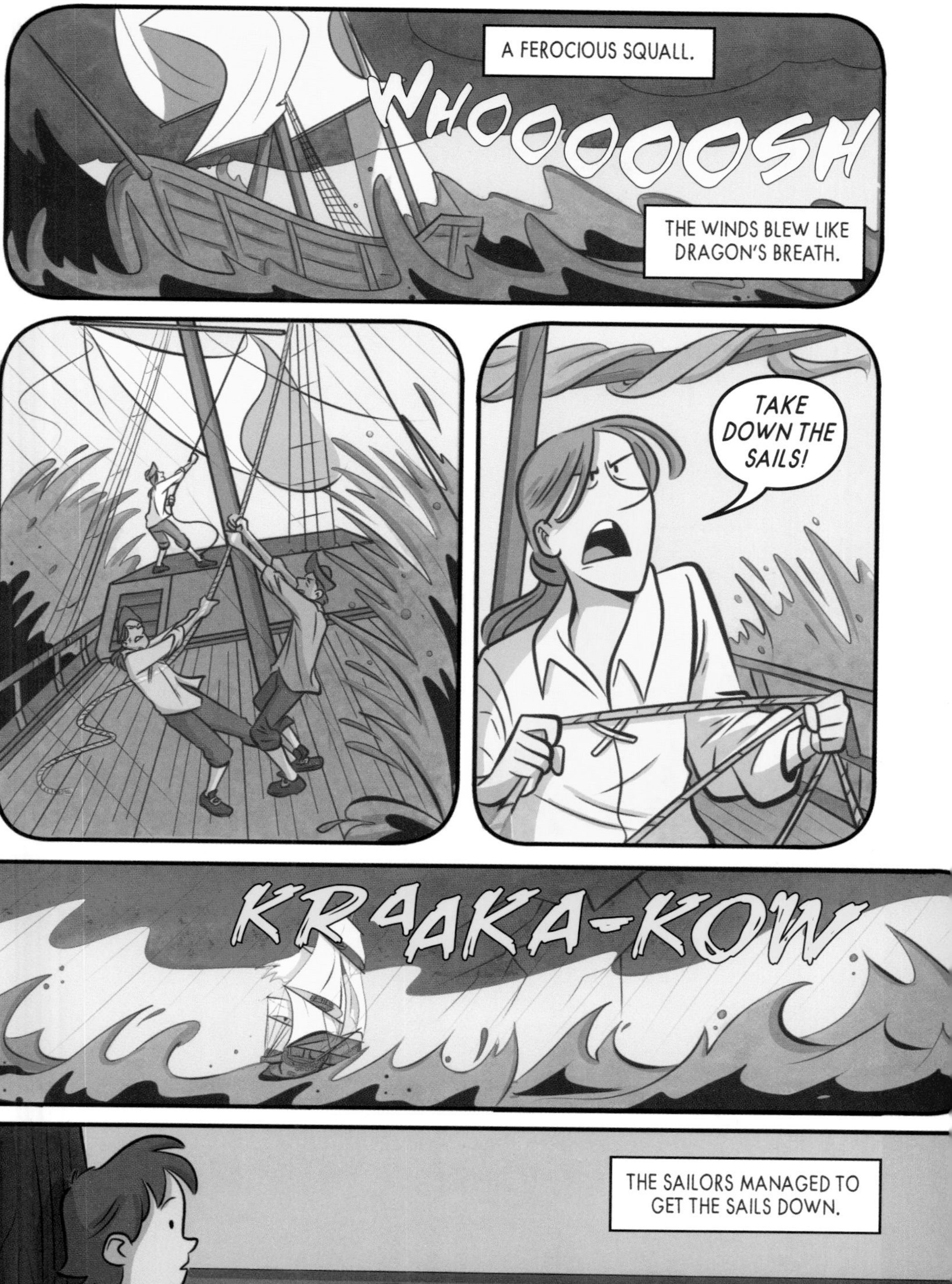
A FEROCIOUS SQUALL.
WHOOOOOSH
THE WINDS BLEW LIKE DRAGON'S BREATH.
TAKE DOWN THE SAILS!
KRAAKA-KOW
THE SAILORS MANAGED TO GET THE SAILS DOWN.

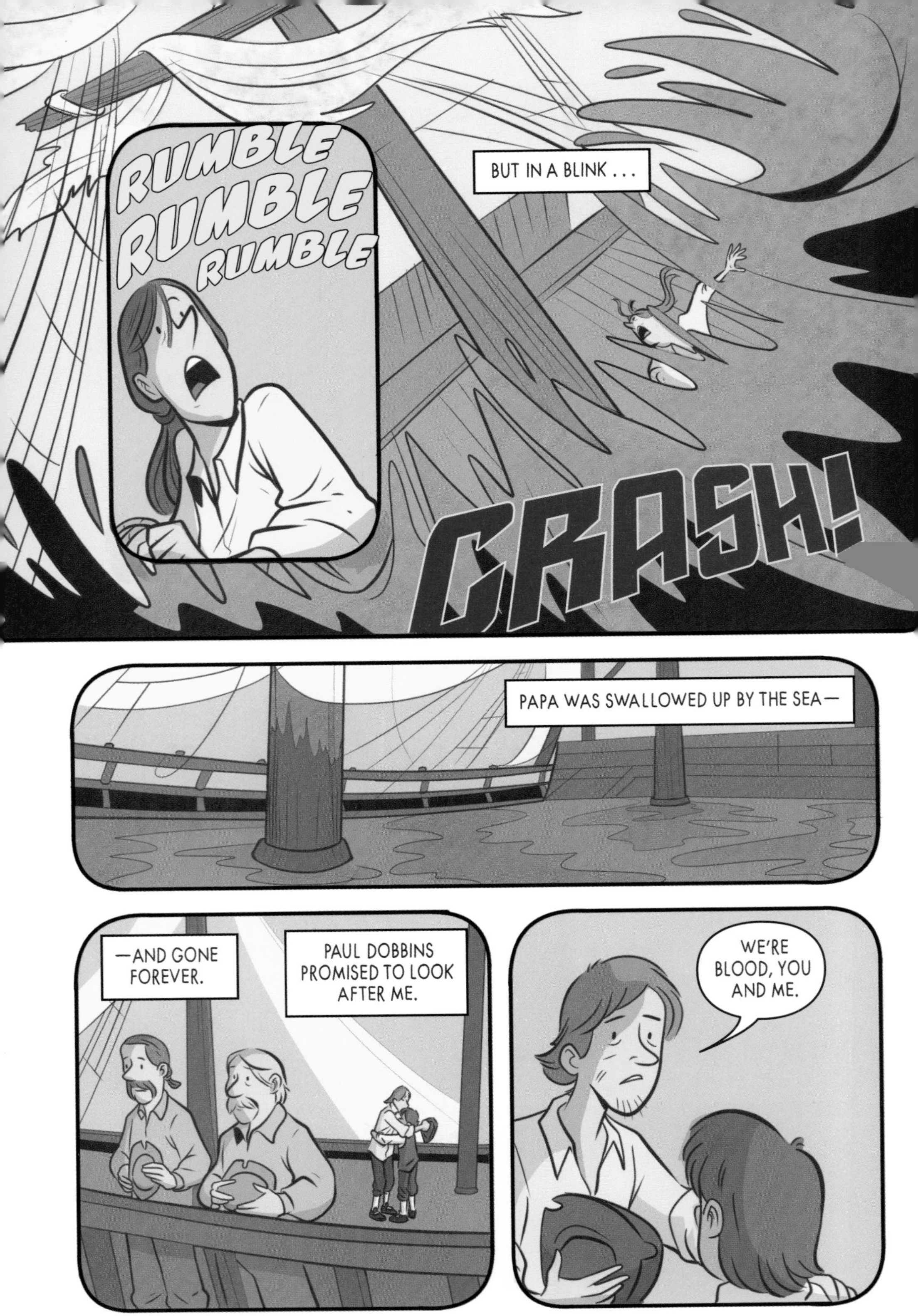
RUMBLE
RUMBLE
RUMBLE
BUT IN A BLINK . . .
CRASH!
PAPA WAS SWALLOWED UP BY THE SEA—
—AND GONE FOREVER.
PAUL DOBBINS PROMISED TO LOOK AFTER ME.
WE'RE BLOOD, YOU AND ME.

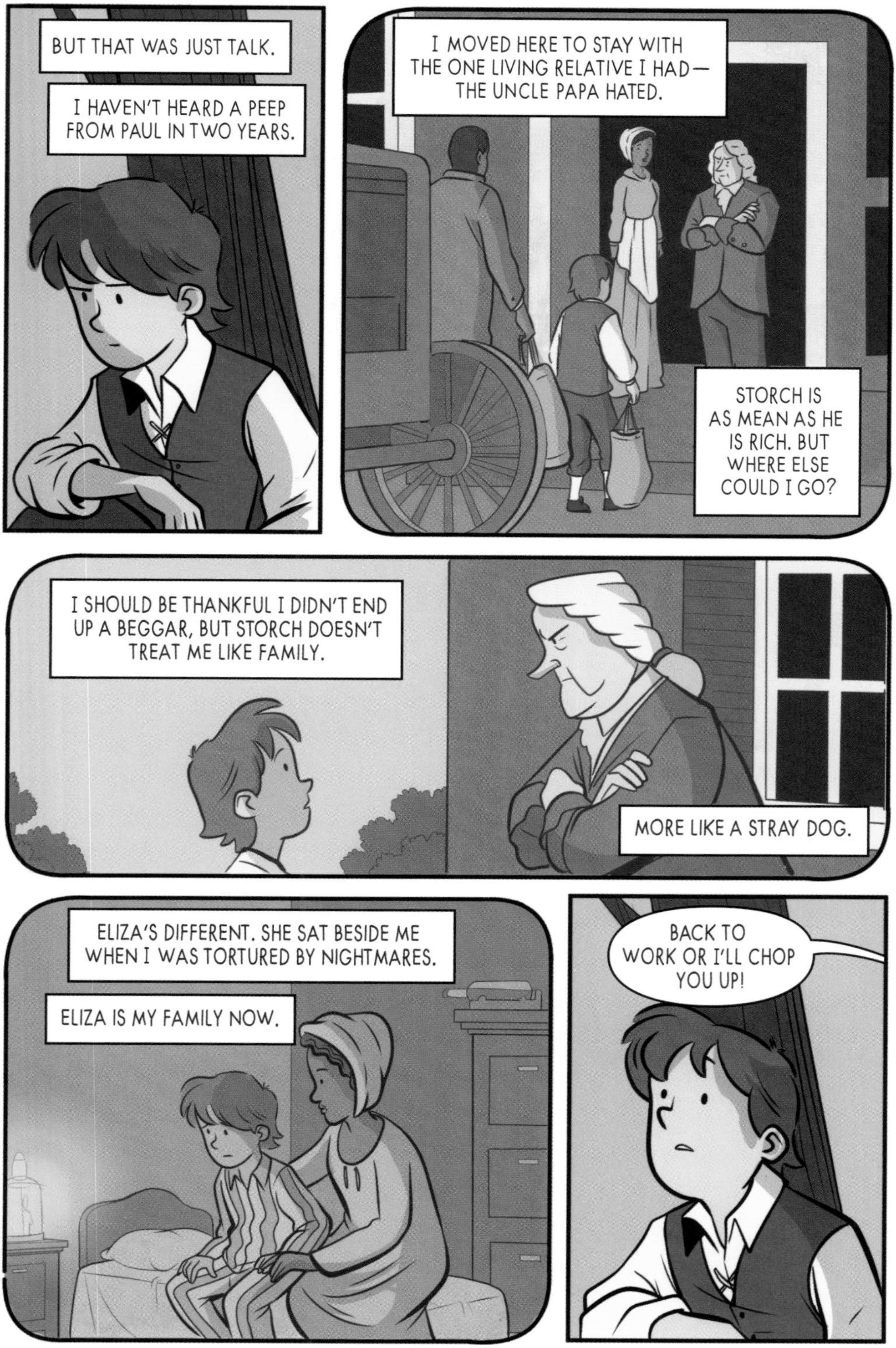
BUT THAT WAS JUST TALK.
I HAVEN'T HEARD A PEEP FROM PAUL IN TWO YEARS.
I MOVED HERE TO STAY WITH THE ONE LIVING RELATIVE I HAD— THE UNCLE PAPA HATED.
STORCH IS AS MEAN AS HE IS RICH. BUT WHERE ELSE COULD I GO?
I SHOULD BE THANKFUL I DIDN'T END UP A BEGGAR, BUT STORCH DOESN'T TREAT ME LIKE FAMILY.
MORE LIKE A STRAY DOG.
ELIZA'S DIFFERENT. SHE SAT BESIDE ME WHEN I WAS TORTURED BY NIGHTMARES.
ELIZA IS MY FAMILY NOW.
BACK TO WORK OR I'LL CHOP YOU UP!

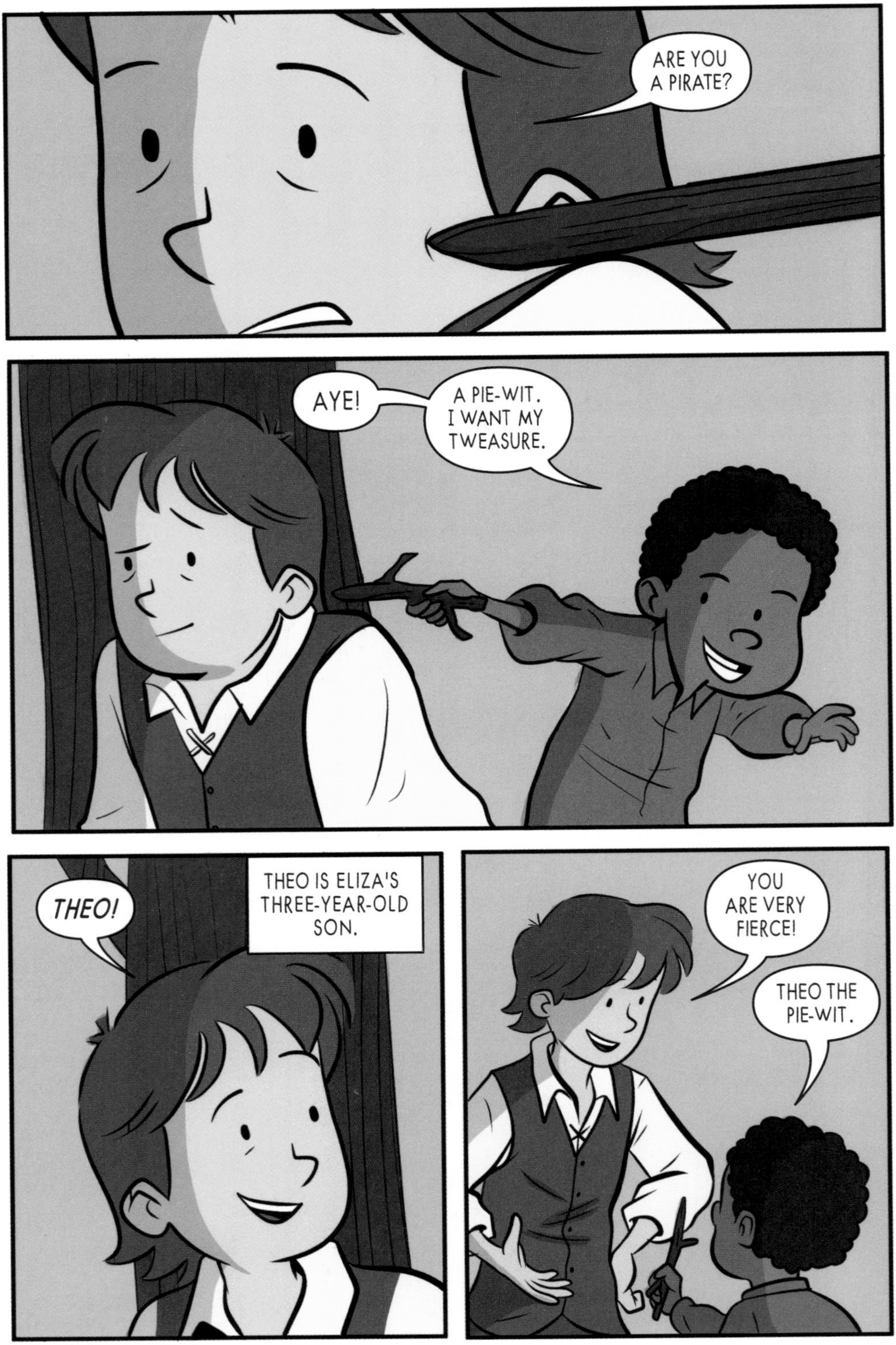
ARE YOU A PIRATE?
AYE!
A PIE-WIT. I WANT MY TWEASURE.
THEO!
THEO IS ELIZA'S THREE-YEAR-OLD SON.
YOU ARE VERY FIERCE!
THEO THE PIE-WIT.

YOU'RE SUPPOSED TO BE NAPPING.

PIE-WITS DON'T NAP!

ARRRRRR!

THEO HAS BEEN WILD ABOUT PIRATES SINCE I TOLD HIM ABOUT MY ADVENTURES AT SEA.

WHOOSH

HEE HEE HEE HEE HEE HEE

NATE! THEO!

YOU BOTH NEED TO HUSH!

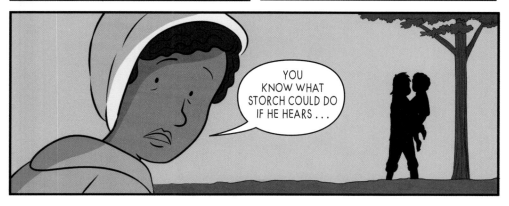

YOU KNOW WHAT STORCH COULD DO IF HE HEARS . . .

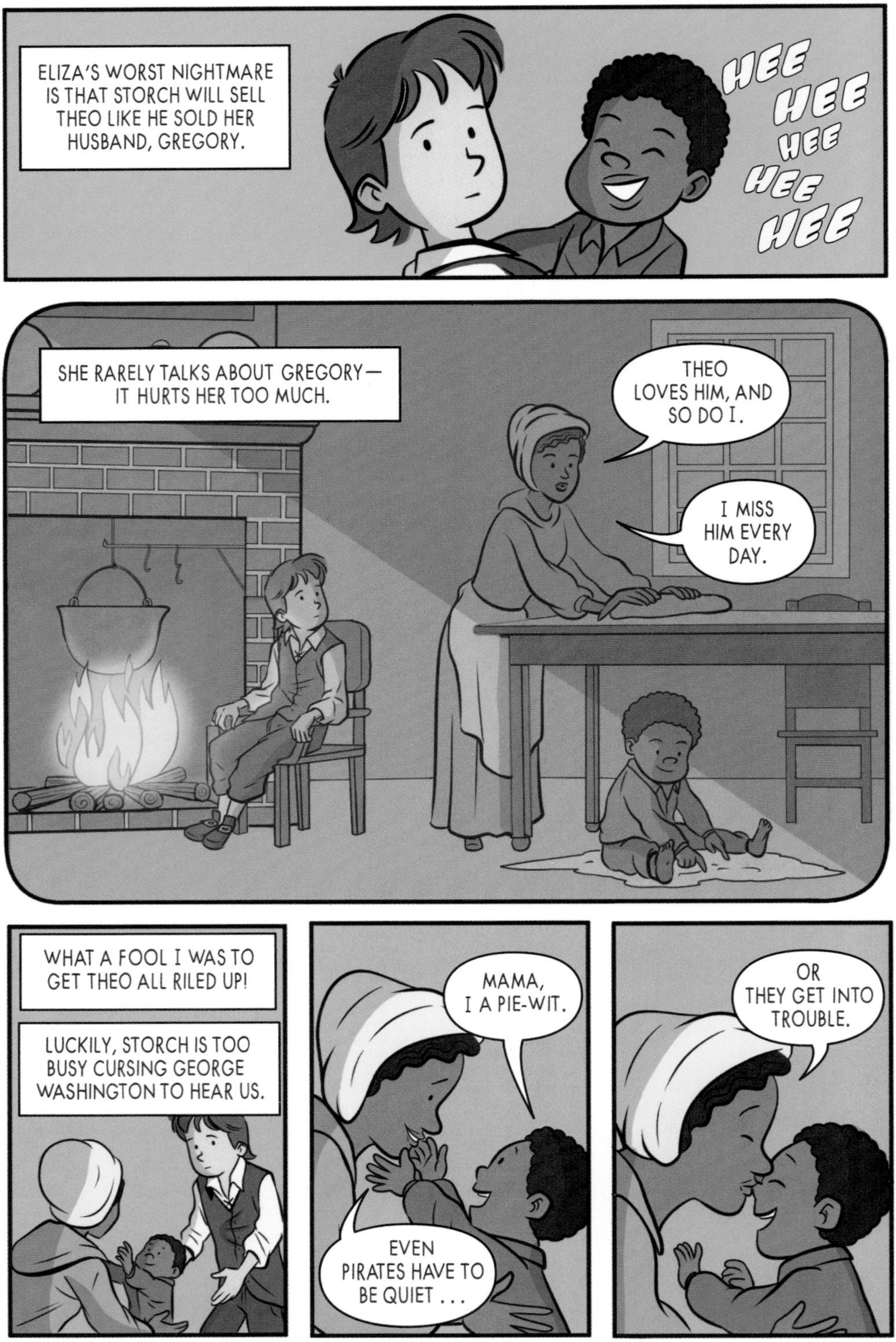
ELIZA'S WORST NIGHTMARE IS THAT STORCH WILL SELL THEO LIKE HE SOLD HER HUSBAND, GREGORY.
HEE HEE HEE HEE HEE
SHE RARELY TALKS ABOUT GREGORY— IT HURTS HER TOO MUCH.
THEO LOVES HIM, AND SO DO I.
I MISS HIM EVERY DAY.
WHAT A FOOL I WAS TO GET THEO ALL RILED UP!
LUCKILY, STORCH IS TOO BUSY CURSING GEORGE WASHINGTON TO HEAR US.
MAMA, I A PIE-WIT.
EVEN PIRATES HAVE TO BE QUIET . . .
OR THEY GET INTO TROUBLE.

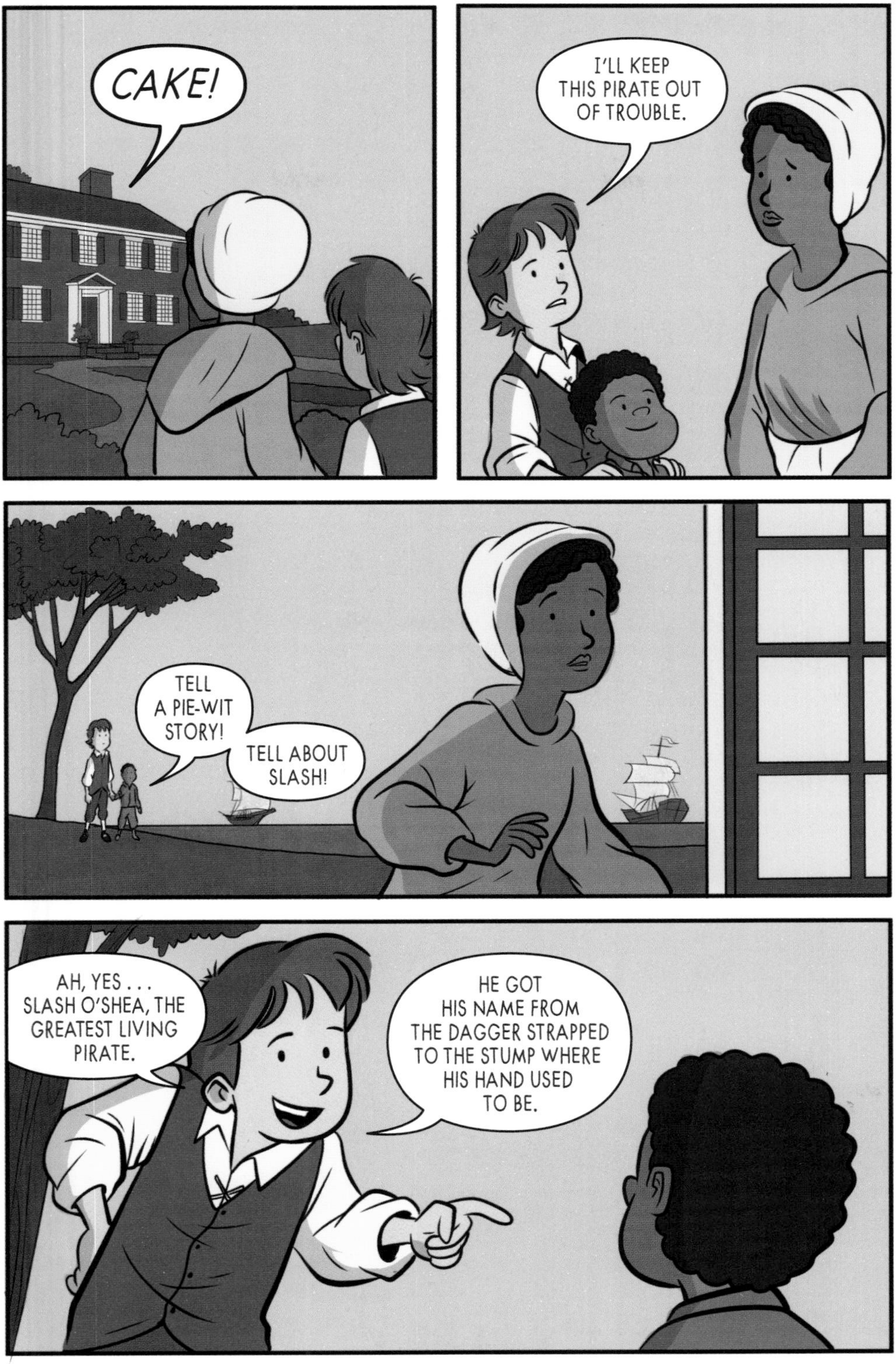
CAKE!
I'LL KEEP THIS PIRATE OUT OF TROUBLE.
TELL A PIE-WIT STORY!
TELL ABOUT SLASH!
AH, YES . . . SLASH O'SHEA, THE GREATEST LIVING PIRATE.
HE GOT HIS NAME FROM THE DAGGER STRAPPED TO THE STUMP WHERE HIS HAND USED TO BE.

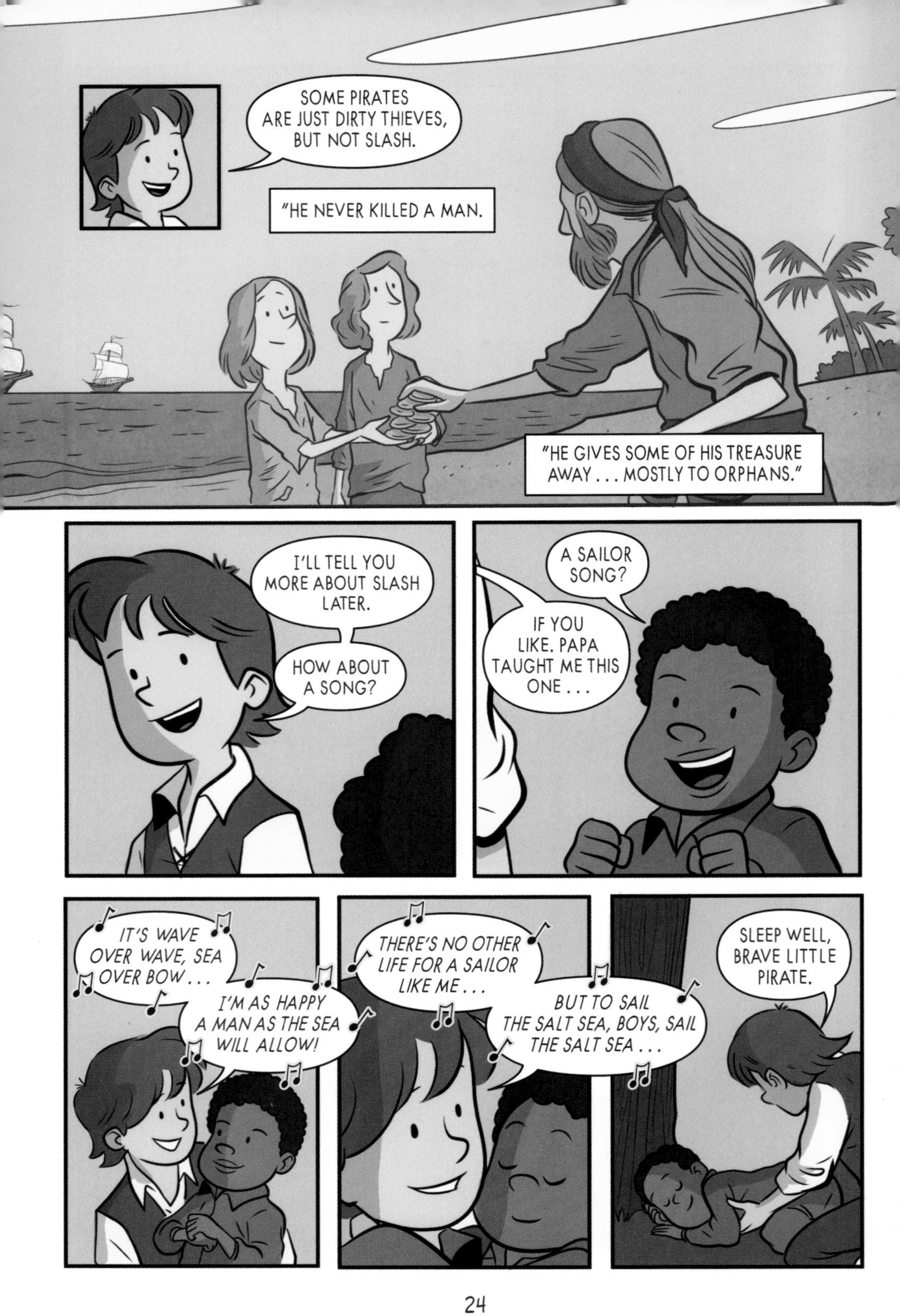
SOME PIRATES ARE JUST DIRTY THIEVES, BUT NOT SLASH.
"HE NEVER KILLED A MAN.
"HE GIVES SOME OF HIS TREASURE AWAY . . . MOSTLY TO ORPHANS."
I'LL TELL YOU MORE ABOUT SLASH LATER.
HOW ABOUT A SONG?
A SAILOR SONG?
IF YOU LIKE. PAPA TAUGHT ME THIS ONE . . .
IT'S WAVE OVER WAVE, SEA OVER BOW . . .
I'M AS HAPPY A MAN AS THE SEA WILL ALLOW!
THERE'S NO OTHER LIFE FOR A SAILOR LIKE ME . . .
BUT TO SAIL THE SALT SEA, BOYS, SAIL THE SALT SEA . . .
SLEEP WELL, BRAVE LITTLE PIRATE.

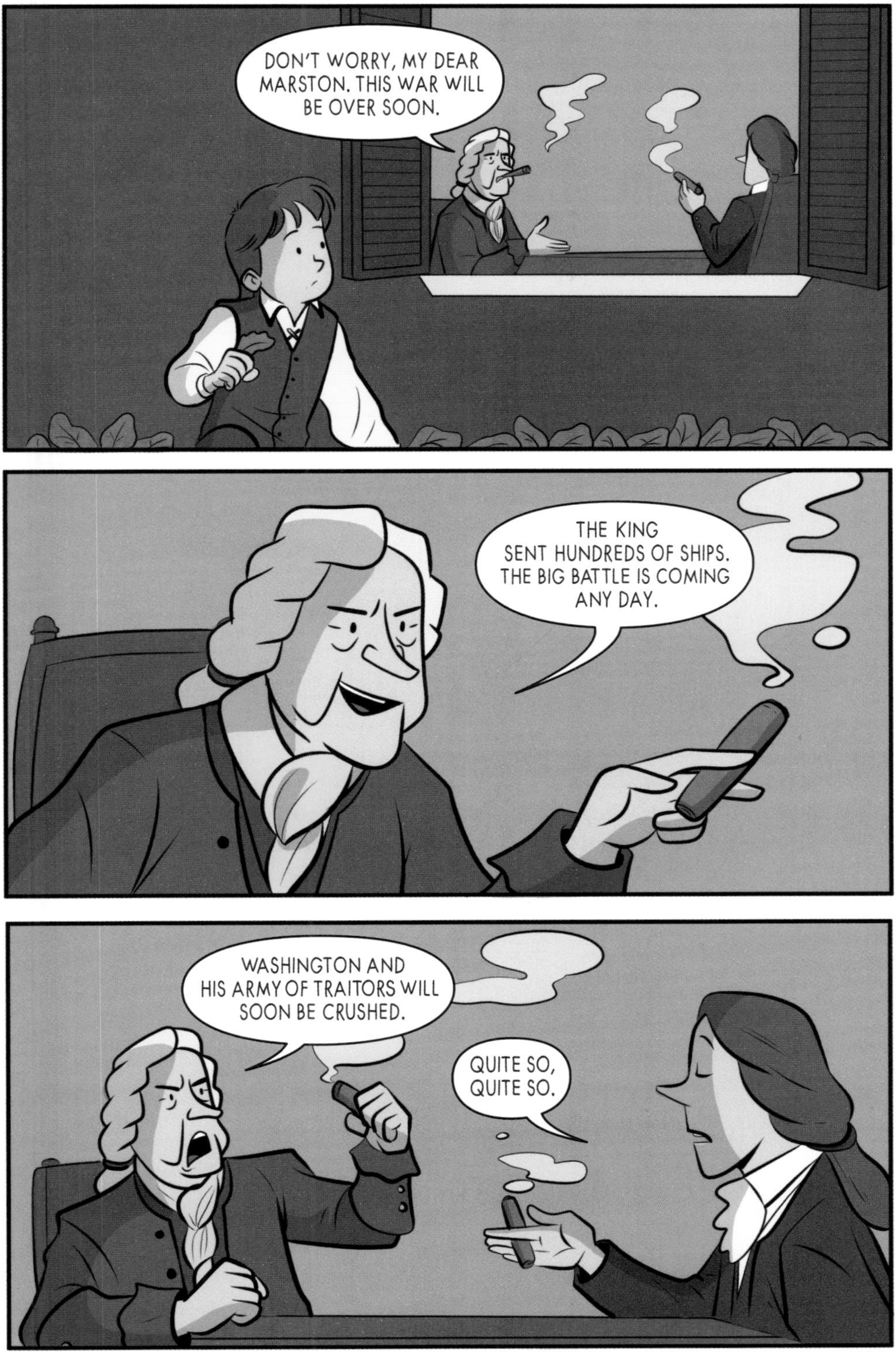
DON'T WORRY, MY DEAR MARSTON. THIS WAR WILL BE OVER SOON.
THE KING SENT HUNDREDS OF SHIPS. THE BIG BATTLE IS COMING ANY DAY.
WASHINGTON AND HIS ARMY OF TRAITORS WILL SOON BE CRUSHED.
QUITE SO, QUITE SO.

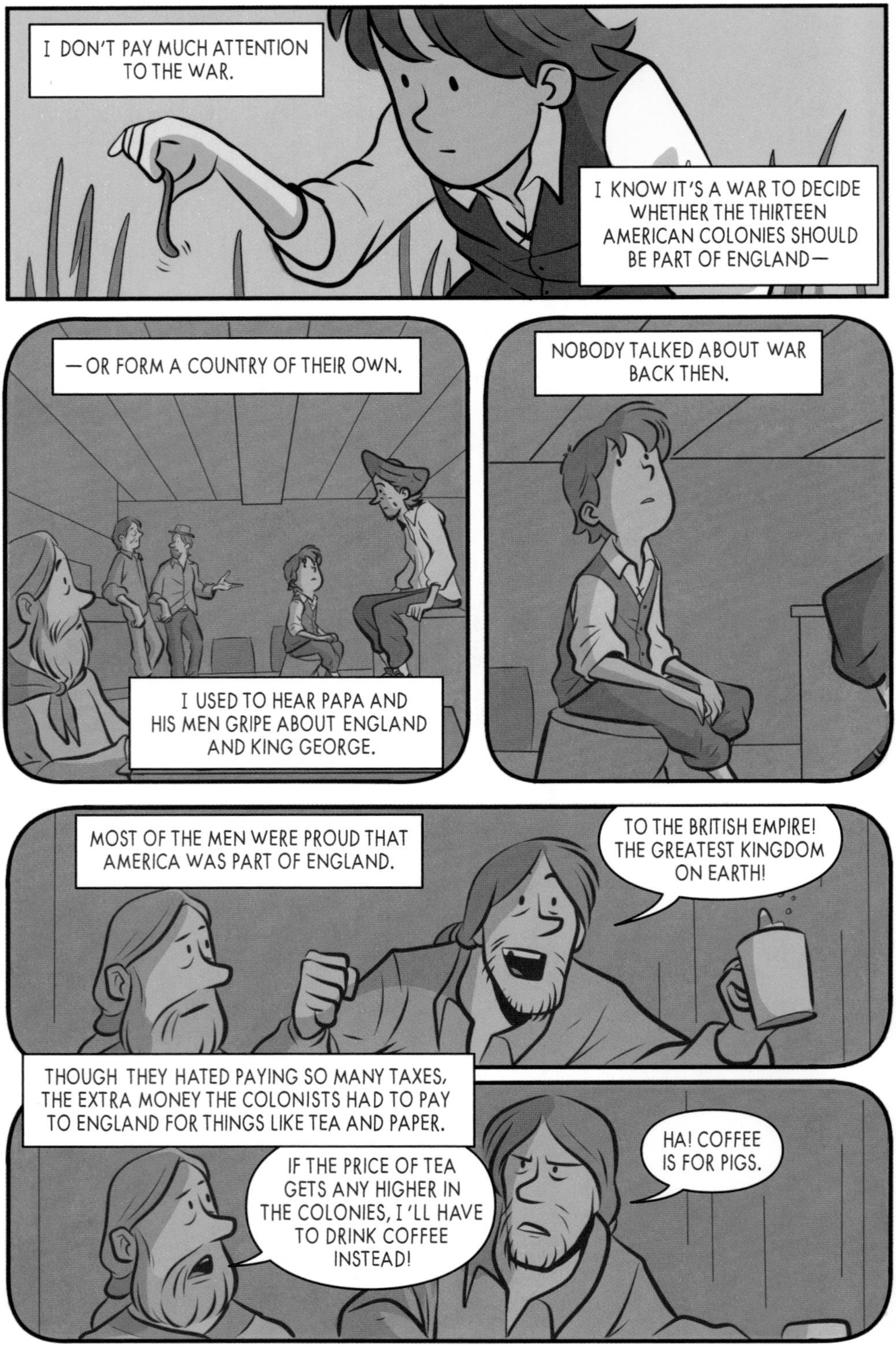

I DON'T PAY MUCH ATTENTION TO THE WAR.
I KNOW IT'S A WAR TO DECIDE WHETHER THE THIRTEEN AMERICAN COLONIES SHOULD BE PART OF ENGLAND—
—OR FORM A COUNTRY OF THEIR OWN.
I USED TO HEAR PAPA AND HIS MEN GRIPE ABOUT ENGLAND AND KING GEORGE.
NOBODY TALKED ABOUT WAR BACK THEN.
MOST OF THE MEN WERE PROUD THAT AMERICA WAS PART OF ENGLAND.
TO THE BRITISH EMPIRE! THE GREATEST KINGDOM ON EARTH!
THOUGH THEY HATED PAYING SO MANY TAXES, THE EXTRA MONEY THE COLONISTS HAD TO PAY TO ENGLAND FOR THINGS LIKE TEA AND PAPER.
IF THE PRICE OF TEA GETS ANY HIGHER IN THE COLONIES, I'LL HAVE TO DRINK COFFEE INSTEAD!
HA! COFFEE IS FOR PIGS.

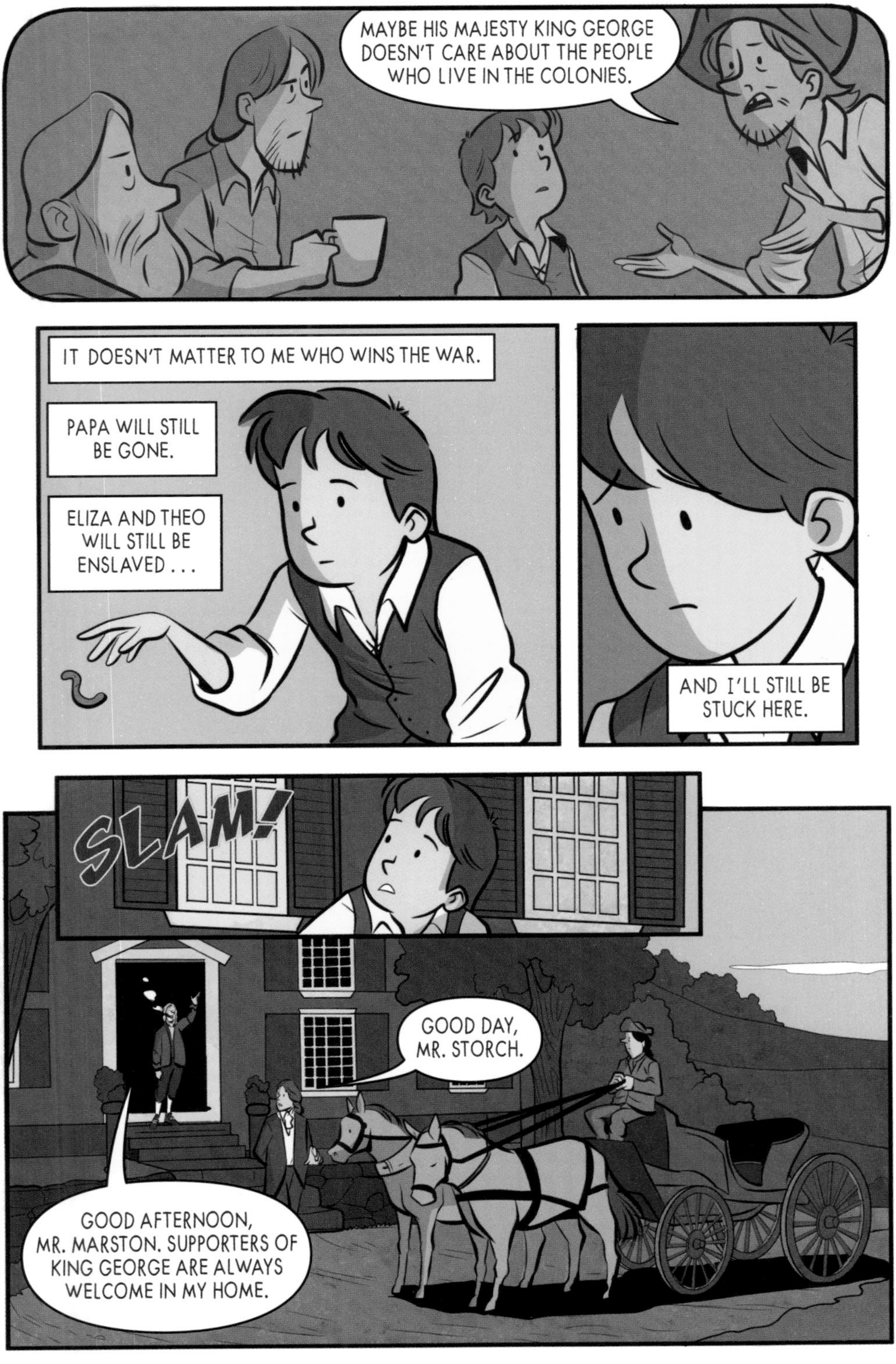
MAYBE HIS MAJESTY KING GEORGE DOESN'T CARE ABOUT THE PEOPLE WHO LIVE IN THE COLONIES.
IT DOESN'T MATTER TO ME WHO WINS THE WAR.
PAPA WILL STILL BE GONE.
ELIZA AND THEO WILL STILL BE ENSLAVED . . .
AND I'LL STILL BE STUCK HERE.
SLAM!
GOOD DAY, MR. STORCH.
GOOD AFTERNOON, MR. MARSTON. SUPPORTERS OF KING GEORGE ARE ALWAYS WELCOME IN MY HOME.

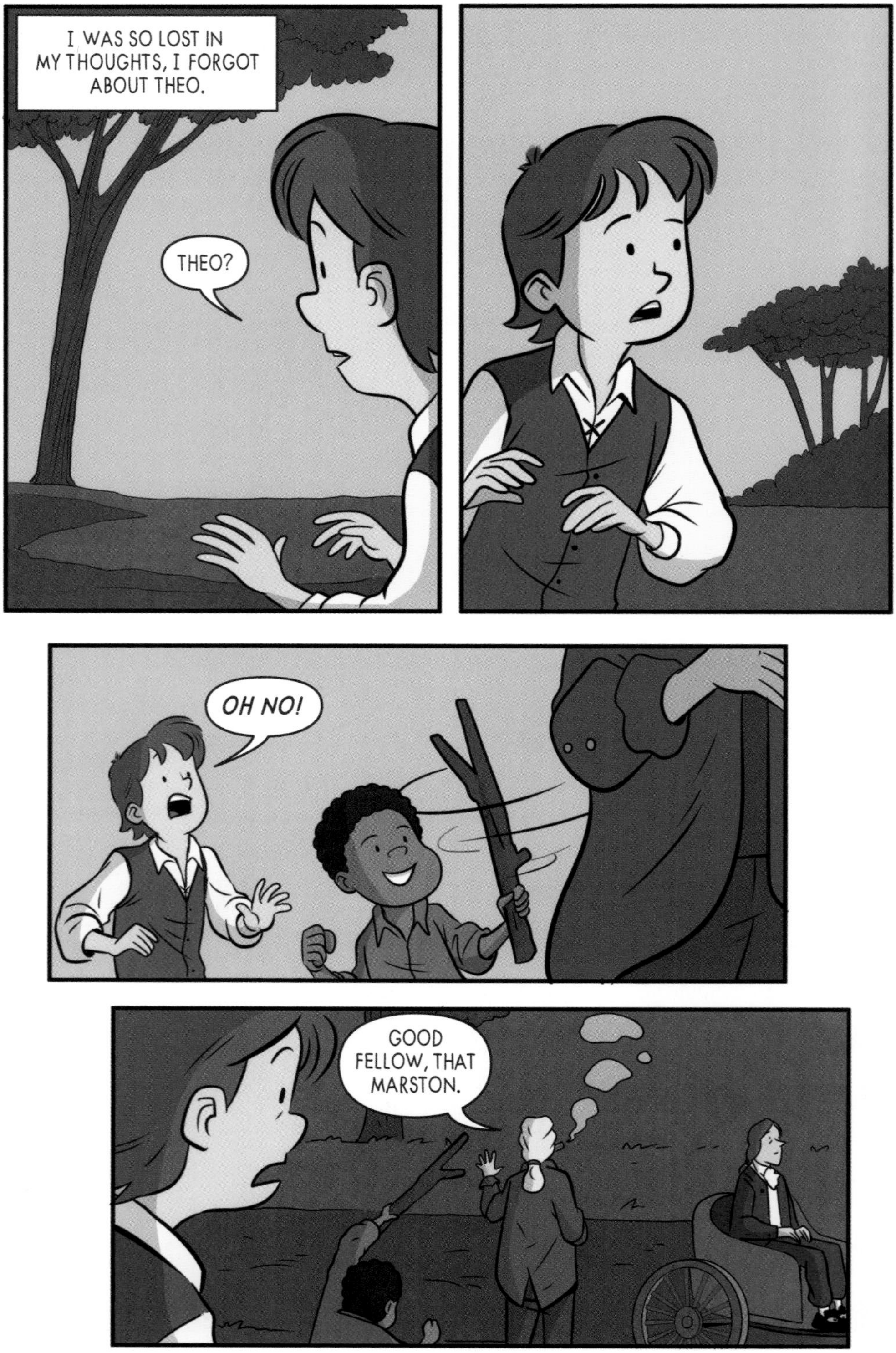
I WAS SO LOST IN MY THOUGHTS, I FORGOT ABOUT THEO.
THEO?
OH NO!
GOOD FELLOW, THAT MARSTON.

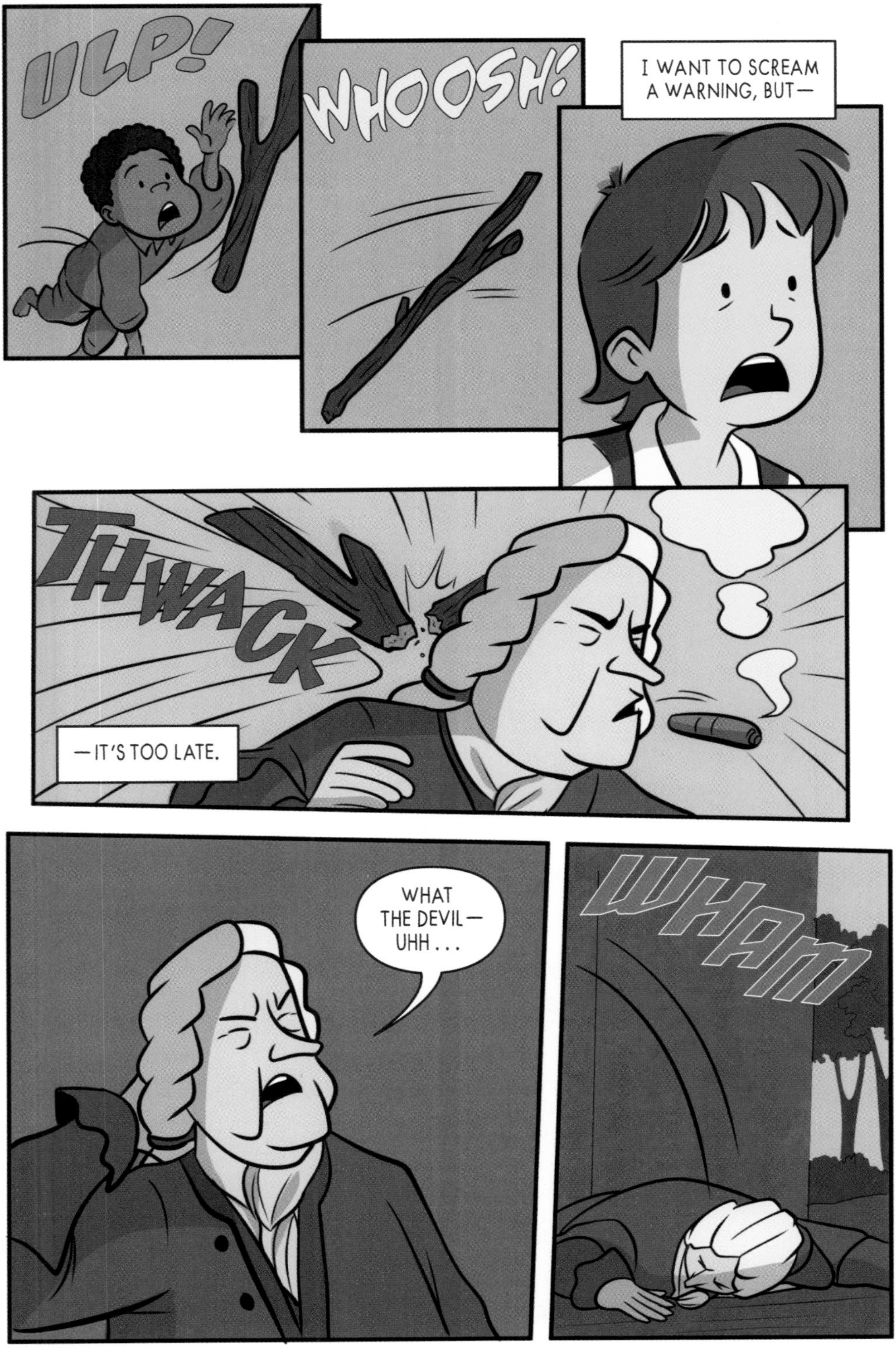
ULP!
WHOOSH!
I WANT TO SCREAM A WARNING, BUT—
THWACK
—IT'S TOO LATE.
WHAT THE DEVIL— UHH . . .
WHAM

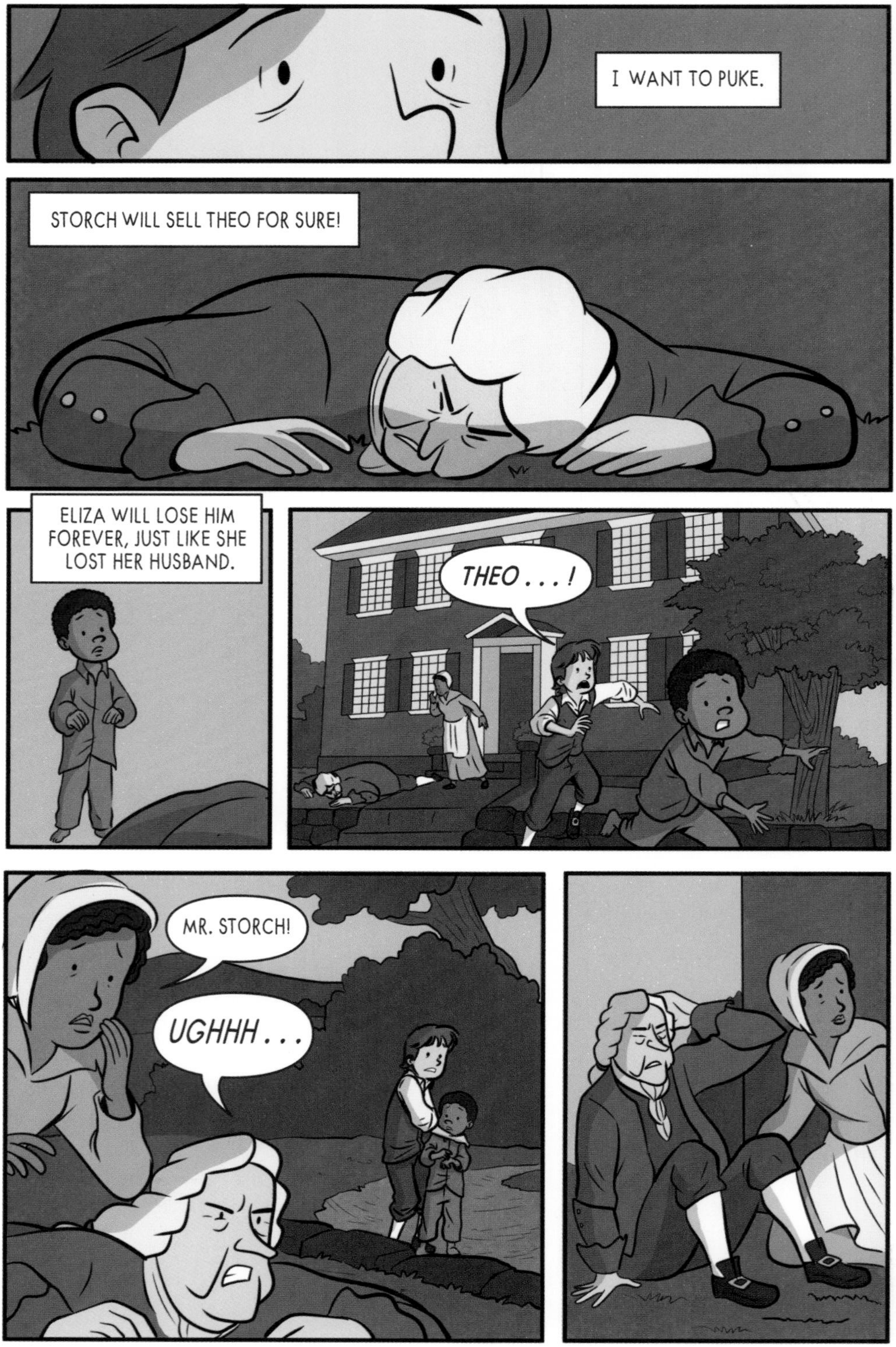

I WANT TO PUKE.
STORCH WILL SELL THEO FOR SURE!
ELIZA WILL LOSE HIM FOREVER, JUST LIKE SHE LOST HER HUSBAND.
THEO . . . !
MR. STORCH!
UGHHH . . .

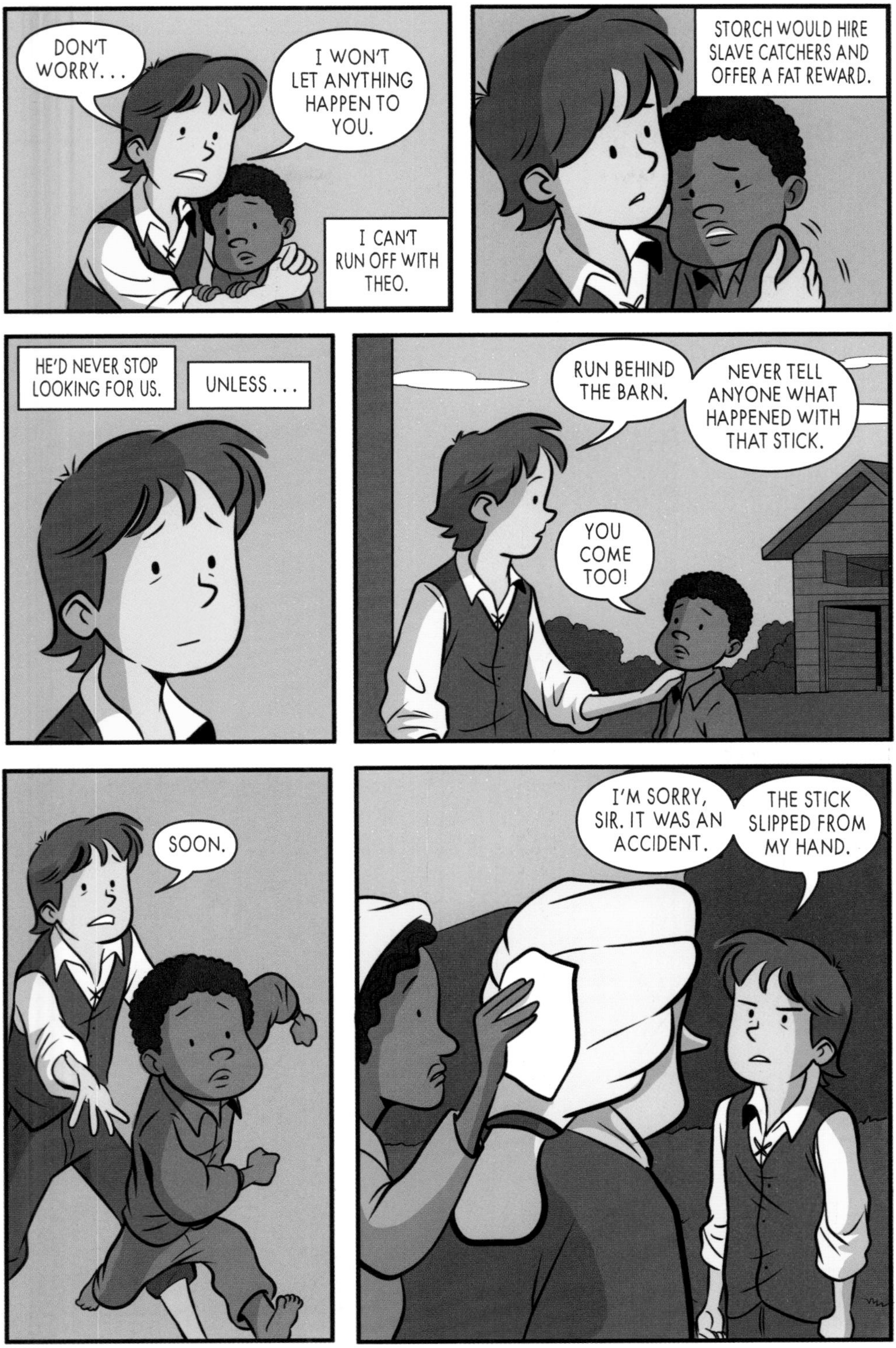
DON'T WORRY. . .
I WON'T LET ANYTHING HAPPEN TO YOU.
I CAN'T RUN OFF WITH THEO.
STORCH WOULD HIRE SLAVE CATCHERS AND OFFER A FAT REWARD.
HE'D NEVER STOP LOOKING FOR US.
UNLESS . . .
RUN BEHIND THE BARN.
NEVER TELL ANYONE WHAT HAPPENED WITH THAT STICK.
YOU COME TOO!
SOON.
I'M SORRY, SIR. IT WAS AN ACCIDENT.
THE STICK SLIPPED FROM MY HAND.

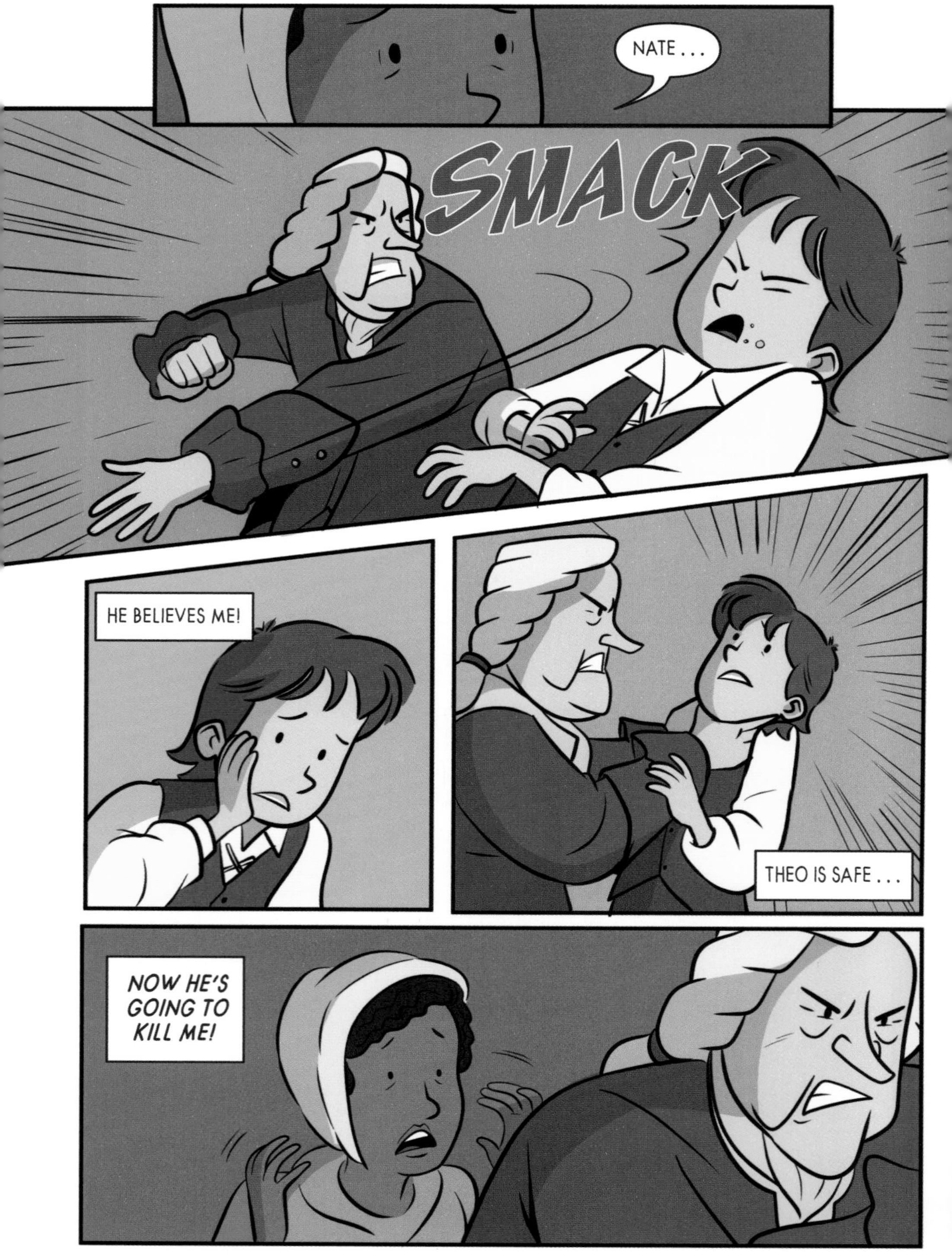
NATE . . .
SMACK
HE BELIEVES ME!
THEO IS SAFE . . .
NOW HE'S GOING TO KILL ME!

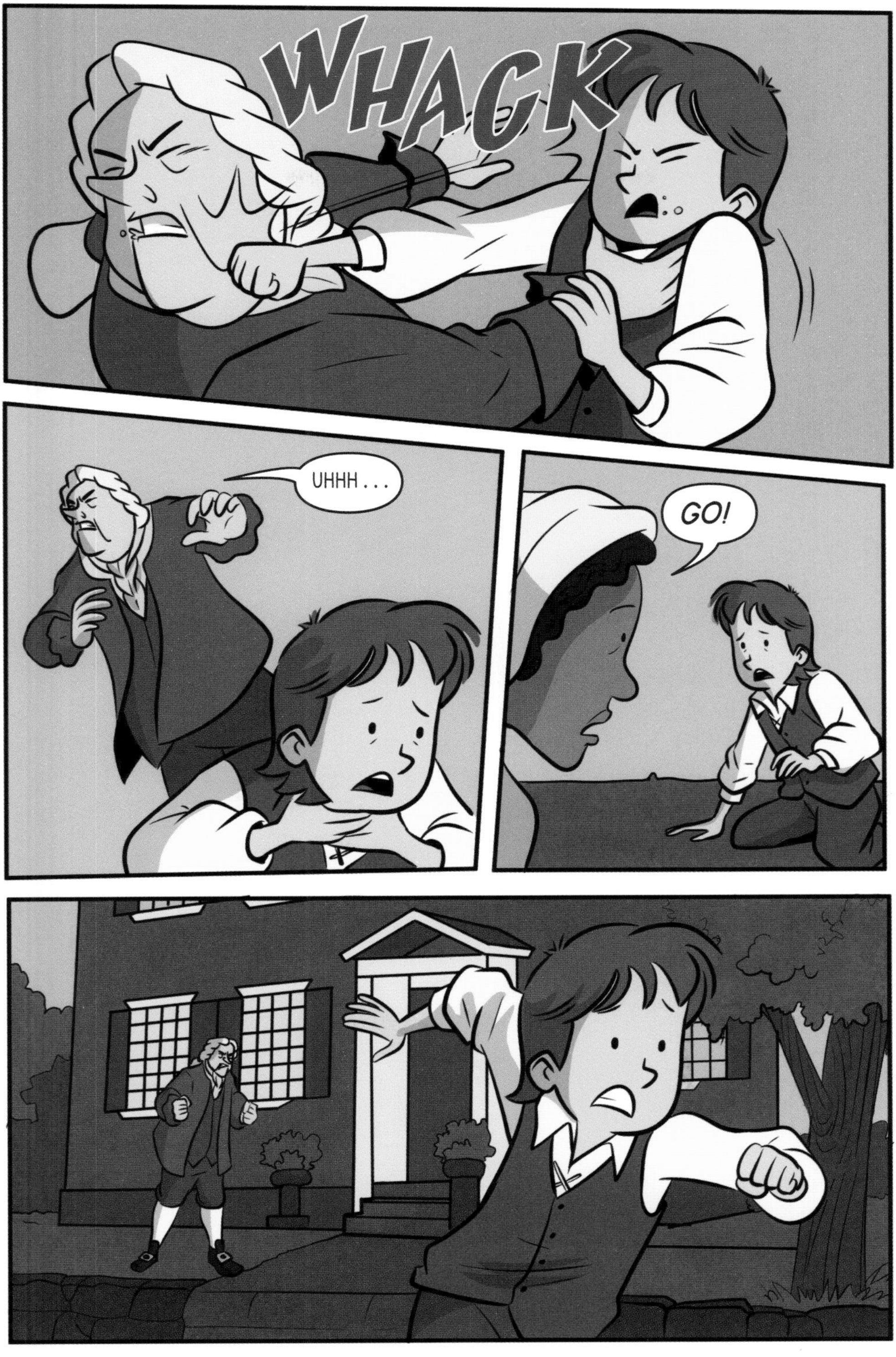
WHACK
UHHH . . .
GO!

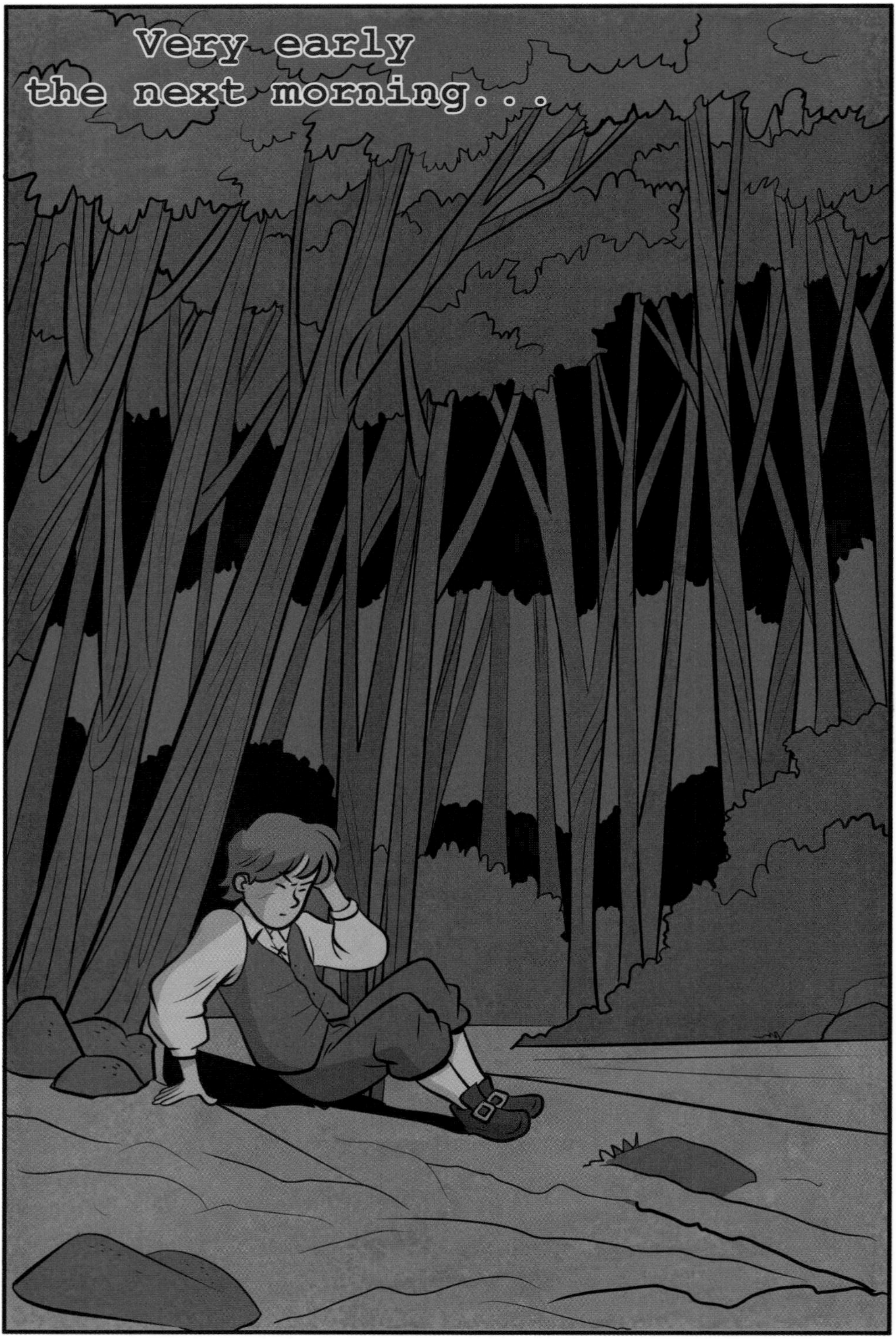
Very early
the next morning...

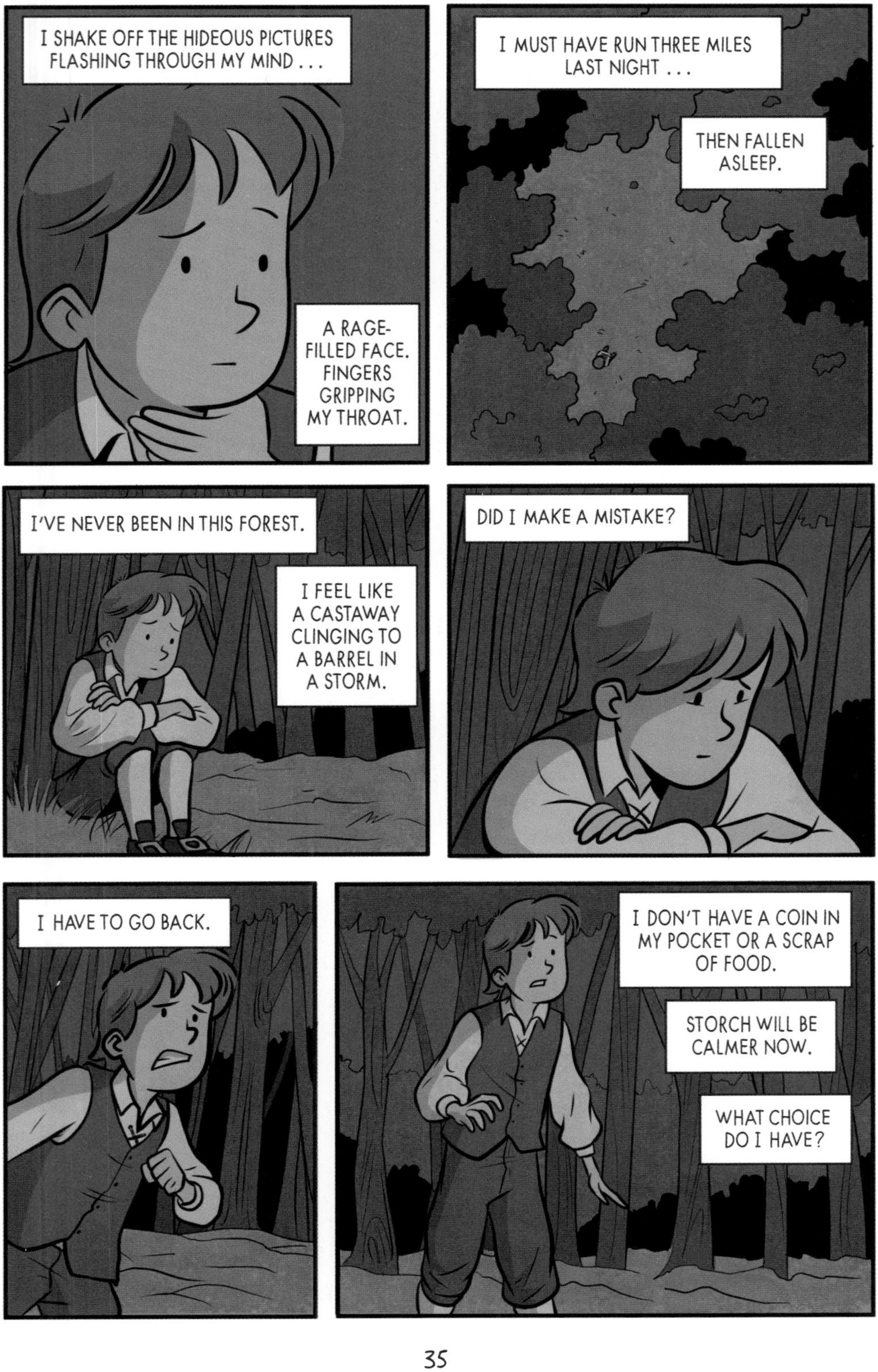
I SHAKE OFF THE HIDEOUS PICTURES FLASHING THROUGH MY MIND . . .
A RAGE-FILLED FACE. FINGERS GRIPPING MY THROAT.
I MUST HAVE RUN THREE MILES LAST NIGHT . . .
THEN FALLEN ASLEEP.
I'VE NEVER BEEN IN THIS FOREST.
I FEEL LIKE A CASTAWAY CLINGING TO A BARREL IN A STORM.
DID I MAKE A MISTAKE?
I HAVE TO GO BACK.
I DON'T HAVE A COIN IN MY POCKET OR A SCRAP OF FOOD.
STORCH WILL BE CALMER NOW.
WHAT CHOICE DO I HAVE?

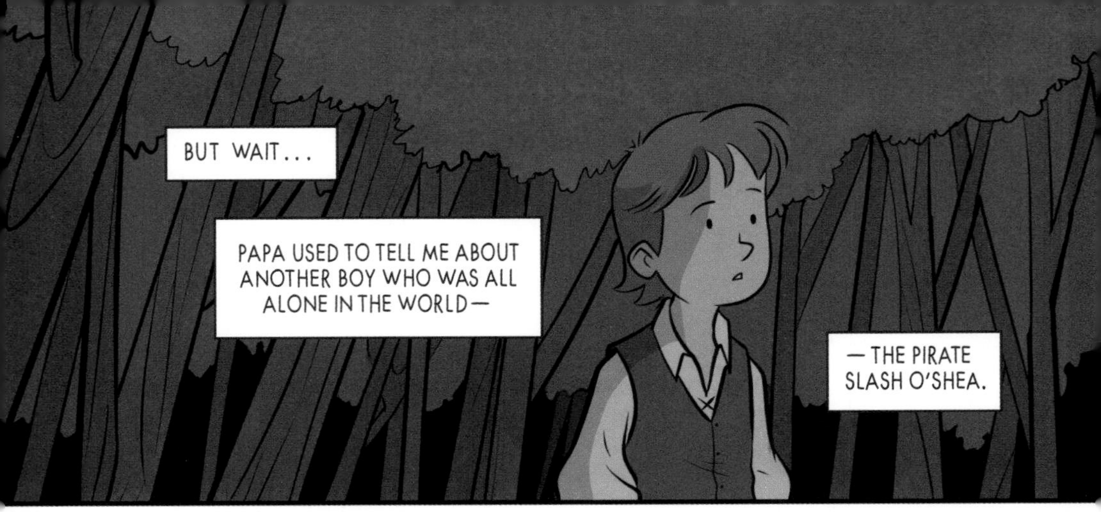
BUT WAIT . . .
PAPA USED TO TELL ME ABOUT ANOTHER BOY WHO WAS ALL ALONE IN THE WORLD—
—THE PIRATE SLASH O'SHEA.

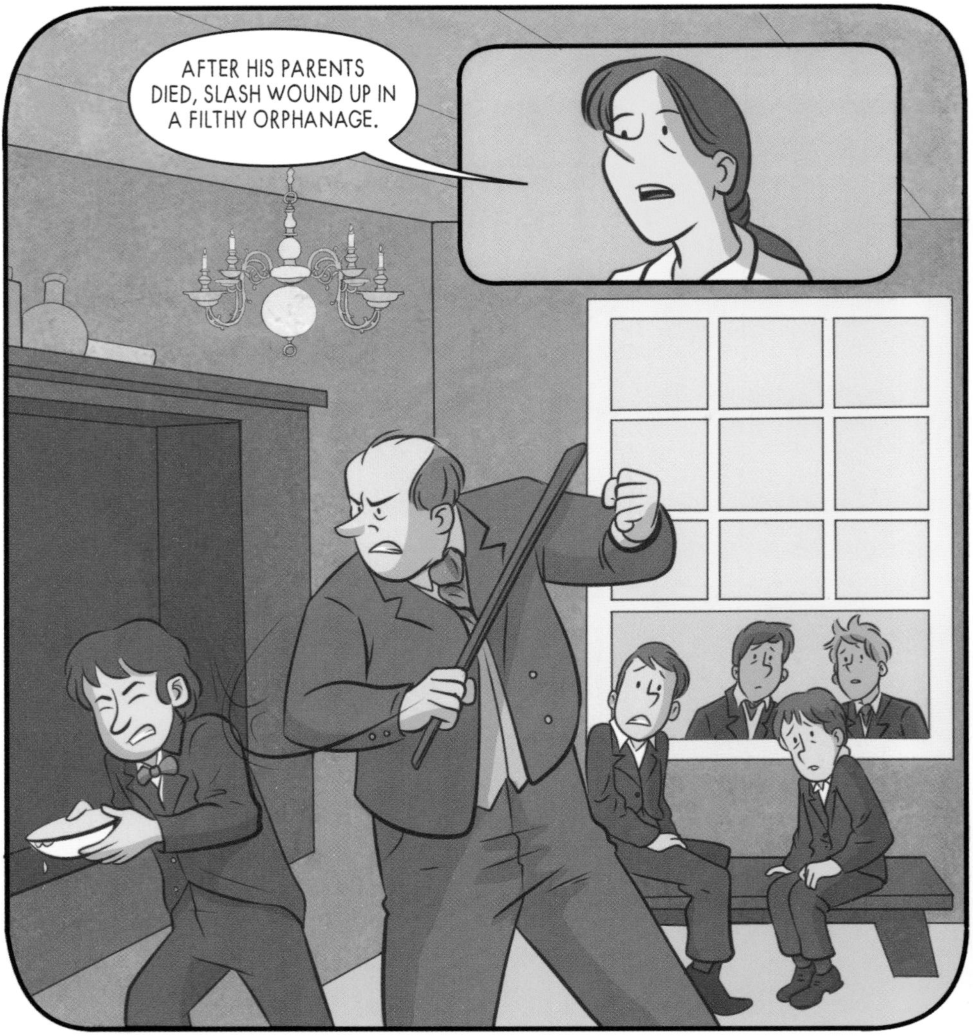
AFTER HIS PARENTS DIED, SLASH WOUND UP IN A FILTHY ORPHANAGE.

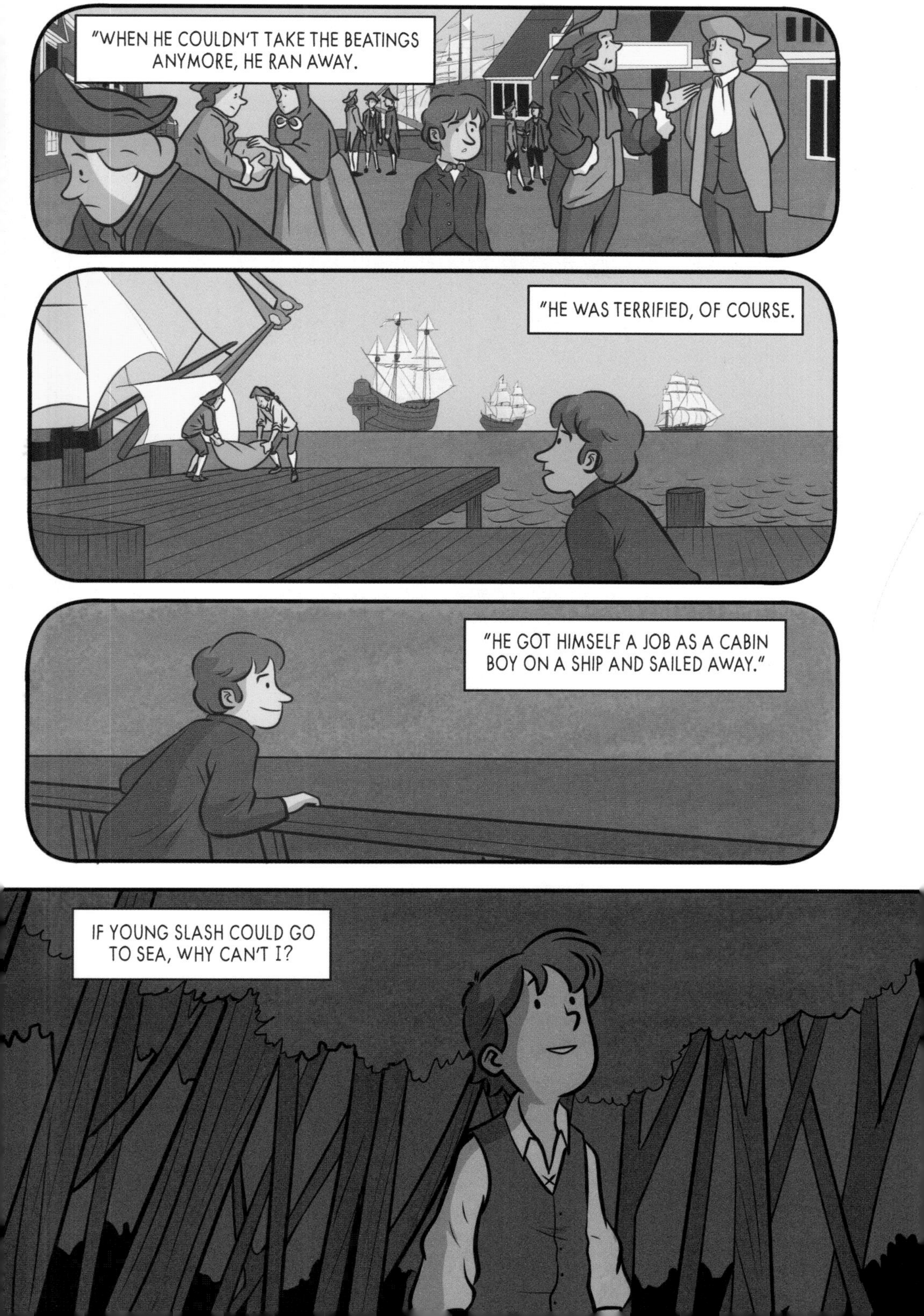
"WHEN HE COULDN'T TAKE THE BEATINGS ANYMORE, HE RAN AWAY.
"HE WAS TERRIFIED, OF COURSE.
"HE GOT HIMSELF A JOB AS A CABIN BOY ON A SHIP AND SAILED AWAY."
IF YOUNG SLASH COULD GO TO SEA, WHY CAN'T I?

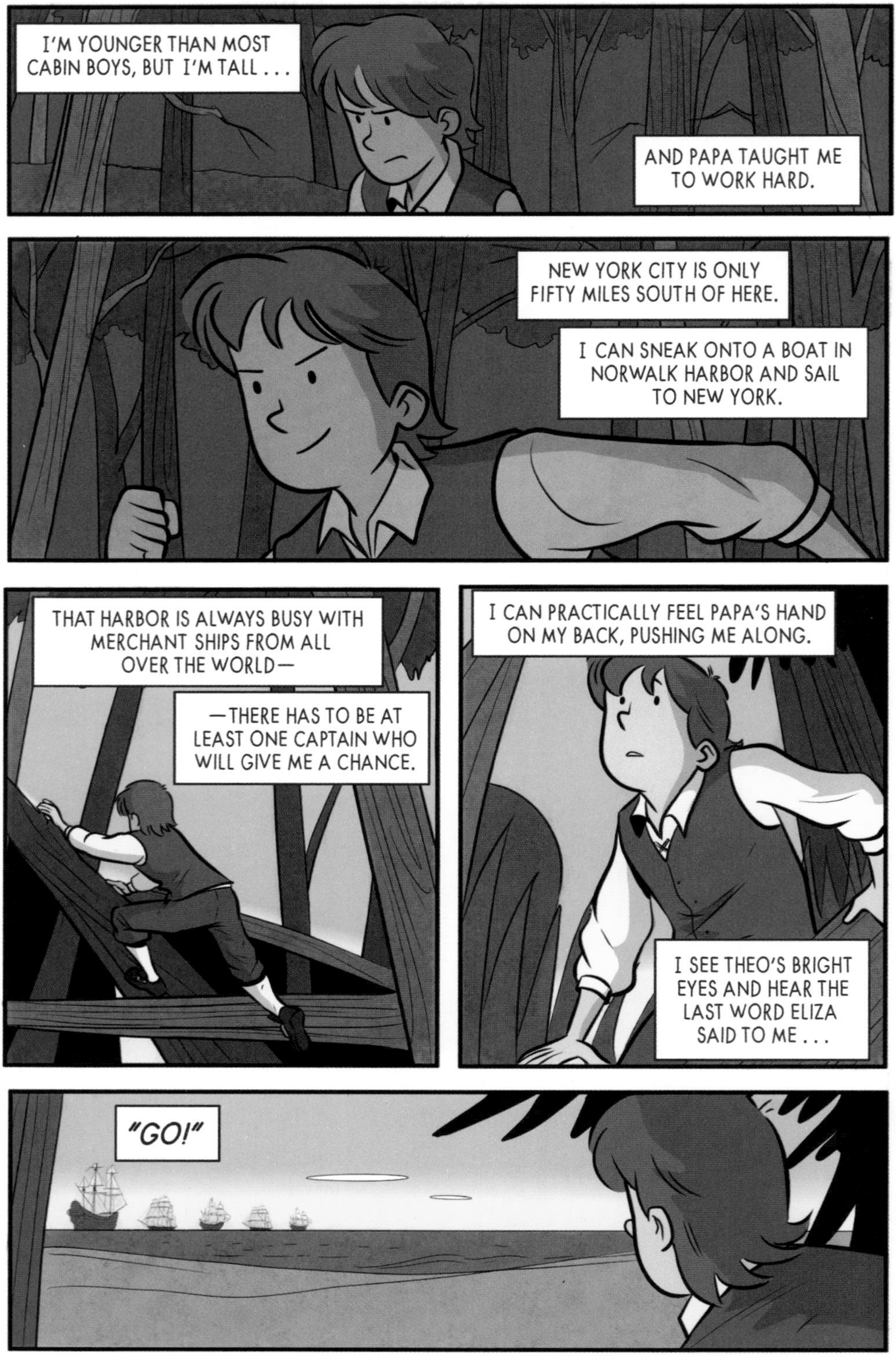
I'M YOUNGER THAN MOST CABIN BOYS, BUT I'M TALL . . .
AND PAPA TAUGHT ME TO WORK HARD.
NEW YORK CITY IS ONLY FIFTY MILES SOUTH OF HERE.
I CAN SNEAK ONTO A BOAT IN NORWALK HARBOR AND SAIL TO NEW YORK.
THAT HARBOR IS ALWAYS BUSY WITH MERCHANT SHIPS FROM ALL OVER THE WORLD—
—THERE HAS TO BE AT LEAST ONE CAPTAIN WHO WILL GIVE ME A CHANCE.
I CAN PRACTICALLY FEEL PAPA'S HAND ON MY BACK, PUSHING ME ALONG.
I SEE THEO'S BRIGHT EYES AND HEAR THE LAST WORD ELIZA SAID TO ME . . .
"GO!"

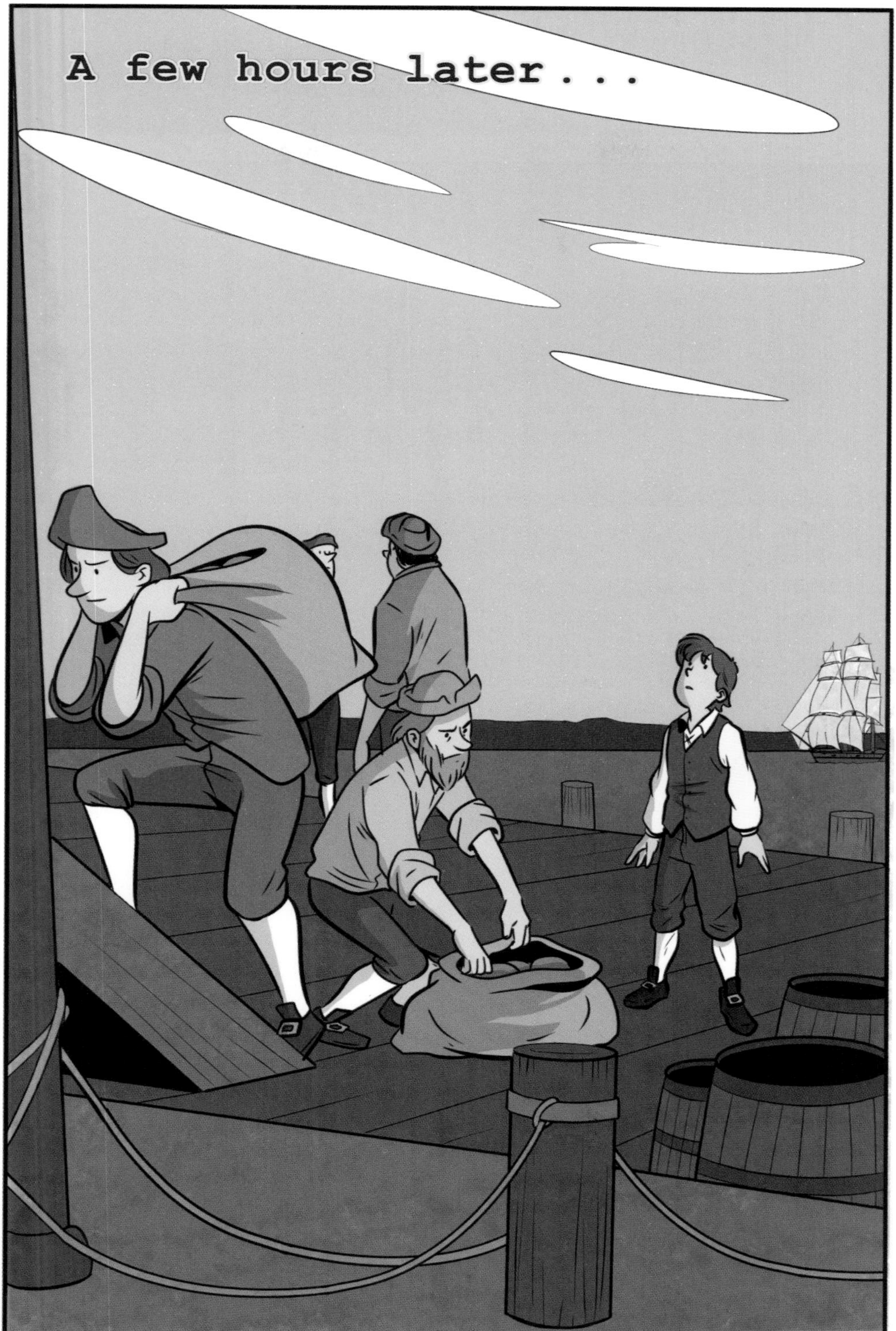
A few hours later . . .

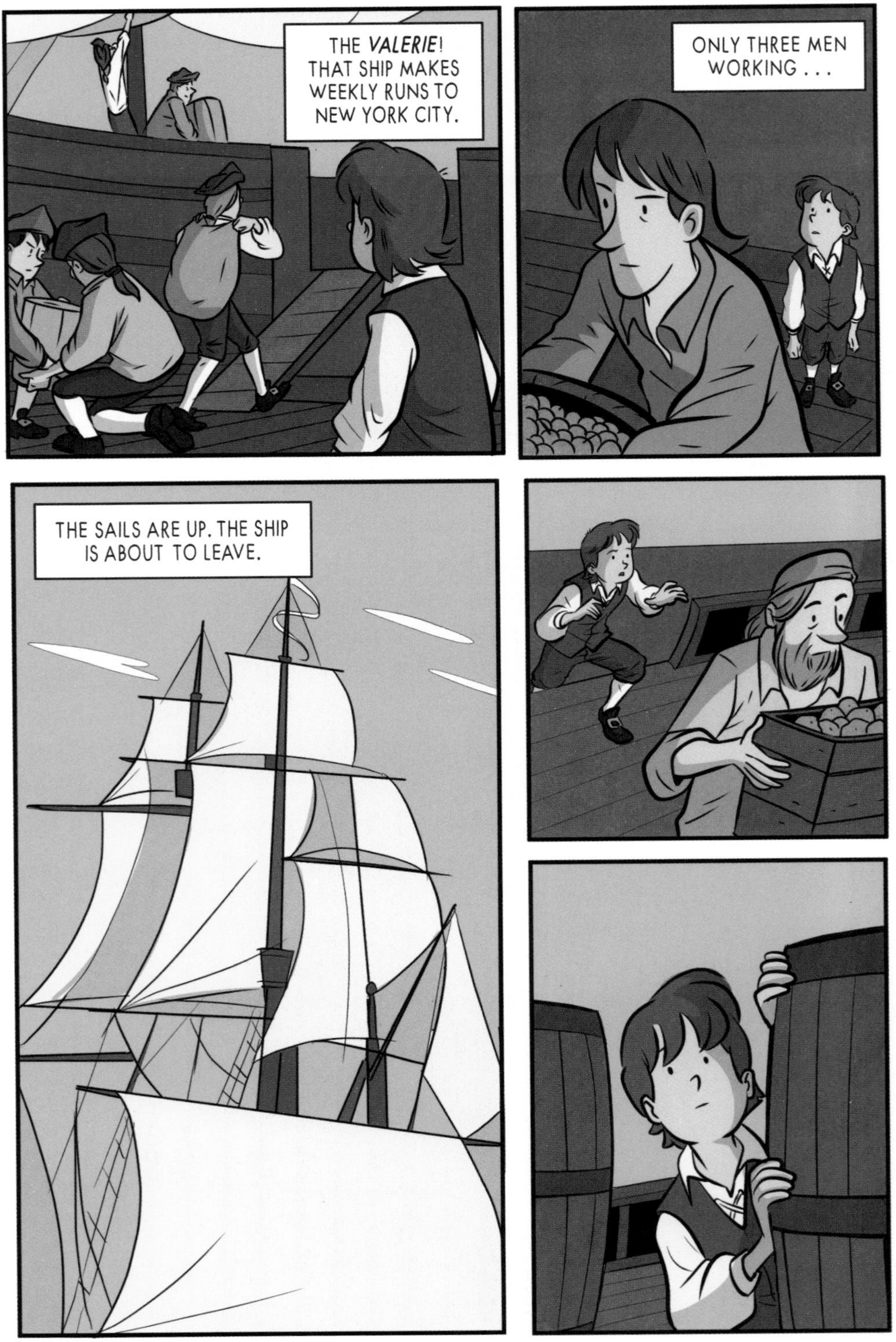
THE *VALERIE*! THAT SHIP MAKES WEEKLY RUNS TO NEW YORK CITY.
ONLY THREE MEN WORKING . . .
THE SAILS ARE UP. THE SHIP IS ABOUT TO LEAVE.

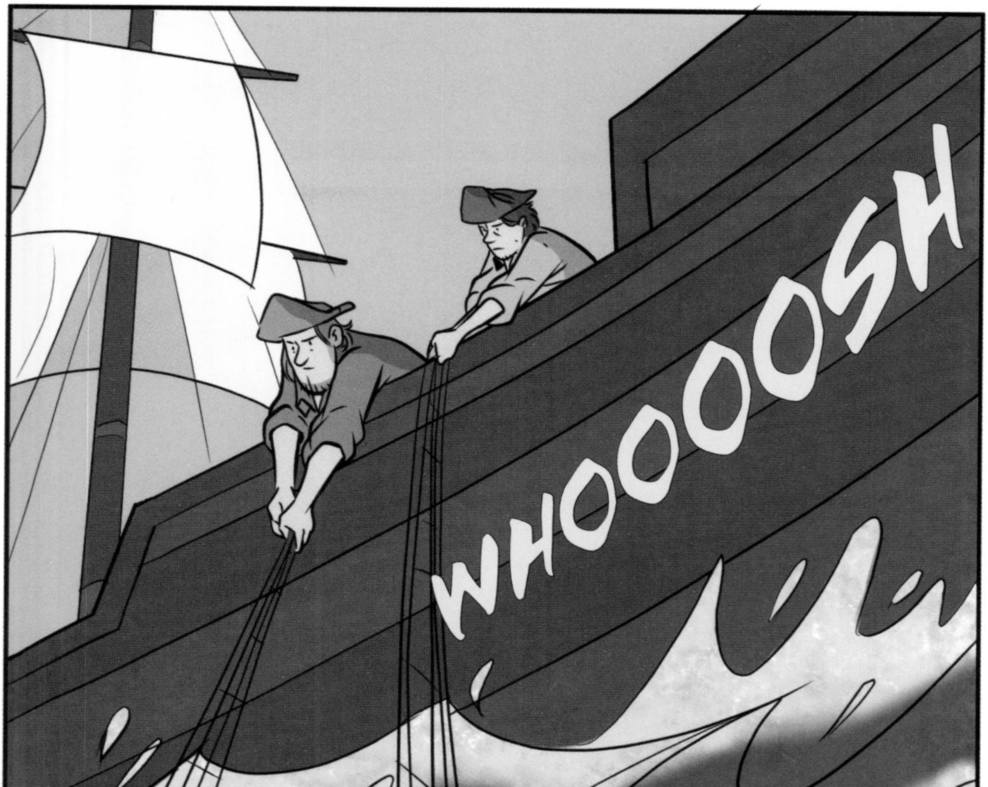
WHOOOOOSH

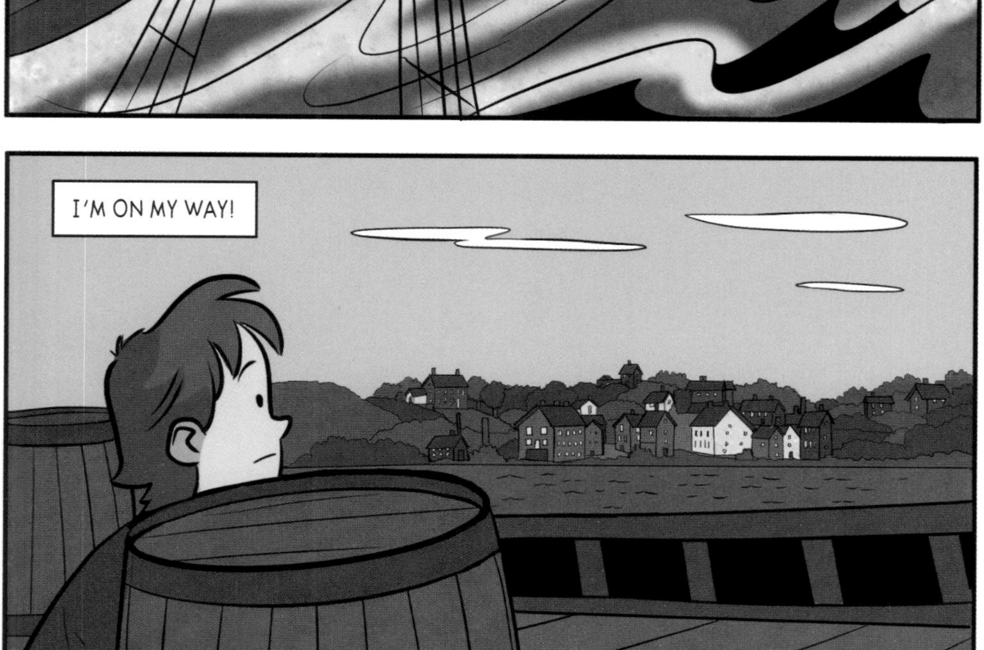
I'M ON MY WAY!

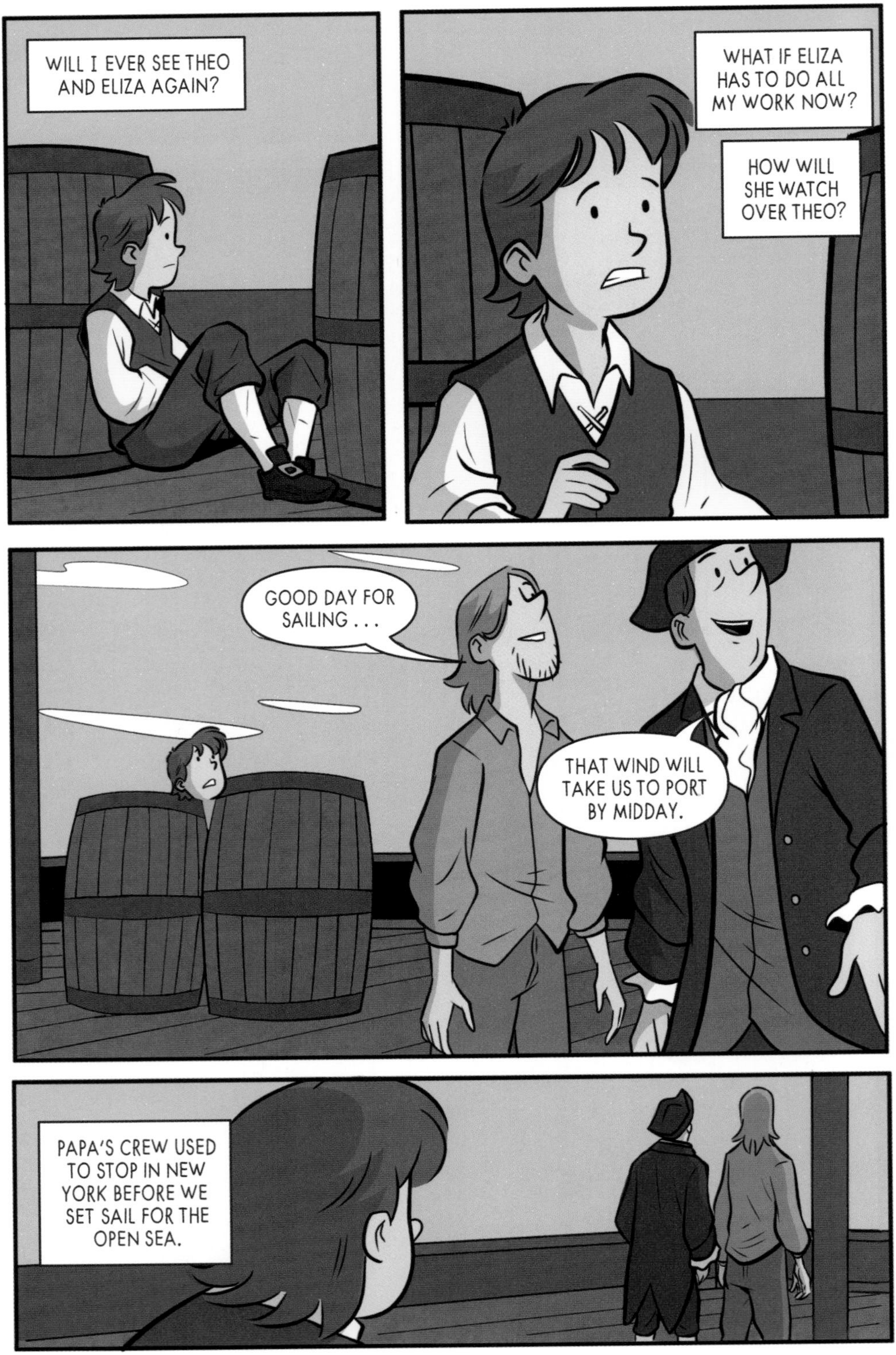
WILL I EVER SEE THEO AND ELIZA AGAIN?
WHAT IF ELIZA HAS TO DO ALL MY WORK NOW?
HOW WILL SHE WATCH OVER THEO?
GOOD DAY FOR SAILING . . .
THAT WIND WILL TAKE US TO PORT BY MIDDAY.
PAPA'S CREW USED TO STOP IN NEW YORK BEFORE WE SET SAIL FOR THE OPEN SEA.

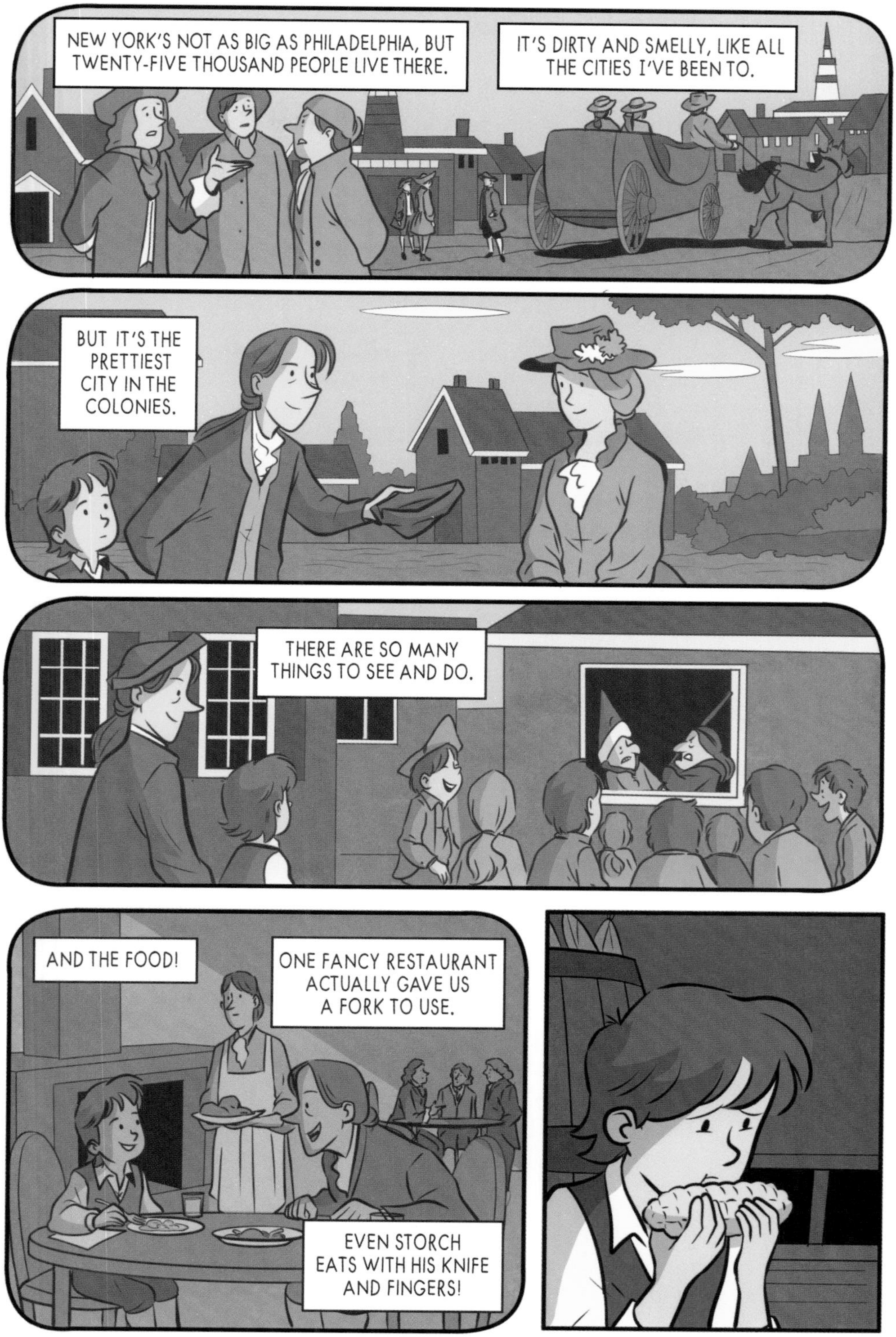
NEW YORK'S NOT AS BIG AS PHILADELPHIA, BUT TWENTY-FIVE THOUSAND PEOPLE LIVE THERE.
IT'S DIRTY AND SMELLY, LIKE ALL THE CITIES I'VE BEEN TO.
BUT IT'S THE PRETTIEST CITY IN THE COLONIES.
THERE ARE SO MANY THINGS TO SEE AND DO.
AND THE FOOD!
ONE FANCY RESTAURANT ACTUALLY GAVE US A FORK TO USE.
EVEN STORCH EATS WITH HIS KNIFE AND FINGERS!

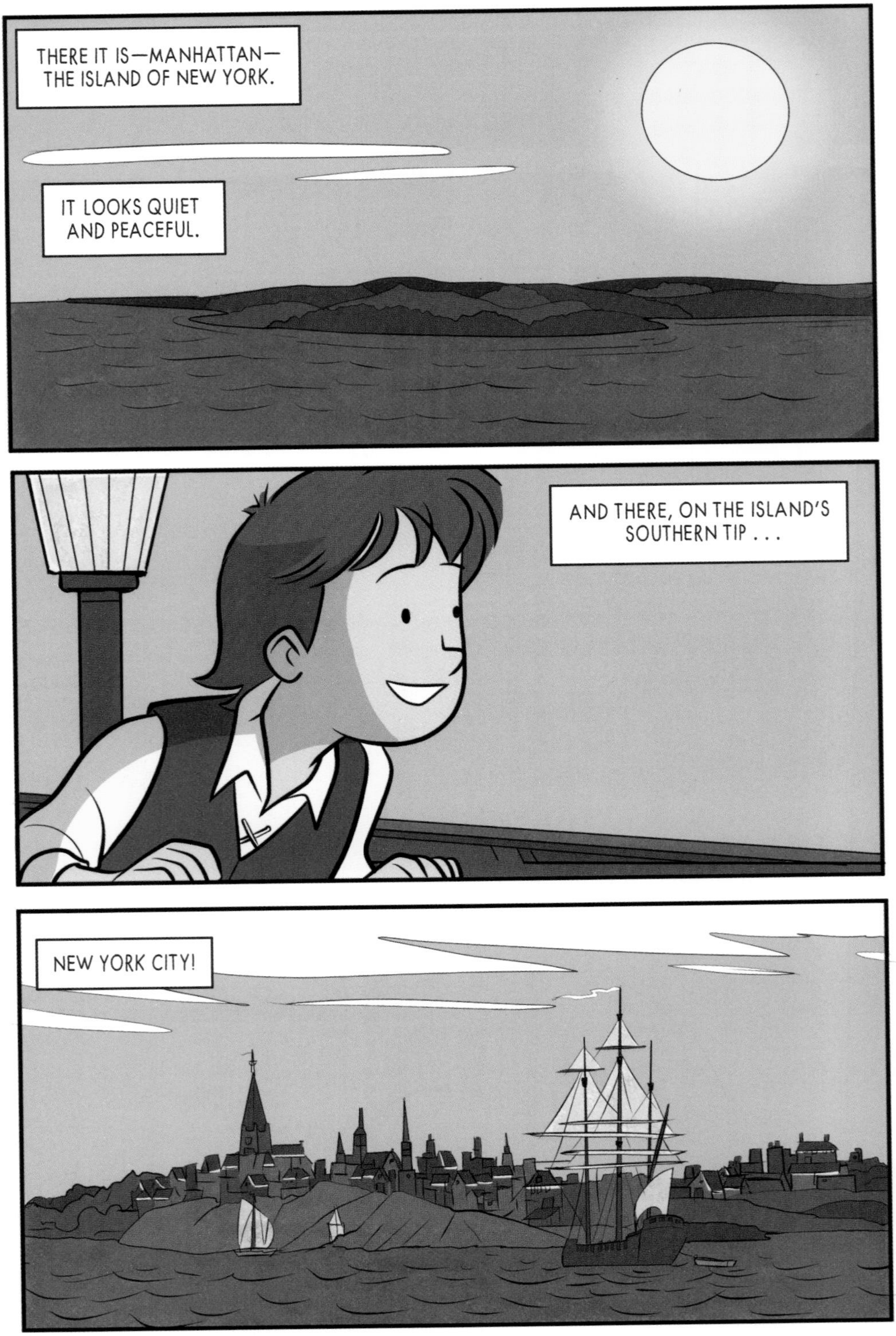
THERE IT IS—MANHATTAN—
THE ISLAND OF NEW YORK.
IT LOOKS QUIET
AND PEACEFUL.
AND THERE, ON THE ISLAND'S
SOUTHERN TIP . . .
NEW YORK CITY!

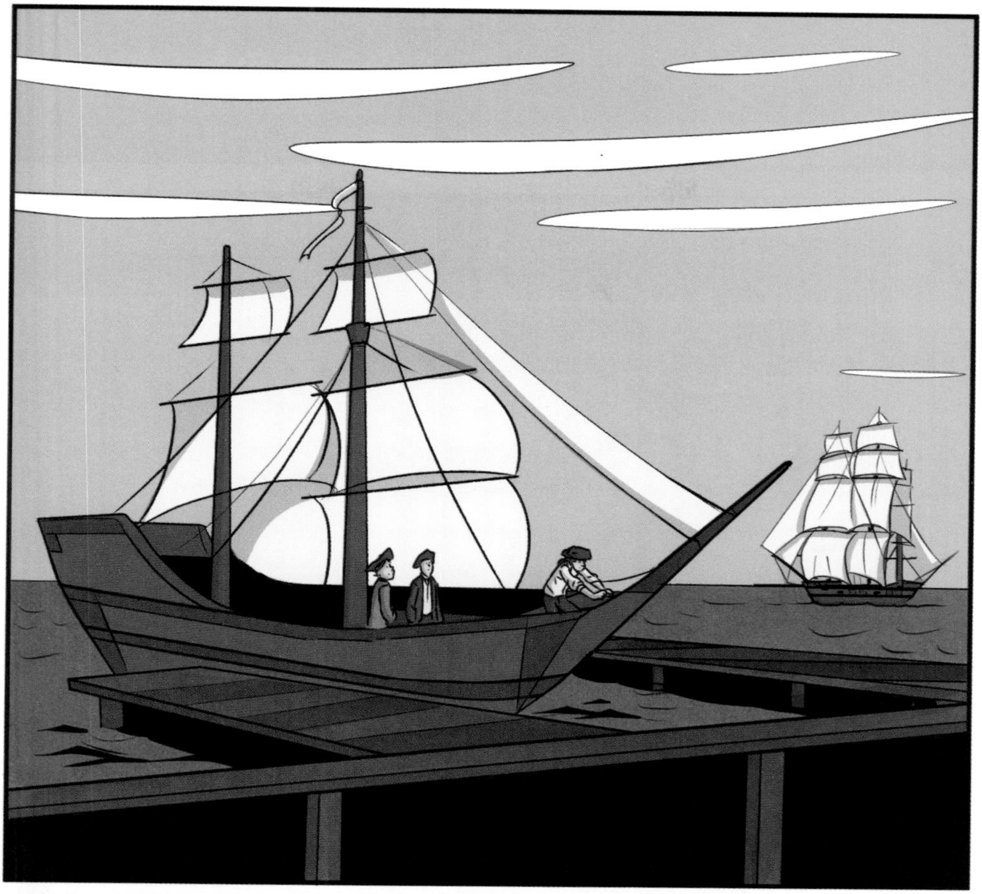

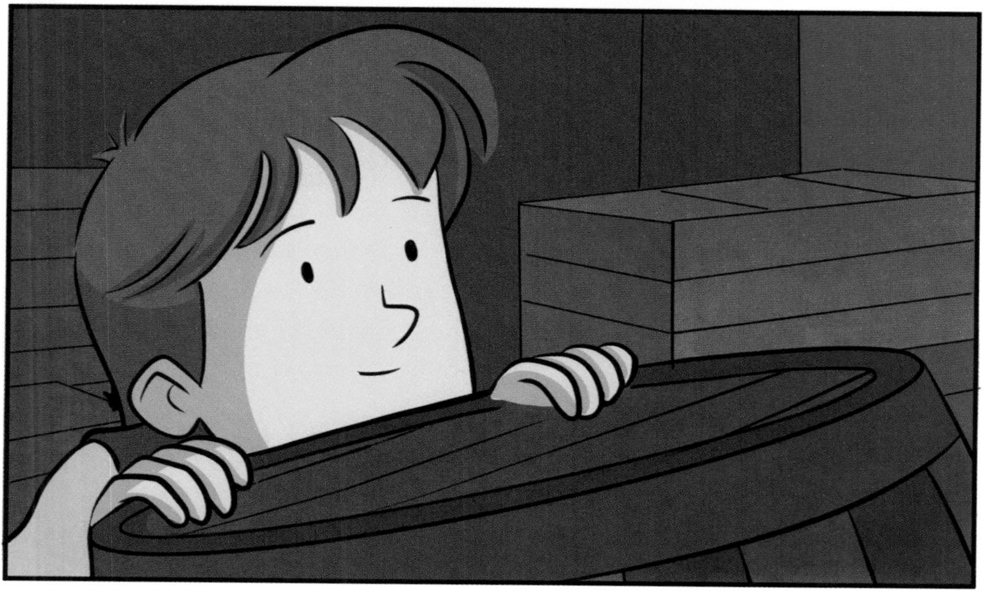

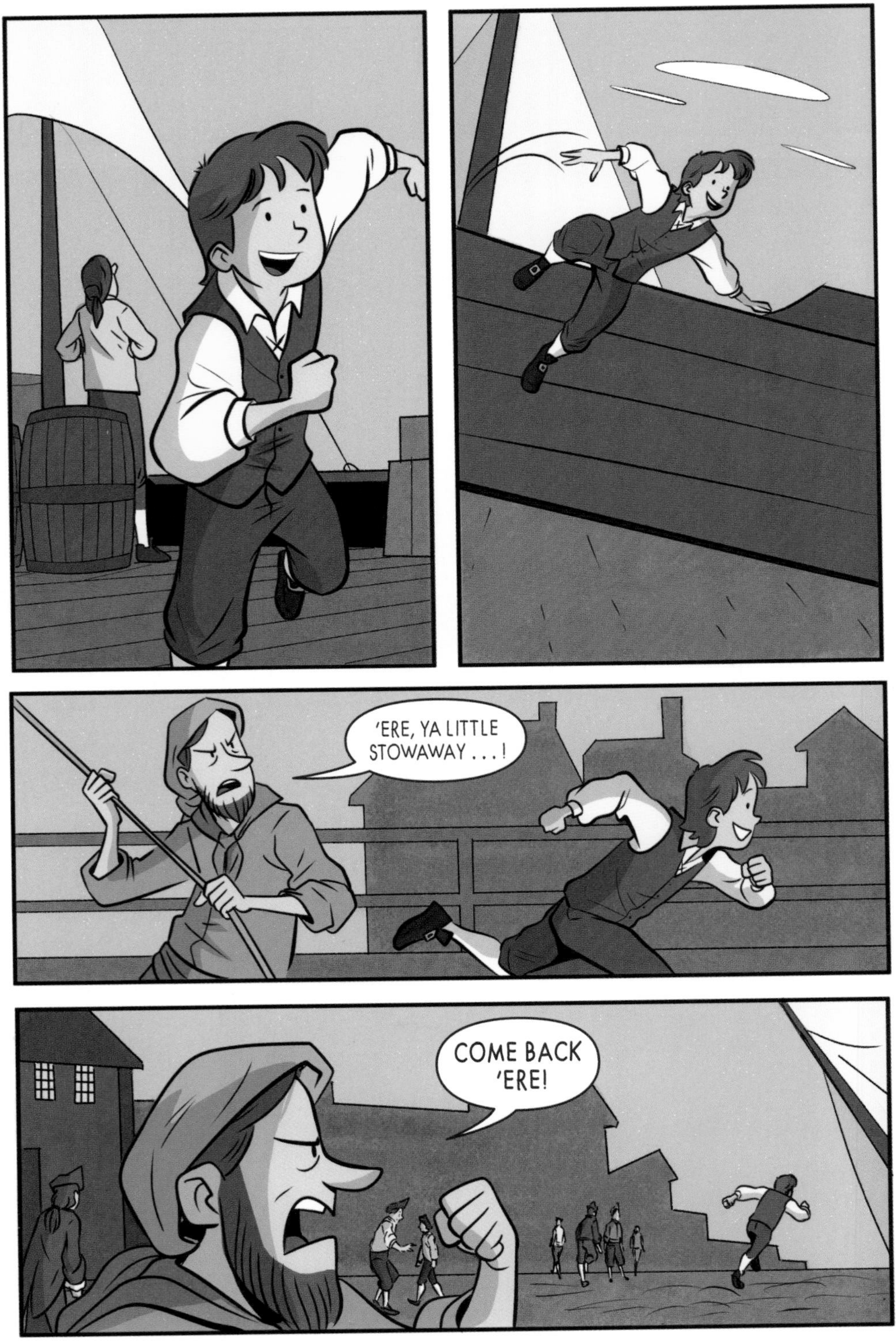
'ERE, YA LITTLE STOWAWAY . . . !
COME BACK 'ERE!

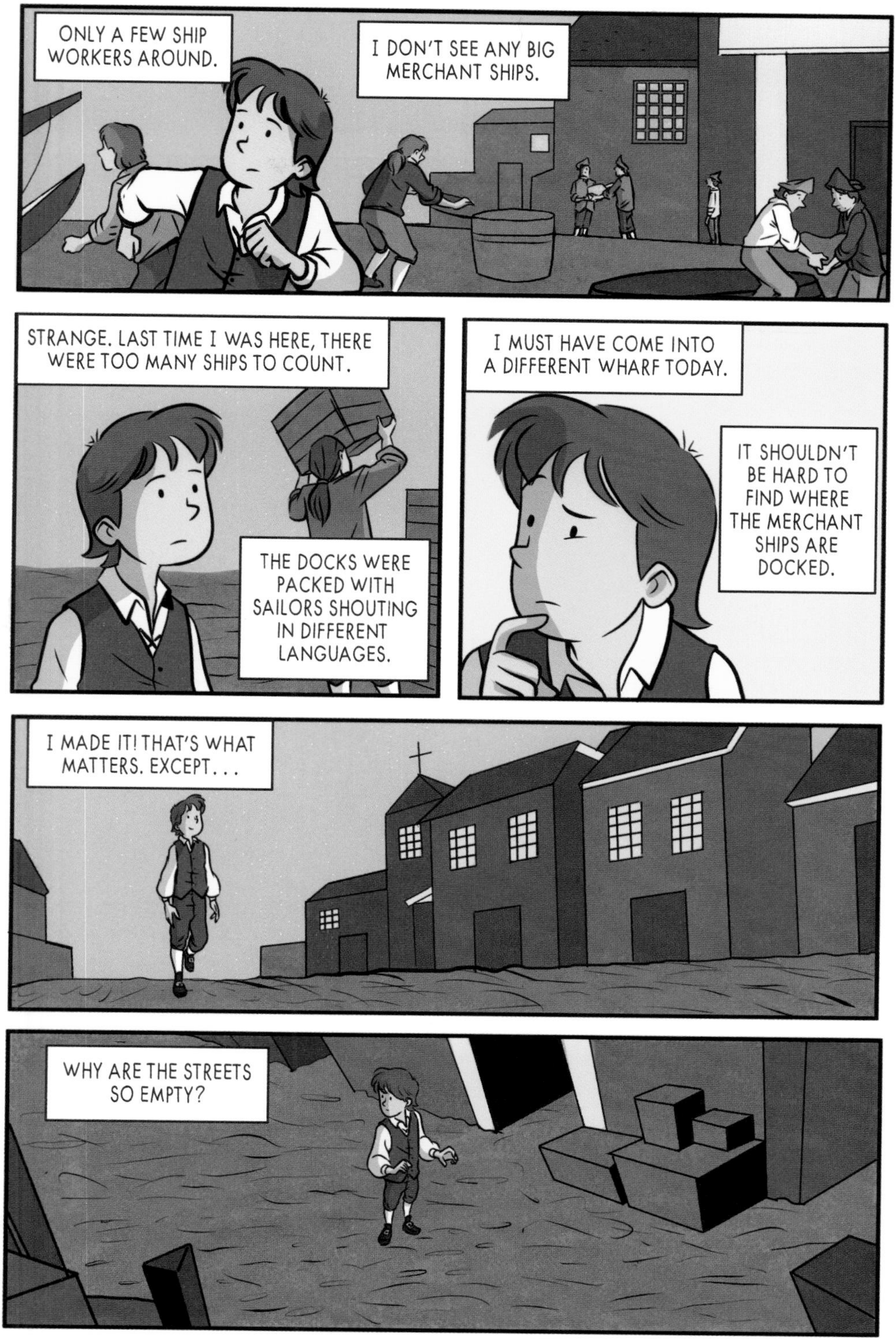
ONLY A FEW SHIP WORKERS AROUND.
I DON'T SEE ANY BIG MERCHANT SHIPS.
STRANGE. LAST TIME I WAS HERE, THERE WERE TOO MANY SHIPS TO COUNT.
THE DOCKS WERE PACKED WITH SAILORS SHOUTING IN DIFFERENT LANGUAGES.
I MUST HAVE COME INTO A DIFFERENT WHARF TODAY.
IT SHOULDN'T BE HARD TO FIND WHERE THE MERCHANT SHIPS ARE DOCKED.
I MADE IT! THAT'S WHAT MATTERS. EXCEPT. . .
WHY ARE THE STREETS SO EMPTY?

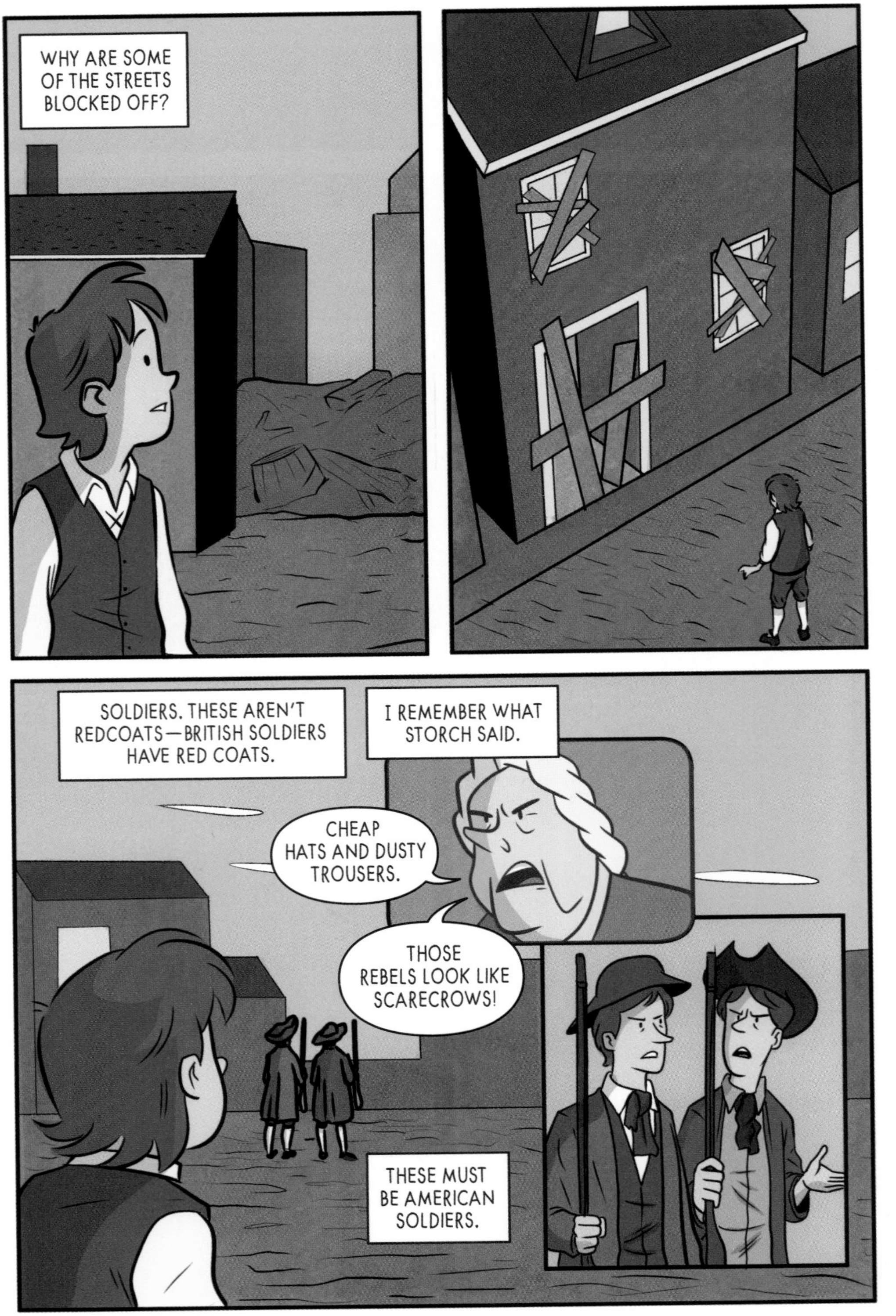
WHY ARE SOME OF THE STREETS BLOCKED OFF?
SOLDIERS. THESE AREN'T REDCOATS—BRITISH SOLDIERS HAVE RED COATS.
I REMEMBER WHAT STORCH SAID.
CHEAP HATS AND DUSTY TROUSERS.
THOSE REBELS LOOK LIKE SCARECROWS!
THESE MUST BE AMERICAN SOLDIERS.

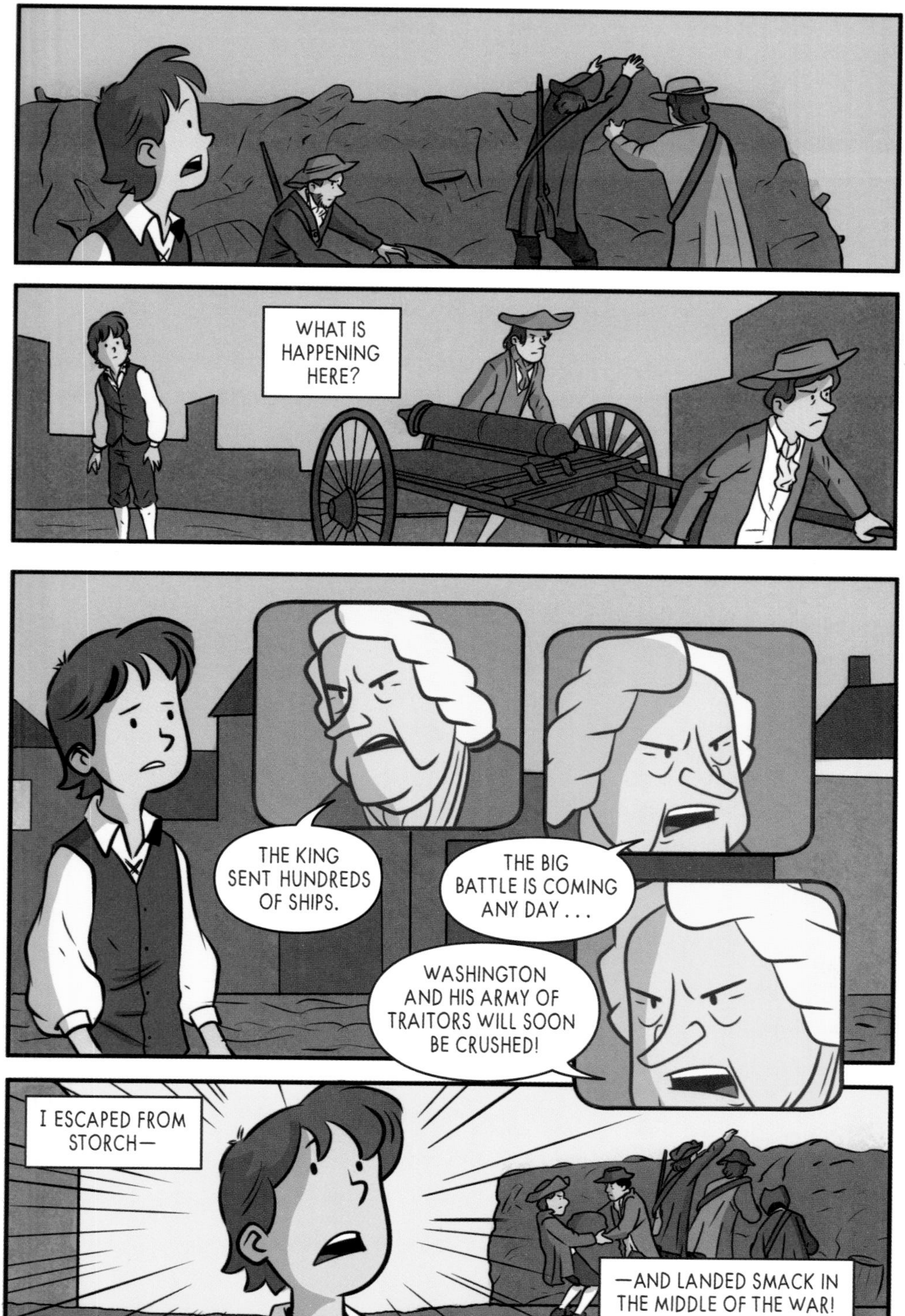
WHAT IS HAPPENING HERE?
THE KING SENT HUNDREDS OF SHIPS.
THE BIG BATTLE IS COMING ANY DAY . . .
WASHINGTON AND HIS ARMY OF TRAITORS WILL SOON BE CRUSHED!
I ESCAPED FROM STORCH—
—AND LANDED SMACK IN THE MIDDLE OF THE WAR!

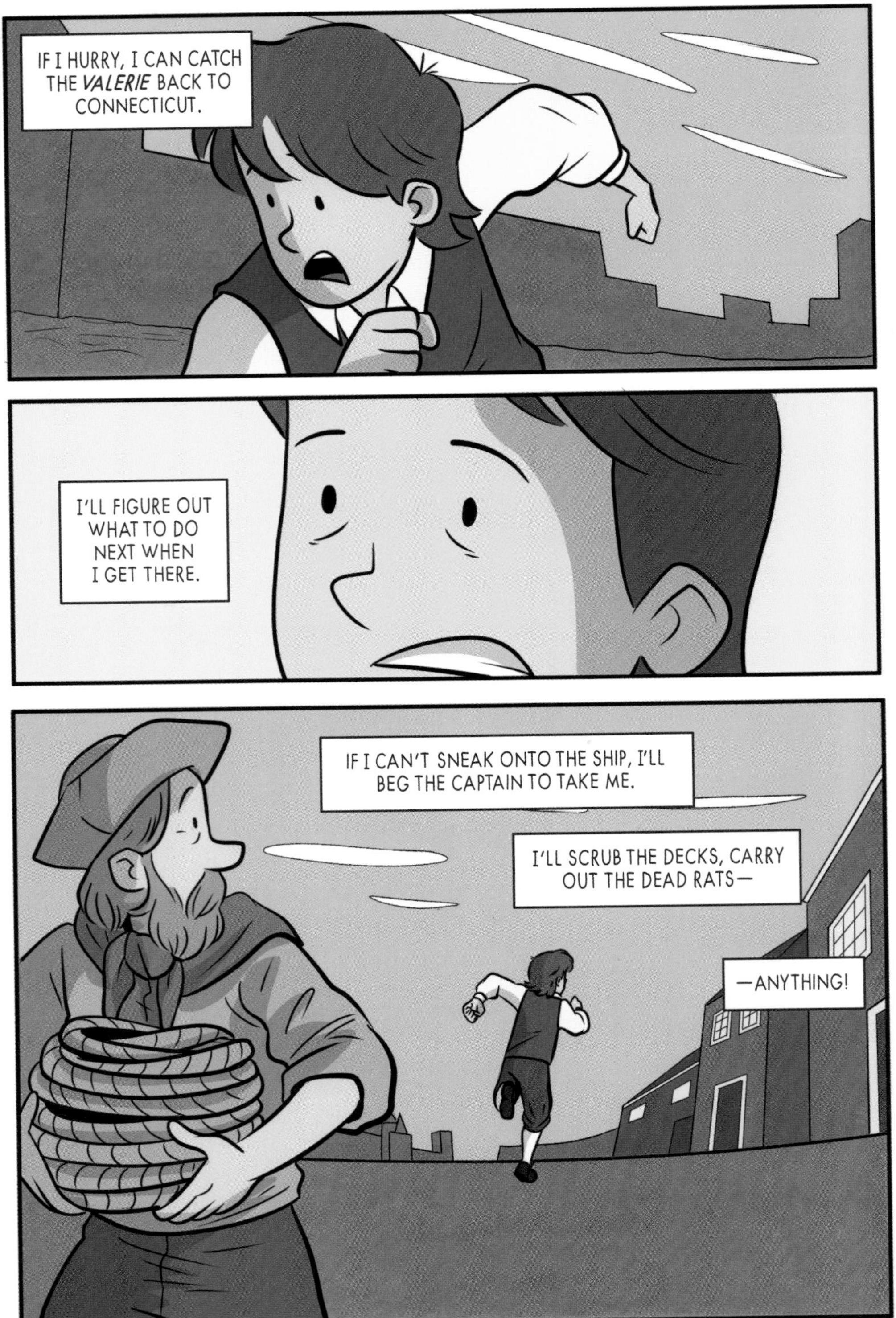
IF I HURRY, I CAN CATCH THE *VALERIE* BACK TO CONNECTICUT.
I'LL FIGURE OUT WHAT TO DO NEXT WHEN I GET THERE.
IF I CAN'T SNEAK ONTO THE SHIP, I'LL BEG THE CAPTAIN TO TAKE ME.
I'LL SCRUB THE DECKS, CARRY OUT THE DEAD RATS—
—ANYTHING!

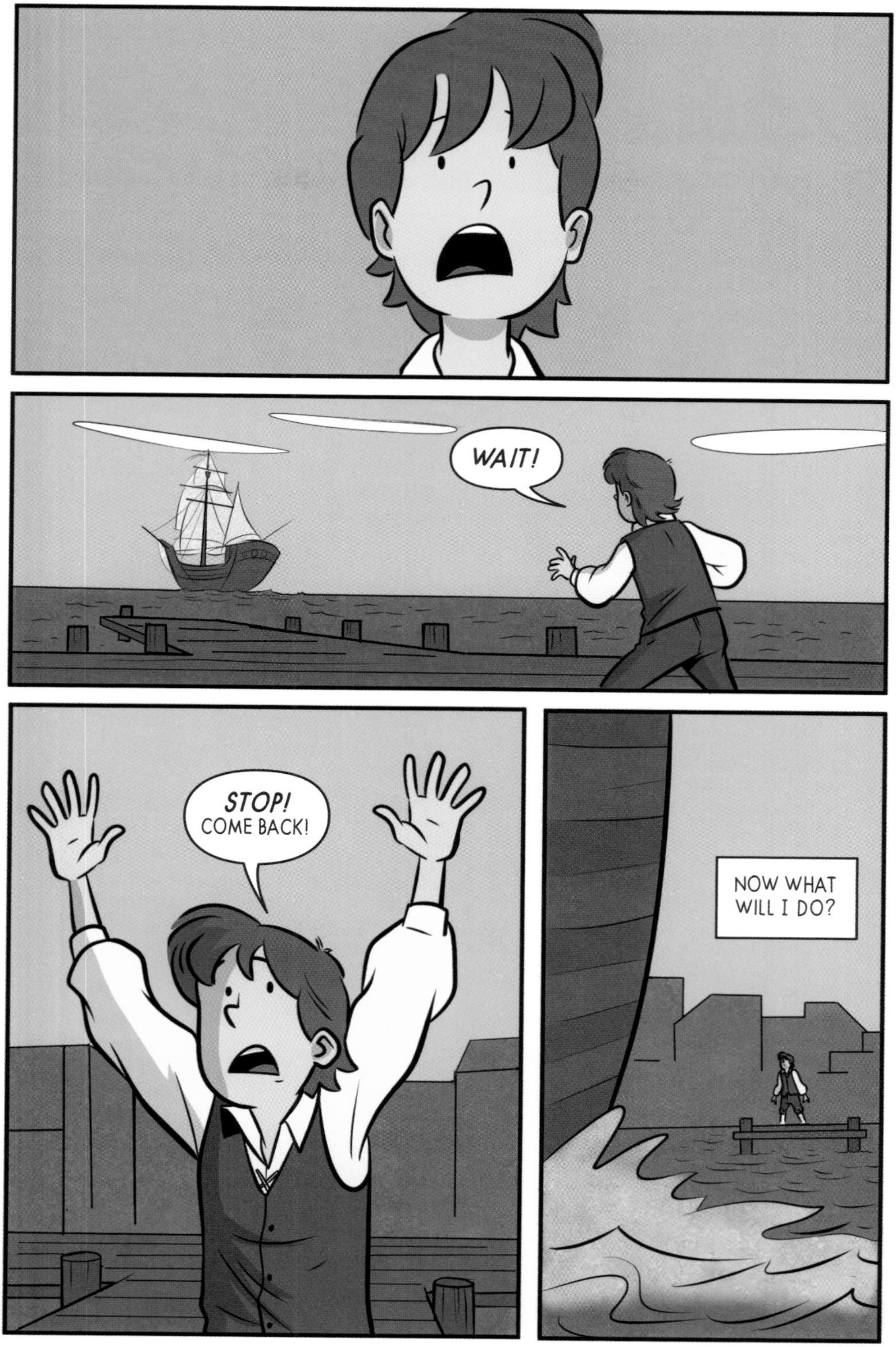
WAIT!
STOP! COME BACK!
NOW WHAT WILL I DO?

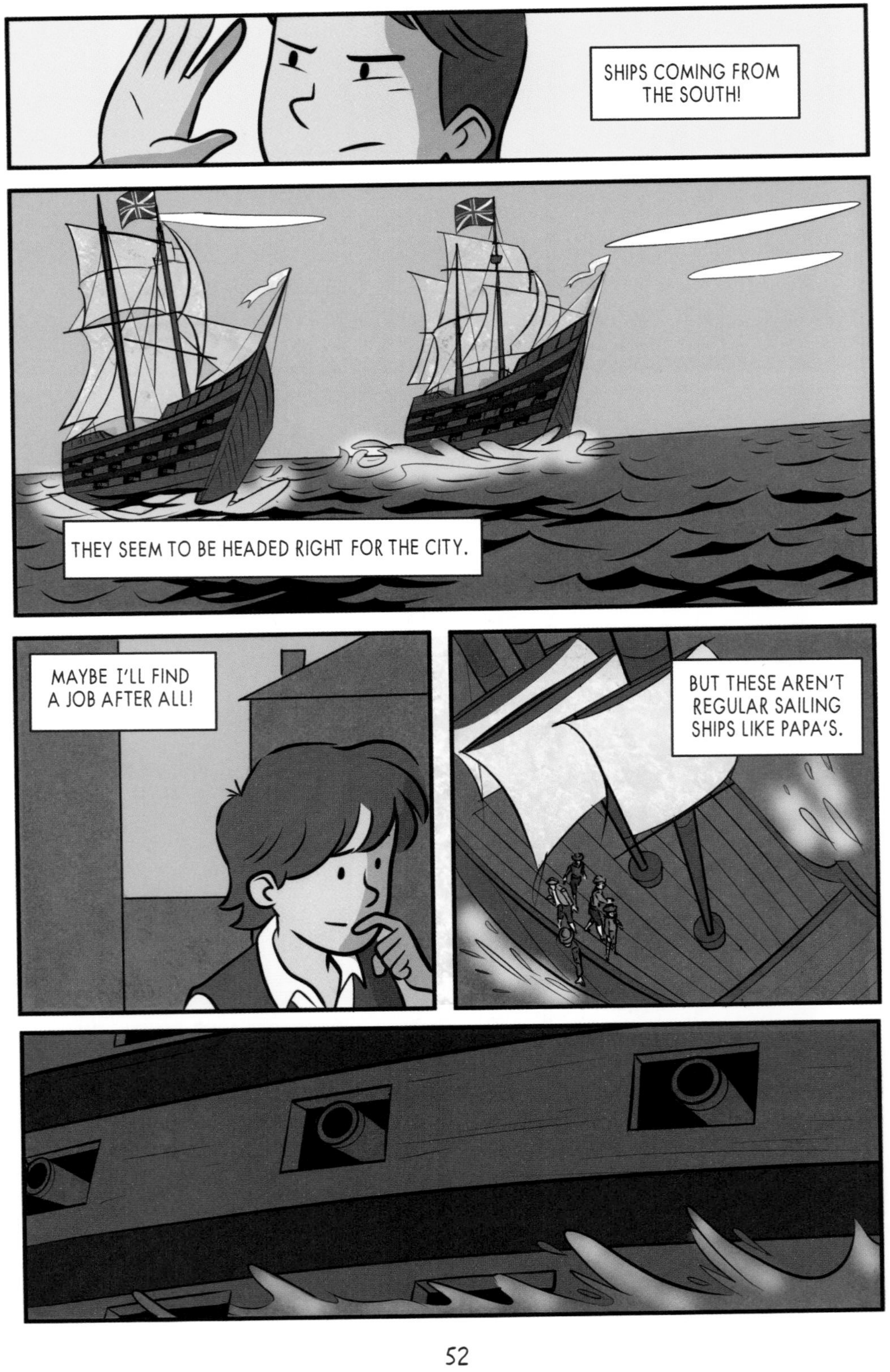
SHIPS COMING FROM THE SOUTH!
THEY SEEM TO BE HEADED RIGHT FOR THE CITY.
MAYBE I'LL FIND A JOB AFTER ALL!
BUT THESE AREN'T REGULAR SAILING SHIPS LIKE PAPA'S.

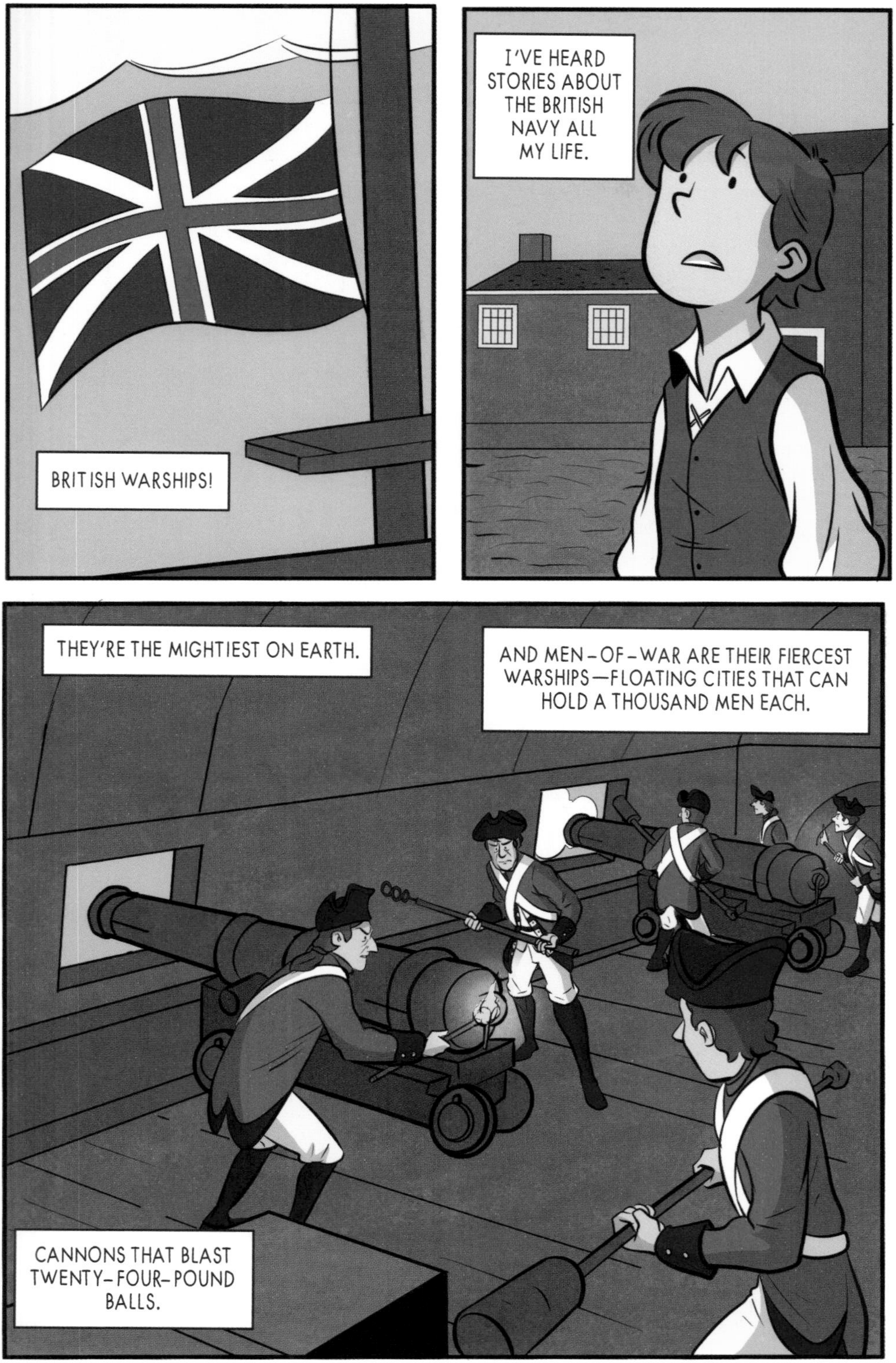
BRITISH WARSHIPS!
I'VE HEARD STORIES ABOUT THE BRITISH NAVY ALL MY LIFE.
THEY'RE THE MIGHTIEST ON EARTH.
AND MEN-OF-WAR ARE THEIR FIERCEST WARSHIPS—FLOATING CITIES THAT CAN HOLD A THOUSAND MEN EACH.
CANNONS THAT BLAST TWENTY-FOUR-POUND BALLS.

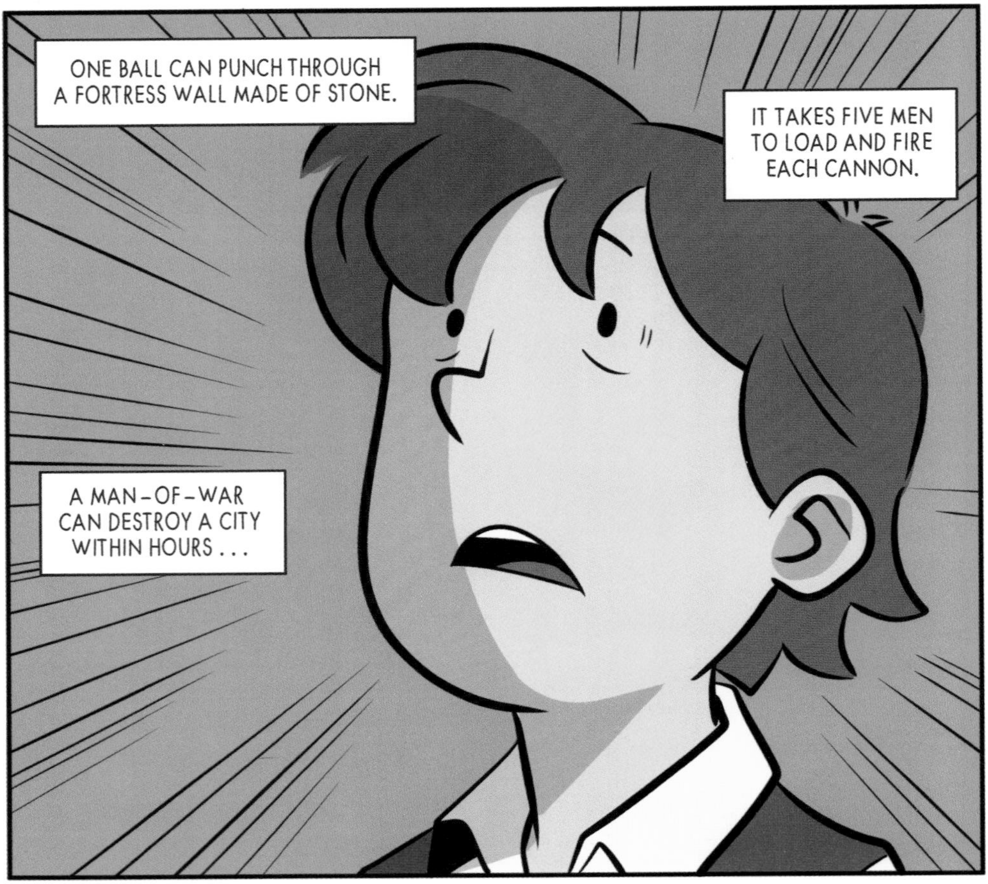
ONE BALL CAN PUNCH THROUGH A FORTRESS WALL MADE OF STONE.
IT TAKES FIVE MEN TO LOAD AND FIRE EACH CANNON.
A MAN-OF-WAR CAN DESTROY A CITY WITHIN HOURS . . .

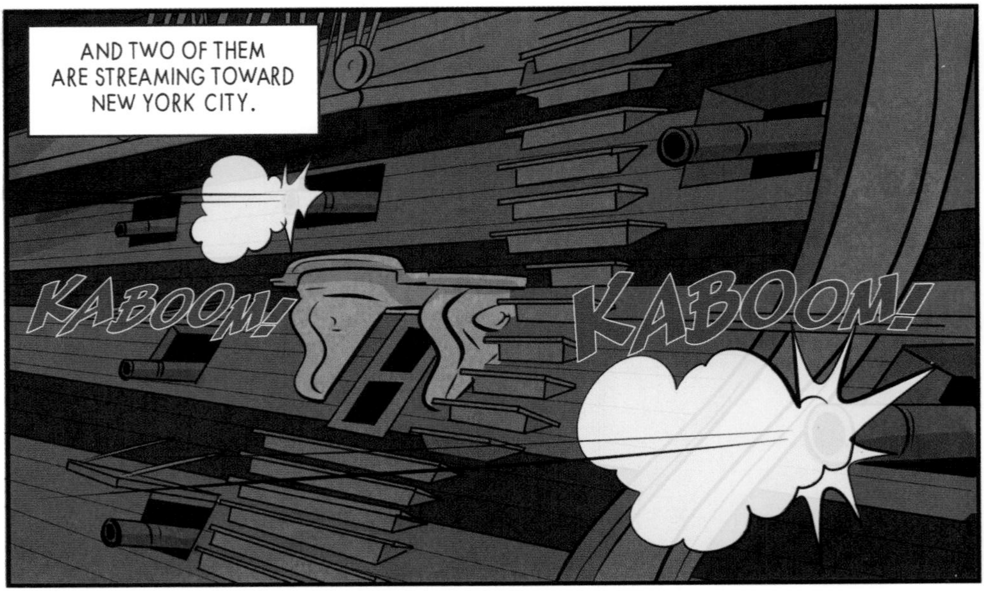
AND TWO OF THEM ARE STREAMING TOWARD NEW YORK CITY.
KABOOM!
KABOOM!

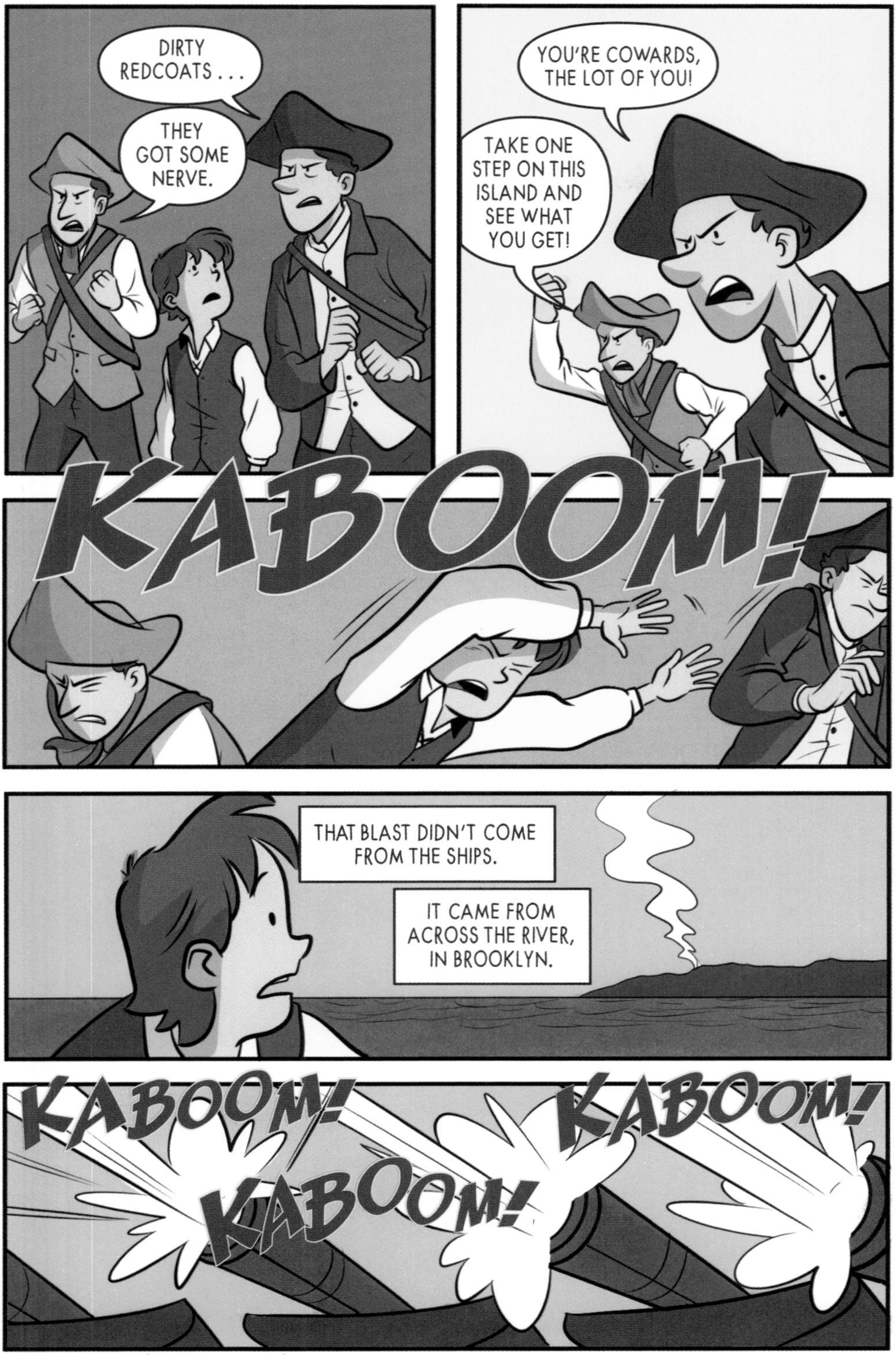
DIRTY REDCOATS . . .
THEY GOT SOME NERVE.
YOU'RE COWARDS, THE LOT OF YOU!
TAKE ONE STEP ON THIS ISLAND AND SEE WHAT YOU GET!
KABOOM!
THAT BLAST DIDN'T COME FROM THE SHIPS.
IT CAME FROM ACROSS THE RIVER, IN BROOKLYN.
KABOOM!
KABOOM!
KABOOM!

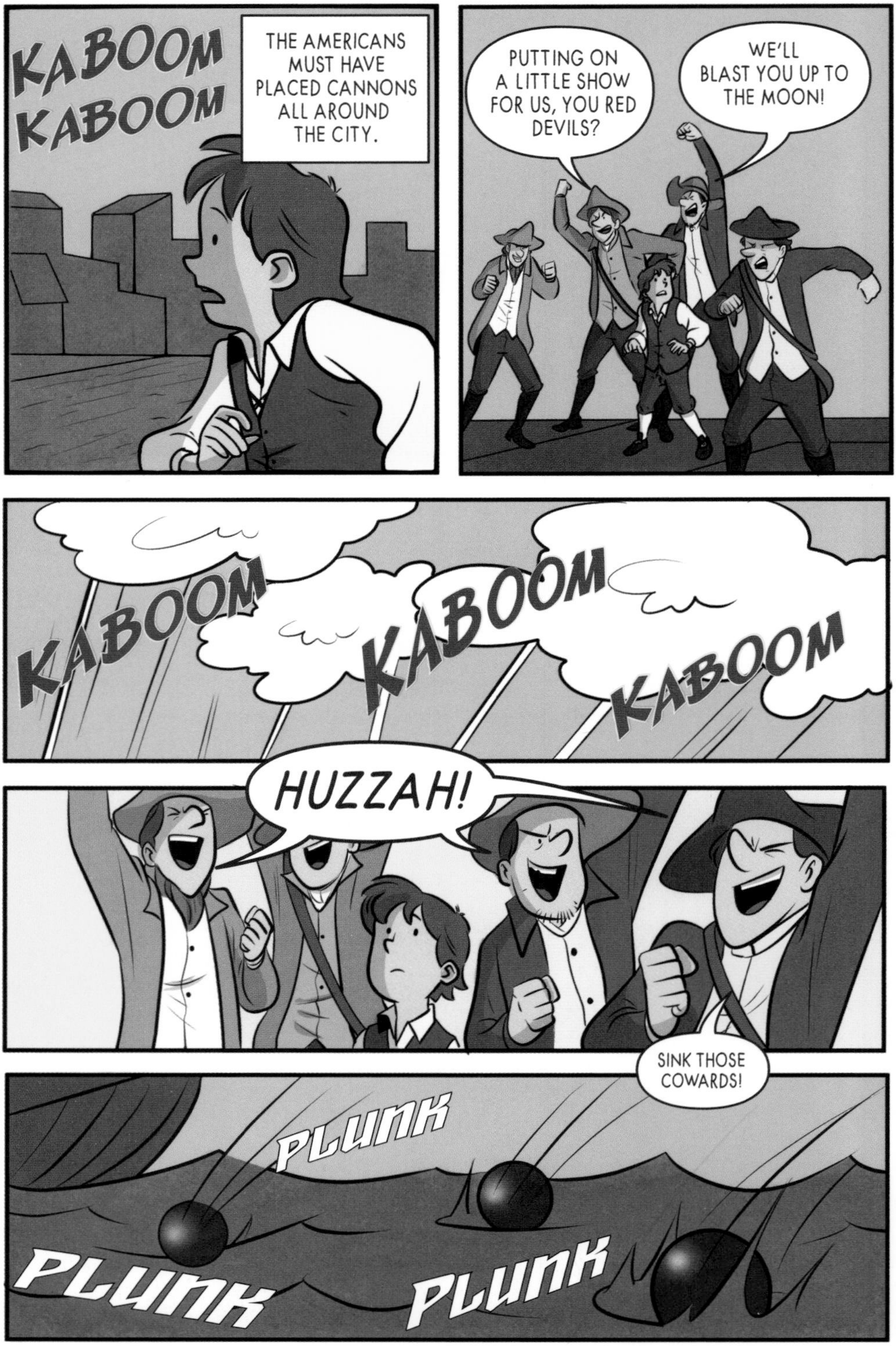
KABOOM
KABOOM
THE AMERICANS MUST HAVE PLACED CANNONS ALL AROUND THE CITY.
PUTTING ON A LITTLE SHOW FOR US, YOU RED DEVILS?
WE'LL BLAST YOU UP TO THE MOON!
KABOOM
KABOOM
KABOOM
HUZZAH!
SINK THOSE COWARDS!
PLUNK
PLUNK
PLUNK

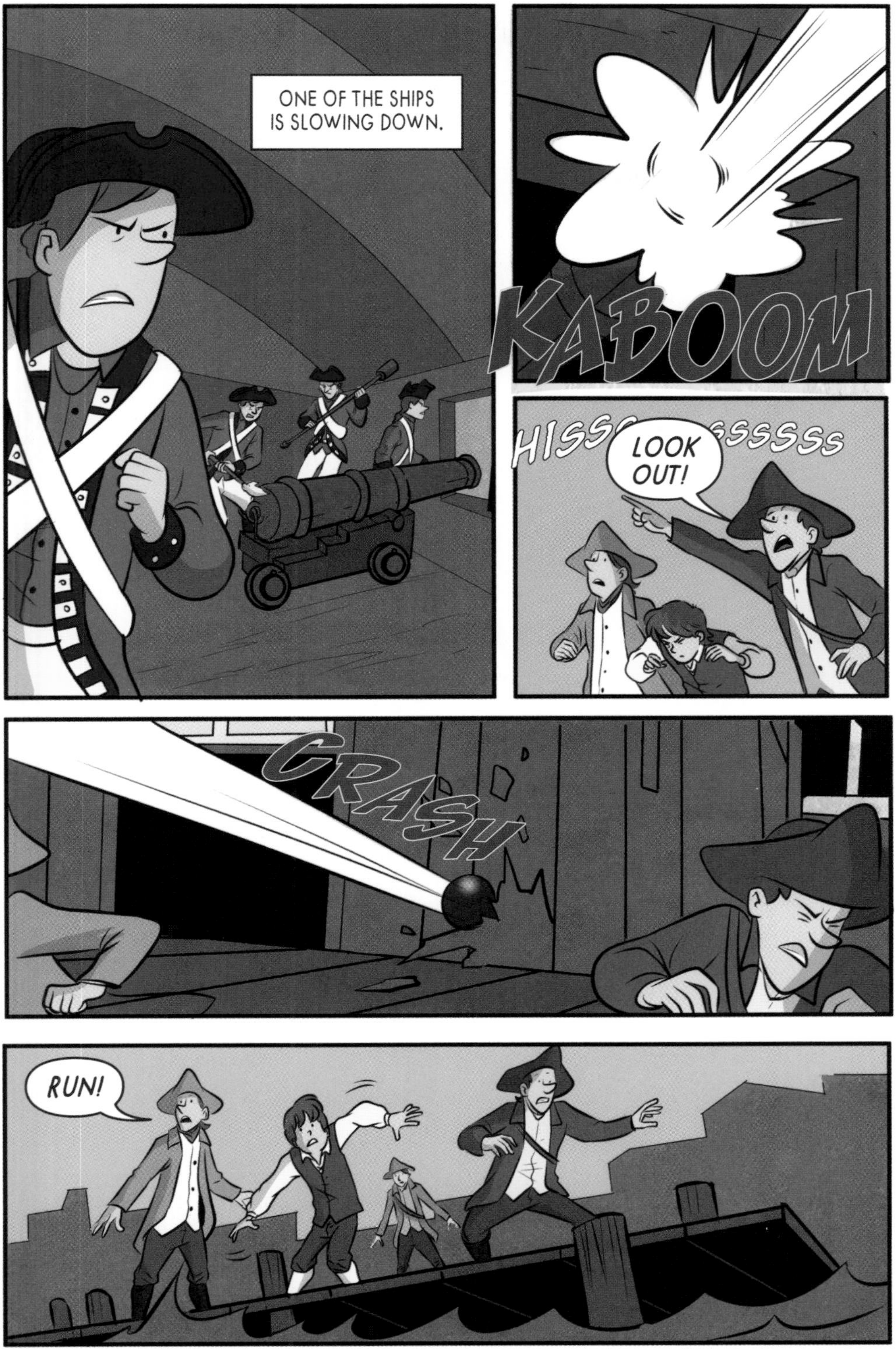
ONE OF THE SHIPS IS SLOWING DOWN.
KABOOM
HISSSSSSSSS
LOOK OUT!
CRASH
RUN!

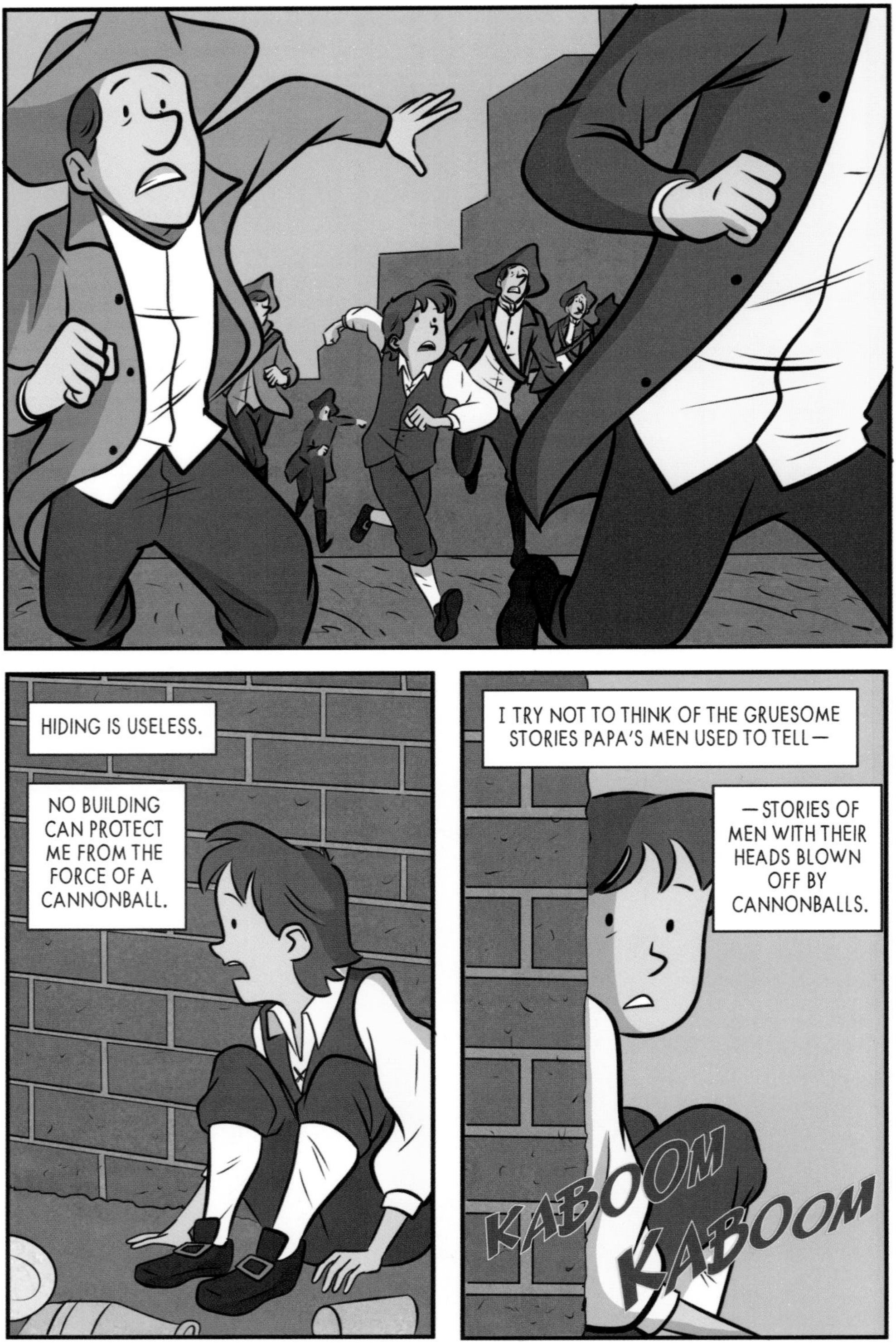
HIDING IS USELESS.
NO BUILDING CAN PROTECT ME FROM THE FORCE OF A CANNONBALL.
I TRY NOT TO THINK OF THE GRUESOME STORIES PAPA'S MEN USED TO TELL—
—STORIES OF MEN WITH THEIR HEADS BLOWN OFF BY CANNONBALLS.
KABOOM
KABOOM

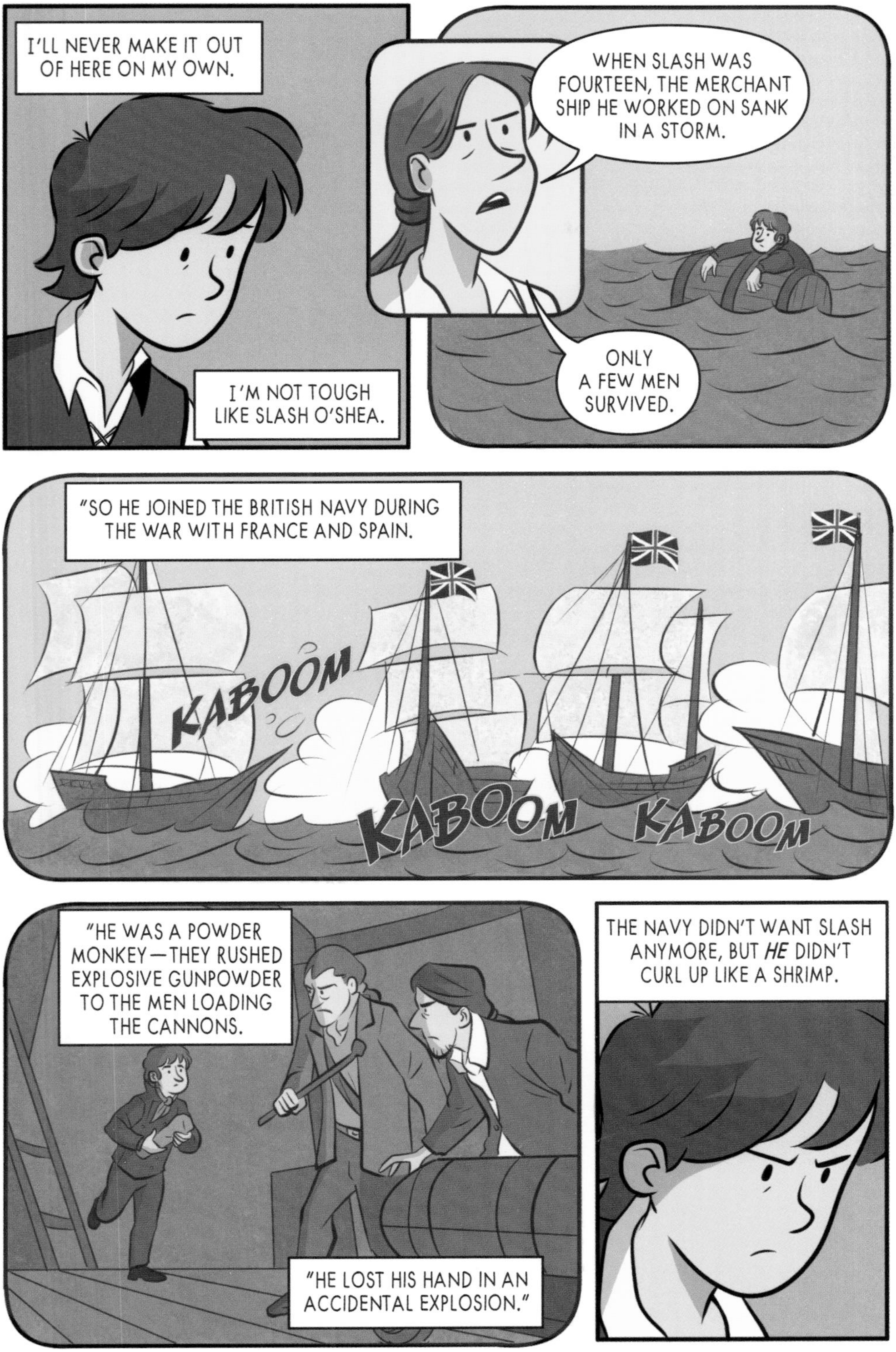
I'LL NEVER MAKE IT OUT OF HERE ON MY OWN.
I'M NOT TOUGH LIKE SLASH O'SHEA.
WHEN SLASH WAS FOURTEEN, THE MERCHANT SHIP HE WORKED ON SANK IN A STORM.
ONLY A FEW MEN SURVIVED.
"SO HE JOINED THE BRITISH NAVY DURING THE WAR WITH FRANCE AND SPAIN.
KABOOM
KABOOM
KABOOM
"HE WAS A POWDER MONKEY—THEY RUSHED EXPLOSIVE GUNPOWDER TO THE MEN LOADING THE CANNONS.
"HE LOST HIS HAND IN AN ACCIDENTAL EXPLOSION."
THE NAVY DIDN'T WANT SLASH ANYMORE, BUT *HE* DIDN'T CURL UP LIKE A SHRIMP.

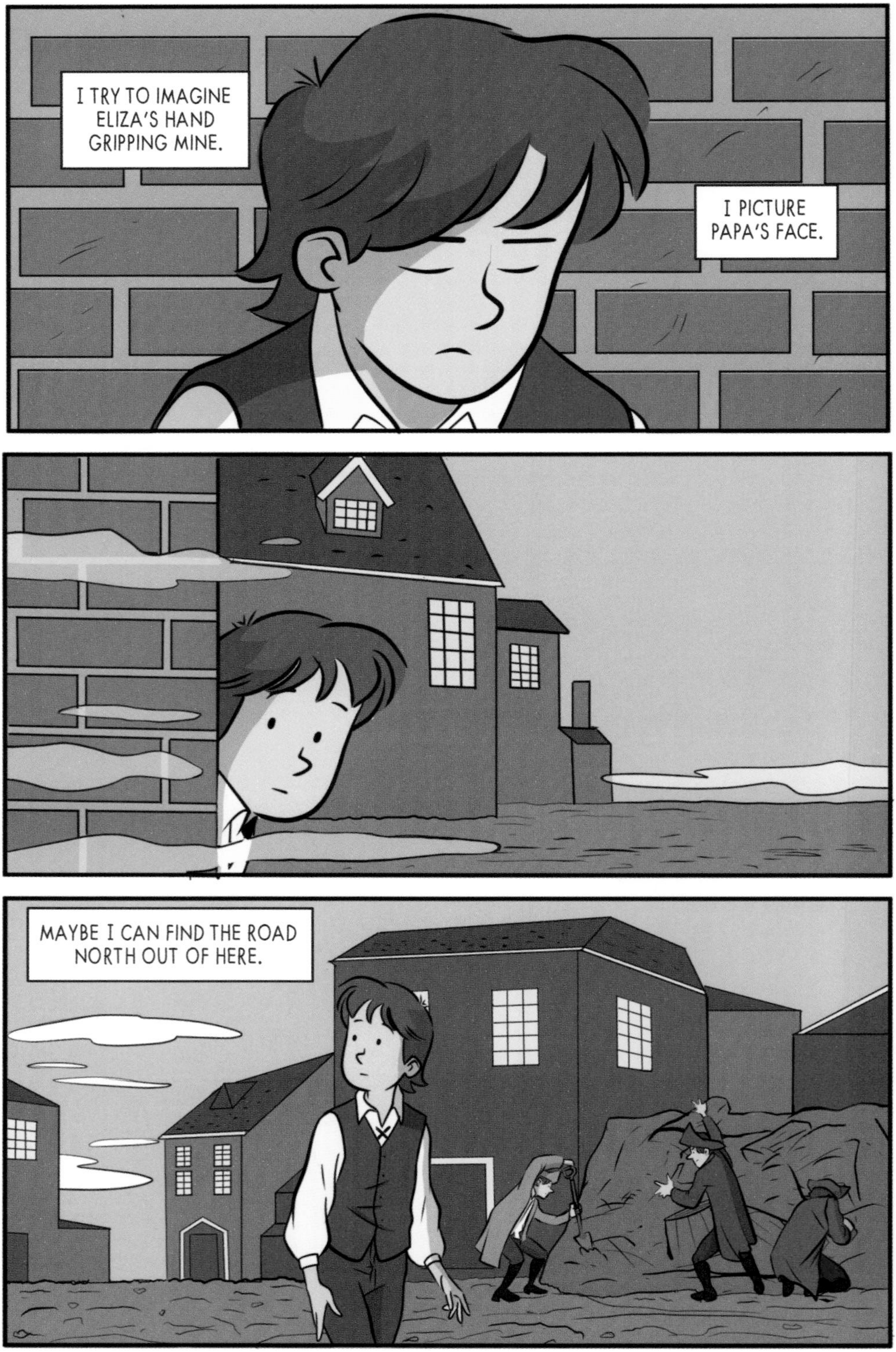
I TRY TO IMAGINE ELIZA'S HAND GRIPPING MINE.
I PICTURE PAPA'S FACE.
MAYBE I CAN FIND THE ROAD NORTH OUT OF HERE.

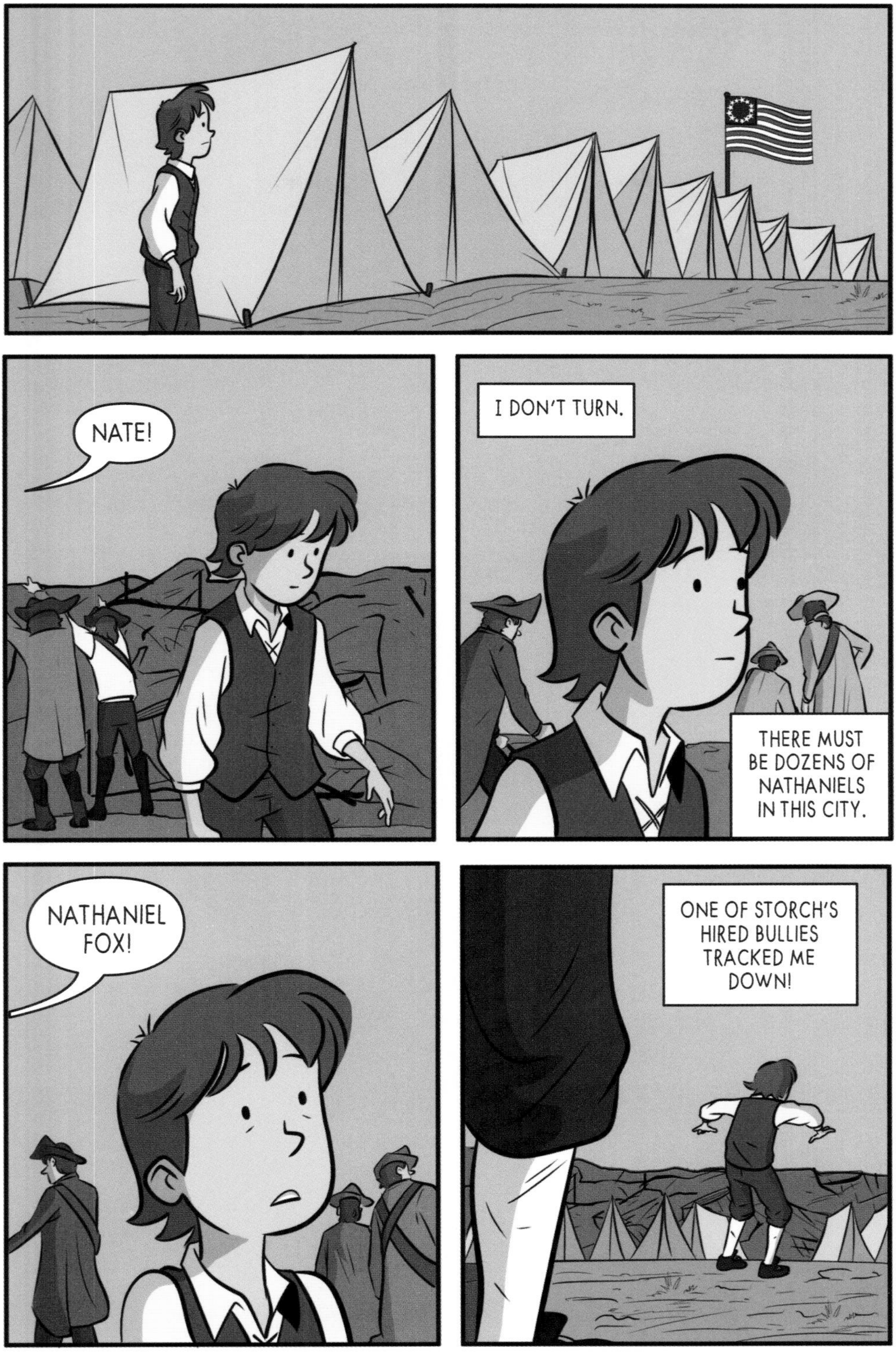
NATE!
I DON'T TURN.
THERE MUST BE DOZENS OF NATHANIELS IN THIS CITY.
NATHANIEL FOX!
ONE OF STORCH'S HIRED BULLIES TRACKED ME DOWN!

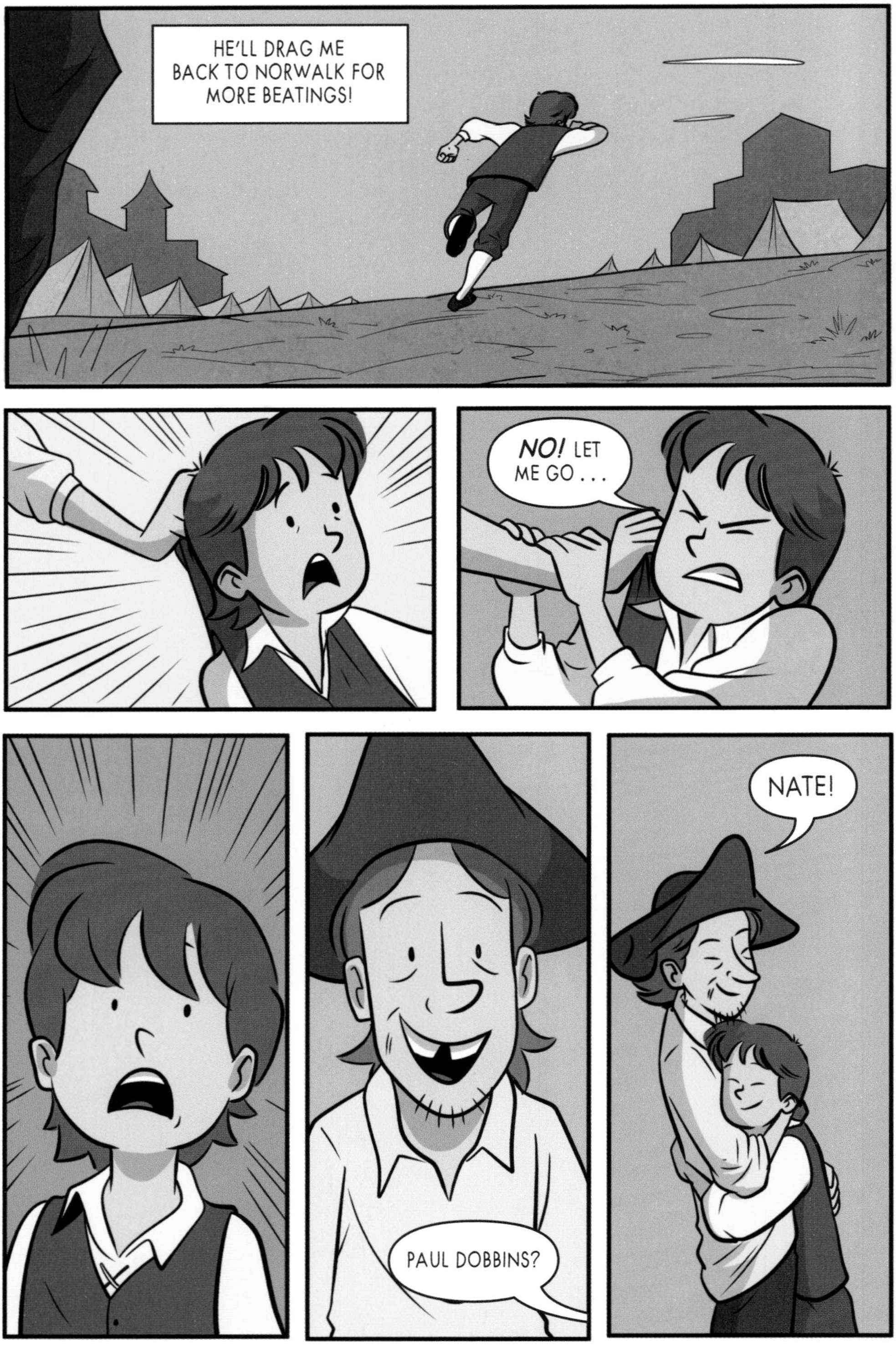
HE'LL DRAG ME BACK TO NORWALK FOR MORE BEATINGS!
NO! LET ME GO . . .
PAUL DOBBINS?
NATE!

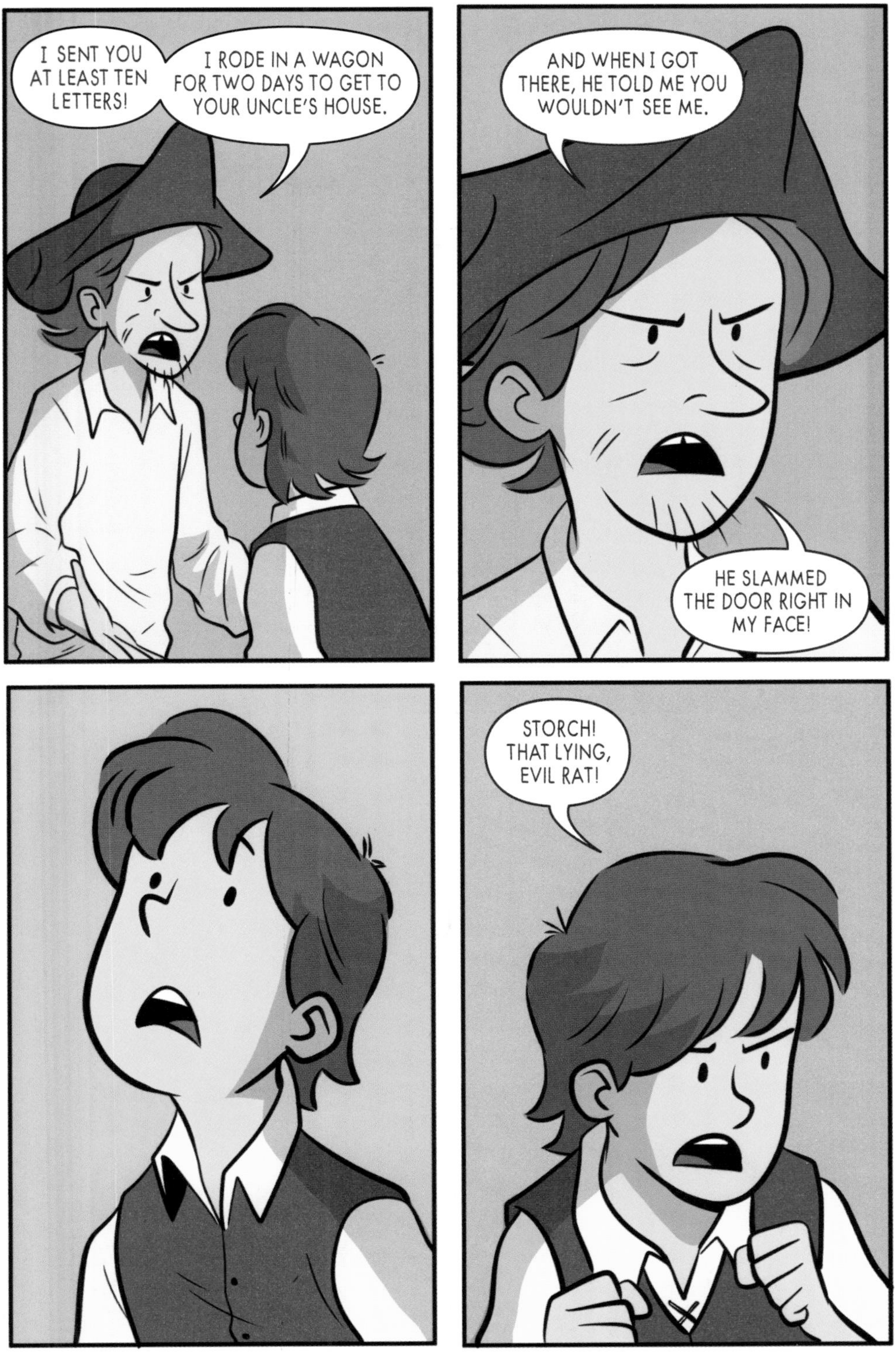
I SENT YOU AT LEAST TEN LETTERS!
I RODE IN A WAGON FOR TWO DAYS TO GET TO YOUR UNCLE'S HOUSE.
AND WHEN I GOT THERE, HE TOLD ME YOU WOULDN'T SEE ME.
HE SLAMMED THE DOOR RIGHT IN MY FACE!
STORCH! THAT LYING, EVIL RAT!

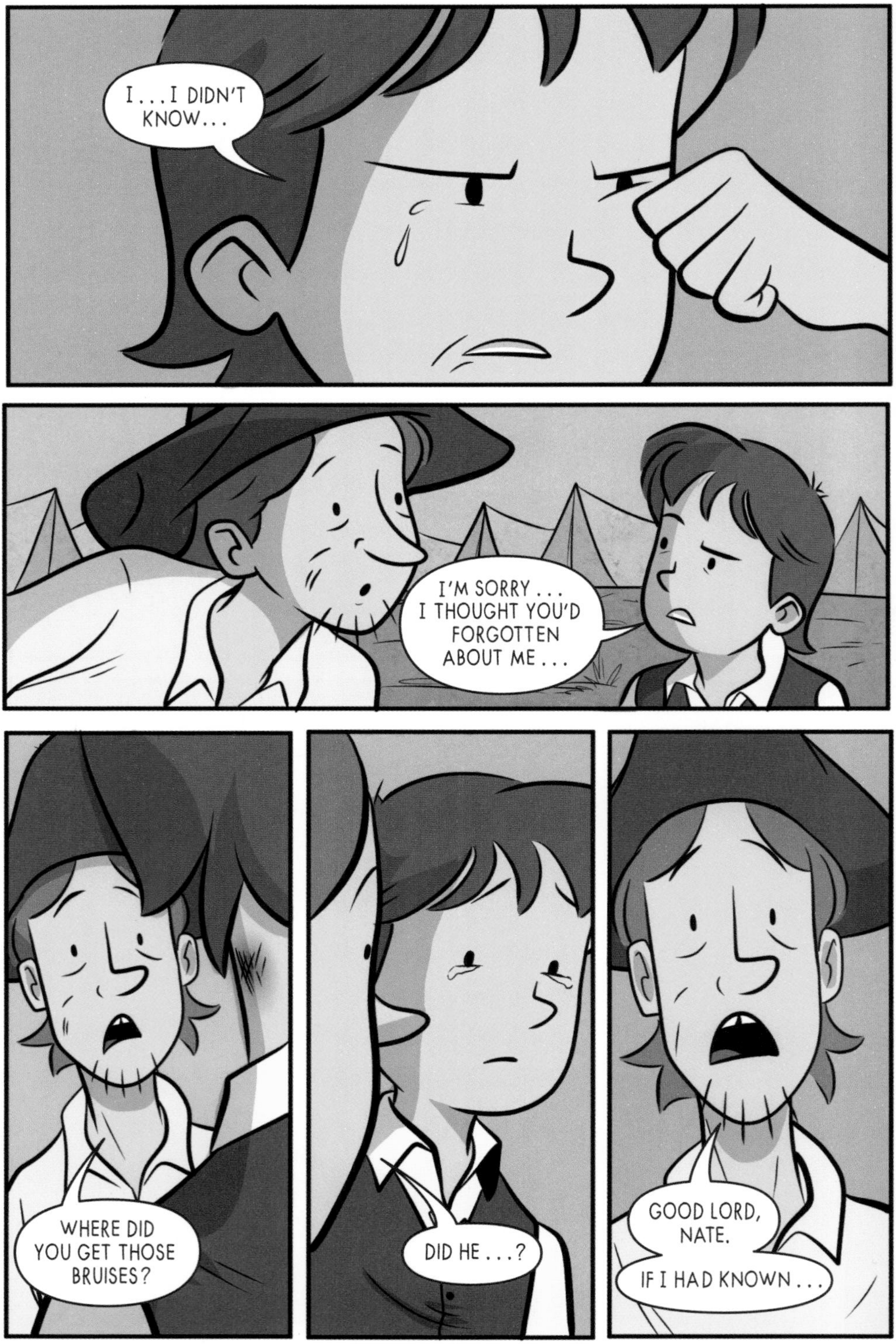
I . . . I DIDN'T KNOW . . .
I'M SORRY . . . I THOUGHT YOU'D FORGOTTEN ABOUT ME . . .
WHERE DID YOU GET THOSE BRUISES?
DID HE . . . ?
GOOD LORD, NATE.
IF I HAD KNOWN . . .

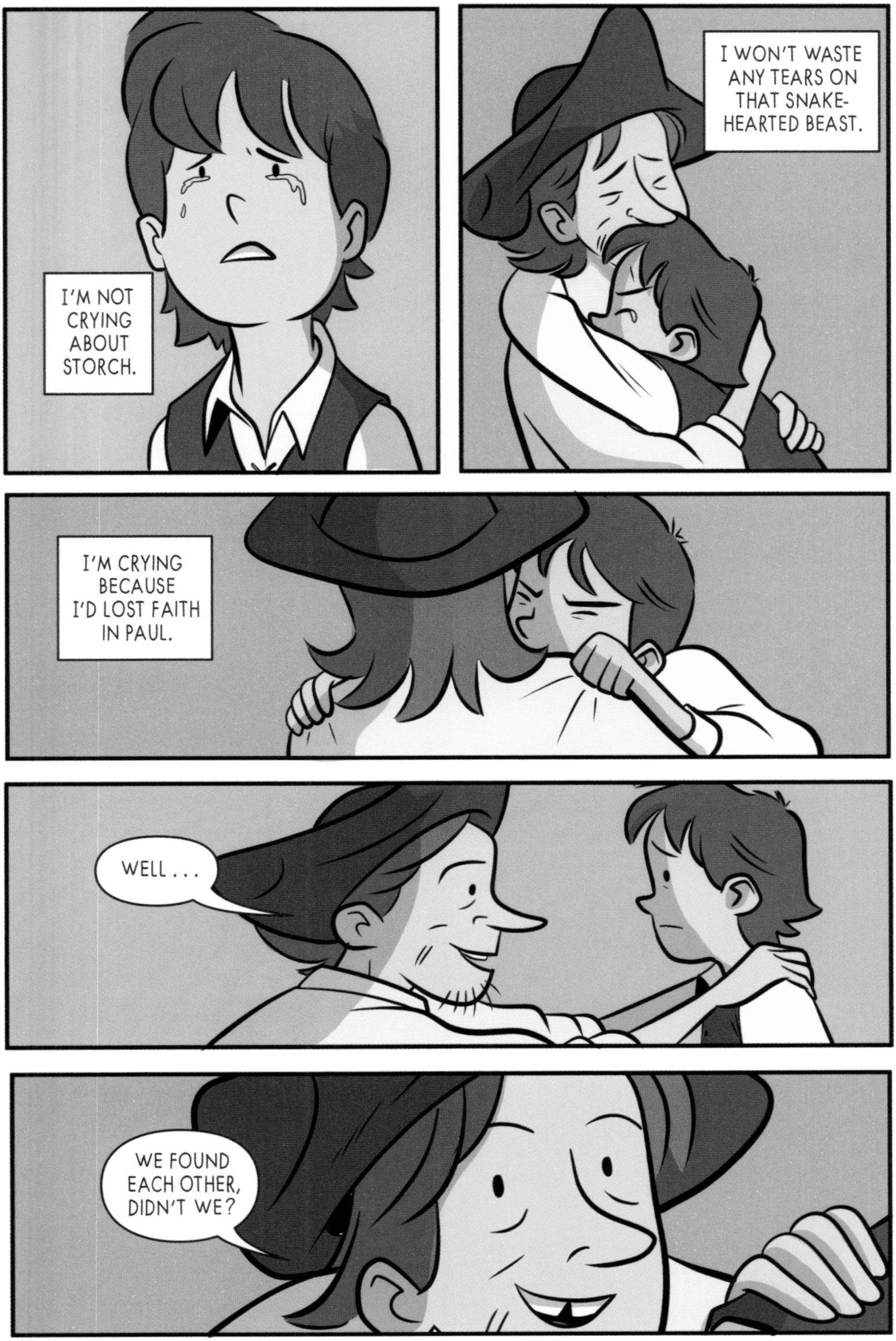
I'M NOT CRYING ABOUT STORCH.
I WON'T WASTE ANY TEARS ON THAT SNAKE-HEARTED BEAST.
I'M CRYING BECAUSE I'D LOST FAITH IN PAUL.
WELL . . .
WE FOUND EACH OTHER, DIDN'T WE?

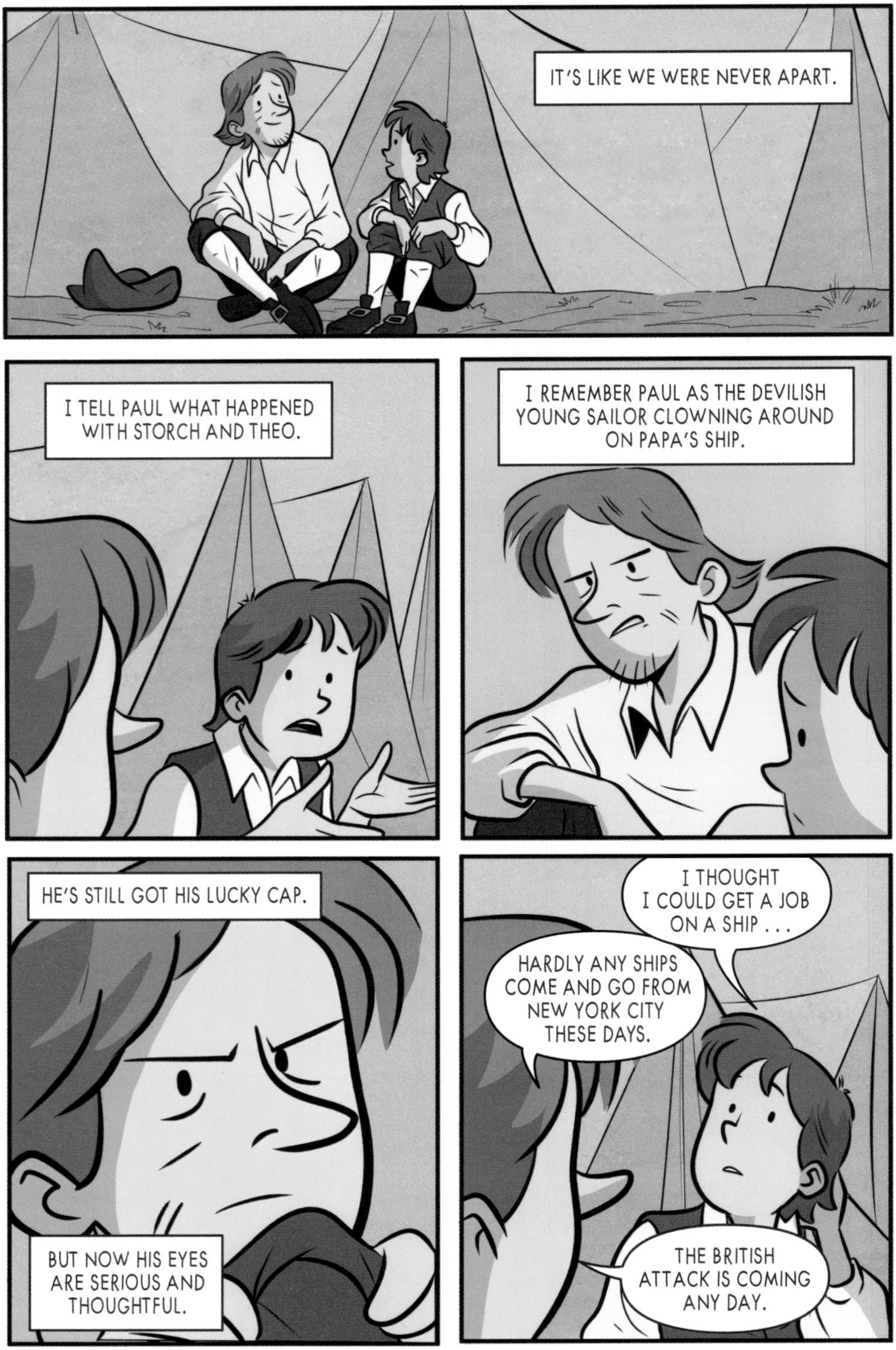
IT'S LIKE WE WERE NEVER APART.
I TELL PAUL WHAT HAPPENED WITH STORCH AND THEO.
I REMEMBER PAUL AS THE DEVILISH YOUNG SAILOR CLOWNING AROUND ON PAPA'S SHIP.
HE'S STILL GOT HIS LUCKY CAP.
BUT NOW HIS EYES ARE SERIOUS AND THOUGHTFUL.
I THOUGHT I COULD GET A JOB ON A SHIP . . .
HARDLY ANY SHIPS COME AND GO FROM NEW YORK CITY THESE DAYS.
THE BRITISH ATTACK IS COMING ANY DAY.

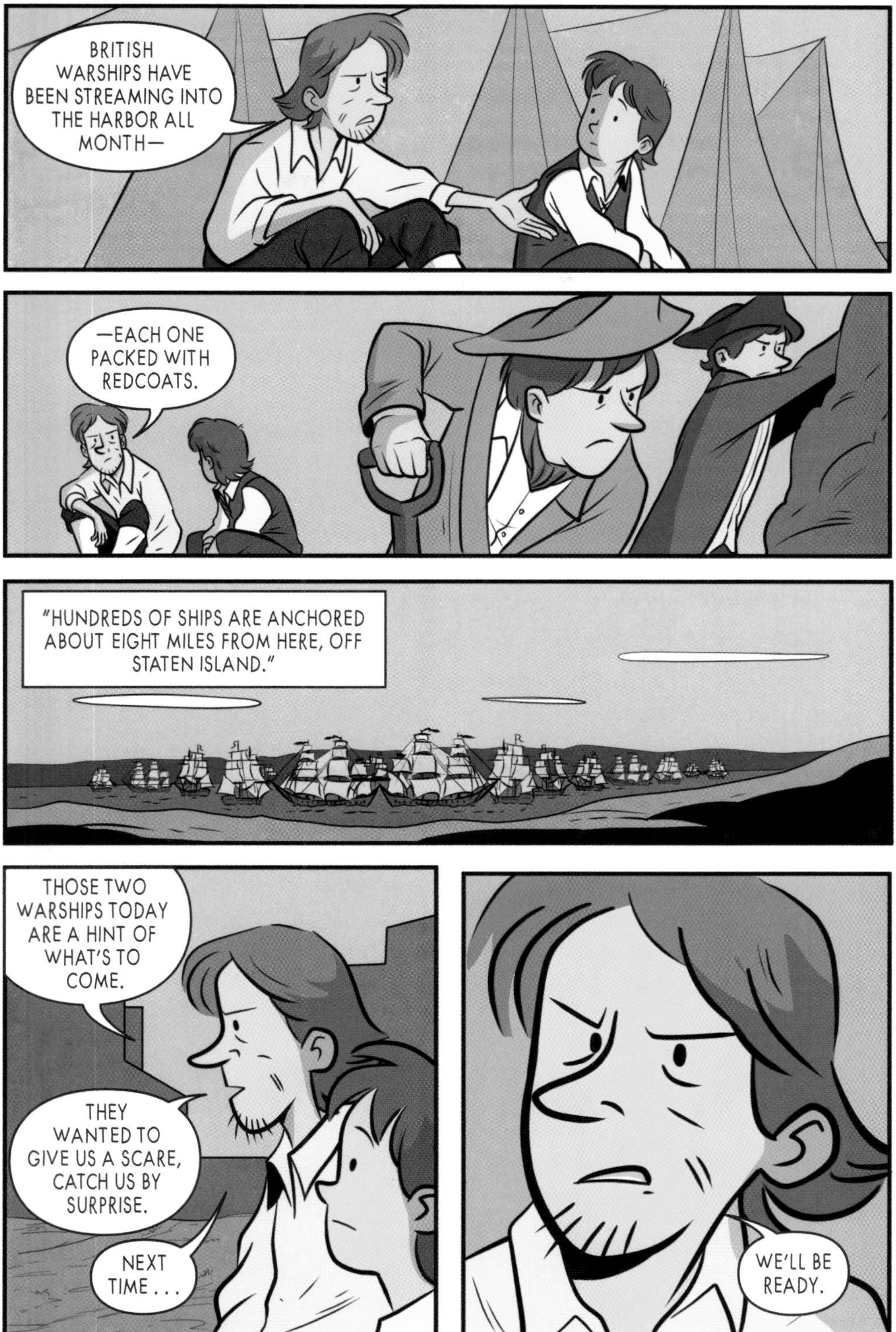
BRITISH WARSHIPS HAVE BEEN STREAMING INTO THE HARBOR ALL MONTH—
—EACH ONE PACKED WITH REDCOATS.
"HUNDREDS OF SHIPS ARE ANCHORED ABOUT EIGHT MILES FROM HERE, OFF STATEN ISLAND."
THOSE TWO WARSHIPS TODAY ARE A HINT OF WHAT'S TO COME.
THEY WANTED TO GIVE US A SCARE, CATCH US BY SURPRISE.
NEXT TIME . . .
WE'LL BE READY.

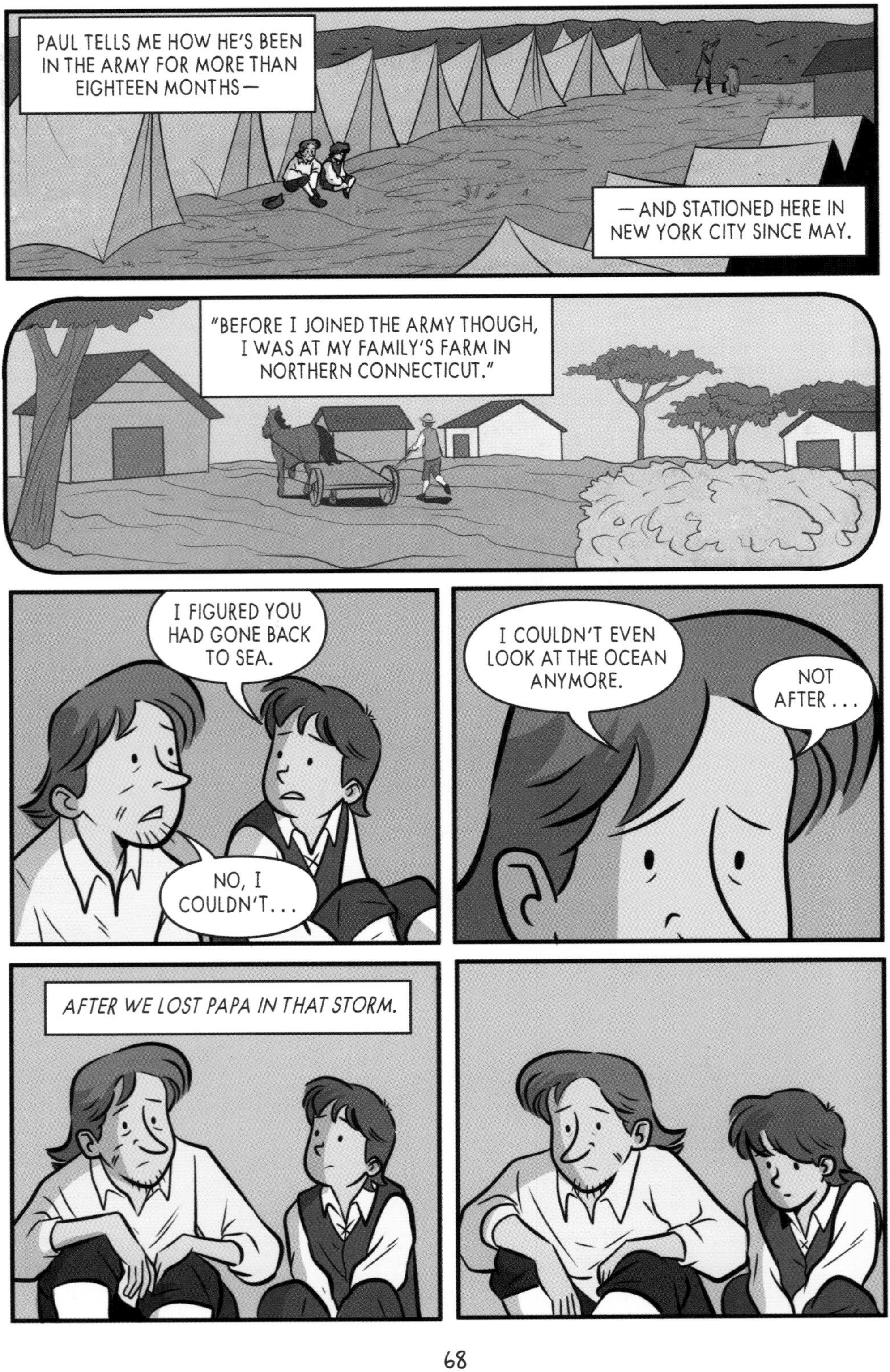
PAUL TELLS ME HOW HE'S BEEN IN THE ARMY FOR MORE THAN EIGHTEEN MONTHS—
—AND STATIONED HERE IN NEW YORK CITY SINCE MAY.
"BEFORE I JOINED THE ARMY THOUGH, I WAS AT MY FAMILY'S FARM IN NORTHERN CONNECTICUT."
I FIGURED YOU HAD GONE BACK TO SEA.
NO, I COULDN'T. . .
I COULDN'T EVEN LOOK AT THE OCEAN ANYMORE.
NOT AFTER . . .
AFTER WE LOST PAPA IN THAT STORM.

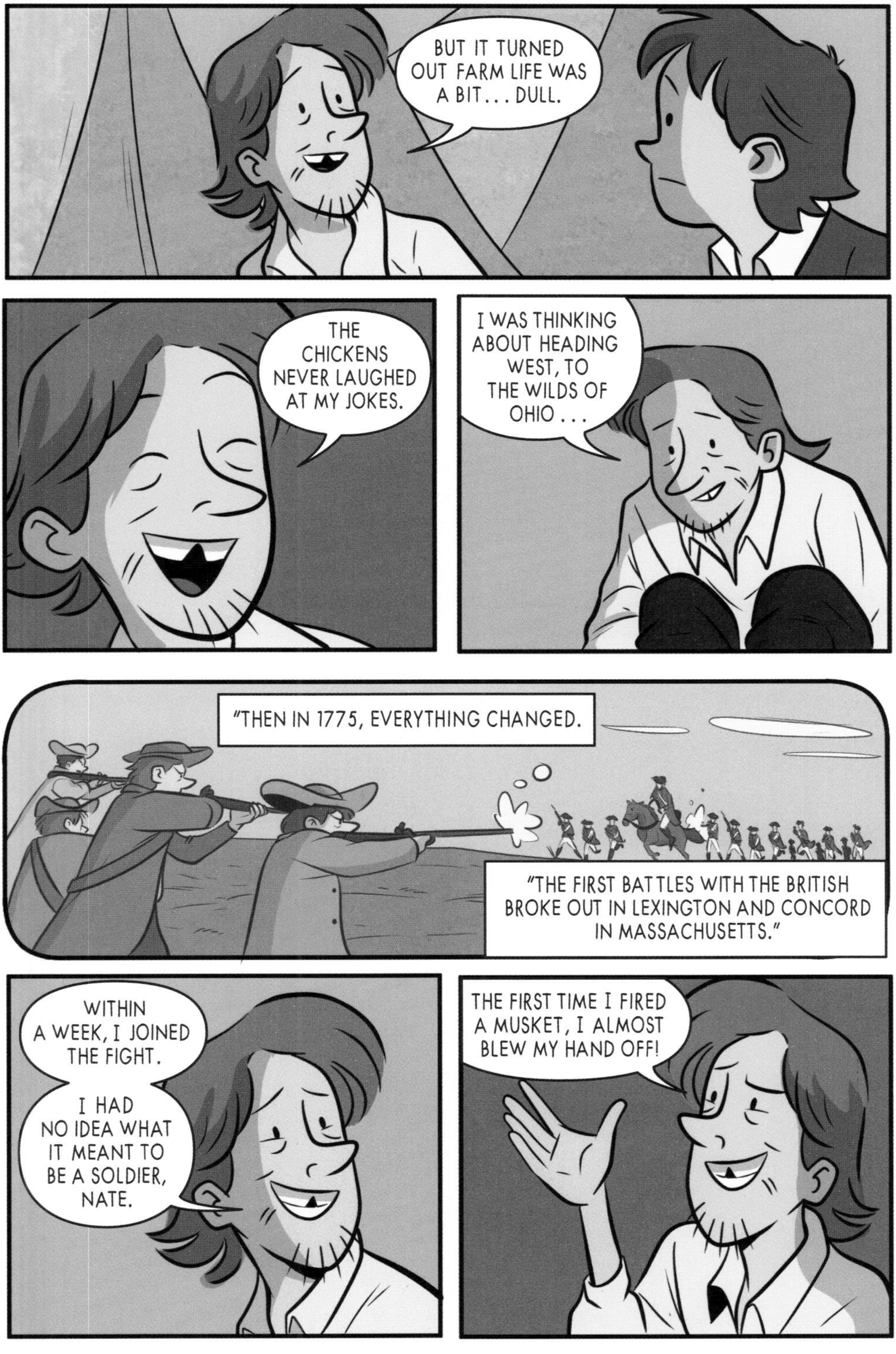
BUT IT TURNED OUT FARM LIFE WAS A BIT . . . DULL.
THE CHICKENS NEVER LAUGHED AT MY JOKES.
I WAS THINKING ABOUT HEADING WEST, TO THE WILDS OF OHIO . . .
"THEN IN 1775, EVERYTHING CHANGED.
"THE FIRST BATTLES WITH THE BRITISH BROKE OUT IN LEXINGTON AND CONCORD IN MASSACHUSETTS."
WITHIN A WEEK, I JOINED THE FIGHT.
I HAD NO IDEA WHAT IT MEANT TO BE A SOLDIER, NATE.
THE FIRST TIME I FIRED A MUSKET, I ALMOST BLEW MY HAND OFF!

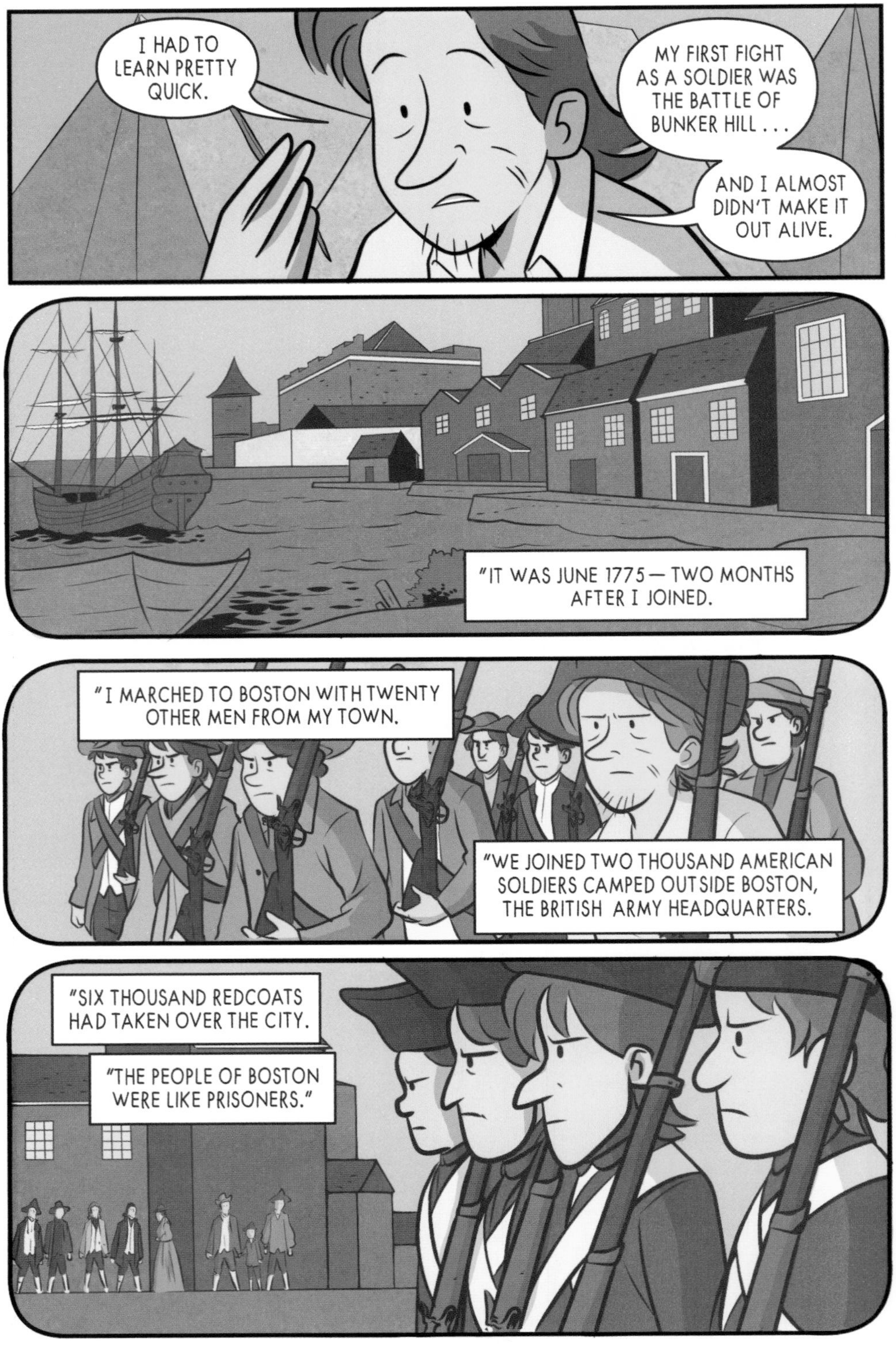
I HAD TO LEARN PRETTY QUICK.
MY FIRST FIGHT AS A SOLDIER WAS THE BATTLE OF BUNKER HILL . . .
AND I ALMOST DIDN'T MAKE IT OUT ALIVE.
"IT WAS JUNE 1775 — TWO MONTHS AFTER I JOINED.
"I MARCHED TO BOSTON WITH TWENTY OTHER MEN FROM MY TOWN.
"WE JOINED TWO THOUSAND AMERICAN SOLDIERS CAMPED OUTSIDE BOSTON, THE BRITISH ARMY HEADQUARTERS.
"SIX THOUSAND REDCOATS HAD TAKEN OVER THE CITY.
"THE PEOPLE OF BOSTON WERE LIKE PRISONERS."

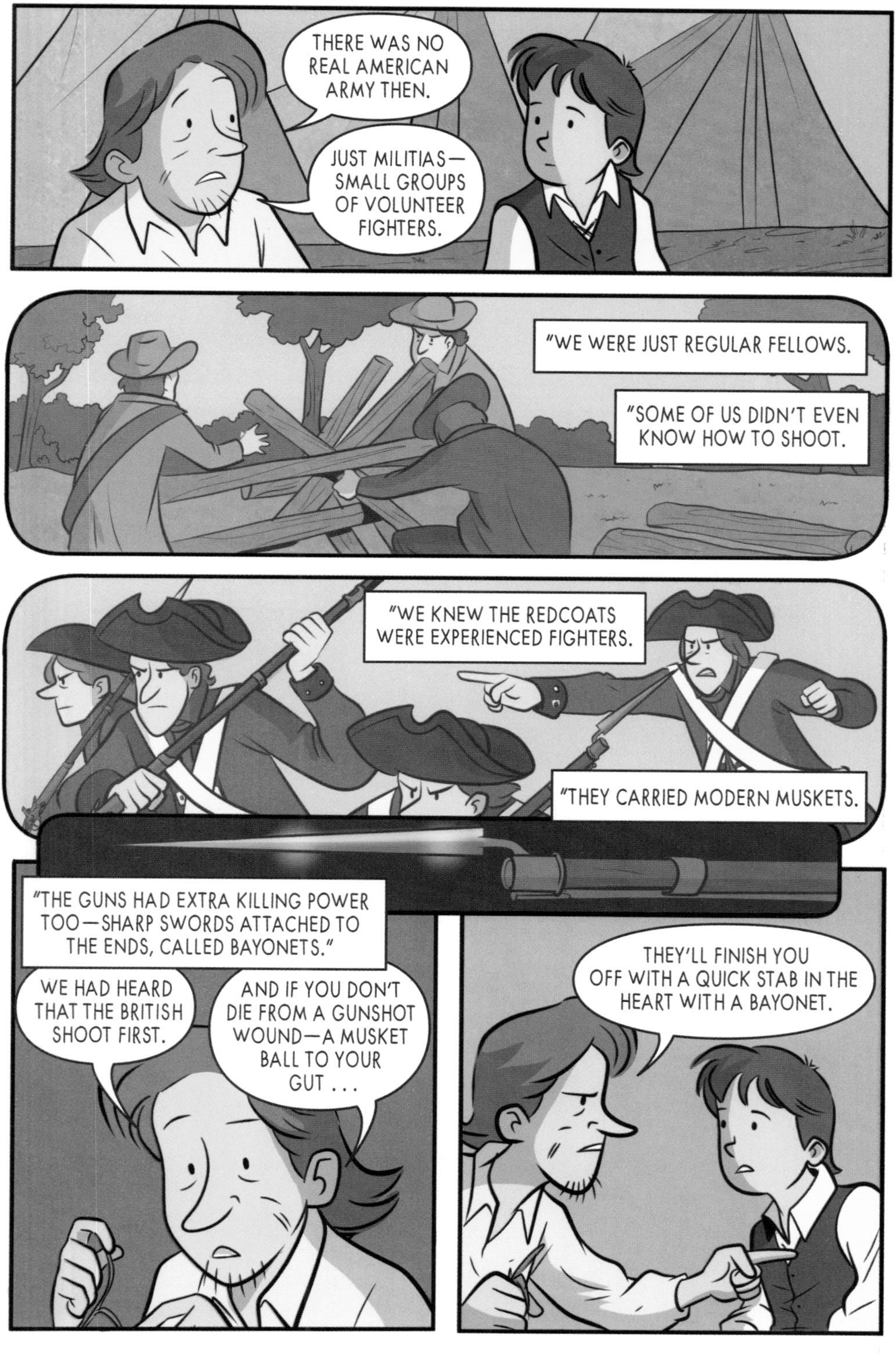
THERE WAS NO REAL AMERICAN ARMY THEN.
JUST MILITIAS—SMALL GROUPS OF VOLUNTEER FIGHTERS.
"WE WERE JUST REGULAR FELLOWS.
"SOME OF US DIDN'T EVEN KNOW HOW TO SHOOT.
"WE KNEW THE REDCOATS WERE EXPERIENCED FIGHTERS.
"THEY CARRIED MODERN MUSKETS.
"THE GUNS HAD EXTRA KILLING POWER TOO—SHARP SWORDS ATTACHED TO THE ENDS, CALLED BAYONETS."
WE HAD HEARD THAT THE BRITISH SHOOT FIRST.
AND IF YOU DON'T DIE FROM A GUNSHOT WOUND—A MUSKET BALL TO YOUR GUT . . .
THEY'LL FINISH YOU OFF WITH A QUICK STAB IN THE HEART WITH A BAYONET.

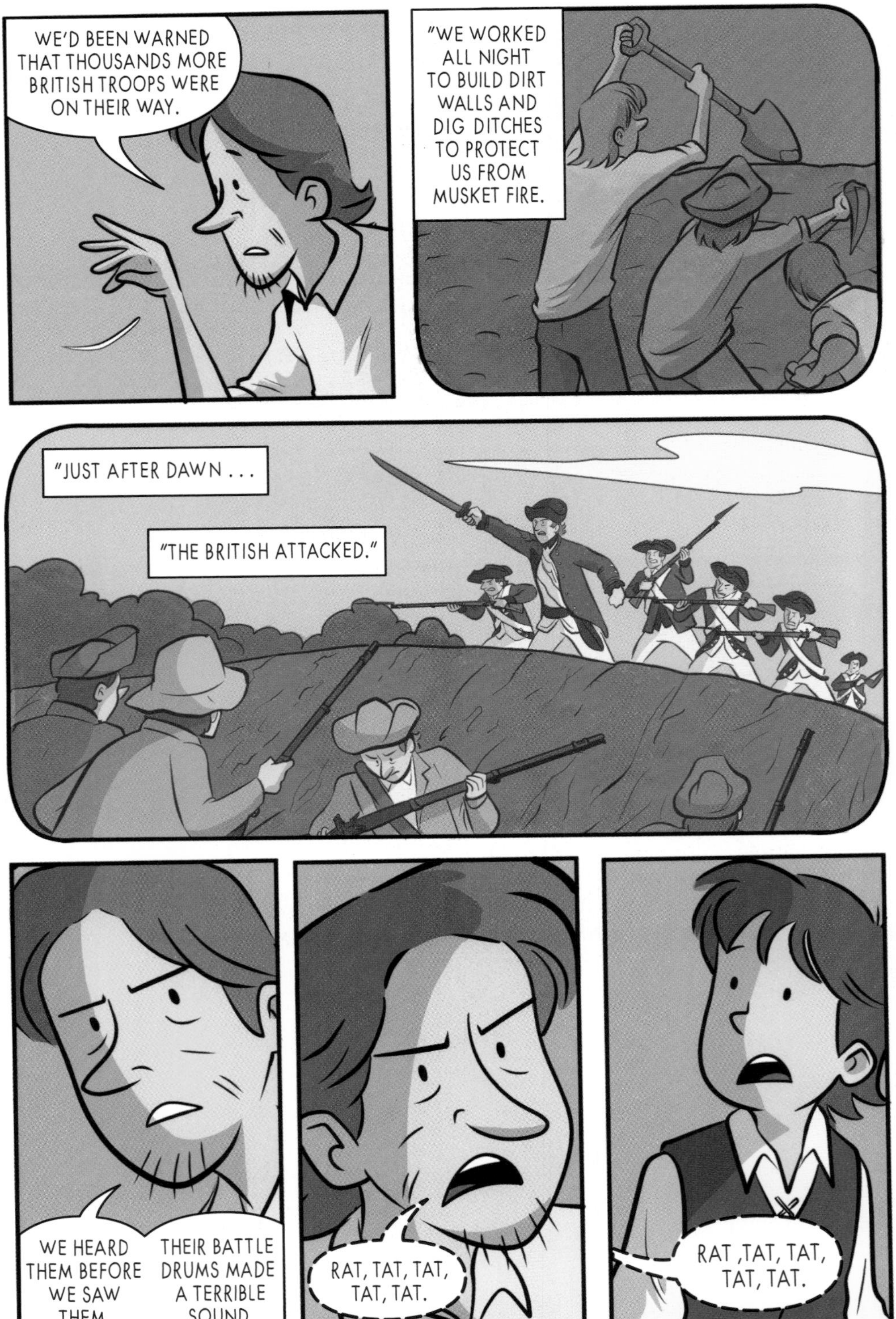
WE'D BEEN WARNED THAT THOUSANDS MORE BRITISH TROOPS WERE ON THEIR WAY.
"WE WORKED ALL NIGHT TO BUILD DIRT WALLS AND DIG DITCHES TO PROTECT US FROM MUSKET FIRE.
"JUST AFTER DAWN . . .
"THE BRITISH ATTACKED."
WE HEARD THEM BEFORE WE SAW THEM.
THEIR BATTLE DRUMS MADE A TERRIBLE SOUND.
RAT, TAT, TAT, TAT, TAT.
RAT ,TAT, TAT, TAT, TAT.

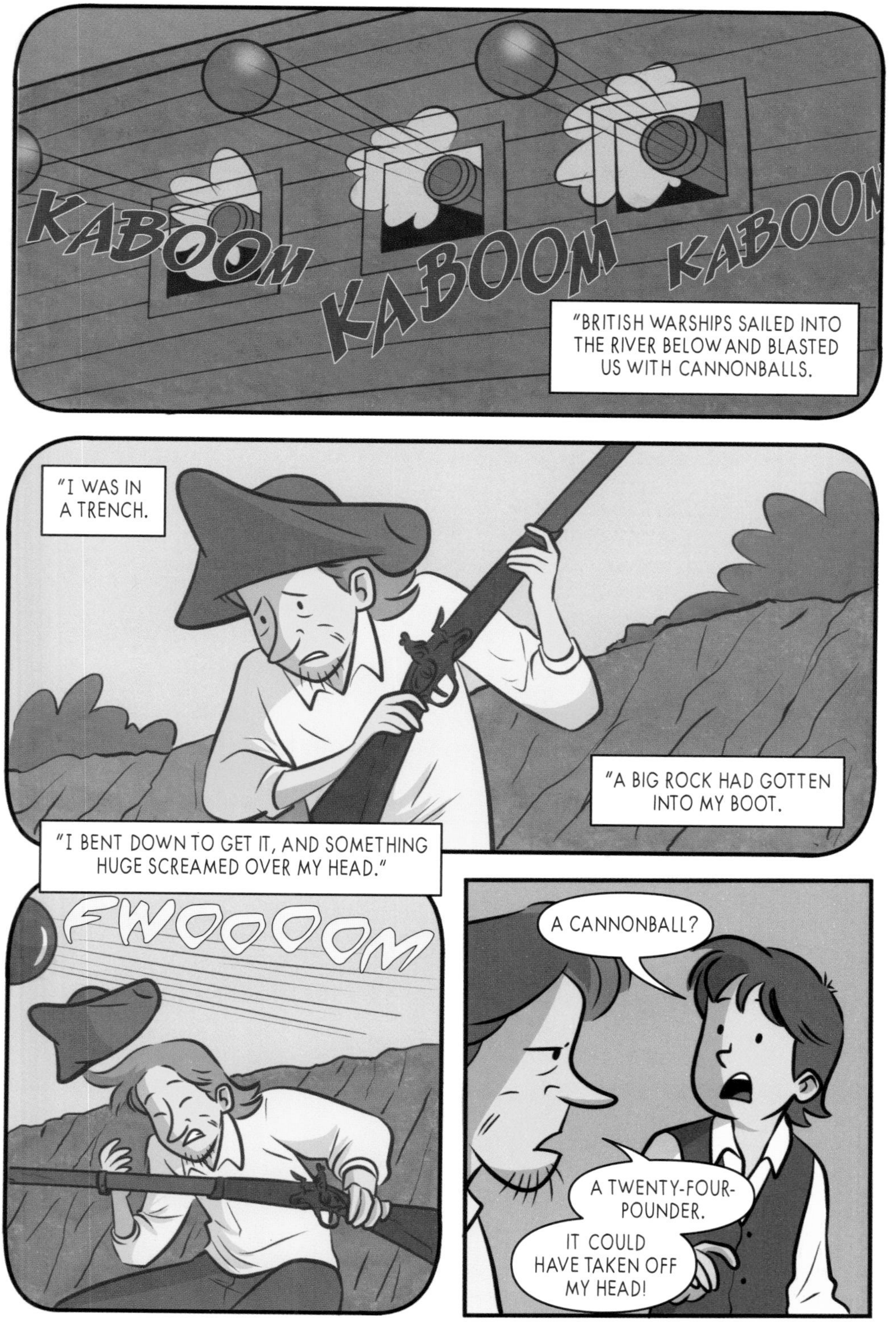
KABOOM
KABOOM
KABOOM
"BRITISH WARSHIPS SAILED INTO THE RIVER BELOW AND BLASTED US WITH CANNONBALLS.
"I WAS IN A TRENCH.
"A BIG ROCK HAD GOTTEN INTO MY BOOT.
"I BENT DOWN TO GET IT, AND SOMETHING HUGE SCREAMED OVER MY HEAD."
FWOOOOM
A CANNONBALL?
A TWENTY-FOUR-POUNDER.
IT COULD HAVE TAKEN OFF MY HEAD!

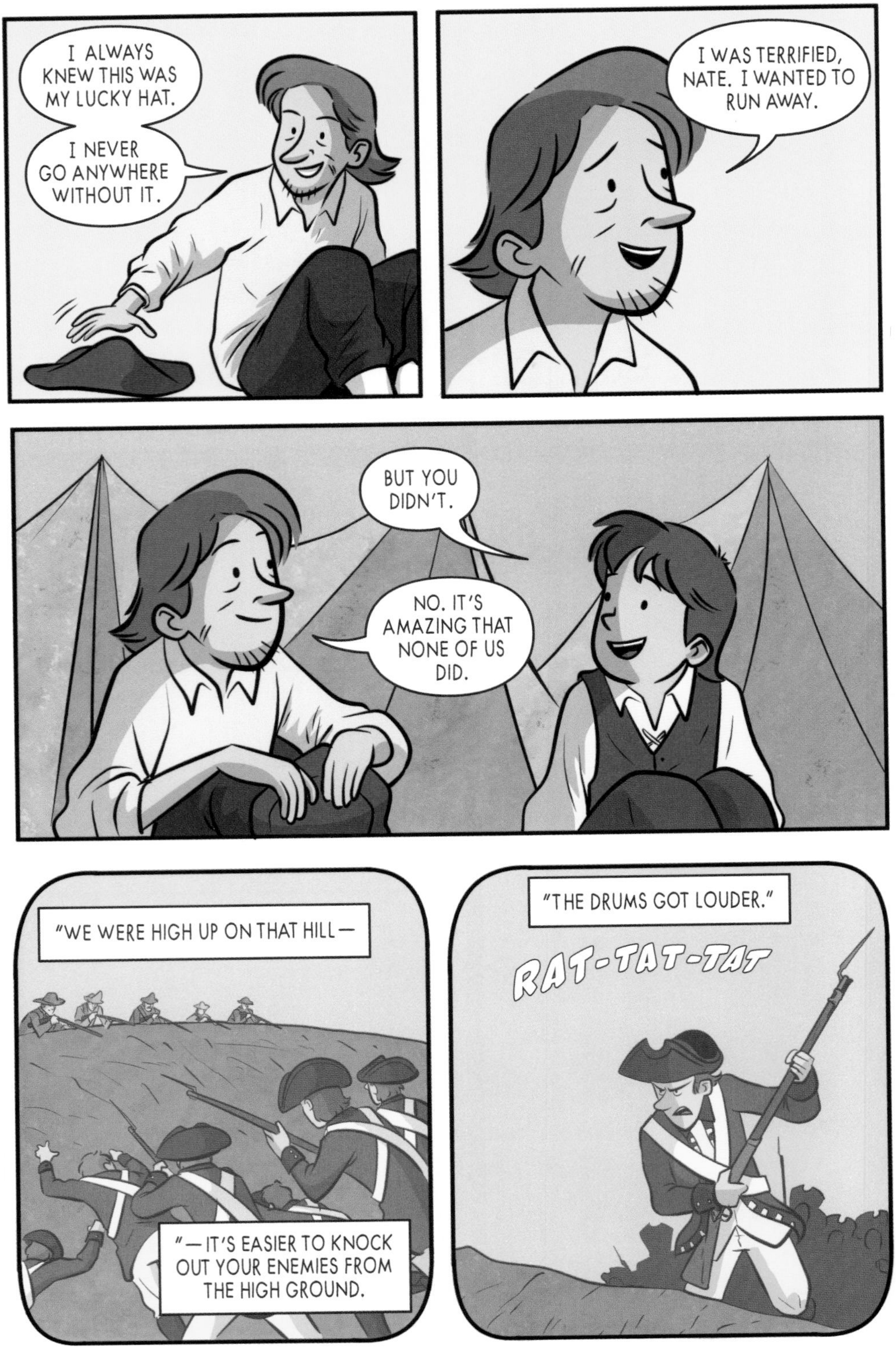
I ALWAYS KNEW THIS WAS MY LUCKY HAT.
I NEVER GO ANYWHERE WITHOUT IT.
I WAS TERRIFIED, NATE. I WANTED TO RUN AWAY.
BUT YOU DIDN'T.
NO. IT'S AMAZING THAT NONE OF US DID.
"WE WERE HIGH UP ON THAT HILL—
"—IT'S EASIER TO KNOCK OUT YOUR ENEMIES FROM THE HIGH GROUND.
"THE DRUMS GOT LOUDER."
RAT-TAT-TAT

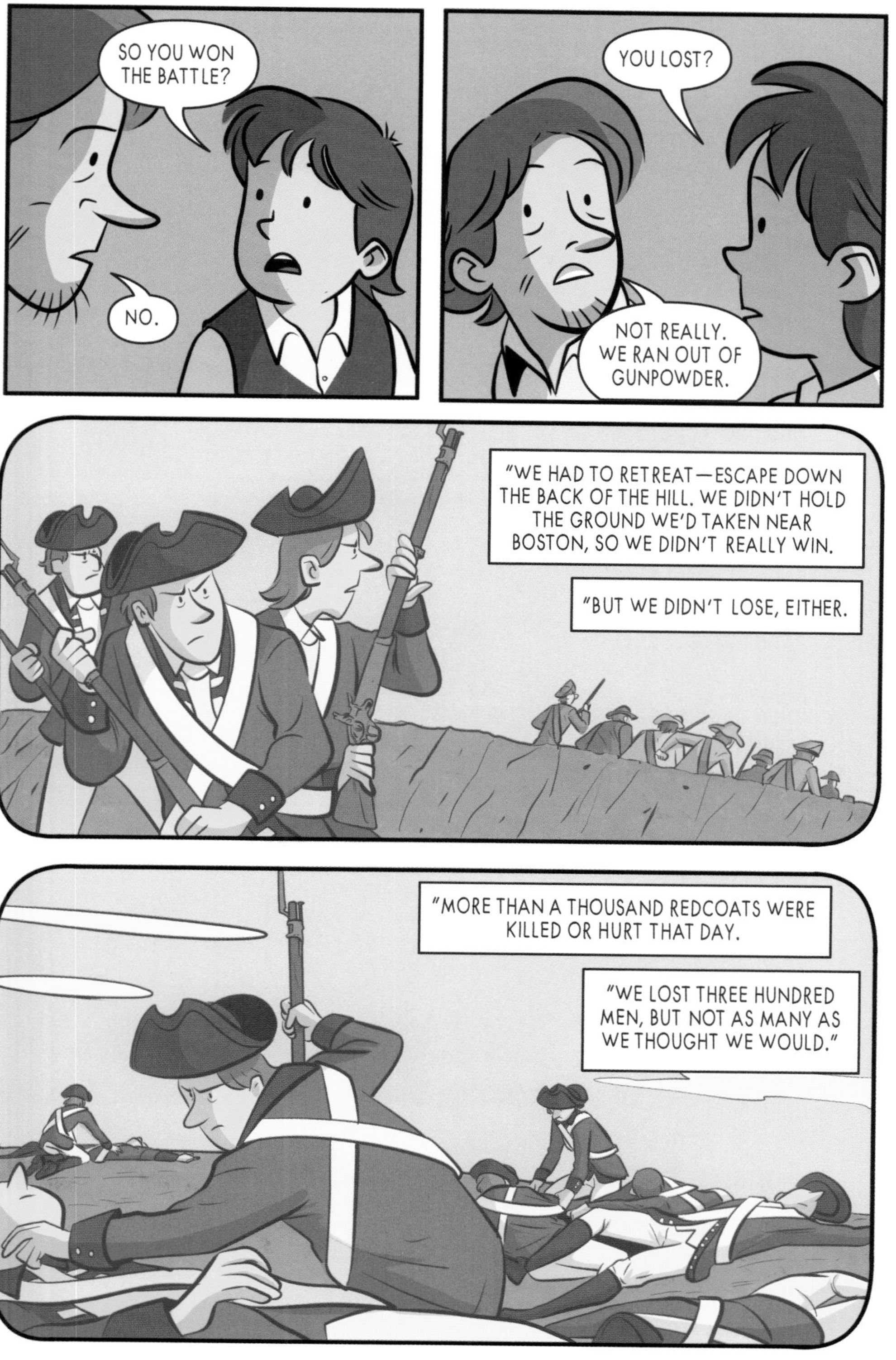
SO YOU WON THE BATTLE?
NO.
YOU LOST?
NOT REALLY. WE RAN OUT OF GUNPOWDER.
"WE HAD TO RETREAT—ESCAPE DOWN THE BACK OF THE HILL. WE DIDN'T HOLD THE GROUND WE'D TAKEN NEAR BOSTON, SO WE DIDN'T REALLY WIN.
"BUT WE DIDN'T LOSE, EITHER.
"MORE THAN A THOUSAND REDCOATS WERE KILLED OR HURT THAT DAY.
"WE LOST THREE HUNDRED MEN, BUT NOT AS MANY AS WE THOUGHT WE WOULD."

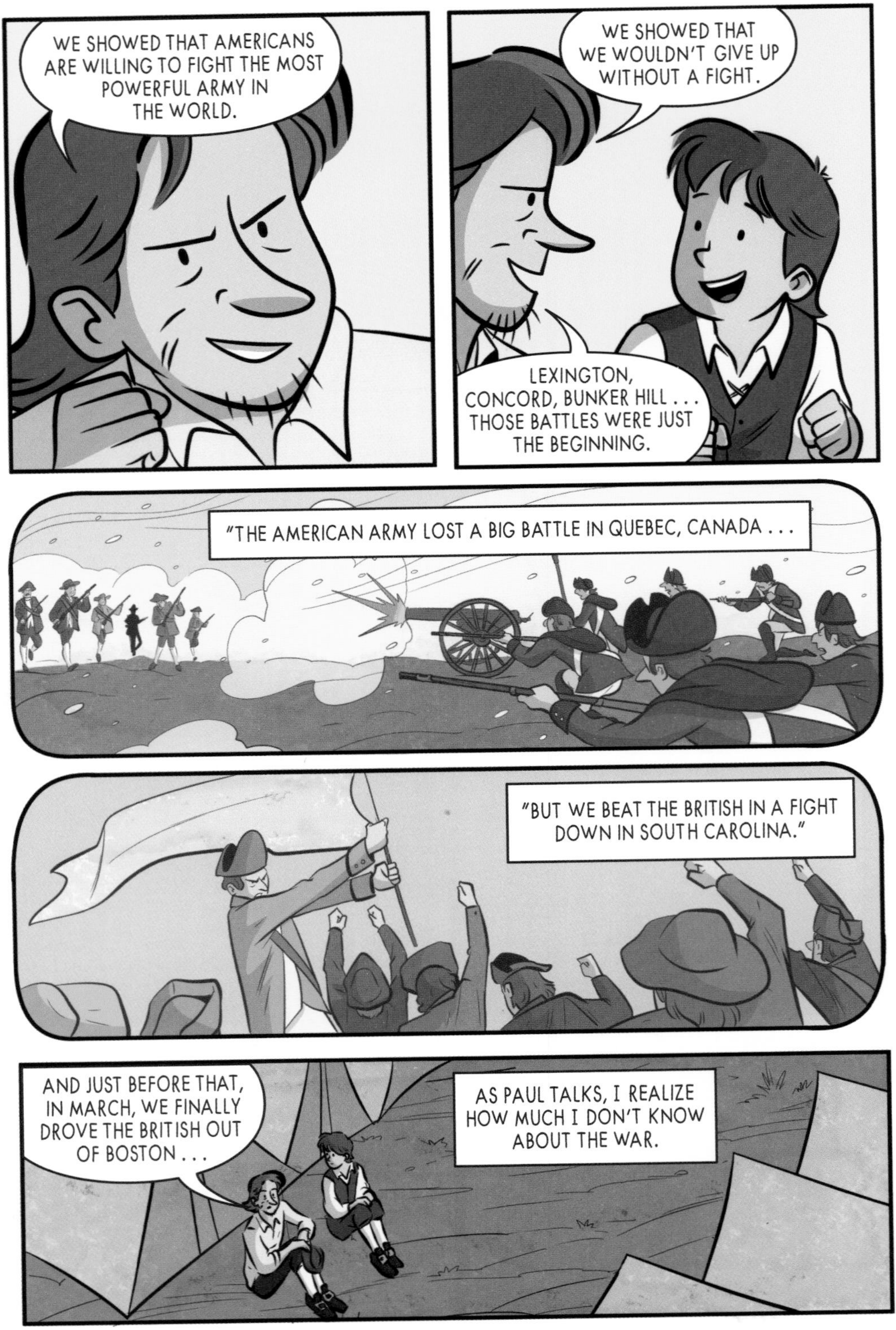
WE SHOWED THAT AMERICANS ARE WILLING TO FIGHT THE MOST POWERFUL ARMY IN THE WORLD.
WE SHOWED THAT WE WOULDN'T GIVE UP WITHOUT A FIGHT.
LEXINGTON, CONCORD, BUNKER HILL . . . THOSE BATTLES WERE JUST THE BEGINNING.
"THE AMERICAN ARMY LOST A BIG BATTLE IN QUEBEC, CANADA . . .
"BUT WE BEAT THE BRITISH IN A FIGHT DOWN IN SOUTH CAROLINA."
AND JUST BEFORE THAT, IN MARCH, WE FINALLY DROVE THE BRITISH OUT OF BOSTON . . .
AS PAUL TALKS, I REALIZE HOW MUCH I DON'T KNOW ABOUT THE WAR.

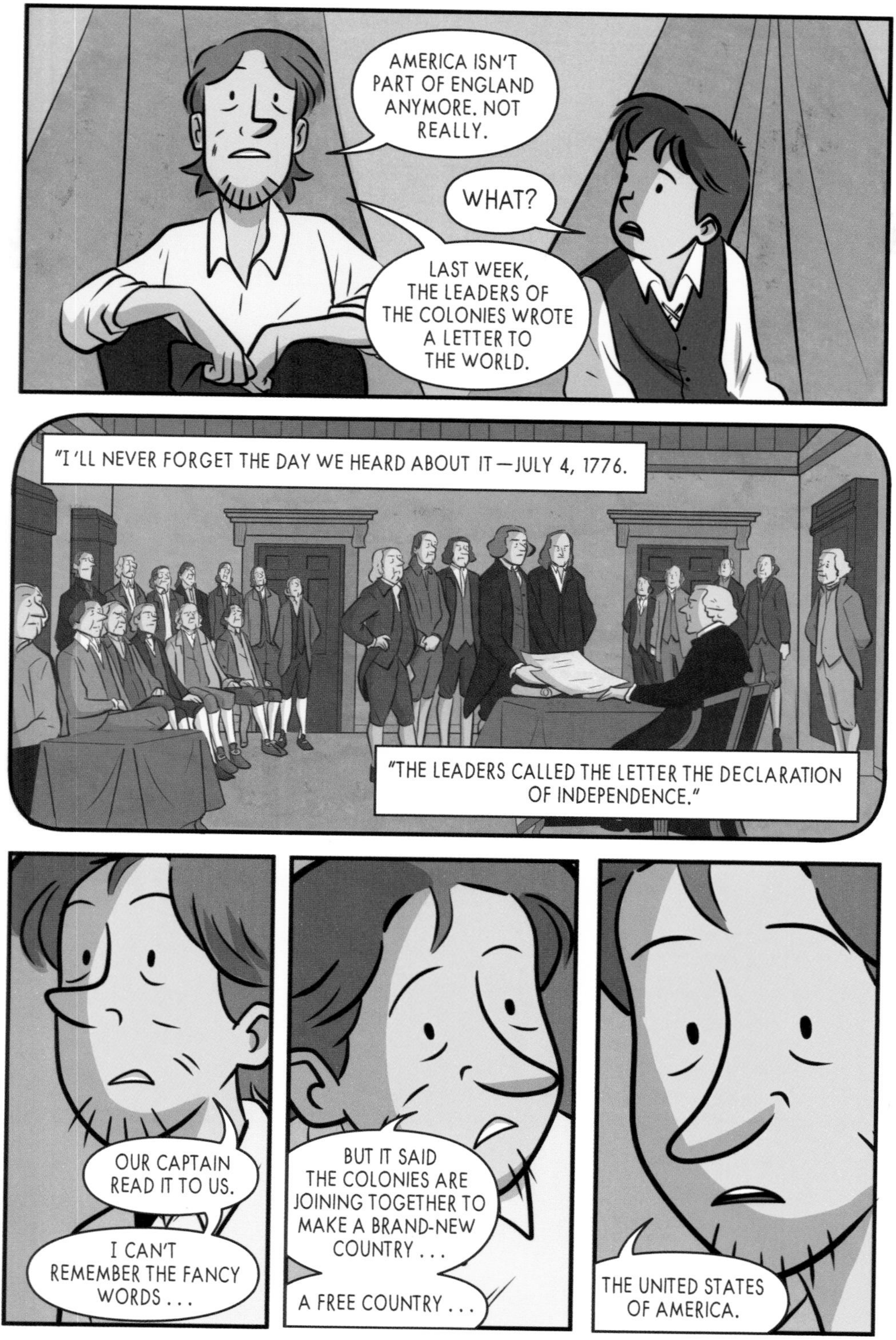
AMERICA ISN'T PART OF ENGLAND ANYMORE. NOT REALLY.
WHAT?
LAST WEEK, THE LEADERS OF THE COLONIES WROTE A LETTER TO THE WORLD.
"I'LL NEVER FORGET THE DAY WE HEARD ABOUT IT—JULY 4, 1776.
"THE LEADERS CALLED THE LETTER THE DECLARATION OF INDEPENDENCE."
OUR CAPTAIN READ IT TO US.
I CAN'T REMEMBER THE FANCY WORDS . . .
BUT IT SAID THE COLONIES ARE JOINING TOGETHER TO MAKE A BRAND-NEW COUNTRY . . .
A FREE COUNTRY . . .
THE UNITED STATES OF AMERICA.

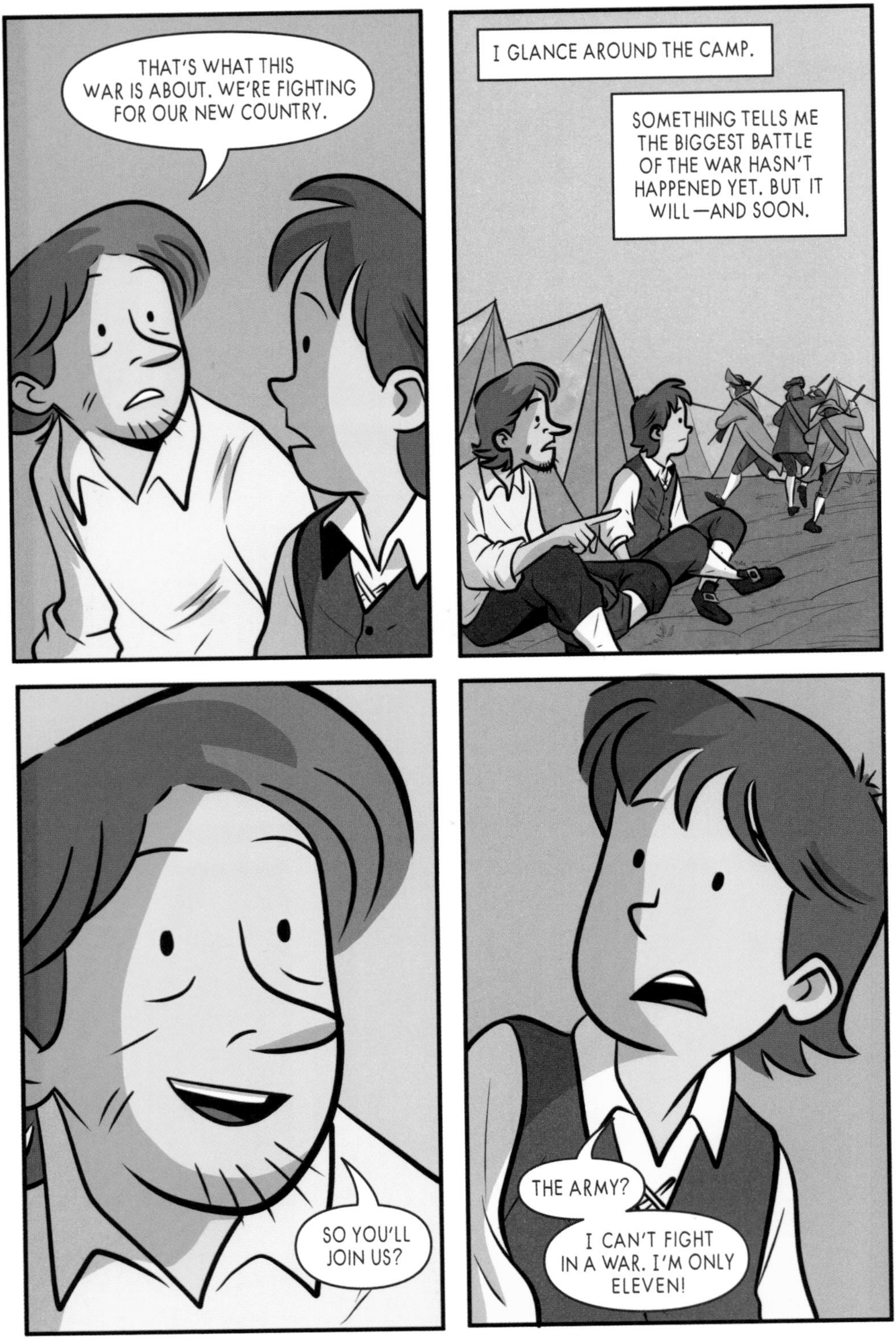

THAT'S WHAT THIS WAR IS ABOUT. WE'RE FIGHTING FOR OUR NEW COUNTRY.
I GLANCE AROUND THE CAMP.
SOMETHING TELLS ME THE BIGGEST BATTLE OF THE WAR HASN'T HAPPENED YET. BUT IT WILL—AND SOON.
SO YOU'LL JOIN US?
THE ARMY?
I CAN'T FIGHT IN A WAR. I'M ONLY ELEVEN!

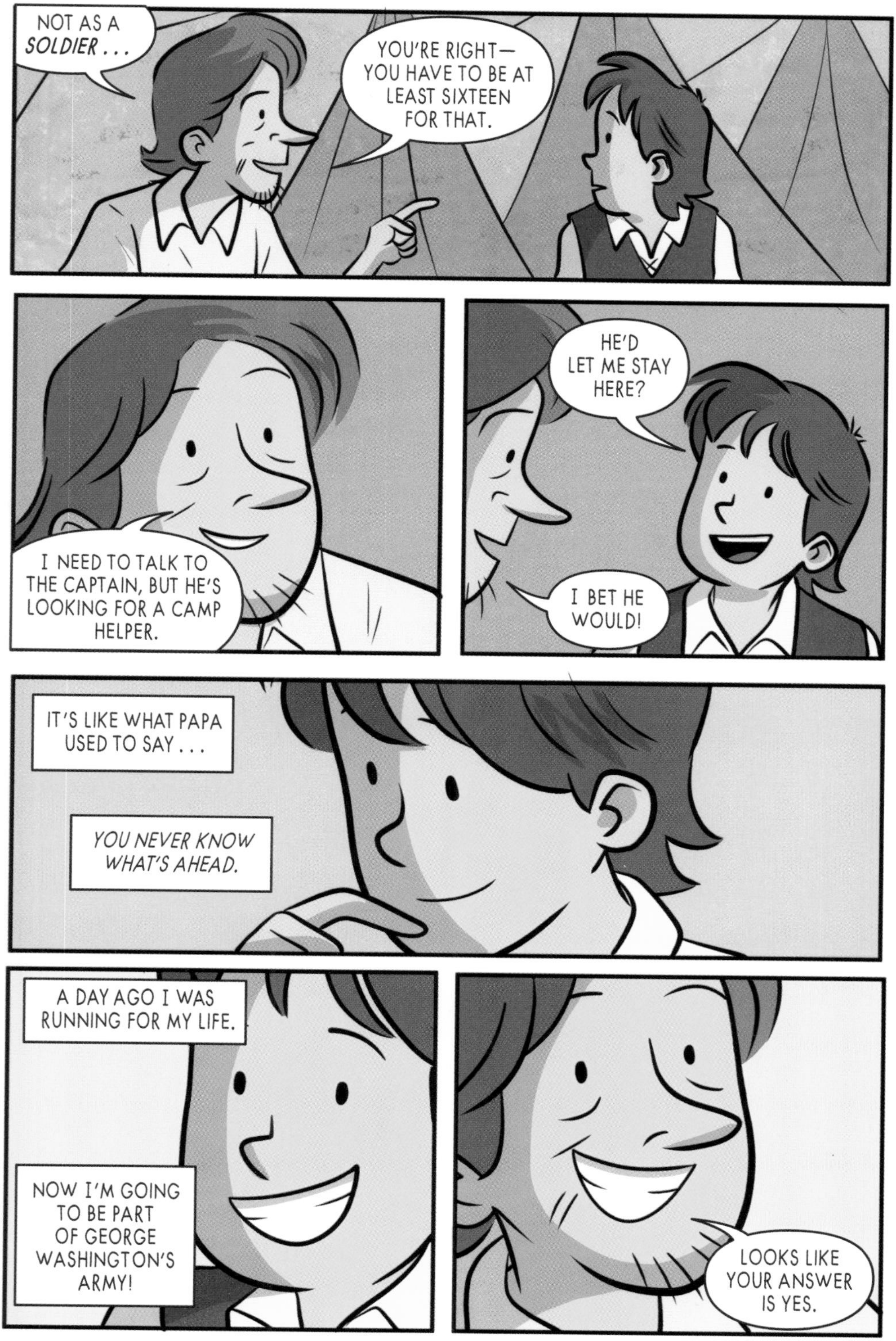

NOT AS A *SOLDIER . . .*
YOU'RE RIGHT—YOU HAVE TO BE AT LEAST SIXTEEN FOR THAT.
I NEED TO TALK TO THE CAPTAIN, BUT HE'S LOOKING FOR A CAMP HELPER.
HE'D LET ME STAY HERE?
I BET HE WOULD!
IT'S LIKE WHAT PAPA USED TO SAY . . .
YOU NEVER KNOW WHAT'S AHEAD.
A DAY AGO I WAS RUNNING FOR MY LIFE.
NOW I'M GOING TO BE PART OF GEORGE WASHINGTON'S ARMY!
LOOKS LIKE YOUR ANSWER IS YES.

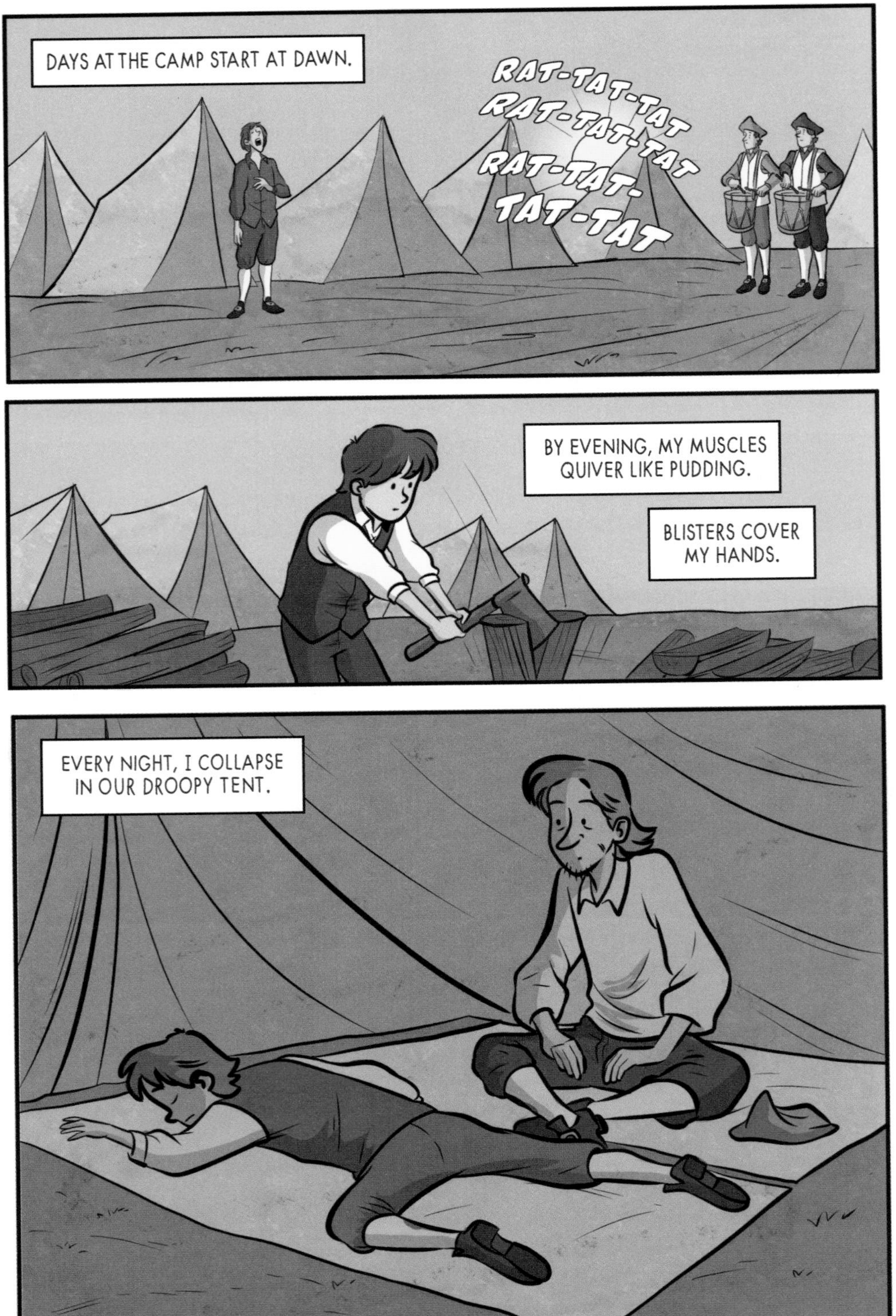
DAYS AT THE CAMP START AT DAWN.
RAT-TAT-TAT
RAT-TAT-TAT
RAT-TAT-
TAT-TAT
BY EVENING, MY MUSCLES QUIVER LIKE PUDDING.
BLISTERS COVER MY HANDS.
EVERY NIGHT, I COLLAPSE IN OUR DROOPY TENT.

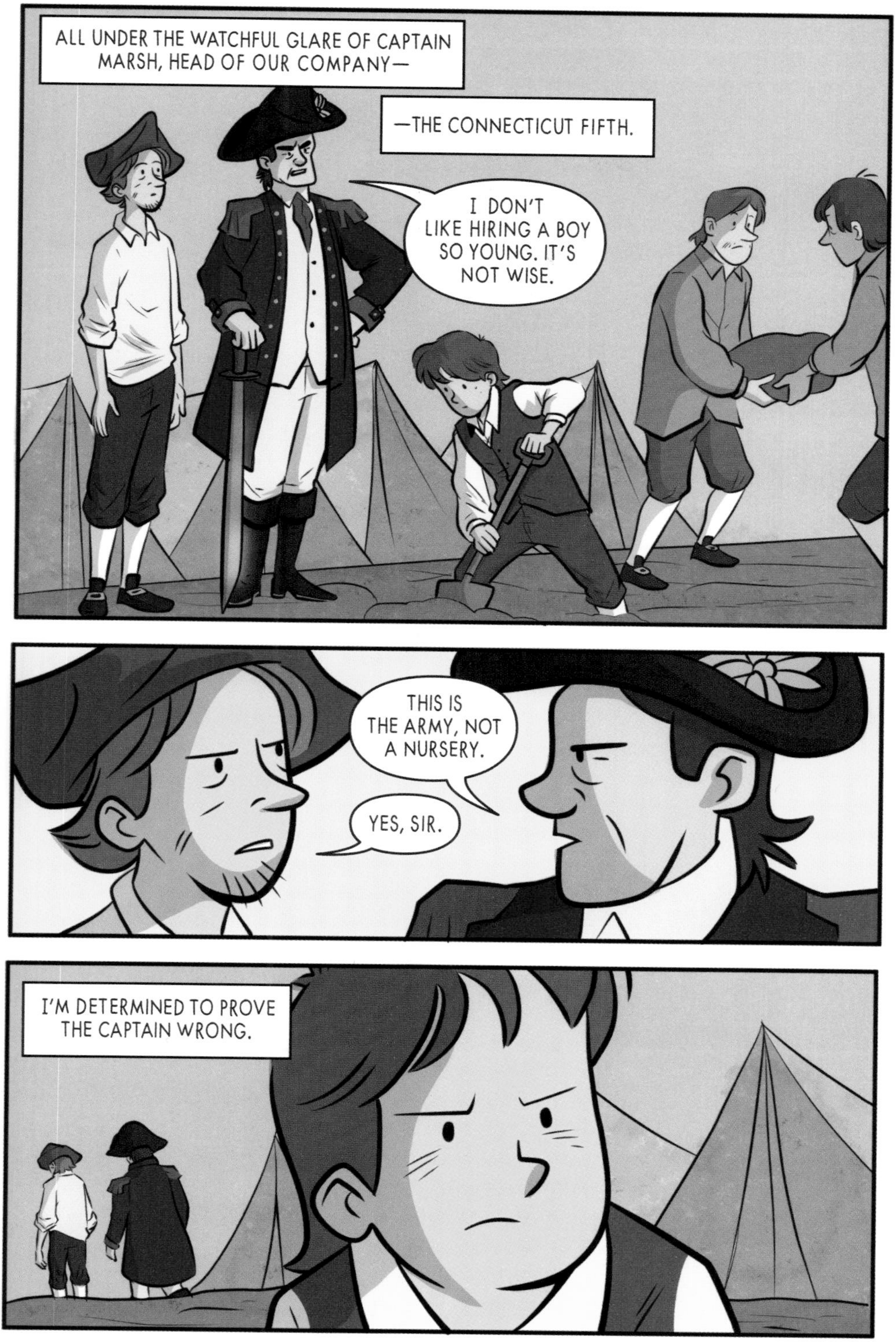
ALL UNDER THE WATCHFUL GLARE OF CAPTAIN MARSH, HEAD OF OUR COMPANY—
—THE CONNECTICUT FIFTH.
I DON'T LIKE HIRING A BOY SO YOUNG. IT'S NOT WISE.
THIS IS THE ARMY, NOT A NURSERY.
YES, SIR.
I'M DETERMINED TO PROVE THE CAPTAIN WRONG.

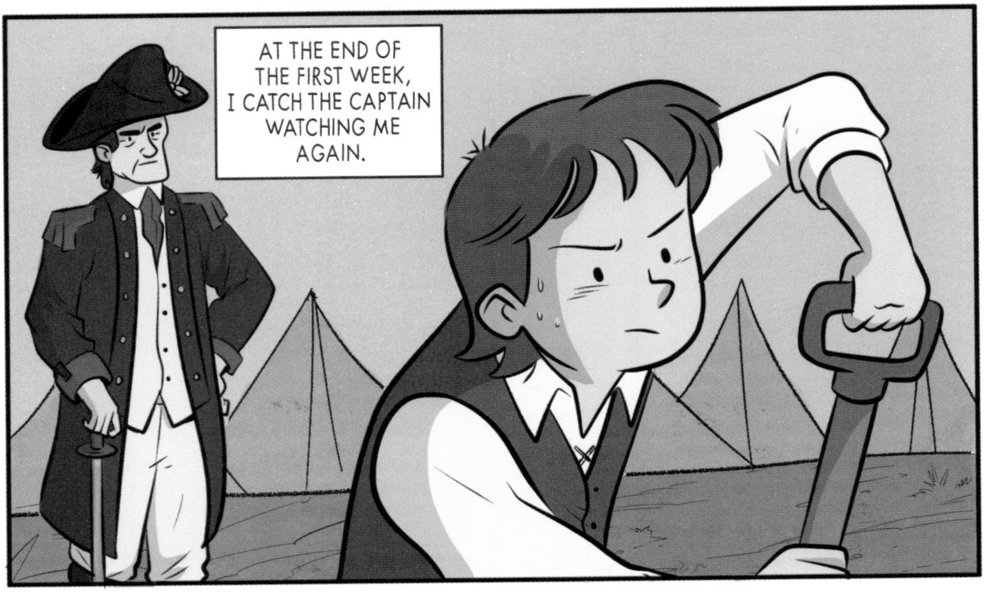
AT THE END OF THE FIRST WEEK, I CATCH THE CAPTAIN WATCHING ME AGAIN.

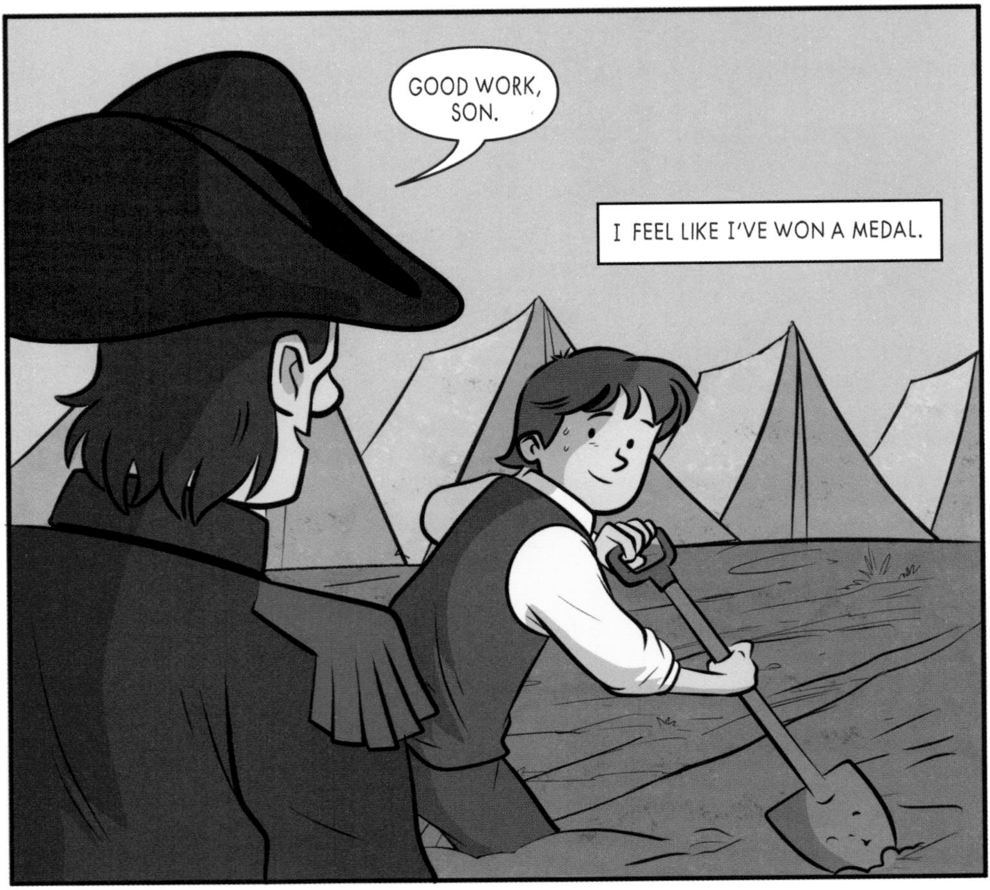
GOOD WORK, SON.
I FEEL LIKE I'VE WON A MEDAL.

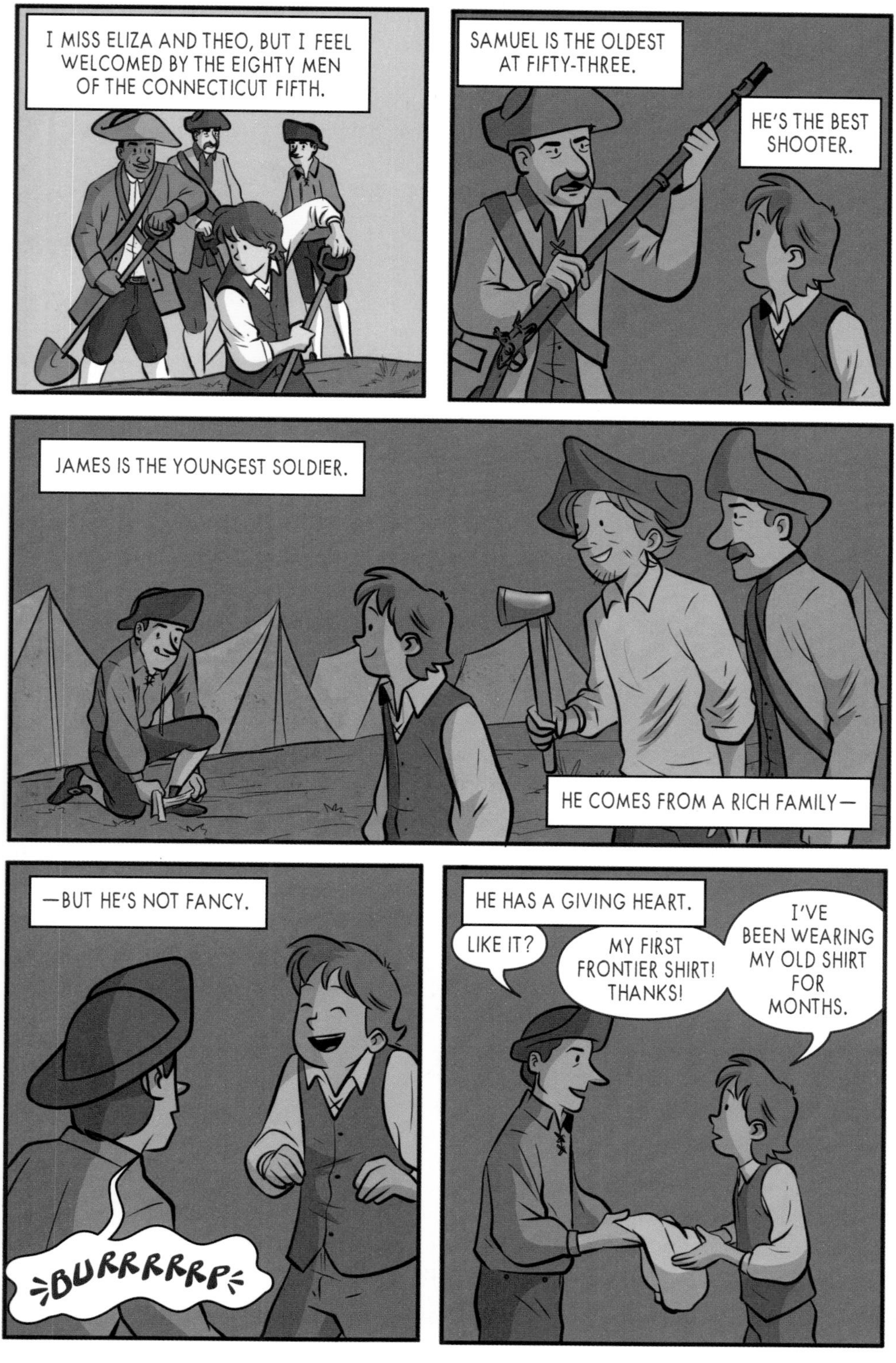
I MISS ELIZA AND THEO, BUT I FEEL WELCOMED BY THE EIGHTY MEN OF THE CONNECTICUT FIFTH.
SAMUEL IS THE OLDEST AT FIFTY-THREE.
HE'S THE BEST SHOOTER.
JAMES IS THE YOUNGEST SOLDIER.
HE COMES FROM A RICH FAMILY—
—BUT HE'S NOT FANCY.
BURRRRRP
HE HAS A GIVING HEART.
LIKE IT?
MY FIRST FRONTIER SHIRT! THANKS!
I'VE BEEN WEARING MY OLD SHIRT FOR MONTHS.

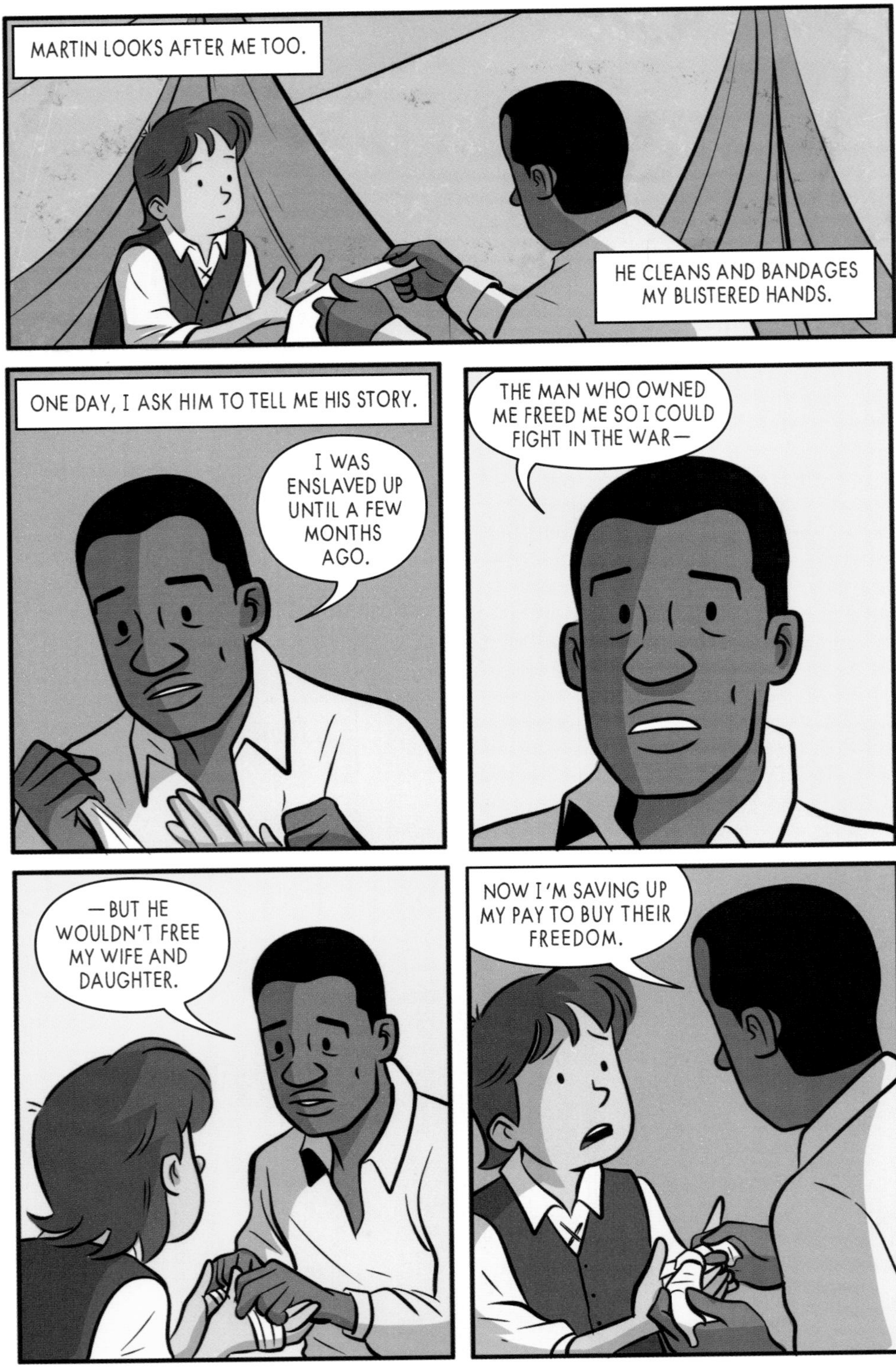

MARTIN LOOKS AFTER ME TOO.
HE CLEANS AND BANDAGES MY BLISTERED HANDS.
ONE DAY, I ASK HIM TO TELL ME HIS STORY.
I WAS ENSLAVED UP UNTIL A FEW MONTHS AGO.
THE MAN WHO OWNED ME FREED ME SO I COULD FIGHT IN THE WAR—
—BUT HE WOULDN'T FREE MY WIFE AND DAUGHTER.
NOW I'M SAVING UP MY PAY TO BUY THEIR FREEDOM.

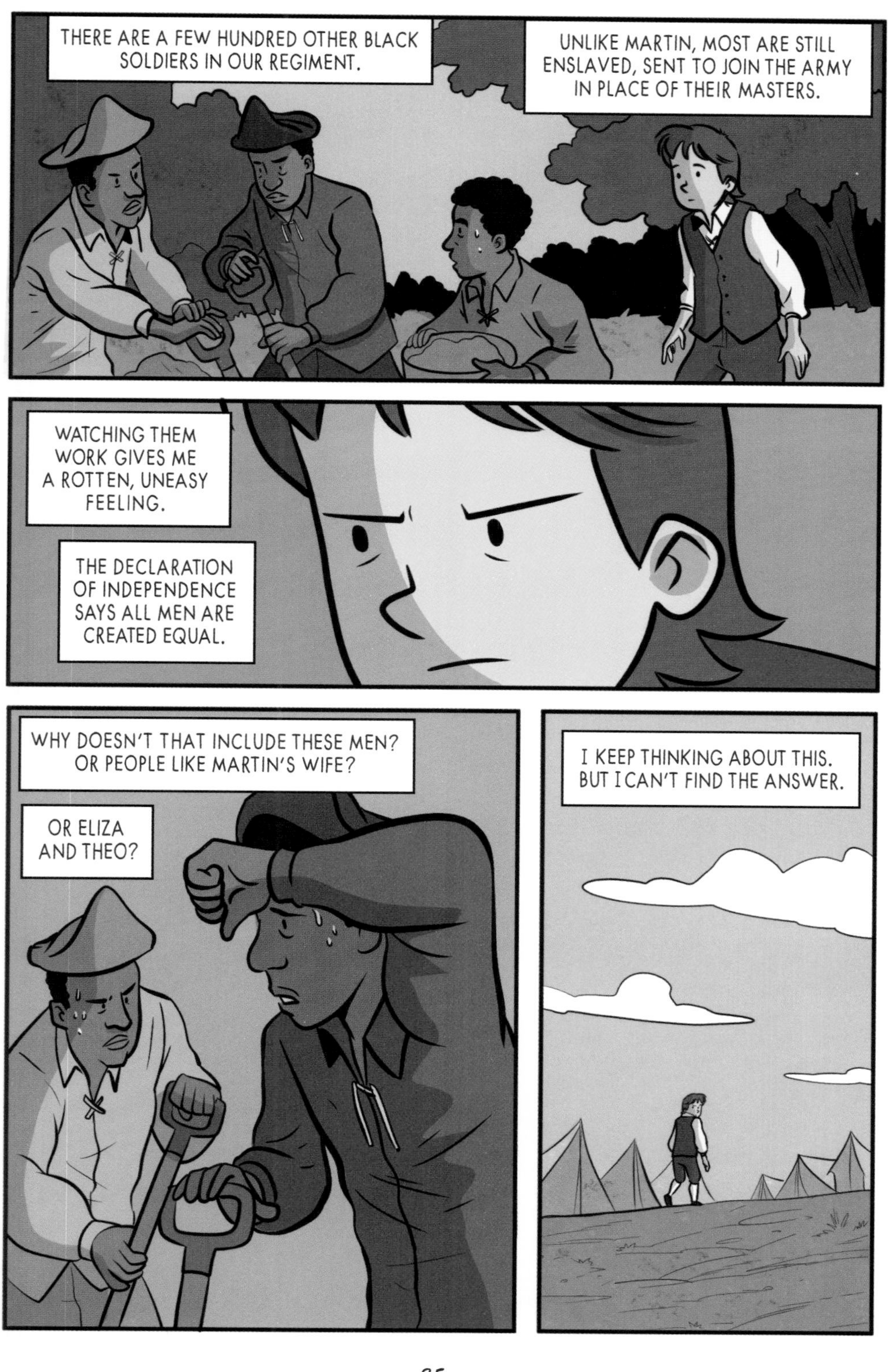
THERE ARE A FEW HUNDRED OTHER BLACK SOLDIERS IN OUR REGIMENT.
UNLIKE MARTIN, MOST ARE STILL ENSLAVED, SENT TO JOIN THE ARMY IN PLACE OF THEIR MASTERS.
WATCHING THEM WORK GIVES ME A ROTTEN, UNEASY FEELING.
THE DECLARATION OF INDEPENDENCE SAYS ALL MEN ARE CREATED EQUAL.
WHY DOESN'T THAT INCLUDE THESE MEN? OR PEOPLE LIKE MARTIN'S WIFE?
OR ELIZA AND THEO?
I KEEP THINKING ABOUT THIS. BUT I CAN'T FIND THE ANSWER.

WHEN I'M NOT BUSY WITH CHORES, I WATCH THE MEN DO PRACTICE DRILLS.

THEY MARCH TO DIFFERENT DRUM SONGS.

IN A NOISY BATTLE, THE OFFICERS' VOICES ARE DROWNED OUT.

THE DRUMS TELL THE MEN HOW FAST TO MARCH AND WHEN TO LOAD THEIR MUSKETS.

THE SOLDIERS PRACTICE LOADING THEIR MUSKETS.

THEY HAVE TO DO IT QUICKLY.

THE AMMUNITION COMES WRAPPED IN PAPER PACKETS CALLED CARTRIDGES.

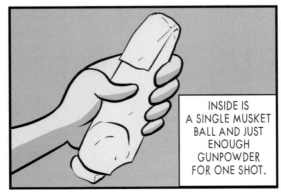

INSIDE IS A SINGLE MUSKET BALL AND JUST ENOUGH GUNPOWDER FOR ONE SHOT.

THE MEN HAVE TO BITE OPEN THE CARTRIDGES.

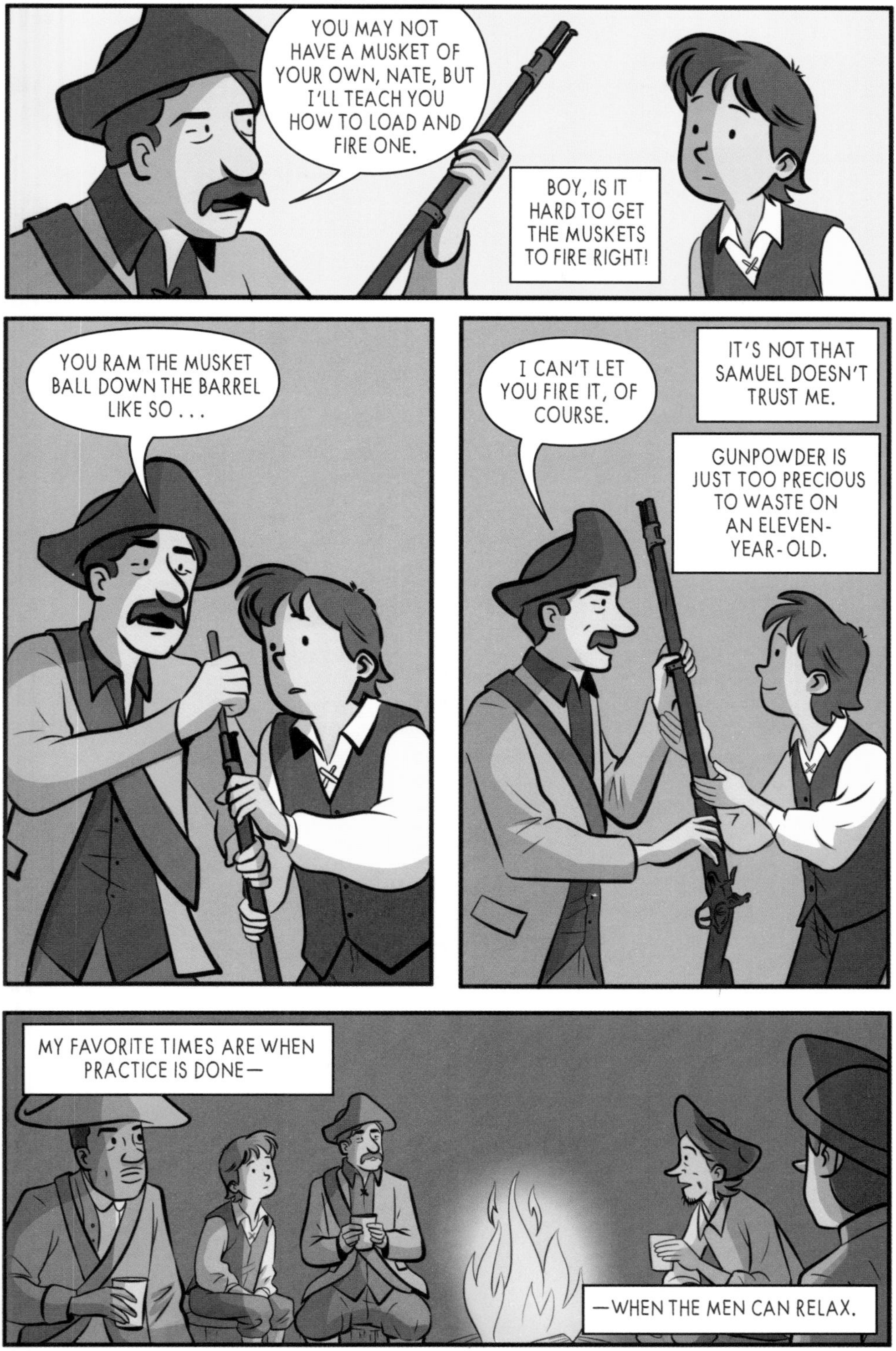
YOU MAY NOT HAVE A MUSKET OF YOUR OWN, NATE, BUT I'LL TEACH YOU HOW TO LOAD AND FIRE ONE.
BOY, IS IT HARD TO GET THE MUSKETS TO FIRE RIGHT!
YOU RAM THE MUSKET BALL DOWN THE BARREL LIKE SO . . .
I CAN'T LET YOU FIRE IT, OF COURSE.
IT'S NOT THAT SAMUEL DOESN'T TRUST ME.
GUNPOWDER IS JUST TOO PRECIOUS TO WASTE ON AN ELEVEN-YEAR-OLD.
MY FAVORITE TIMES ARE WHEN PRACTICE IS DONE—
—WHEN THE MEN CAN RELAX.

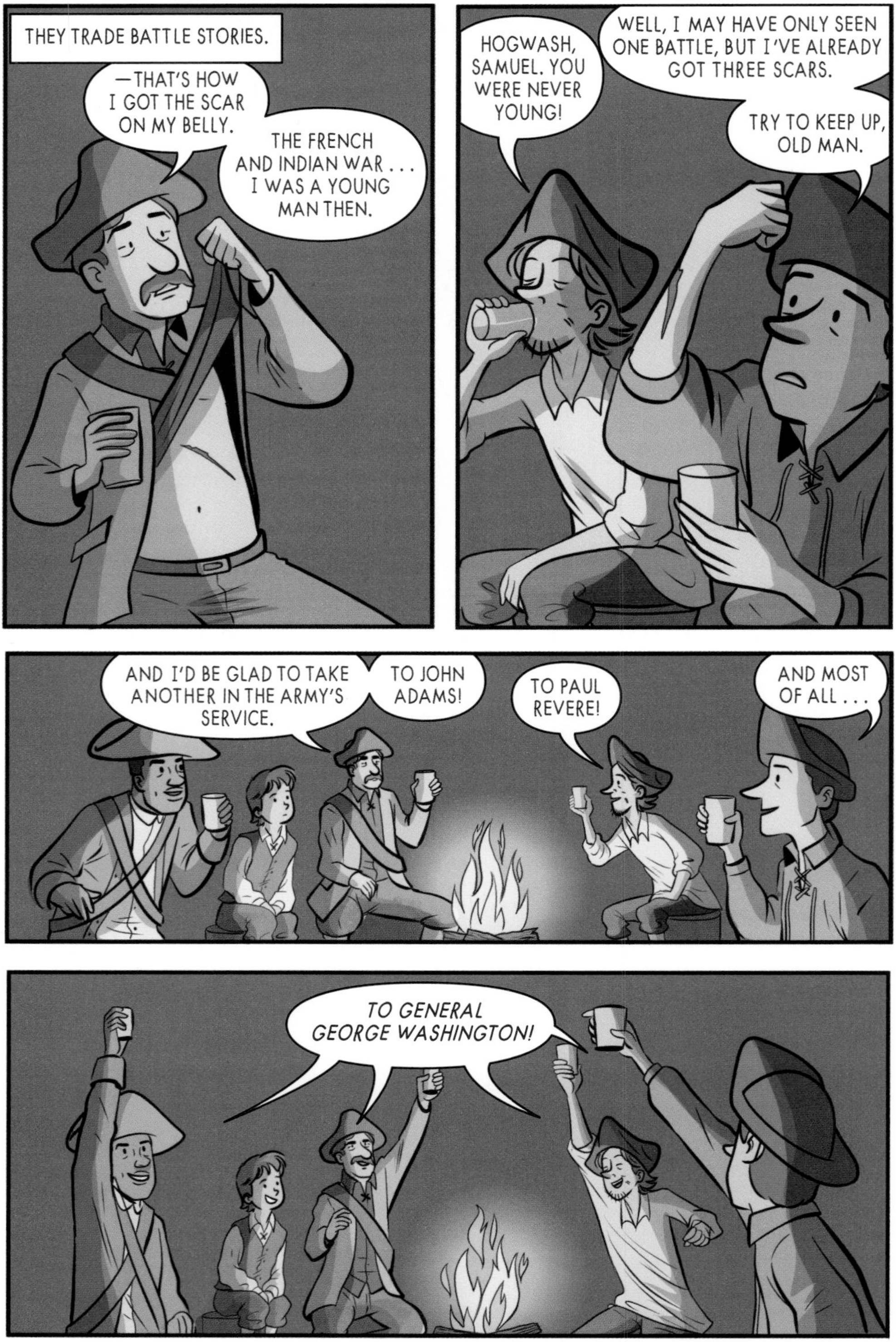
THEY TRADE BATTLE STORIES.
—THAT'S HOW I GOT THE SCAR ON MY BELLY.
THE FRENCH AND INDIAN WAR . . . I WAS A YOUNG MAN THEN.
HOGWASH, SAMUEL. YOU WERE NEVER YOUNG!
WELL, I MAY HAVE ONLY SEEN ONE BATTLE, BUT I'VE ALREADY GOT THREE SCARS.
TRY TO KEEP UP, OLD MAN.
AND I'D BE GLAD TO TAKE ANOTHER IN THE ARMY'S SERVICE.
TO JOHN ADAMS!
TO PAUL REVERE!
AND MOST OF ALL . . .
TO GENERAL GEORGE WASHINGTON!

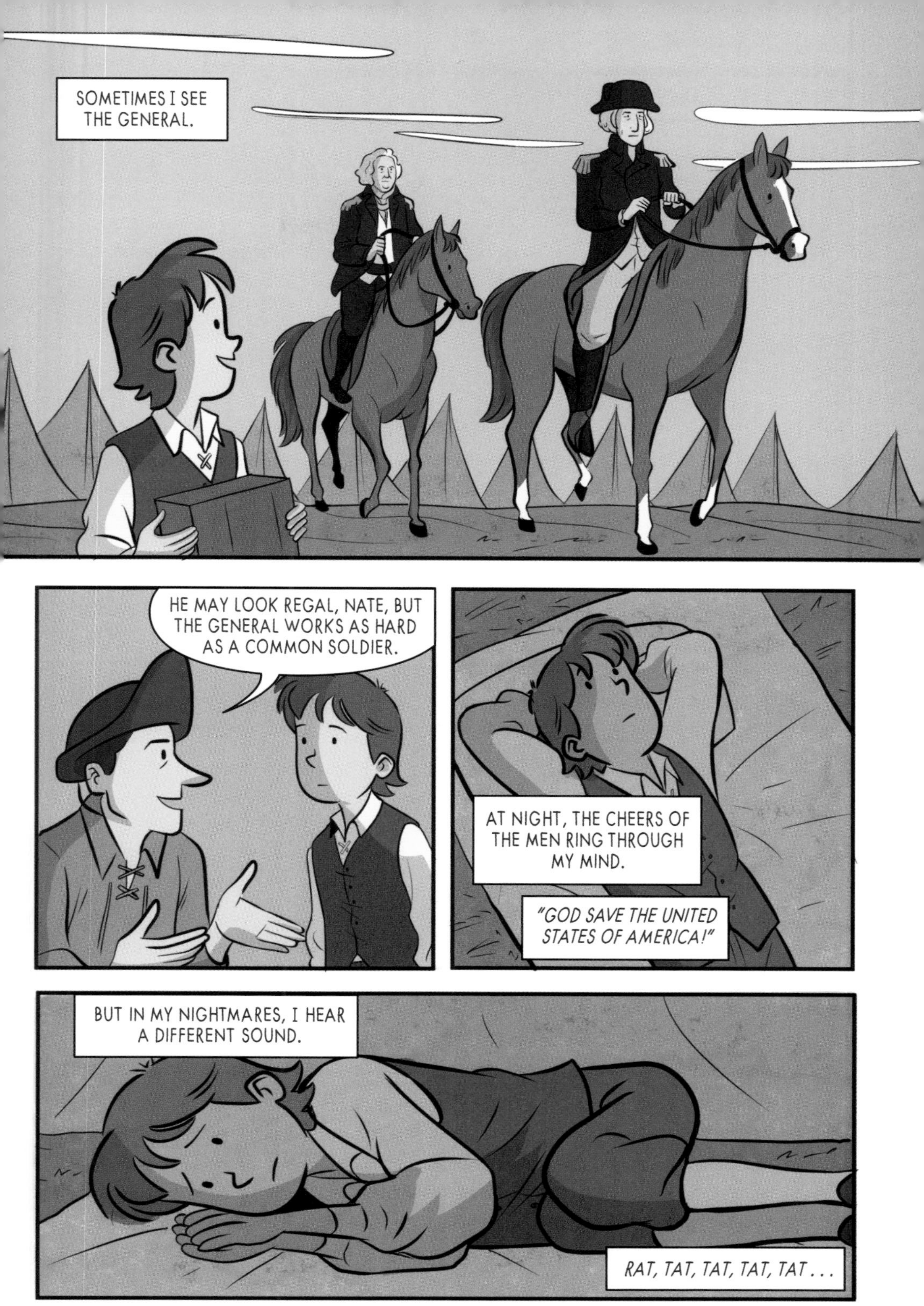
SOMETIMES I SEE THE GENERAL.
HE MAY LOOK REGAL, NATE, BUT THE GENERAL WORKS AS HARD AS A COMMON SOLDIER.
AT NIGHT, THE CHEERS OF THE MEN RING THROUGH MY MIND.
"GOD SAVE THE UNITED STATES OF AMERICA!"
BUT IN MY NIGHTMARES, I HEAR A DIFFERENT SOUND.
RAT, TAT, TAT, TAT, TAT . . .

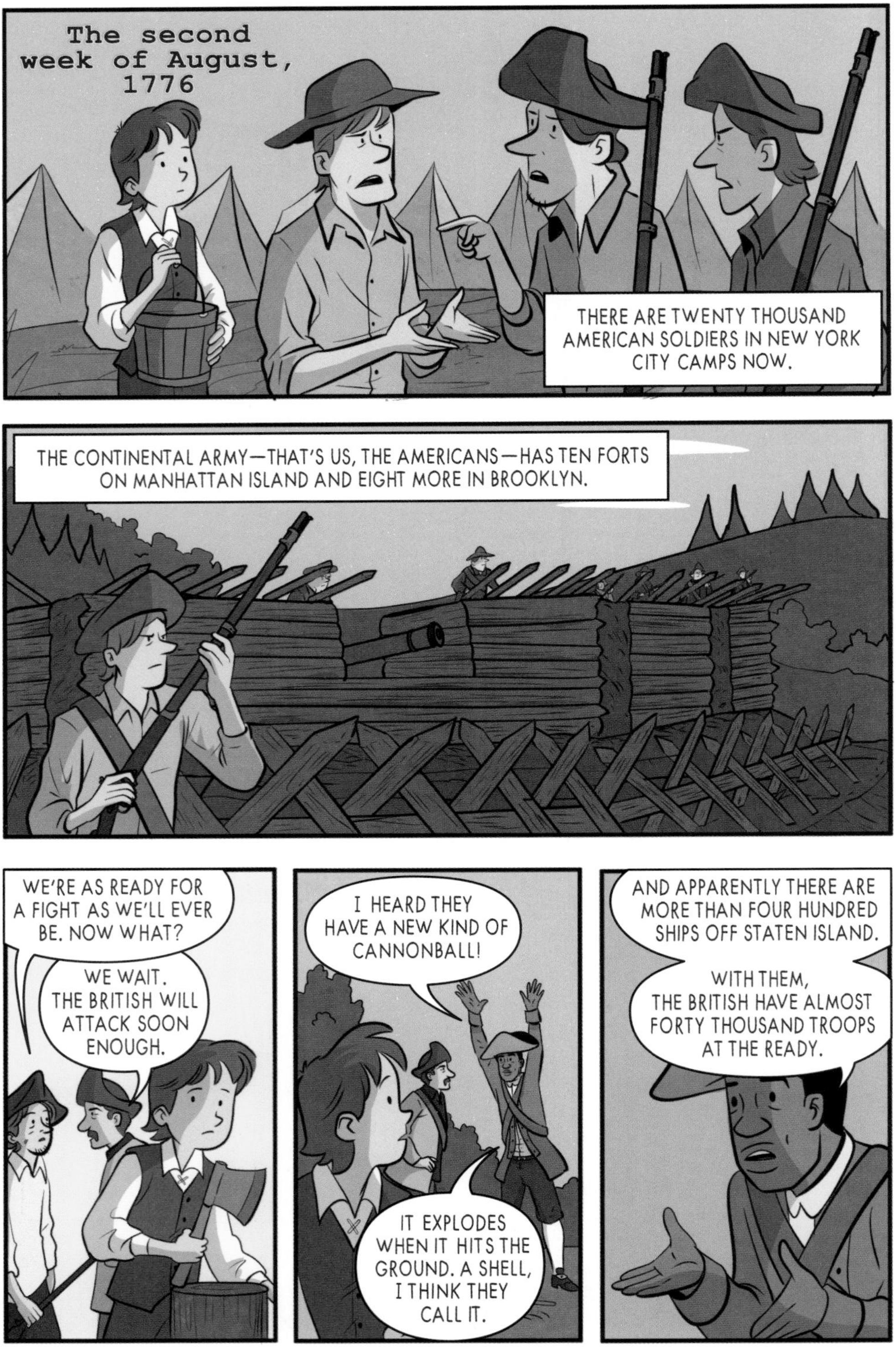
The second week of August, 1776
THERE ARE TWENTY THOUSAND AMERICAN SOLDIERS IN NEW YORK CITY CAMPS NOW.
THE CONTINENTAL ARMY—THAT'S US, THE AMERICANS—HAS TEN FORTS ON MANHATTAN ISLAND AND EIGHT MORE IN BROOKLYN.
WE'RE AS READY FOR A FIGHT AS WE'LL EVER BE. NOW WHAT?
WE WAIT. THE BRITISH WILL ATTACK SOON ENOUGH.
I HEARD THEY HAVE A NEW KIND OF CANNONBALL!
IT EXPLODES WHEN IT HITS THE GROUND. A SHELL, I THINK THEY CALL IT.
AND APPARENTLY THERE ARE MORE THAN FOUR HUNDRED SHIPS OFF STATEN ISLAND.
WITH THEM, THE BRITISH HAVE ALMOST FORTY THOUSAND TROOPS AT THE READY.

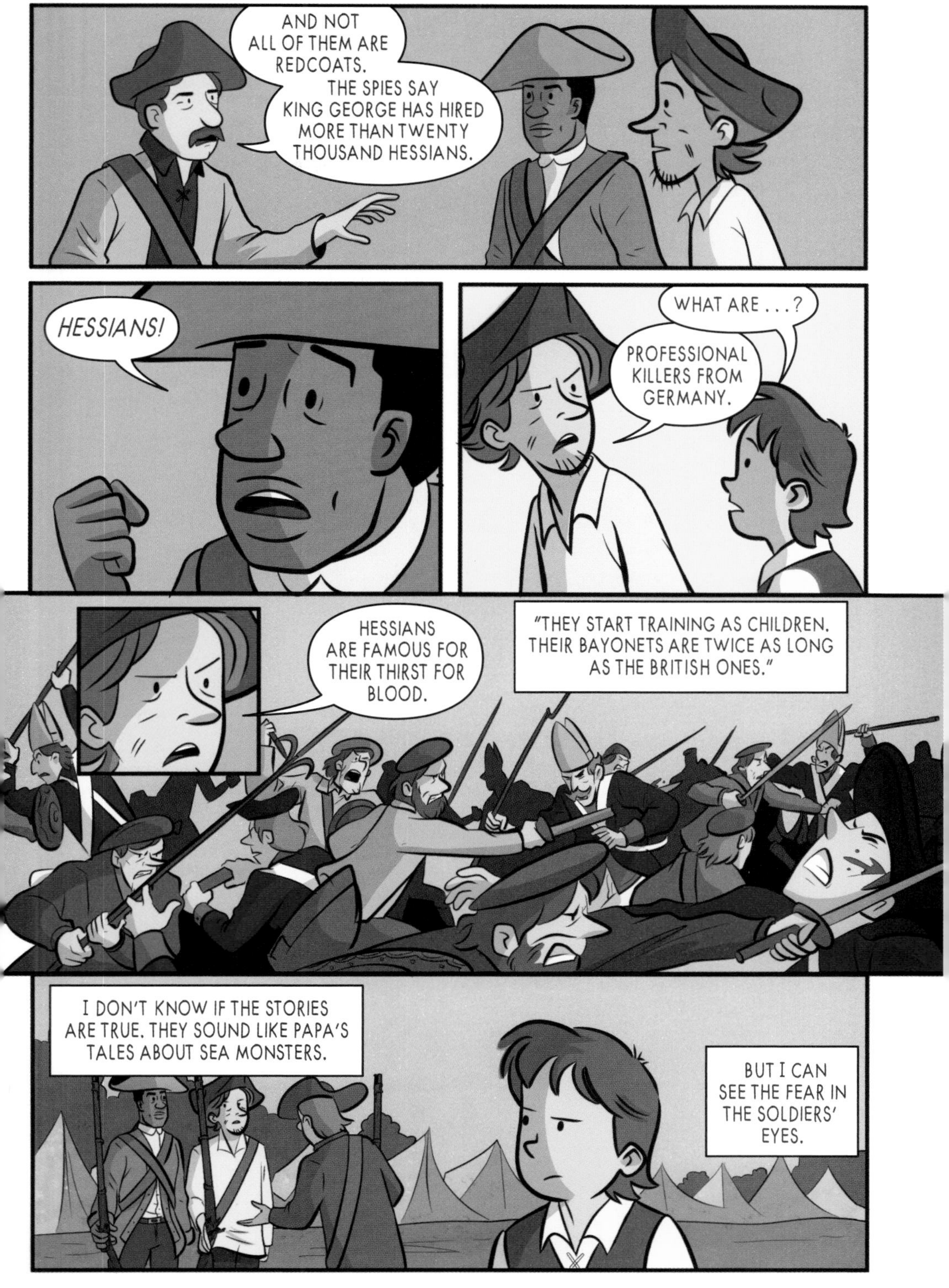
AND NOT ALL OF THEM ARE REDCOATS.
THE SPIES SAY KING GEORGE HAS HIRED MORE THAN TWENTY THOUSAND HESSIANS.
HESSIANS!
WHAT ARE . . . ?
PROFESSIONAL KILLERS FROM GERMANY.
HESSIANS ARE FAMOUS FOR THEIR THIRST FOR BLOOD.
"THEY START TRAINING AS CHILDREN. THEIR BAYONETS ARE TWICE AS LONG AS THE BRITISH ONES."
I DON'T KNOW IF THE STORIES ARE TRUE. THEY SOUND LIKE PAPA'S TALES ABOUT SEA MONSTERS.
BUT I CAN SEE THE FEAR IN THE SOLDIERS' EYES.

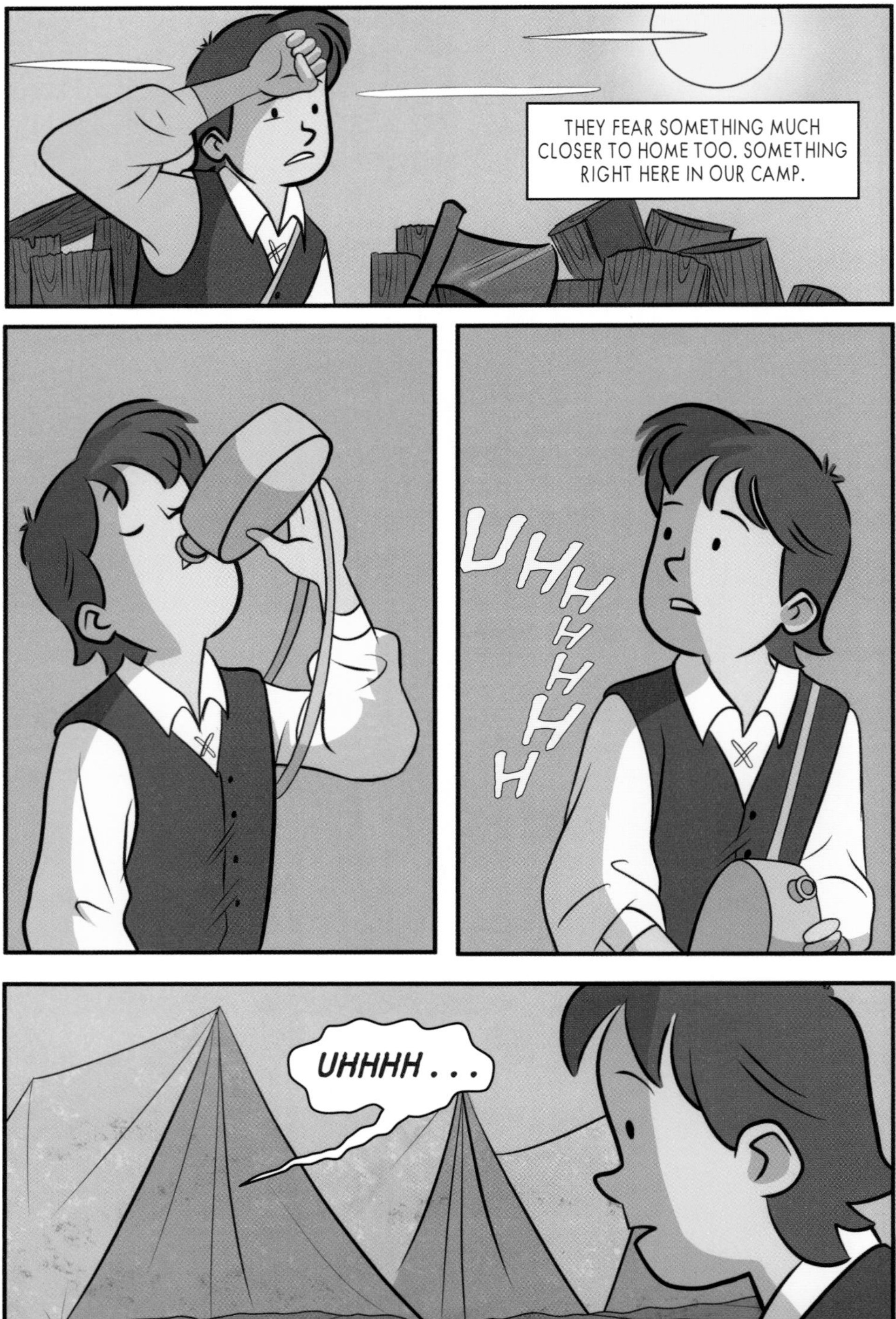
THEY FEAR SOMETHING MUCH CLOSER TO HOME TOO. SOMETHING RIGHT HERE IN OUR CAMP.
UHHHHHHHH
UHHHH . . .

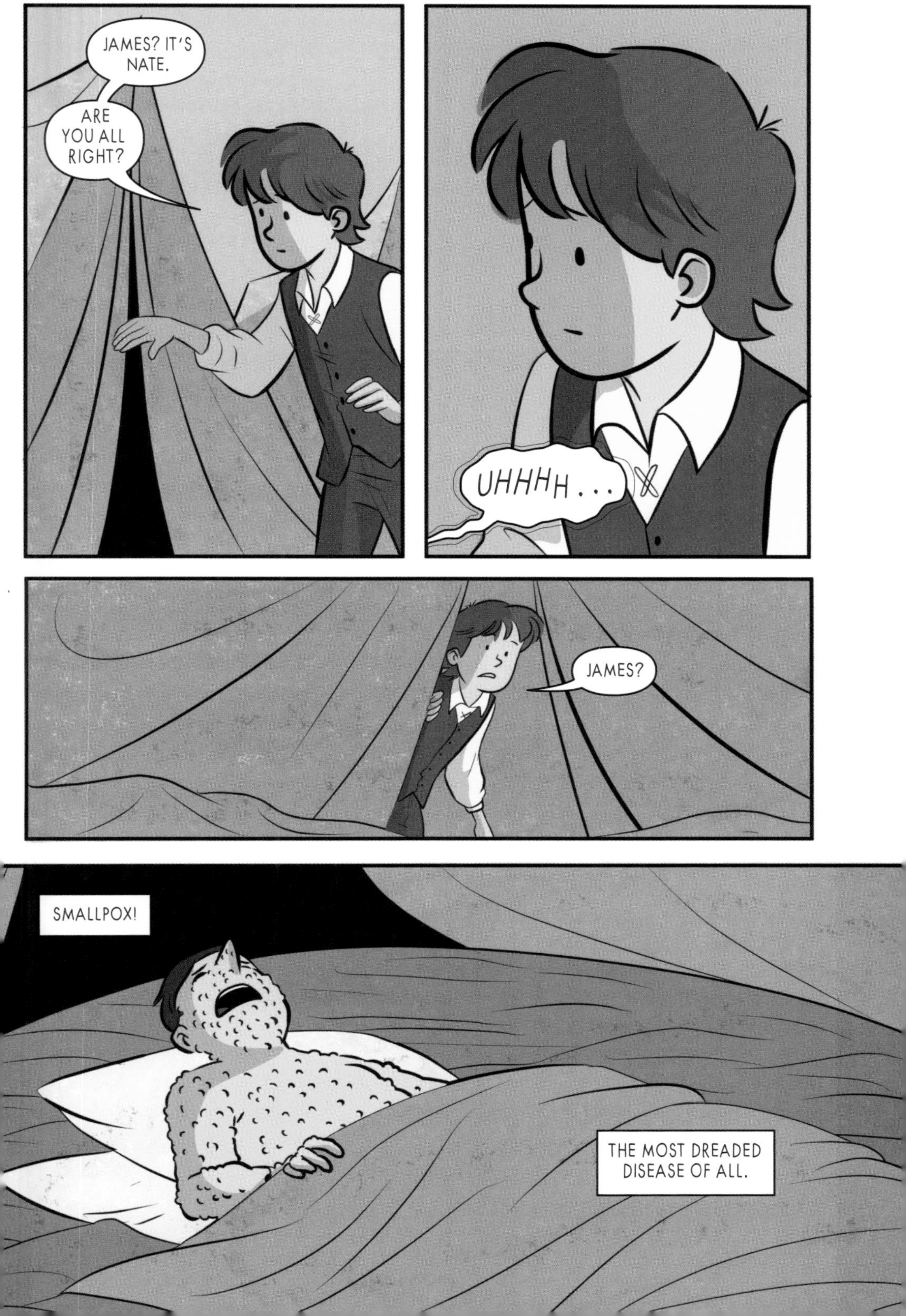
JAMES? IT'S NATE.
ARE YOU ALL RIGHT?
UHHHH . . .
JAMES?
SMALLPOX!
THE MOST DREADED DISEASE OF ALL.

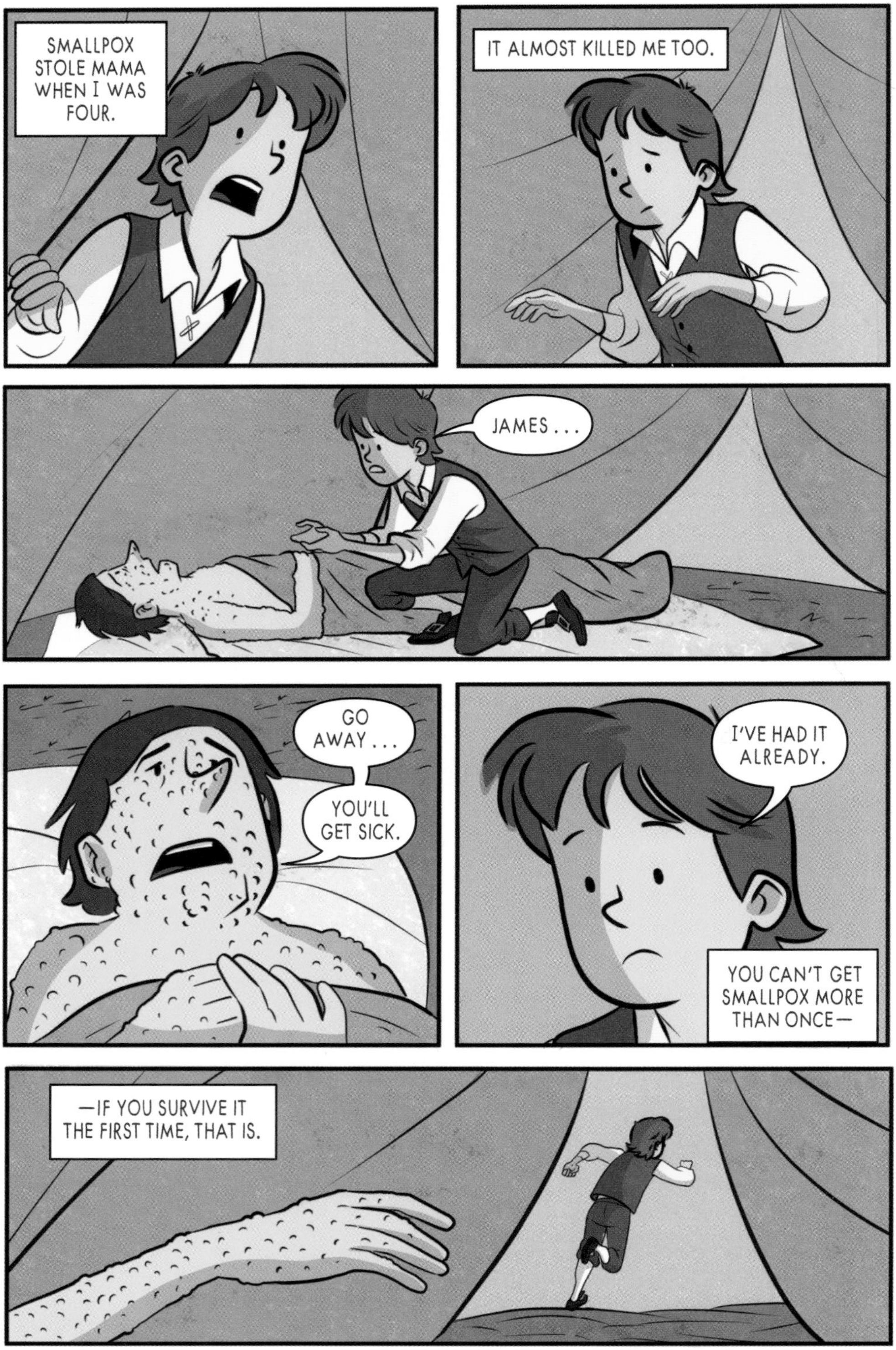
SMALLPOX STOLE MAMA WHEN I WAS FOUR.
IT ALMOST KILLED ME TOO.
JAMES . . .
GO AWAY . . .
YOU'LL GET SICK.
I'VE HAD IT ALREADY.
YOU CAN'T GET SMALLPOX MORE THAN ONCE—
—IF YOU SURVIVE IT THE FIRST TIME, THAT IS.

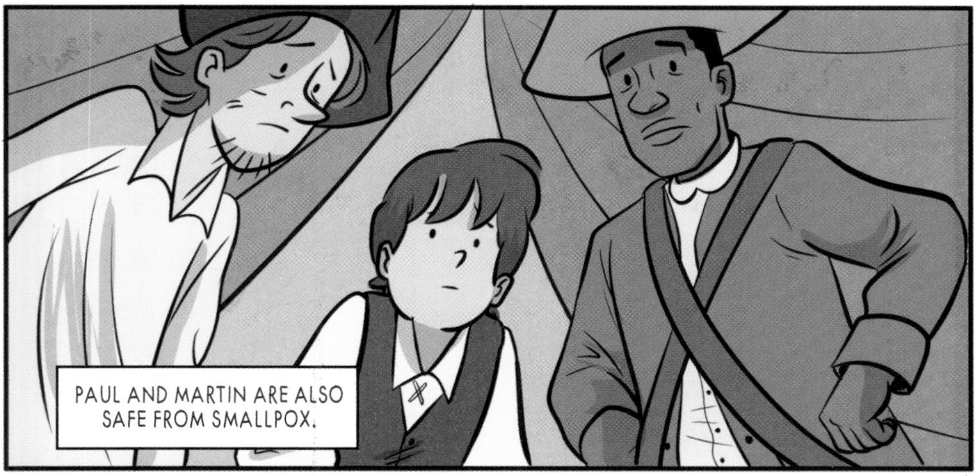
PAUL AND MARTIN ARE ALSO SAFE FROM SMALLPOX.

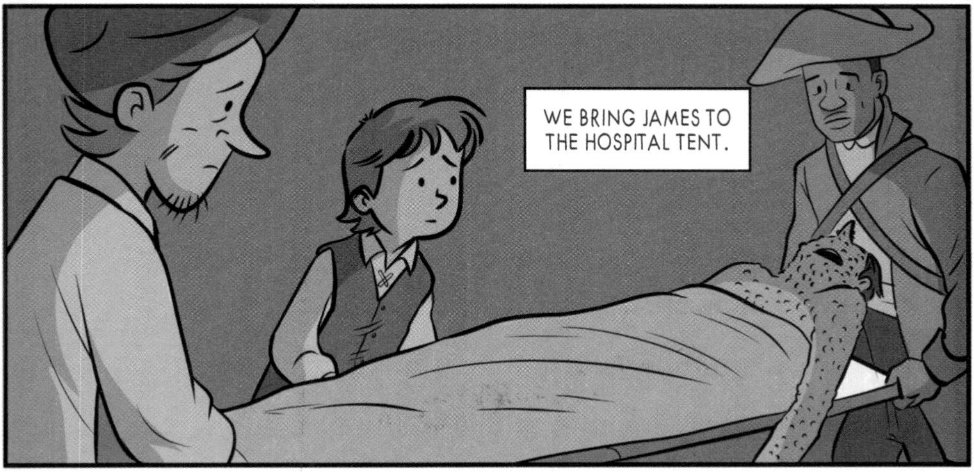
WE BRING JAMES TO THE HOSPITAL TENT.

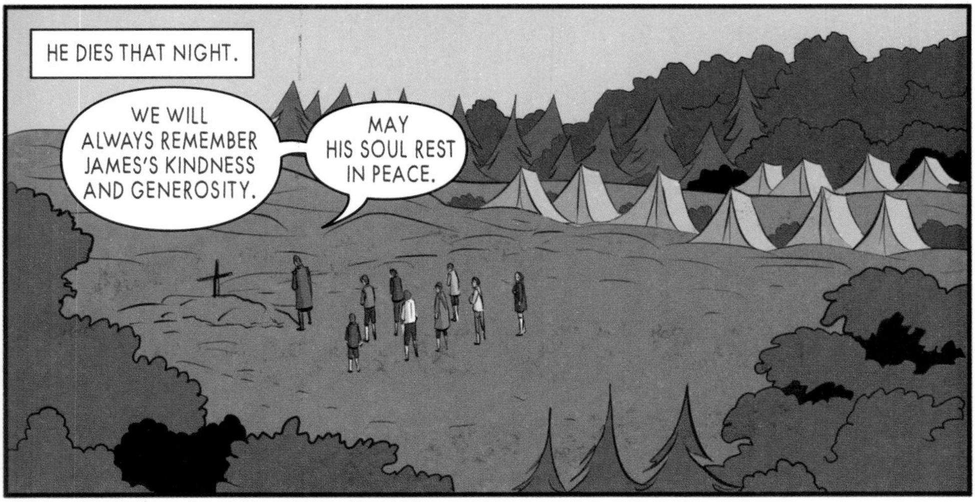
HE DIES THAT NIGHT.
WE WILL ALWAYS REMEMBER JAMES'S KINDNESS AND GENEROSITY.
MAY HIS SOUL REST IN PEACE.

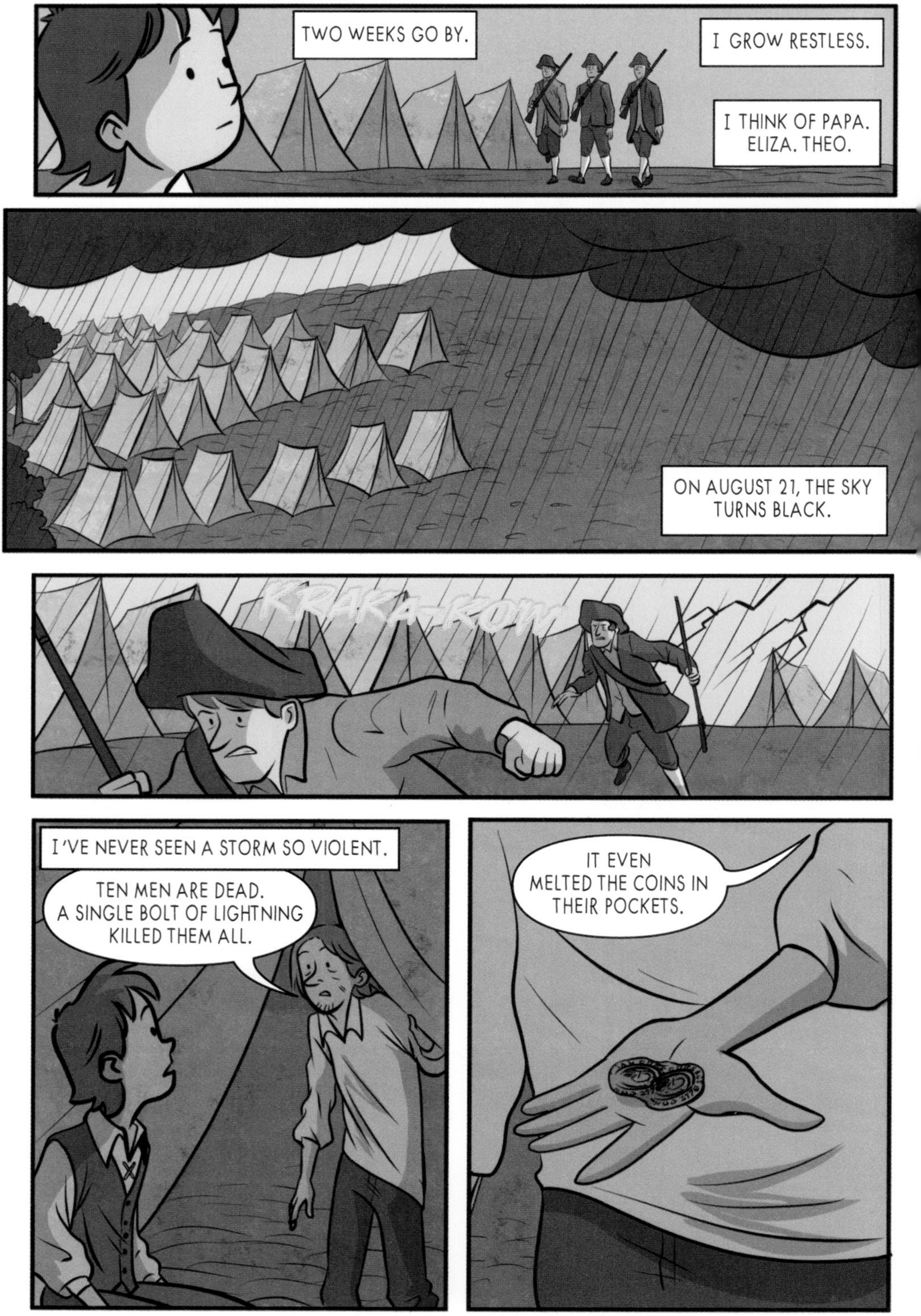
TWO WEEKS GO BY.
I GROW RESTLESS.
I THINK OF PAPA. ELIZA. THEO.
ON AUGUST 21, THE SKY TURNS BLACK.
KRAKA-KOW
I'VE NEVER SEEN A STORM SO VIOLENT.
TEN MEN ARE DEAD. A SINGLE BOLT OF LIGHTNING KILLED THEM ALL.
IT EVEN MELTED THE COINS IN THEIR POCKETS.

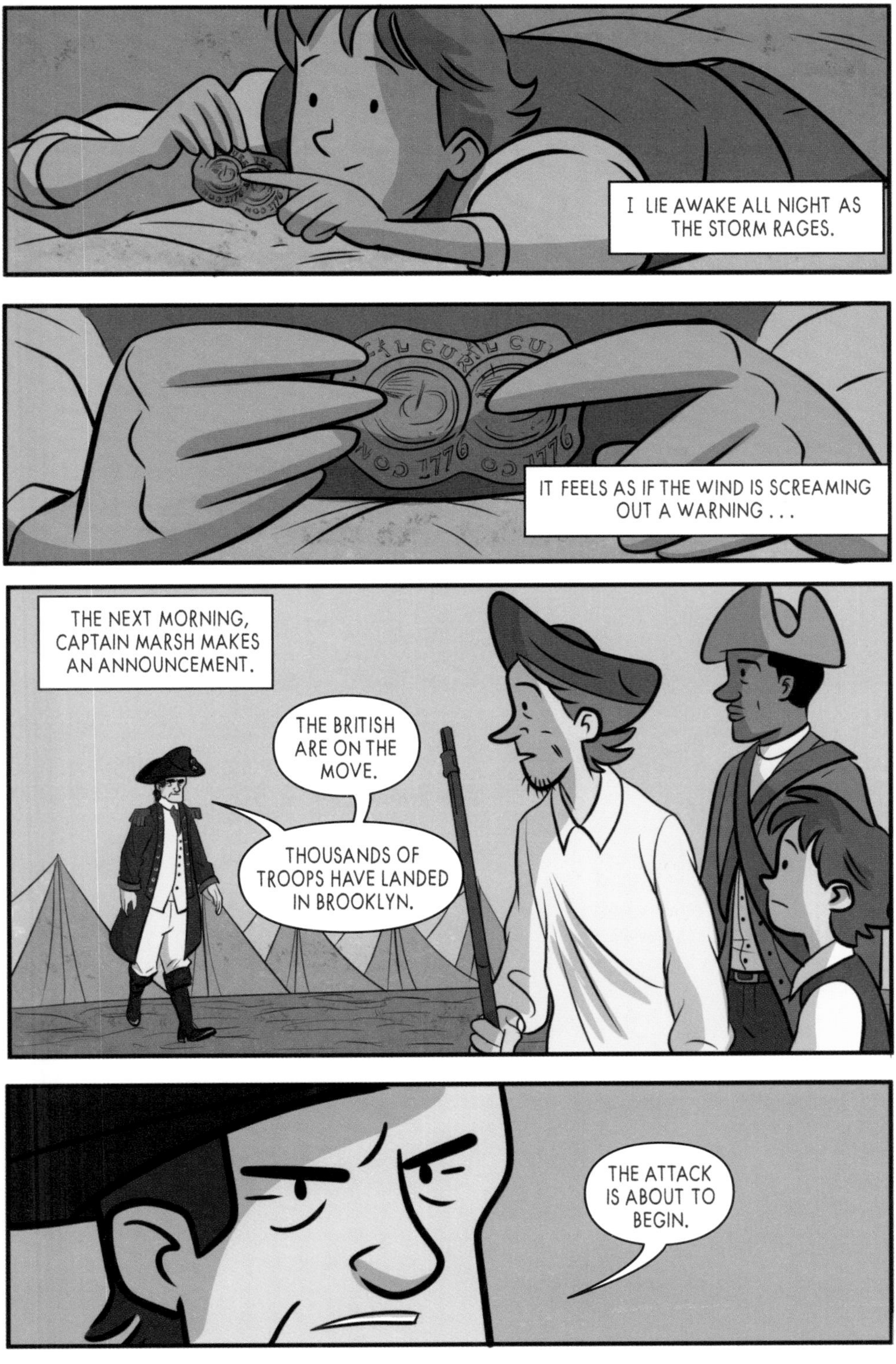
I LIE AWAKE ALL NIGHT AS THE STORM RAGES.
IT FEELS AS IF THE WIND IS SCREAMING OUT A WARNING . . .
THE NEXT MORNING, CAPTAIN MARSH MAKES AN ANNOUNCEMENT.
THE BRITISH ARE ON THE MOVE.
THOUSANDS OF TROOPS HAVE LANDED IN BROOKLYN.
THE ATTACK IS ABOUT TO BEGIN.

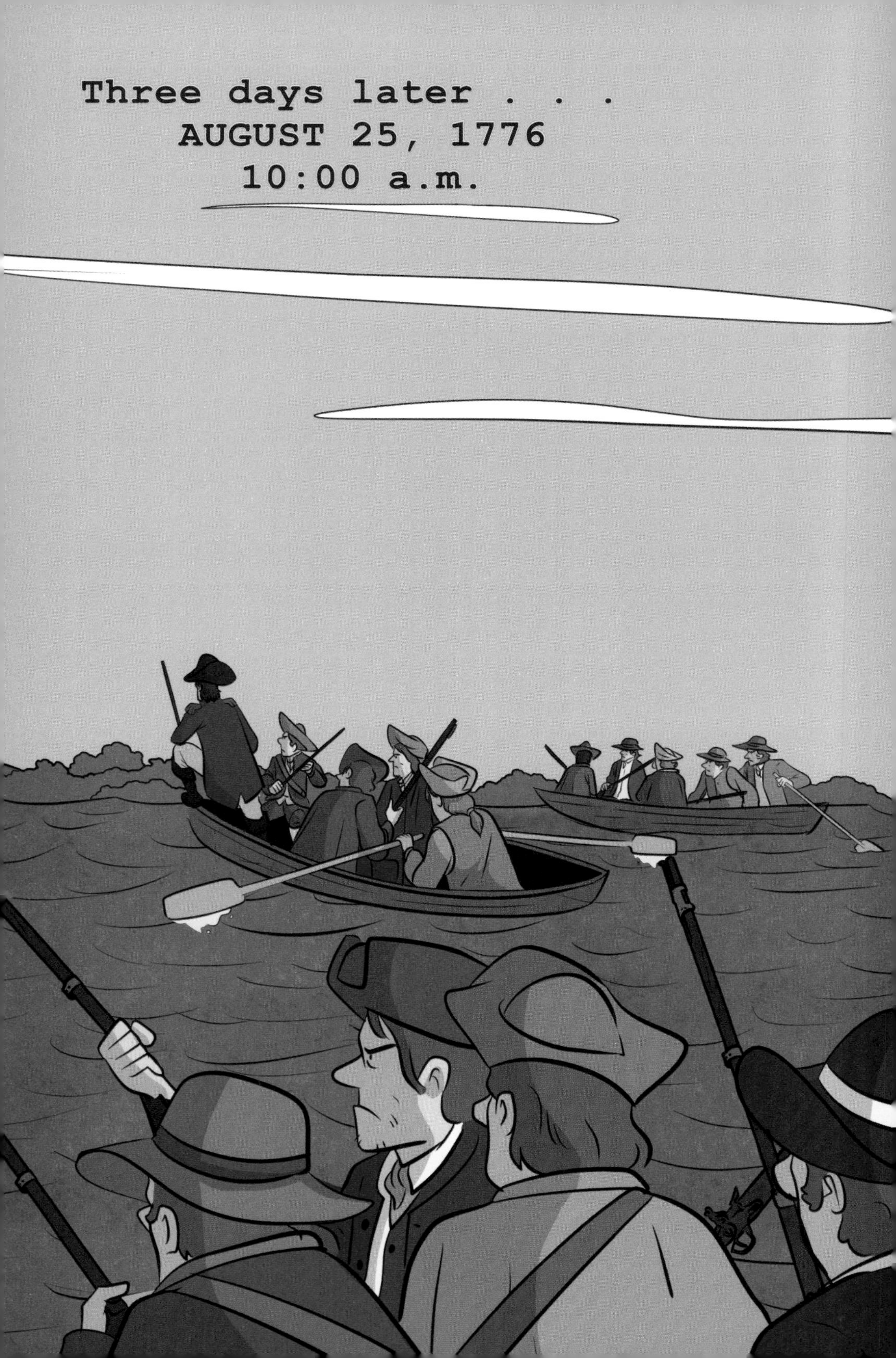
Three days later . . .
AUGUST 25, 1776
10:00 a.m.

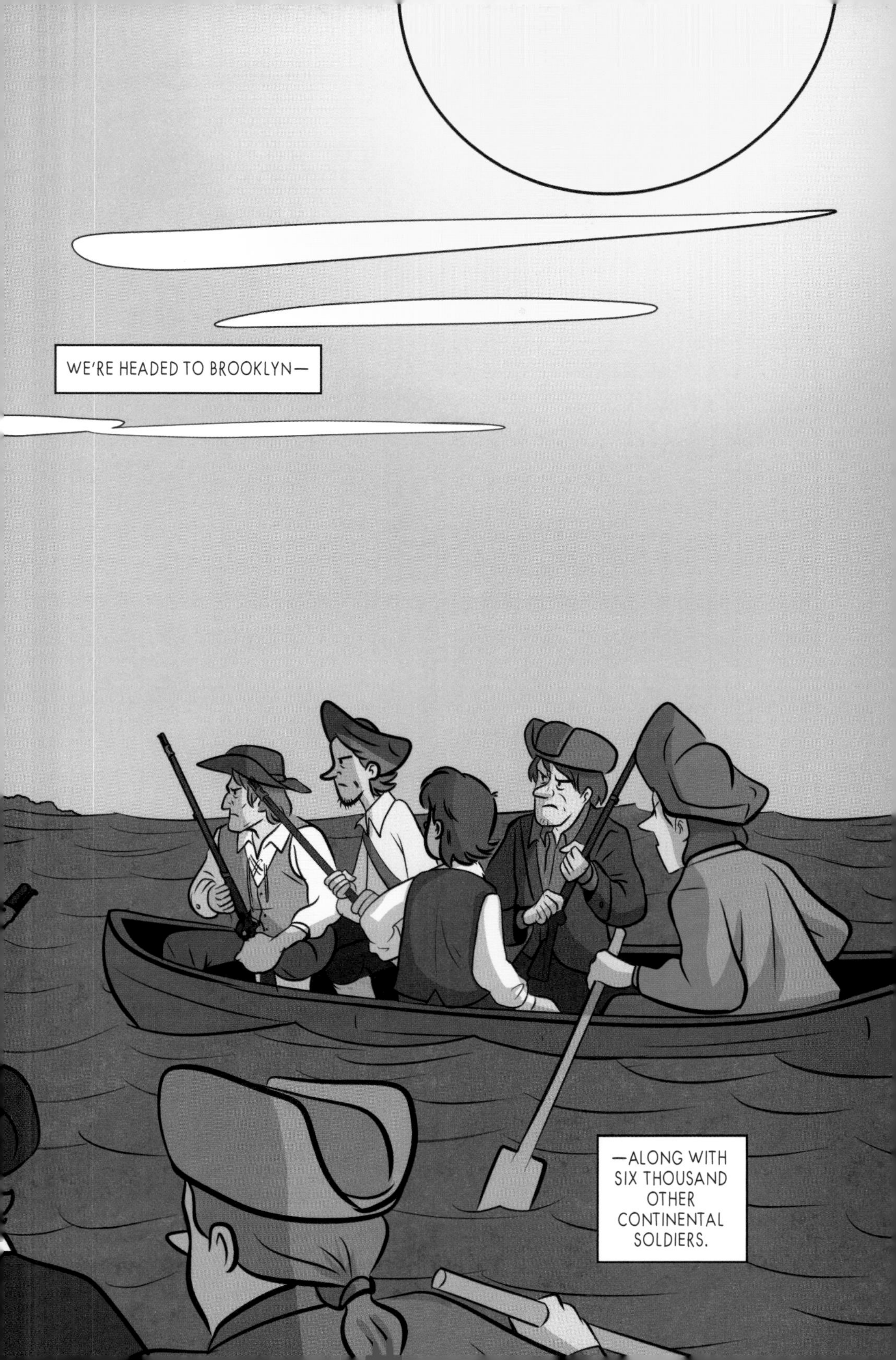
WE'RE HEADED TO BROOKLYN—
—ALONG WITH SIX THOUSAND OTHER CONTINENTAL SOLDIERS.

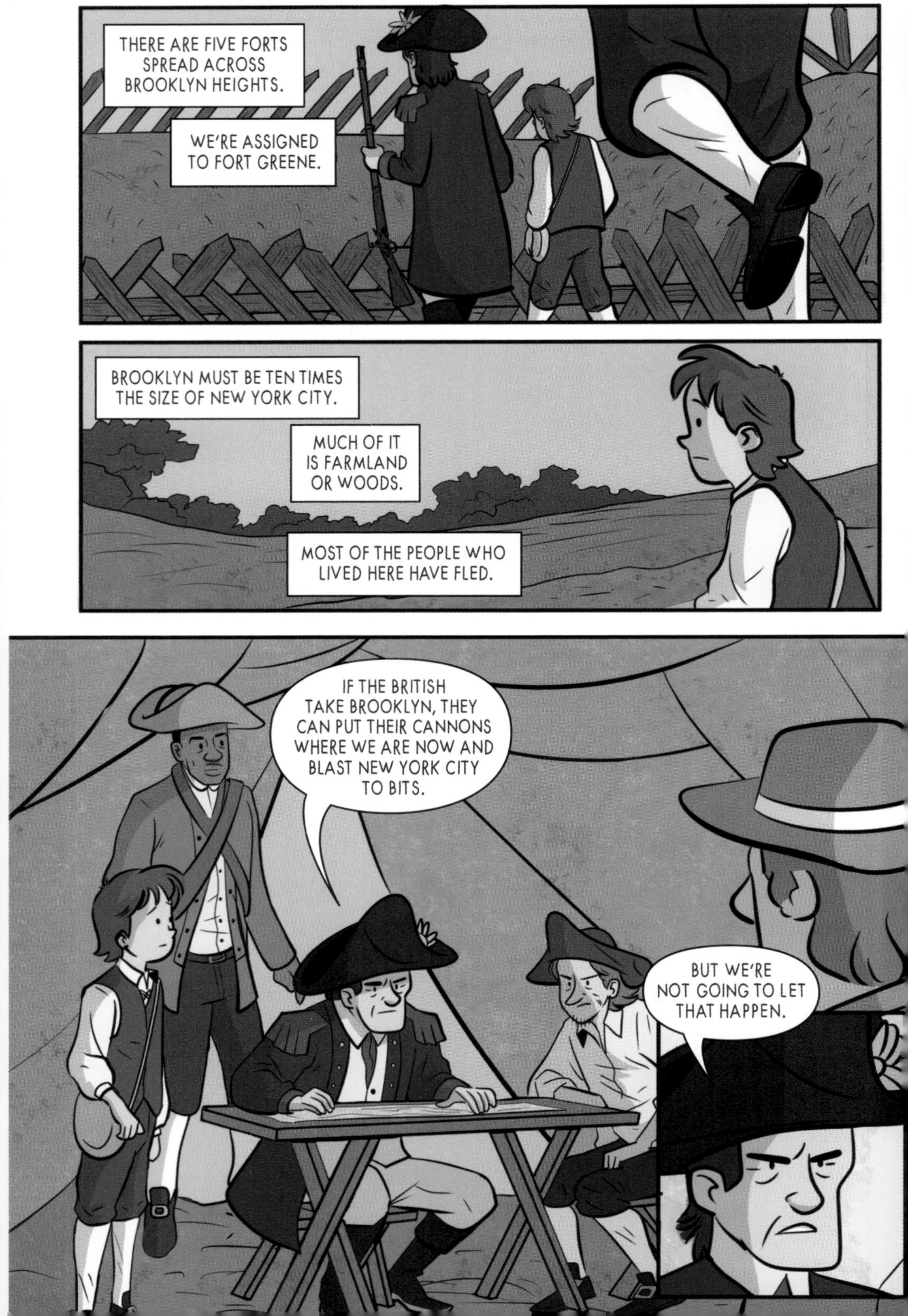
THERE ARE FIVE FORTS SPREAD ACROSS BROOKLYN HEIGHTS.
WE'RE ASSIGNED TO FORT GREENE.
BROOKLYN MUST BE TEN TIMES THE SIZE OF NEW YORK CITY.
MUCH OF IT IS FARMLAND OR WOODS.
MOST OF THE PEOPLE WHO LIVED HERE HAVE FLED.
IF THE BRITISH TAKE BROOKLYN, THEY CAN PUT THEIR CANNONS WHERE WE ARE NOW AND BLAST NEW YORK CITY TO BITS.
BUT WE'RE NOT GOING TO LET THAT HAPPEN.

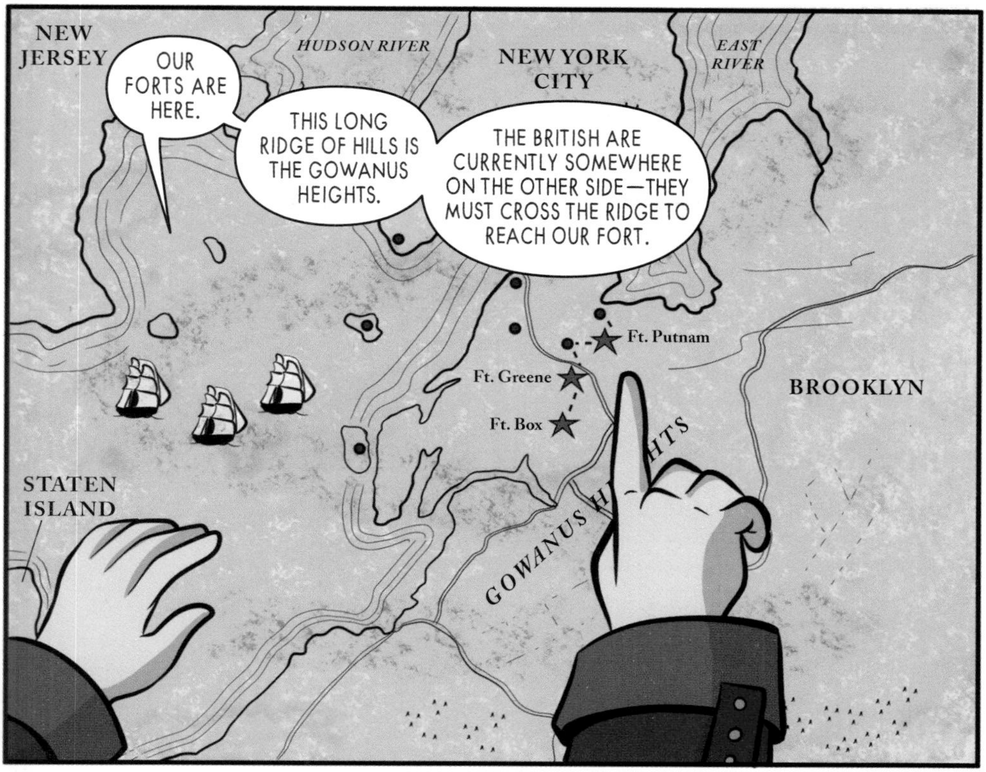
NEW JERSEY
HUDSON RIVER
NEW YORK CITY
EAST RIVER
OUR FORTS ARE HERE.
THIS LONG RIDGE OF HILLS IS THE GOWANUS HEIGHTS.
THE BRITISH ARE CURRENTLY SOMEWHERE ON THE OTHER SIDE—THEY MUST CROSS THE RIDGE TO REACH OUR FORT.
Ft. Putnam
Ft. Greene
Ft. Box
BROOKLYN
STATEN ISLAND
GOWANUS HEIGHTS

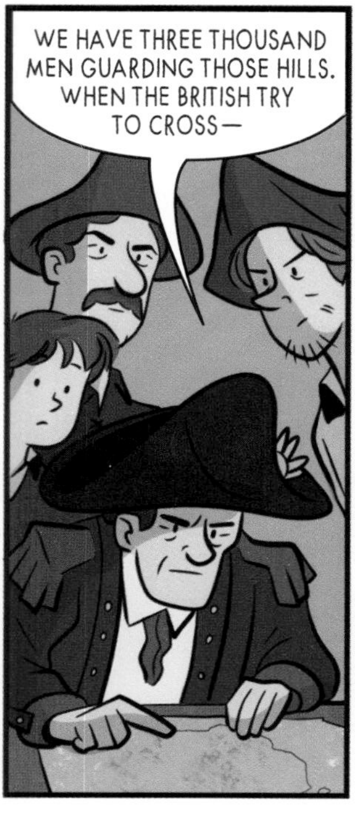
WE HAVE THREE THOUSAND MEN GUARDING THOSE HILLS. WHEN THE BRITISH TRY TO CROSS—

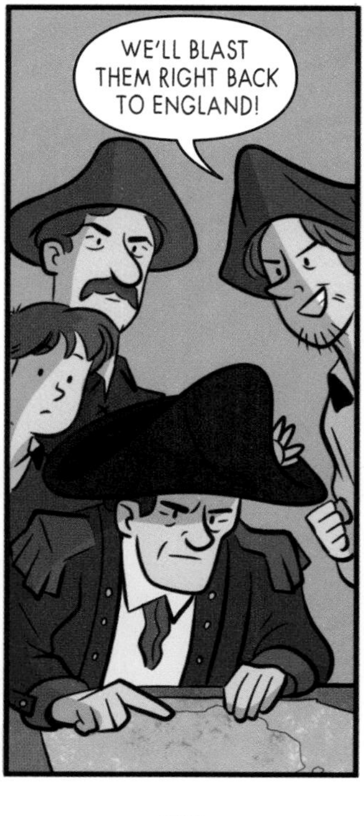
WE'LL BLAST THEM RIGHT BACK TO ENGLAND!

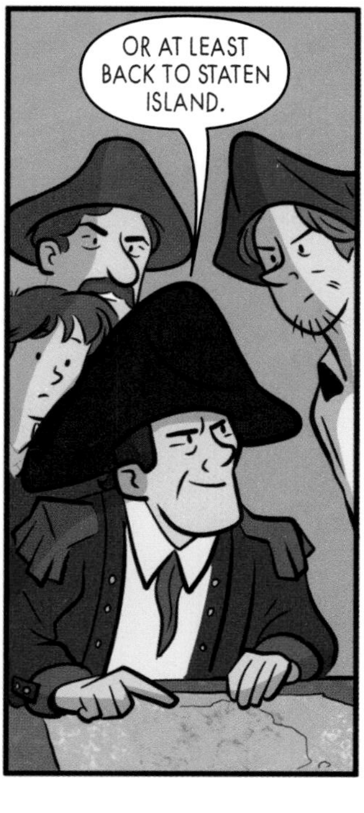
OR AT LEAST BACK TO STATEN ISLAND.

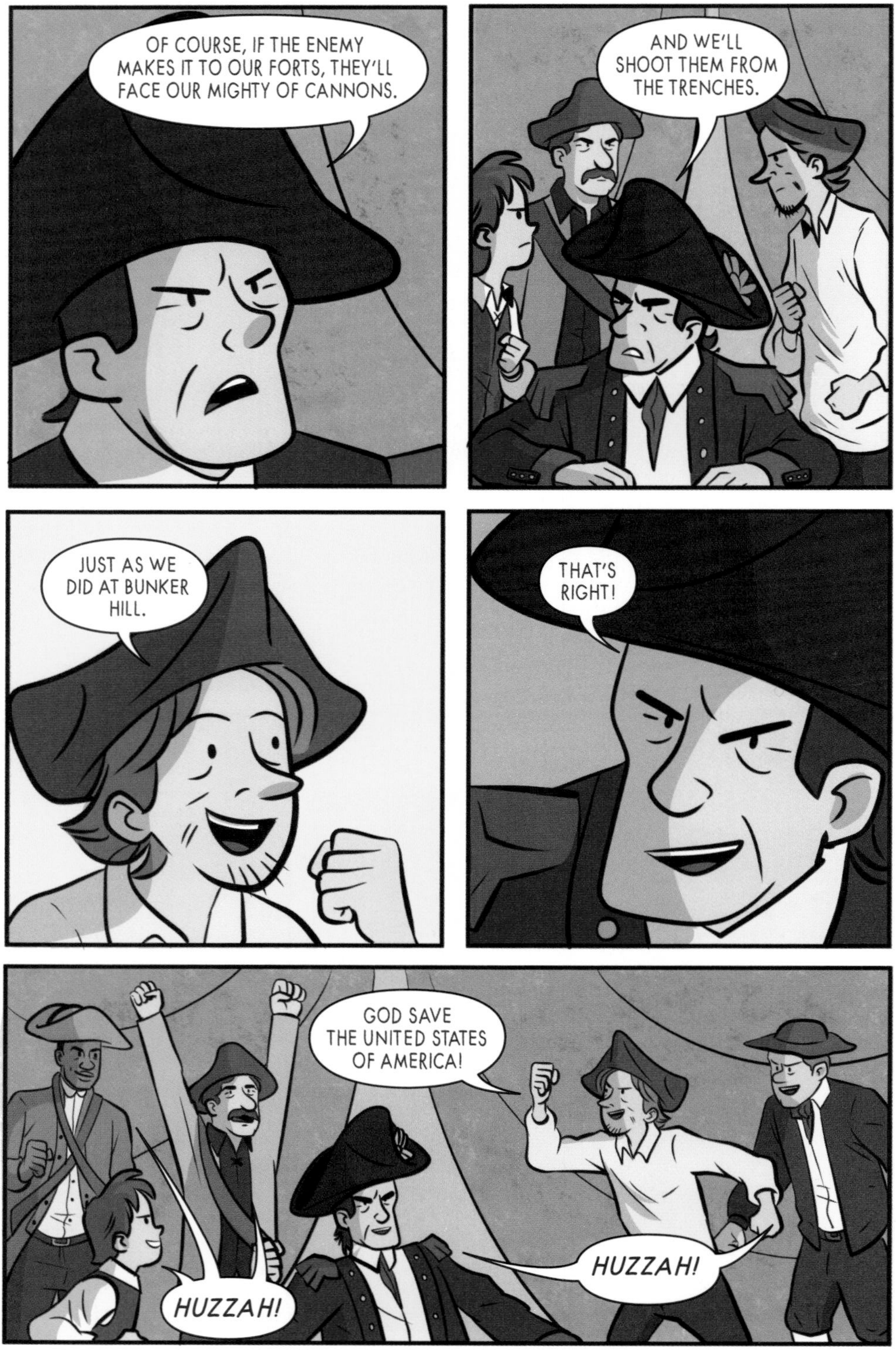
OF COURSE, IF THE ENEMY MAKES IT TO OUR FORTS, THEY'LL FACE OUR MIGHTY OF CANNONS.
AND WE'LL SHOOT THEM FROM THE TRENCHES.
JUST AS WE DID AT BUNKER HILL.
THAT'S RIGHT!
GOD SAVE THE UNITED STATES OF AMERICA!
HUZZAH!
HUZZAH!

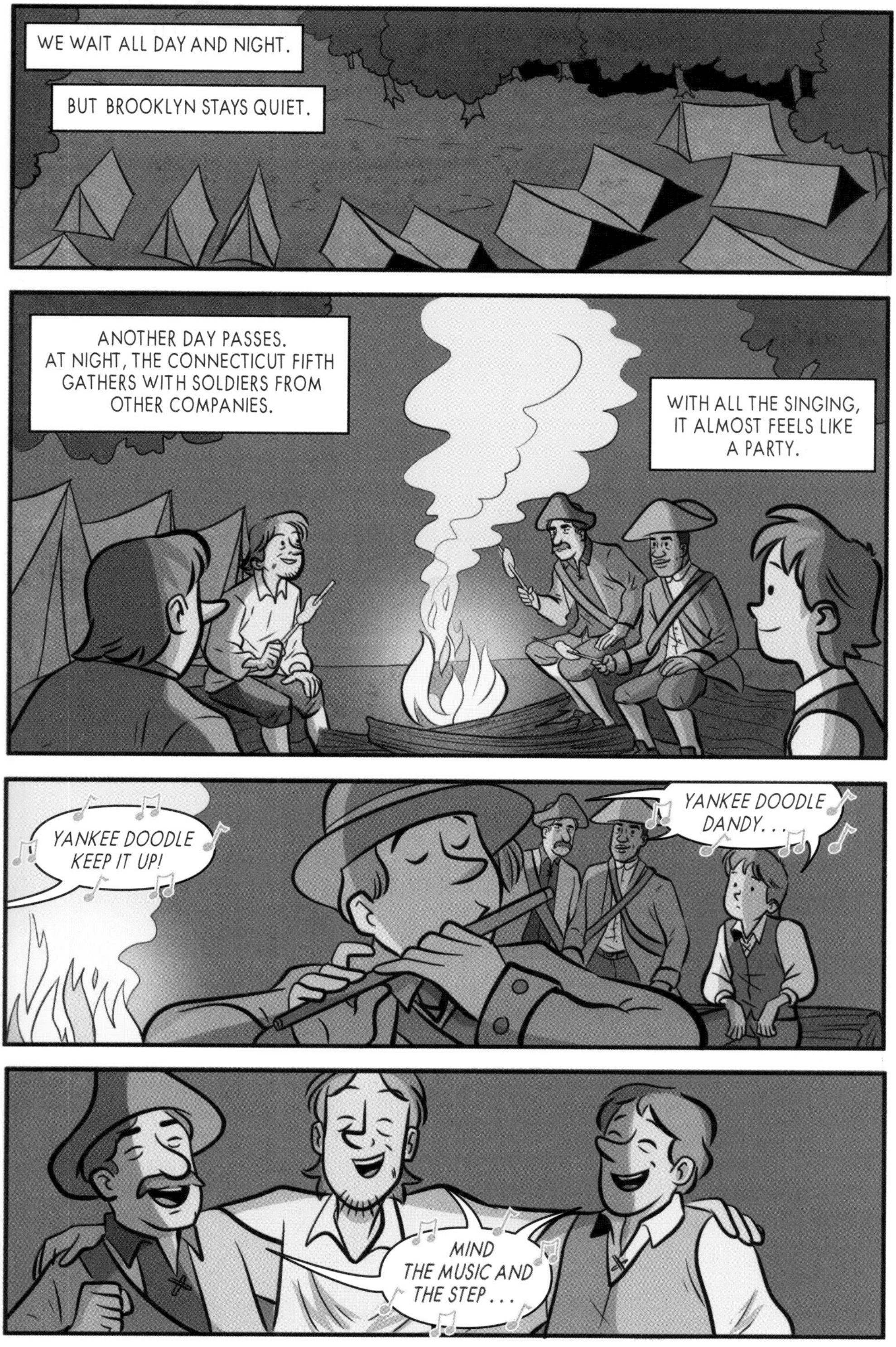
WE WAIT ALL DAY AND NIGHT.
BUT BROOKLYN STAYS QUIET.
ANOTHER DAY PASSES. AT NIGHT, THE CONNECTICUT FIFTH GATHERS WITH SOLDIERS FROM OTHER COMPANIES.
WITH ALL THE SINGING, IT ALMOST FEELS LIKE A PARTY.
YANKEE DOODLE KEEP IT UP!
YANKEE DOODLE DANDY...
MIND THE MUSIC AND THE STEP...

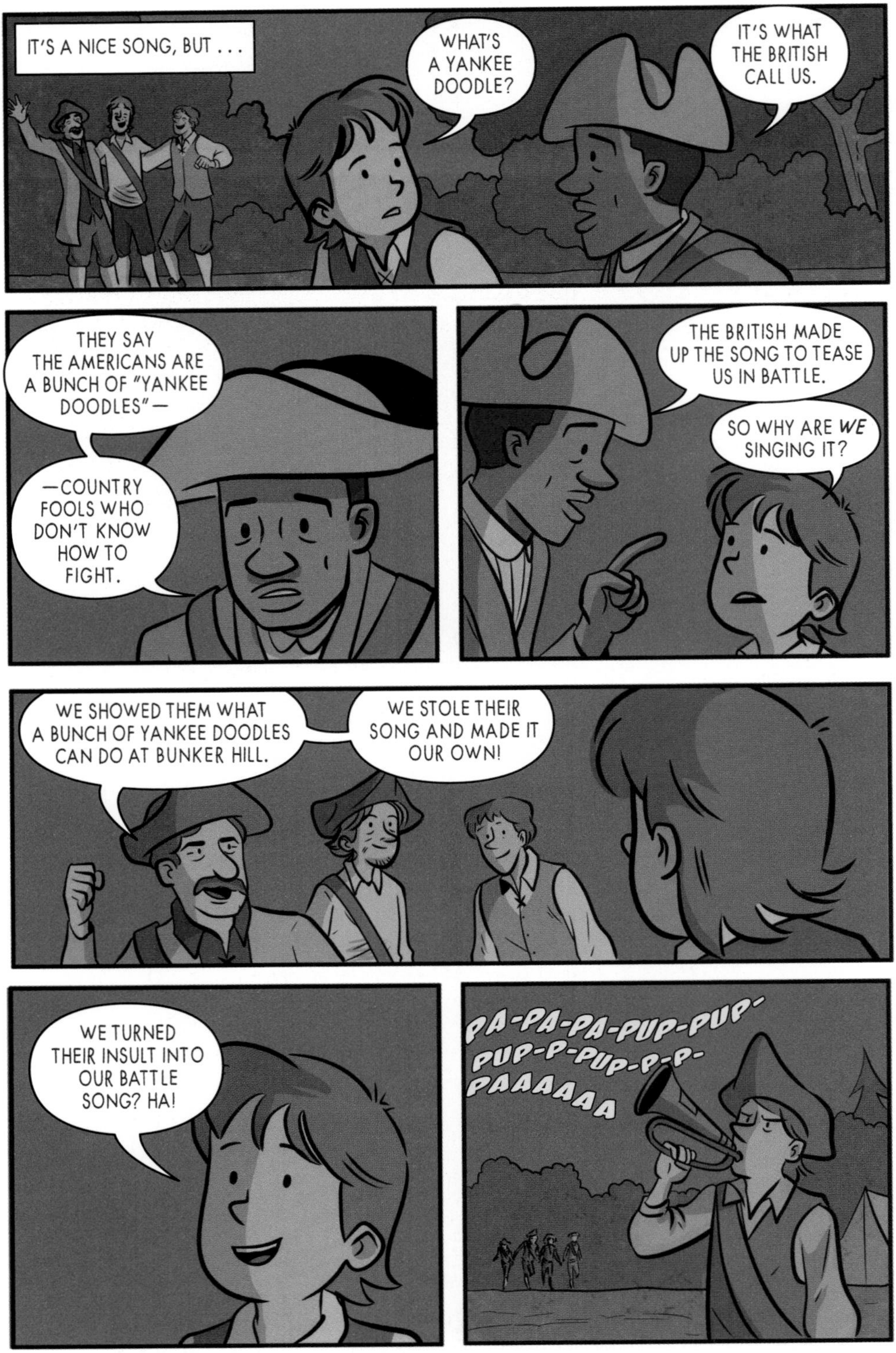
IT'S A NICE SONG, BUT . . .
WHAT'S A YANKEE DOODLE?
IT'S WHAT THE BRITISH CALL US.
THEY SAY THE AMERICANS ARE A BUNCH OF "YANKEE DOODLES"—
—COUNTRY FOOLS WHO DON'T KNOW HOW TO FIGHT.
THE BRITISH MADE UP THE SONG TO TEASE US IN BATTLE.
SO WHY ARE *WE* SINGING IT?
WE SHOWED THEM WHAT A BUNCH OF YANKEE DOODLES CAN DO AT BUNKER HILL.
WE STOLE THEIR SONG AND MADE IT OUR OWN!
WE TURNED THEIR INSULT INTO OUR BATTLE SONG? HA!
PA-PA-PA-PUP-PUP-PUP-P-PUP-P-P-PAAAAAA

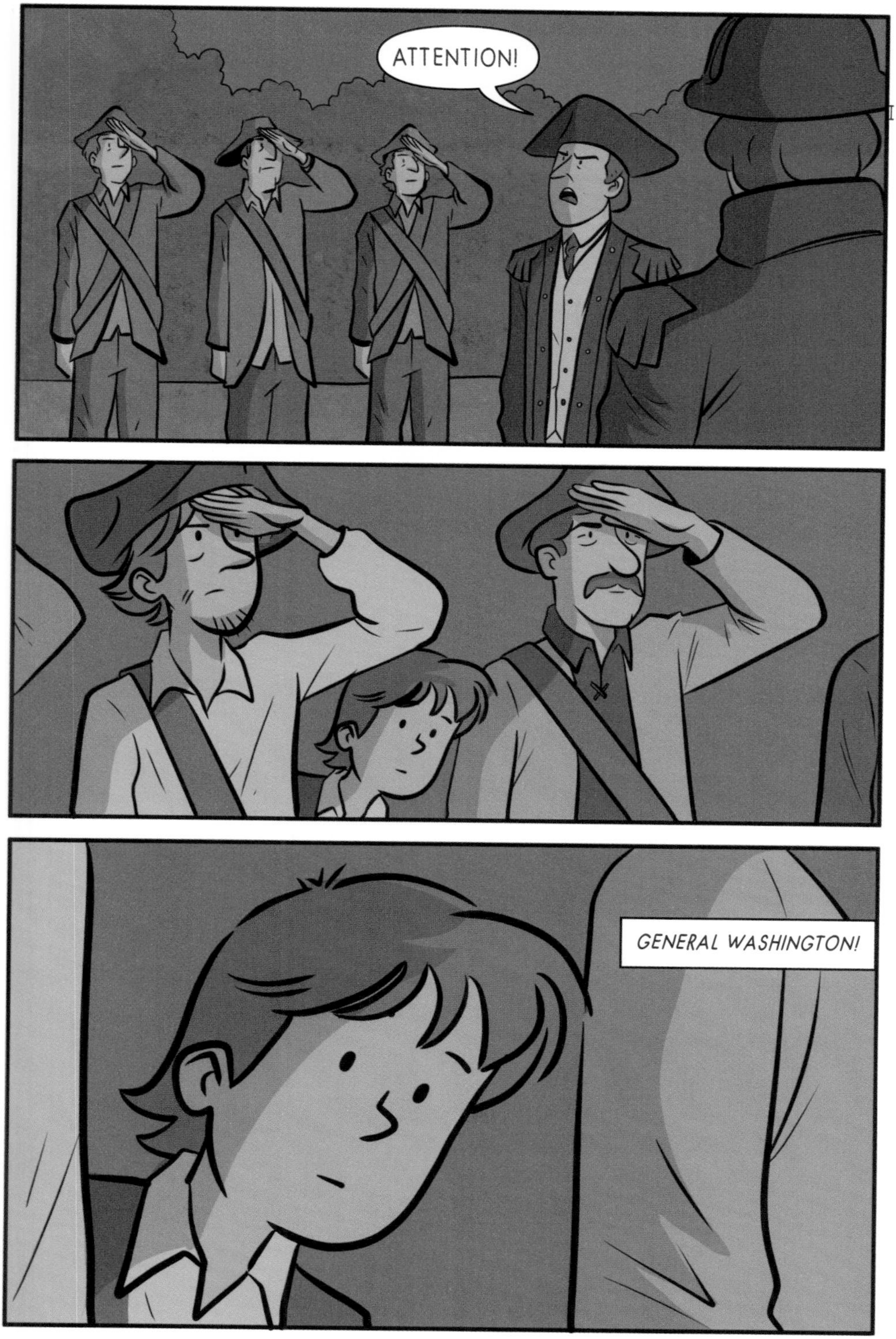
ATTENTION!
GENERAL WASHINGTON!

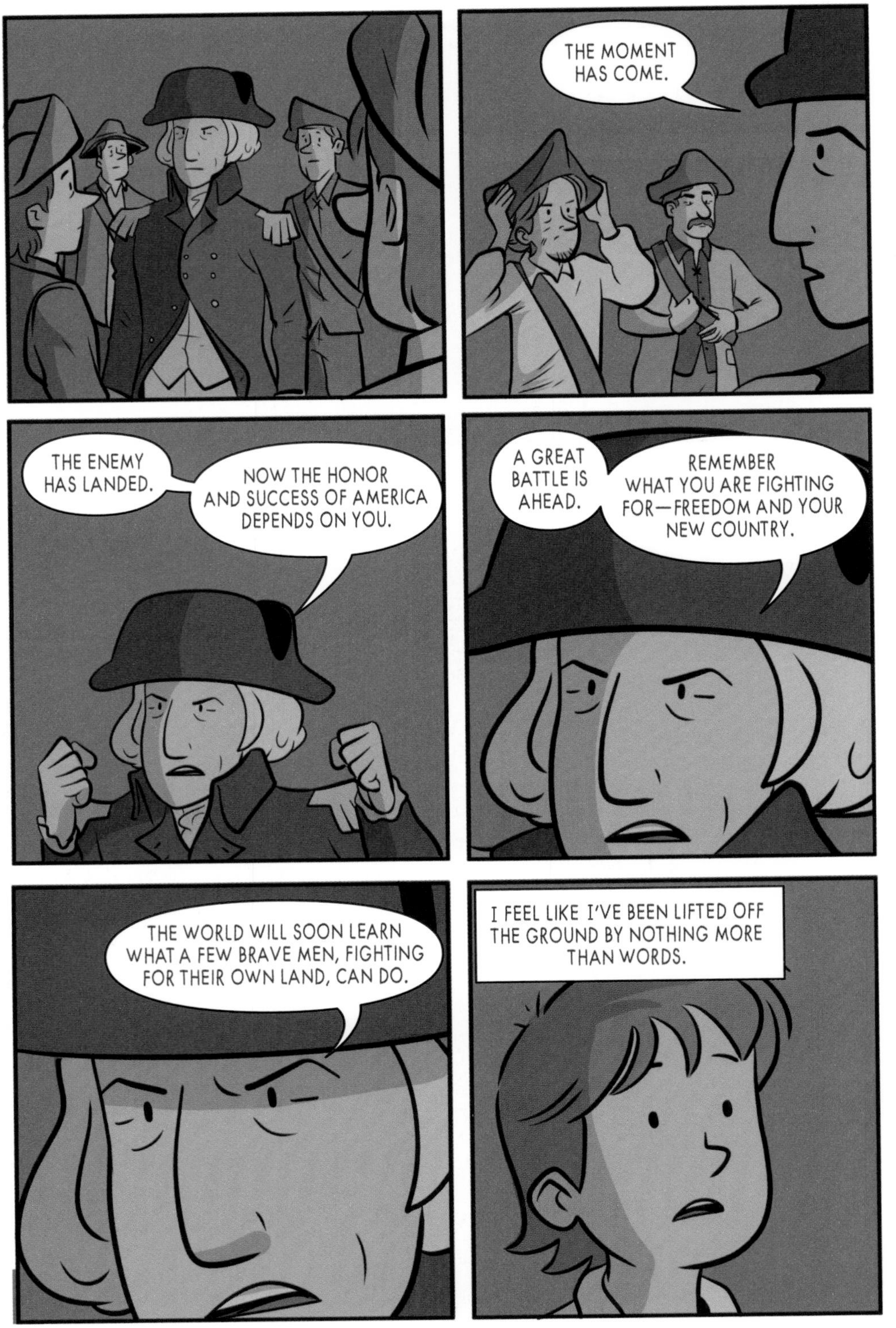
THE MOMENT HAS COME.
THE ENEMY HAS LANDED.
NOW THE HONOR AND SUCCESS OF AMERICA DEPENDS ON YOU.
A GREAT BATTLE IS AHEAD.
REMEMBER WHAT YOU ARE FIGHTING FOR—FREEDOM AND YOUR NEW COUNTRY.
THE WORLD WILL SOON LEARN WHAT A FEW BRAVE MEN, FIGHTING FOR THEIR OWN LAND, CAN DO.
I FEEL LIKE I'VE BEEN LIFTED OFF THE GROUND BY NOTHING MORE THAN WORDS.

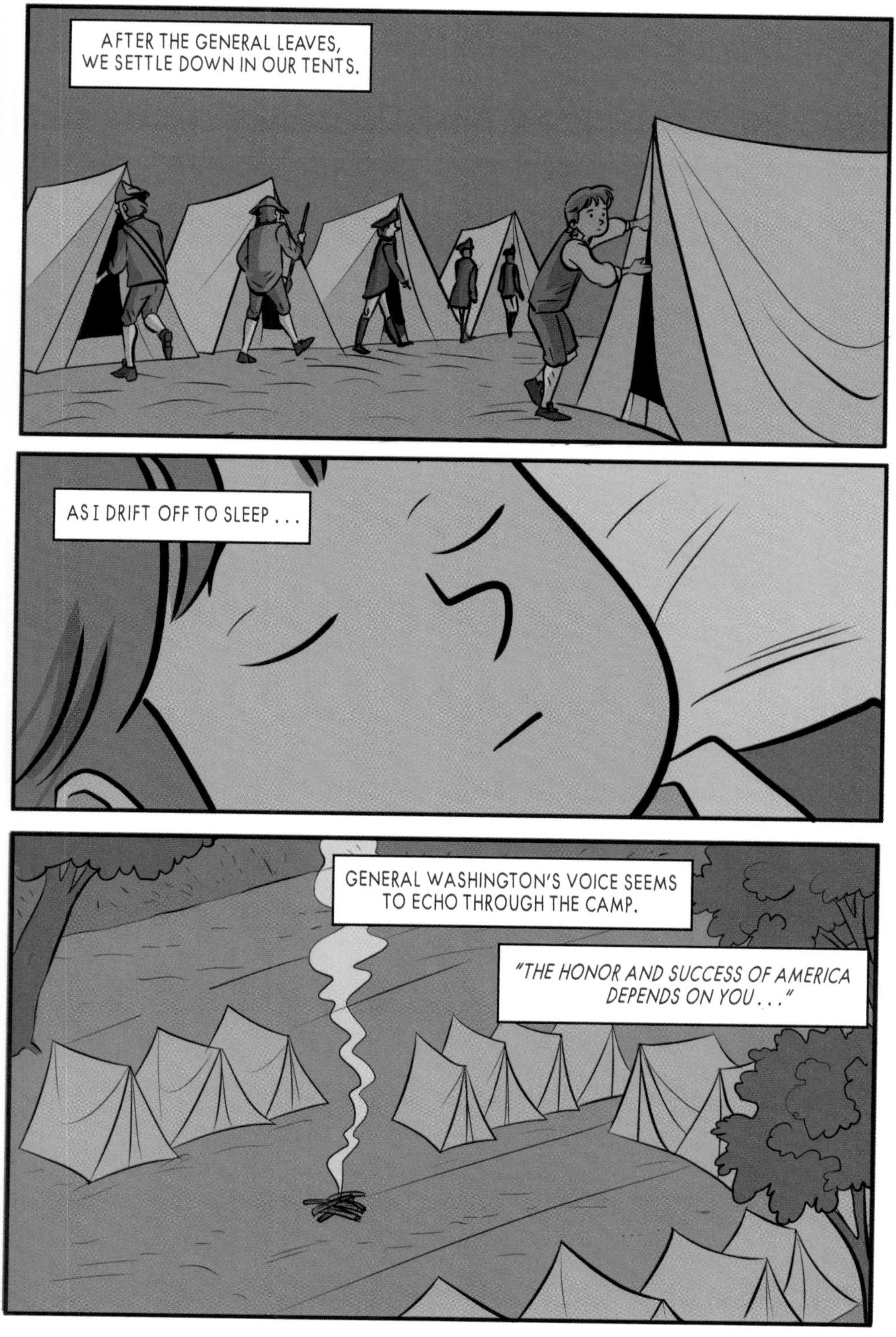
AFTER THE GENERAL LEAVES, WE SETTLE DOWN IN OUR TENTS.
AS I DRIFT OFF TO SLEEP . . .
GENERAL WASHINGTON'S VOICE SEEMS TO ECHO THROUGH THE CAMP.
"THE HONOR AND SUCCESS OF AMERICA DEPENDS ON YOU . . ."

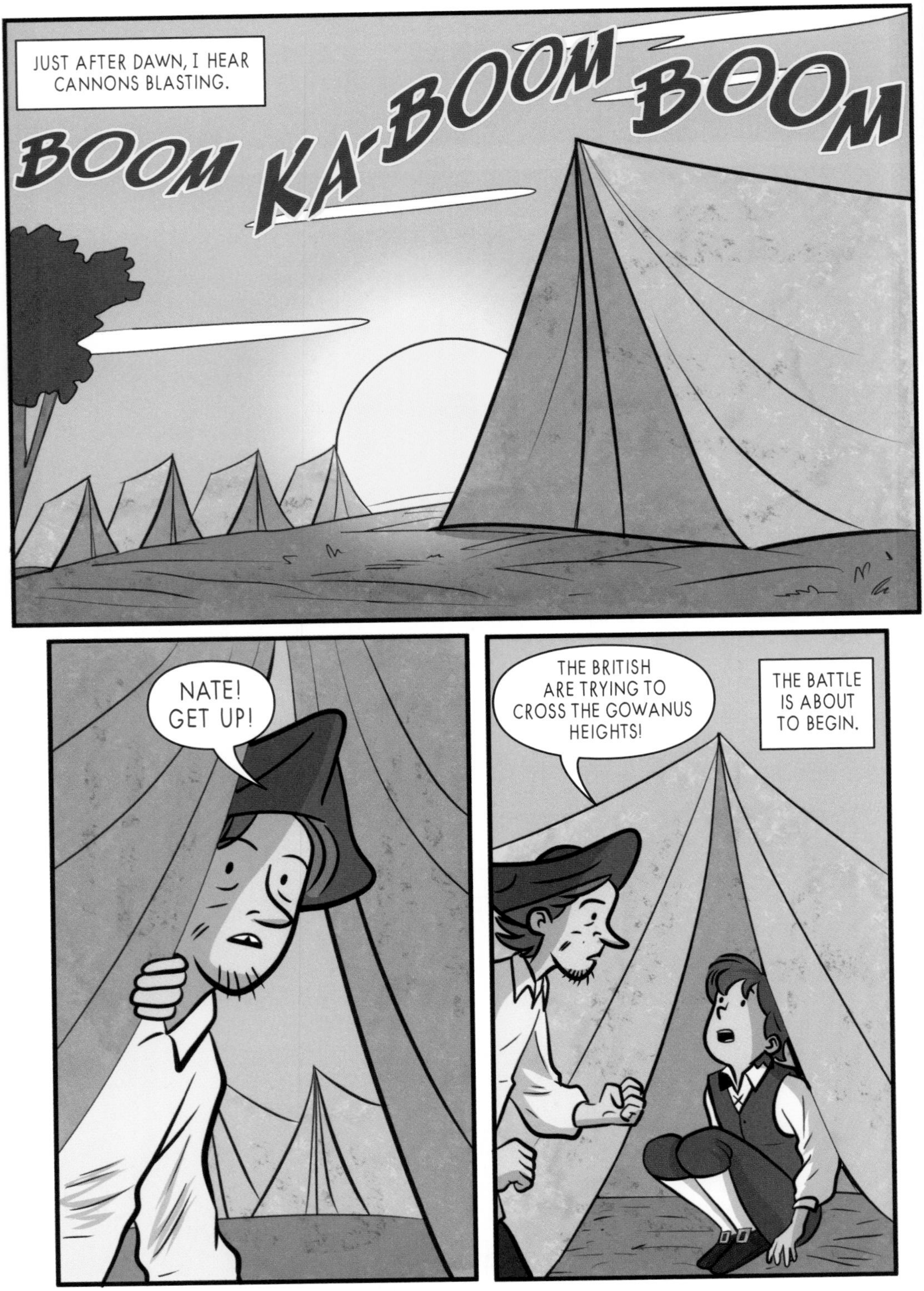
JUST AFTER DAWN, I HEAR CANNONS BLASTING.
BOOM
KA-BOOM
BOOM
NATE! GET UP!
THE BRITISH ARE TRYING TO CROSS THE GOWANUS HEIGHTS!
THE BATTLE IS ABOUT TO BEGIN.

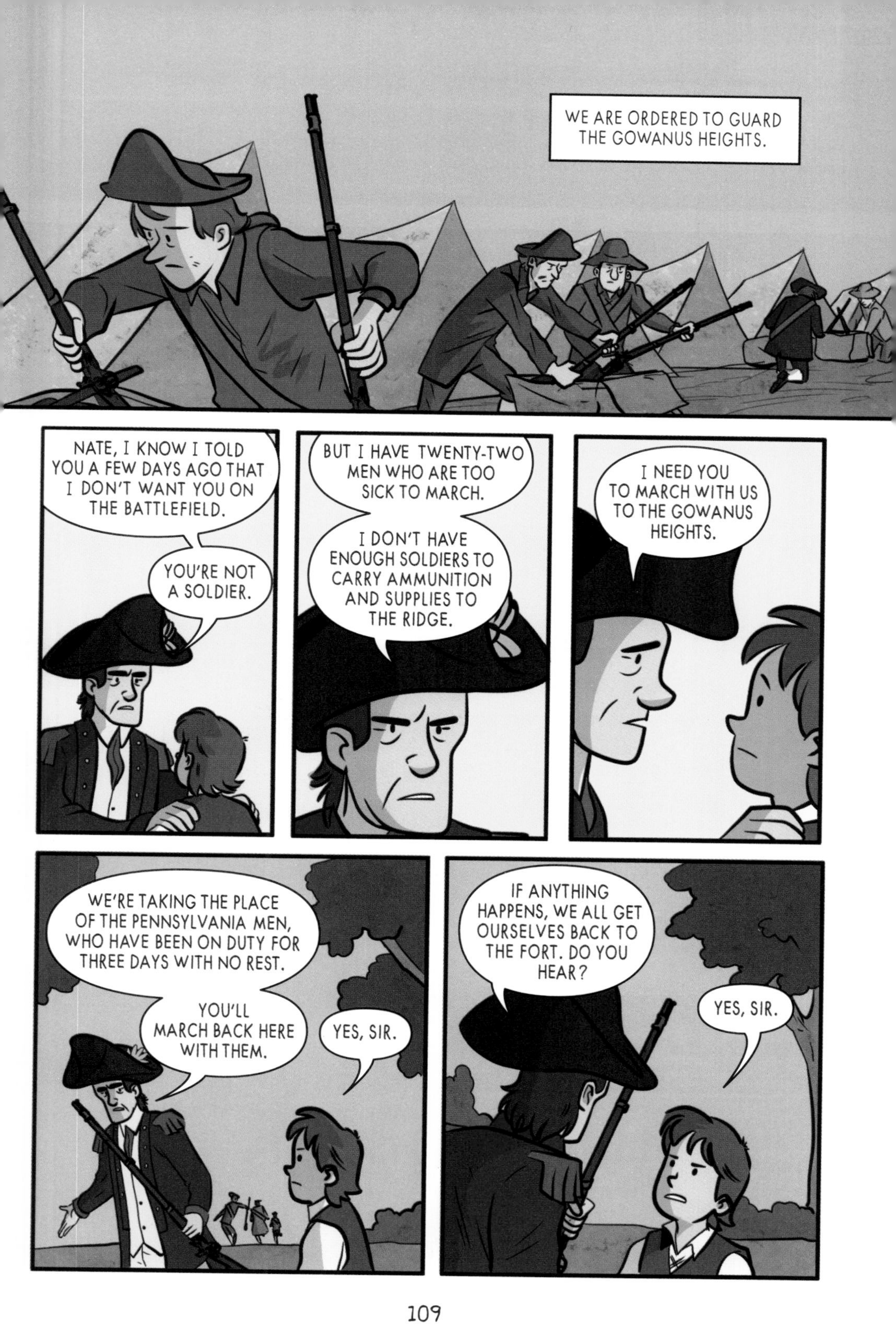
WE ARE ORDERED TO GUARD THE GOWANUS HEIGHTS.
NATE, I KNOW I TOLD YOU A FEW DAYS AGO THAT I DON'T WANT YOU ON THE BATTLEFIELD.
YOU'RE NOT A SOLDIER.
BUT I HAVE TWENTY-TWO MEN WHO ARE TOO SICK TO MARCH.
I DON'T HAVE ENOUGH SOLDIERS TO CARRY AMMUNITION AND SUPPLIES TO THE RIDGE.
I NEED YOU TO MARCH WITH US TO THE GOWANUS HEIGHTS.
WE'RE TAKING THE PLACE OF THE PENNSYLVANIA MEN, WHO HAVE BEEN ON DUTY FOR THREE DAYS WITH NO REST.
YOU'LL MARCH BACK HERE WITH THEM.
YES, SIR.
IF ANYTHING HAPPENS, WE ALL GET OURSELVES BACK TO THE FORT. DO YOU HEAR?
YES, SIR.

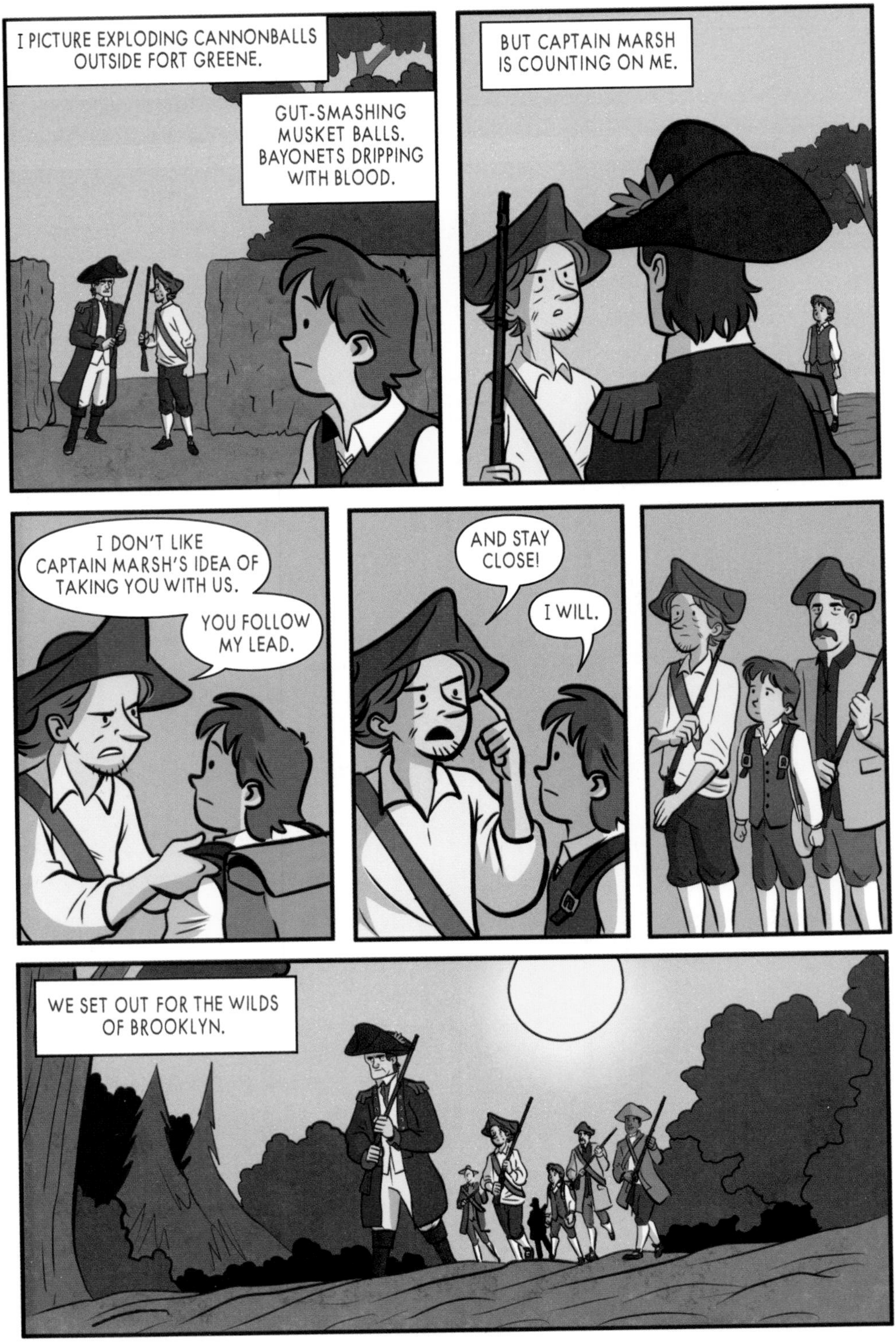
I PICTURE EXPLODING CANNONBALLS OUTSIDE FORT GREENE.
GUT-SMASHING MUSKET BALLS. BAYONETS DRIPPING WITH BLOOD.
BUT CAPTAIN MARSH IS COUNTING ON ME.
I DON'T LIKE CAPTAIN MARSH'S IDEA OF TAKING YOU WITH US.
YOU FOLLOW MY LEAD.
AND STAY CLOSE!
I WILL.
WE SET OUT FOR THE WILDS OF BROOKLYN.

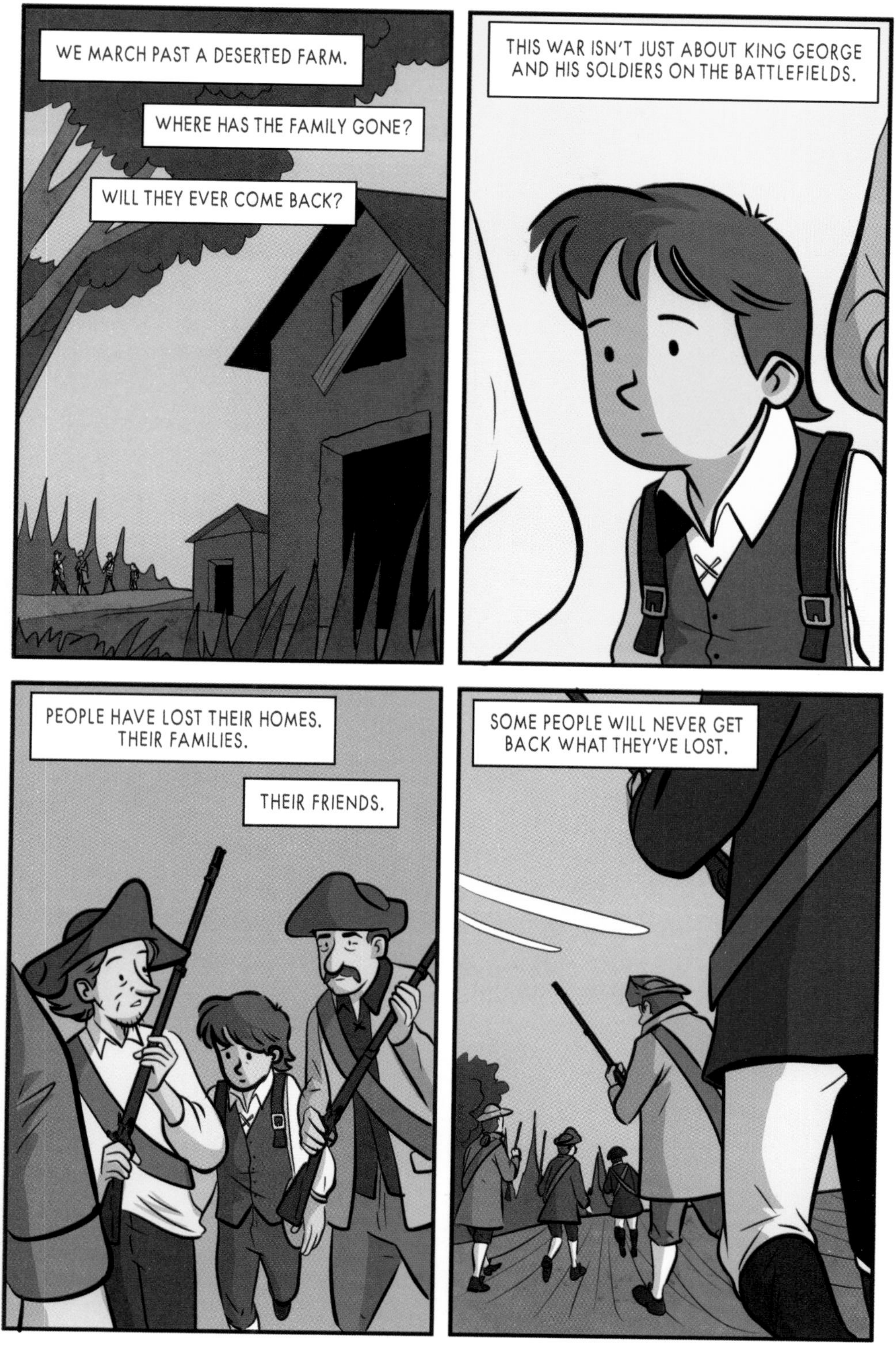
WE MARCH PAST A DESERTED FARM.
WHERE HAS THE FAMILY GONE?
WILL THEY EVER COME BACK?
THIS WAR ISN'T JUST ABOUT KING GEORGE AND HIS SOLDIERS ON THE BATTLEFIELDS.
PEOPLE HAVE LOST THEIR HOMES. THEIR FAMILIES.
THEIR FRIENDS.
SOME PEOPLE WILL NEVER GET BACK WHAT THEY'VE LOST.

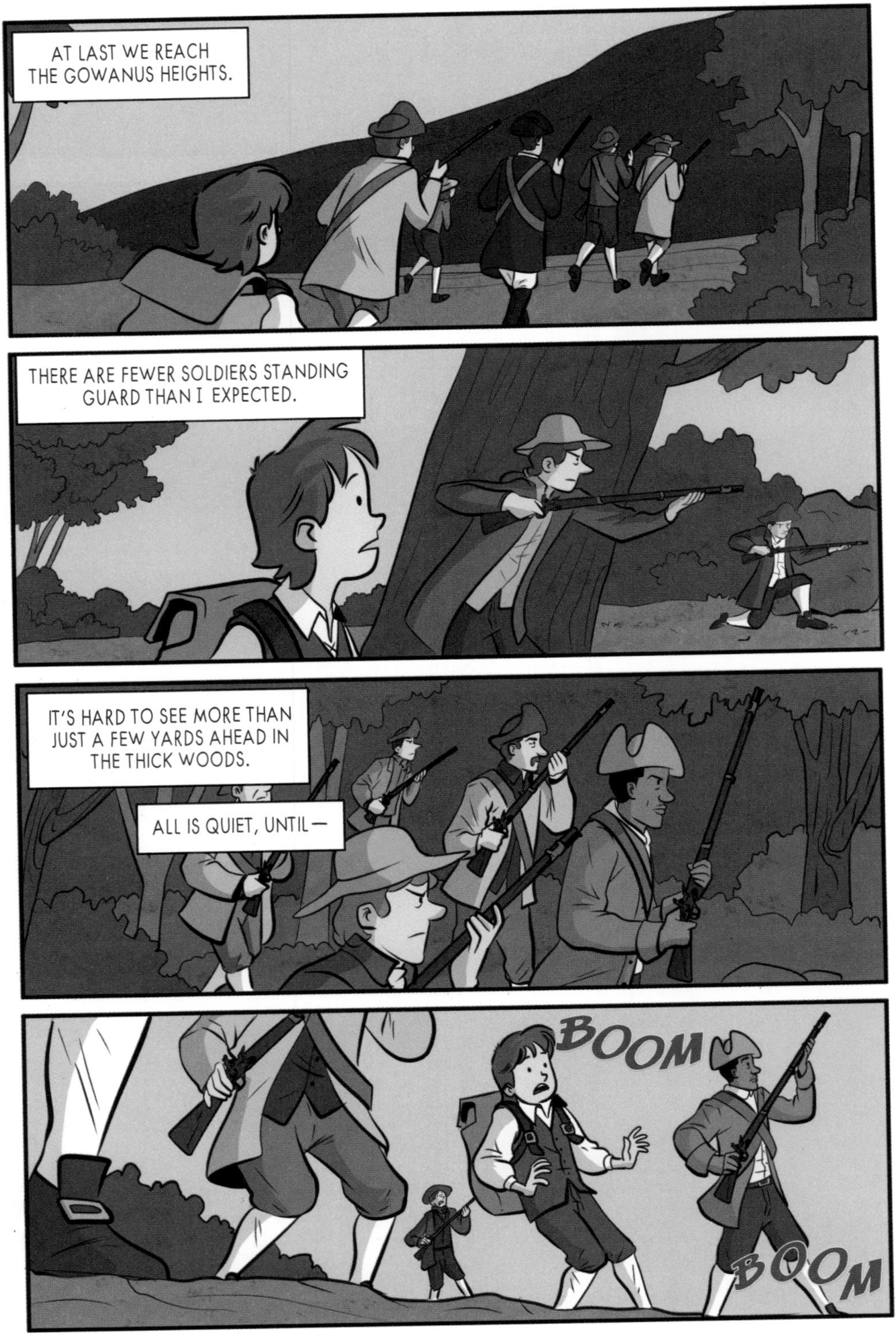
AT LAST WE REACH THE GOWANUS HEIGHTS.
THERE ARE FEWER SOLDIERS STANDING GUARD THAN I EXPECTED.
IT'S HARD TO SEE MORE THAN JUST A FEW YARDS AHEAD IN THE THICK WOODS.
ALL IS QUIET, UNTIL—
BOOM
BOOM

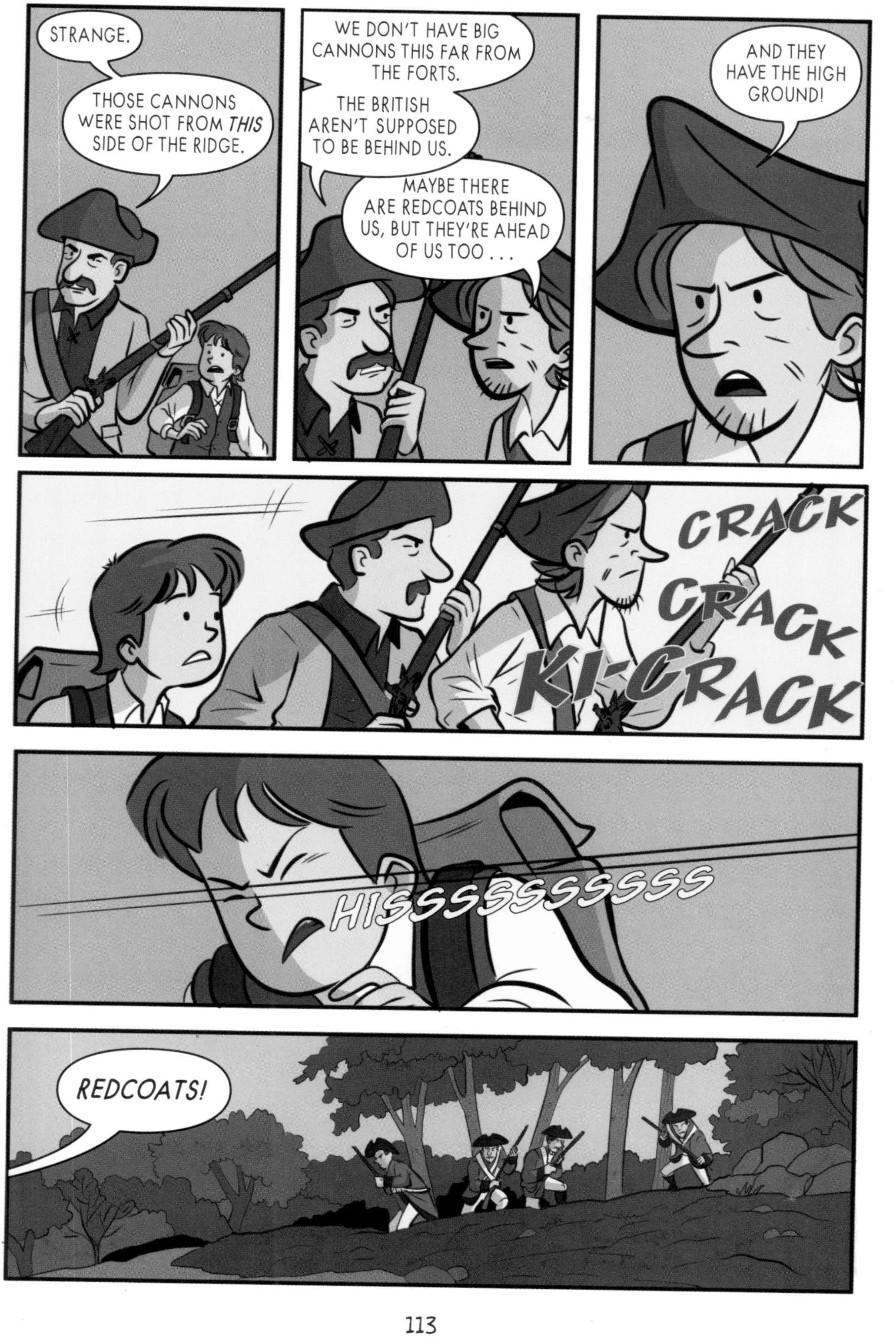

STRANGE.
THOSE CANNONS WERE SHOT FROM *THIS* SIDE OF THE RIDGE.
WE DON'T HAVE BIG CANNONS THIS FAR FROM THE FORTS.
THE BRITISH AREN'T SUPPOSED TO BE BEHIND US.
MAYBE THERE ARE REDCOATS BEHIND US, BUT THEY'RE AHEAD OF US TOO . . .
AND THEY HAVE THE HIGH GROUND!
CRACK
CRACK
KI-CRACK
HISSSSSSSSSS
REDCOATS!

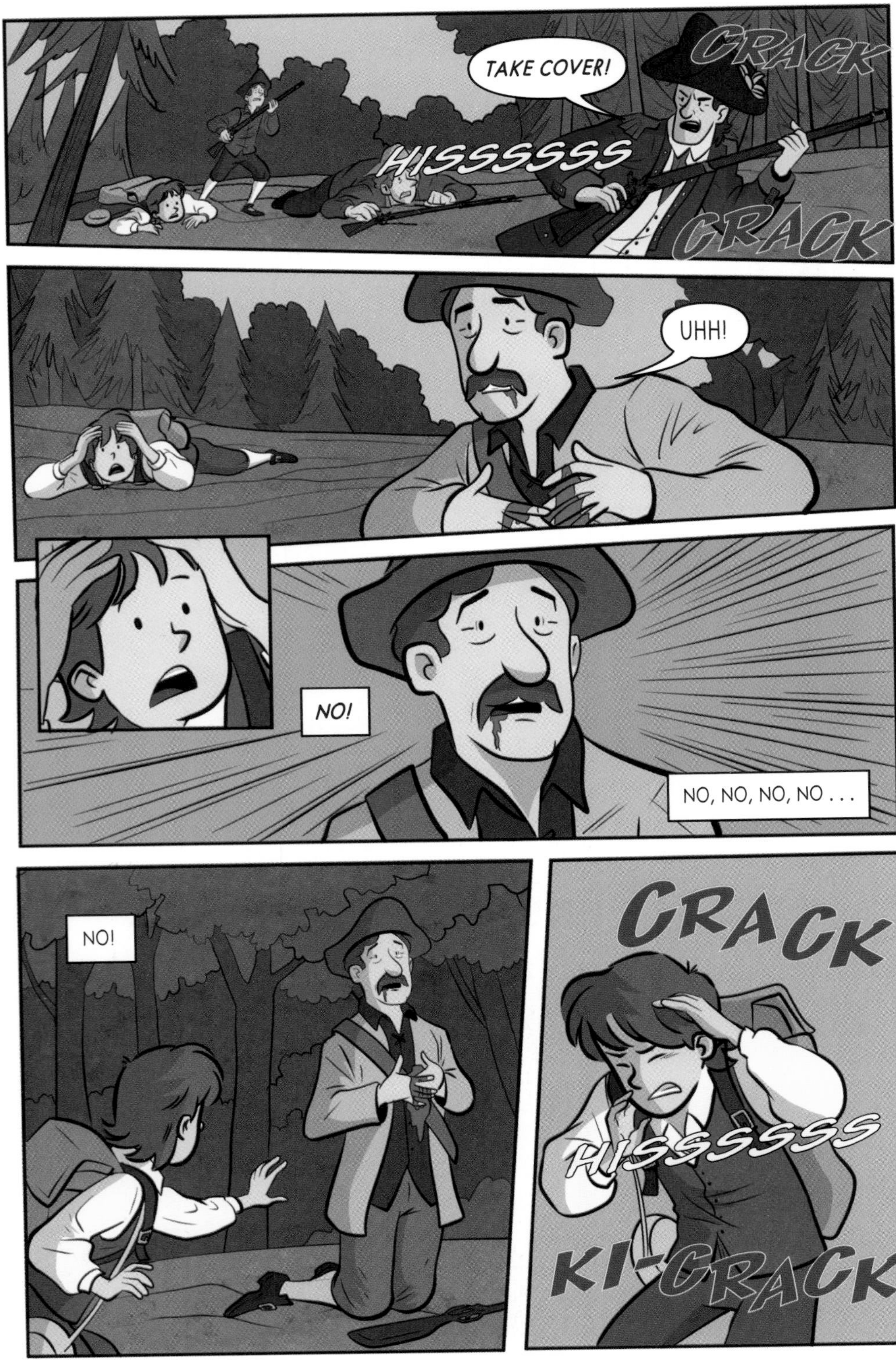
TAKE COVER!
CRACK
HISSSSSS
CRACK
UHH!
NO!
NO, NO, NO, NO . . .
NO!
CRACK
HISSSSSS
KI-CRACK

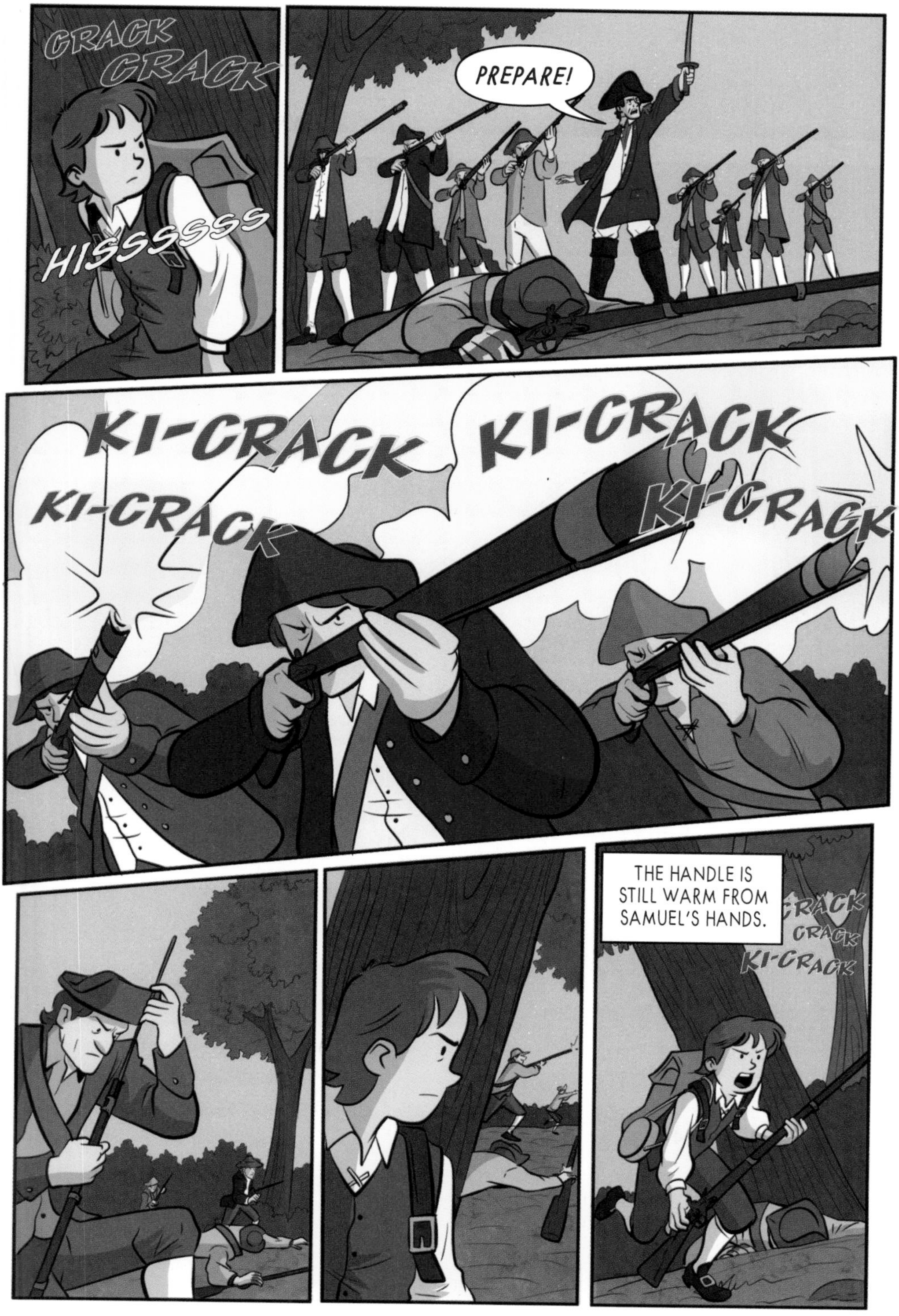
CRACK
CRACK
HISSSSSS
PREPARE!
KI-CRACK
KI-CRACK
KI-CRACK
KI-CRACK
THE HANDLE IS STILL WARM FROM SAMUEL'S HANDS.
CRACK
CRACK
KI-CRACK

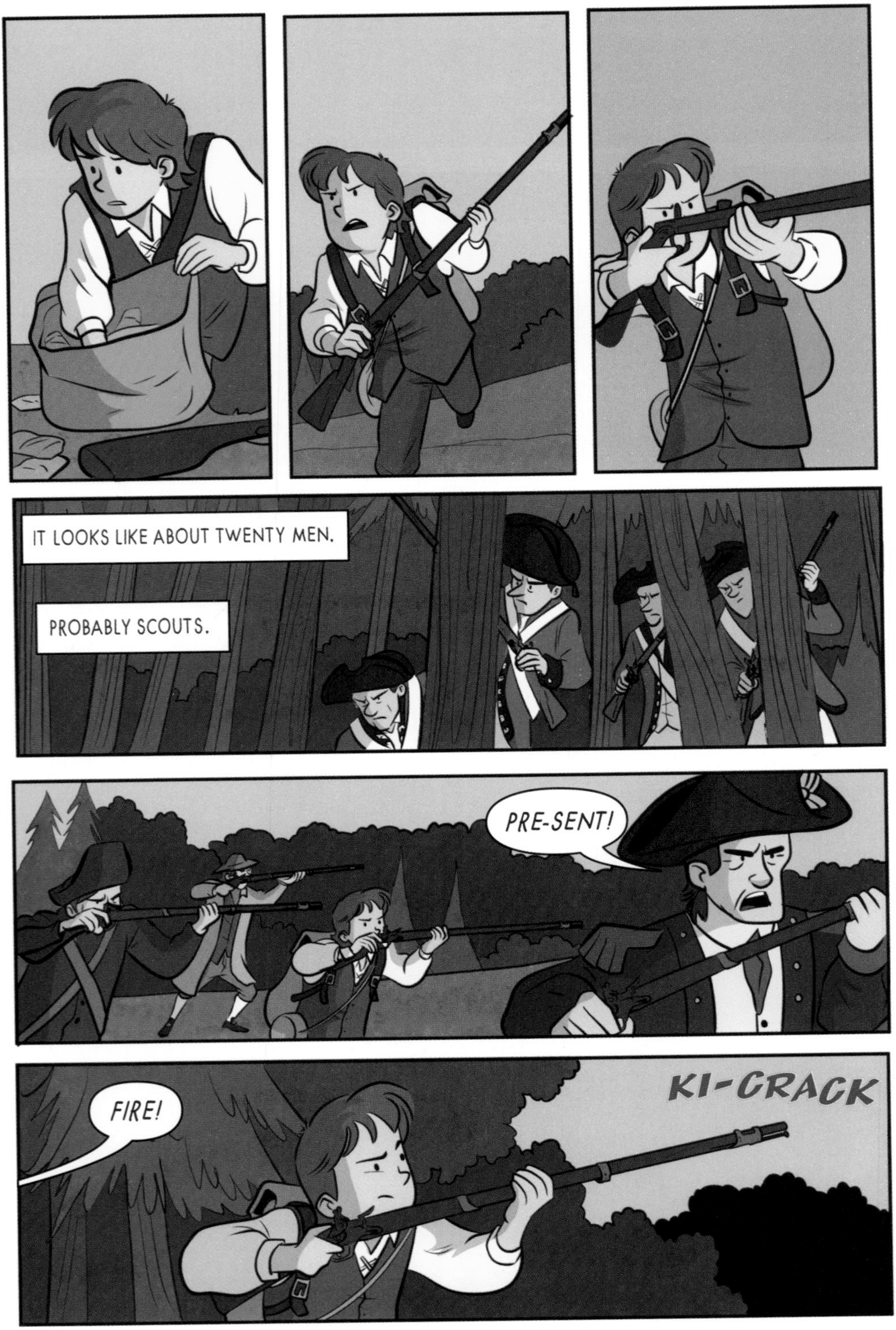
IT LOOKS LIKE ABOUT TWENTY MEN.
PROBABLY SCOUTS.
PRE-SENT!
FIRE!
KI-CRACK

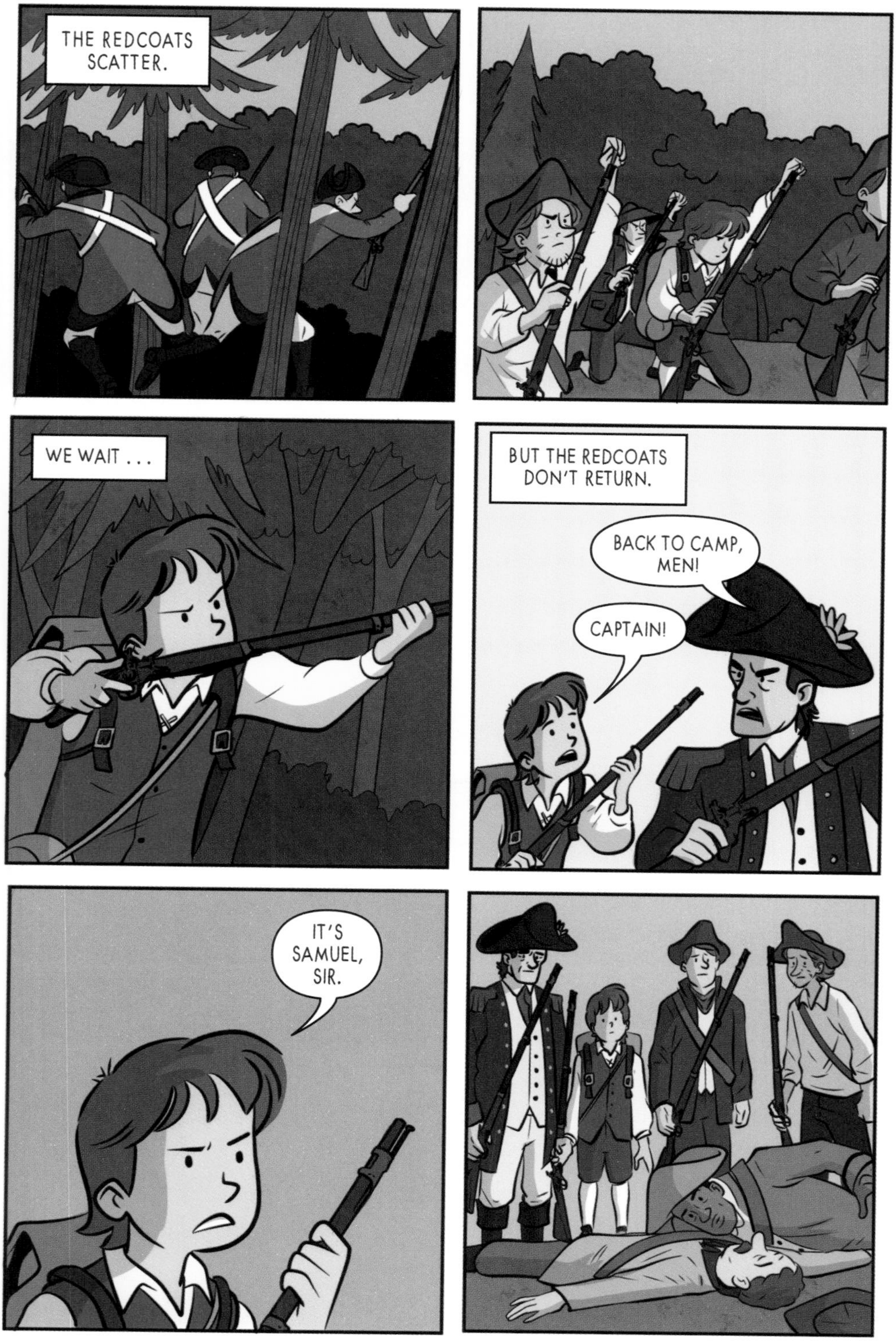
THE REDCOATS SCATTER.
WE WAIT . . .
BUT THE REDCOATS DON'T RETURN.
BACK TO CAMP, MEN!
CAPTAIN!
IT'S SAMUEL, SIR.

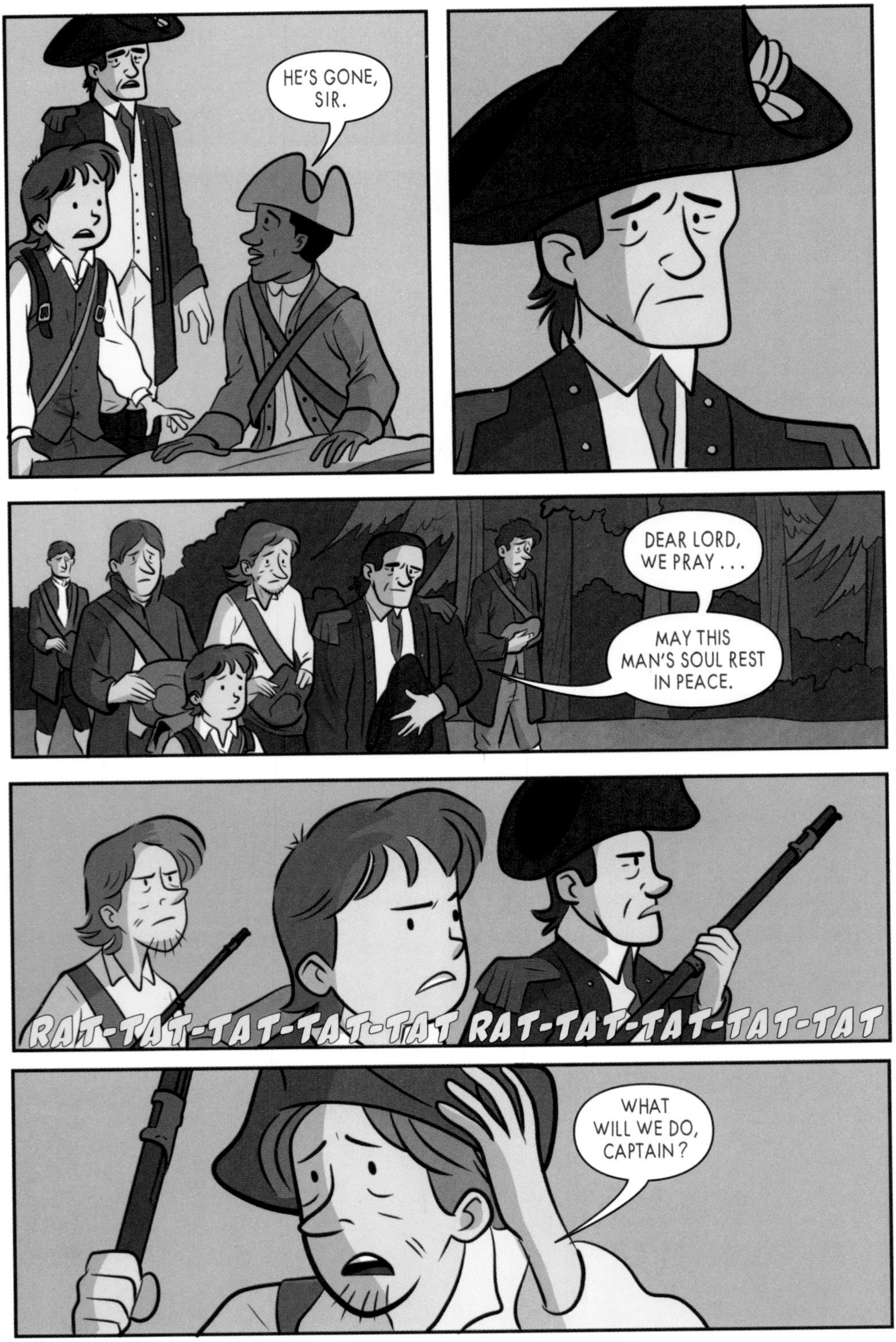

HE'S GONE, SIR.
DEAR LORD, WE PRAY . . .
MAY THIS MAN'S SOUL REST IN PEACE.
RAT-TAT-TAT-TAT-TAT RAT-TAT-TAT-TAT-TAT
WHAT WILL WE DO, CAPTAIN?

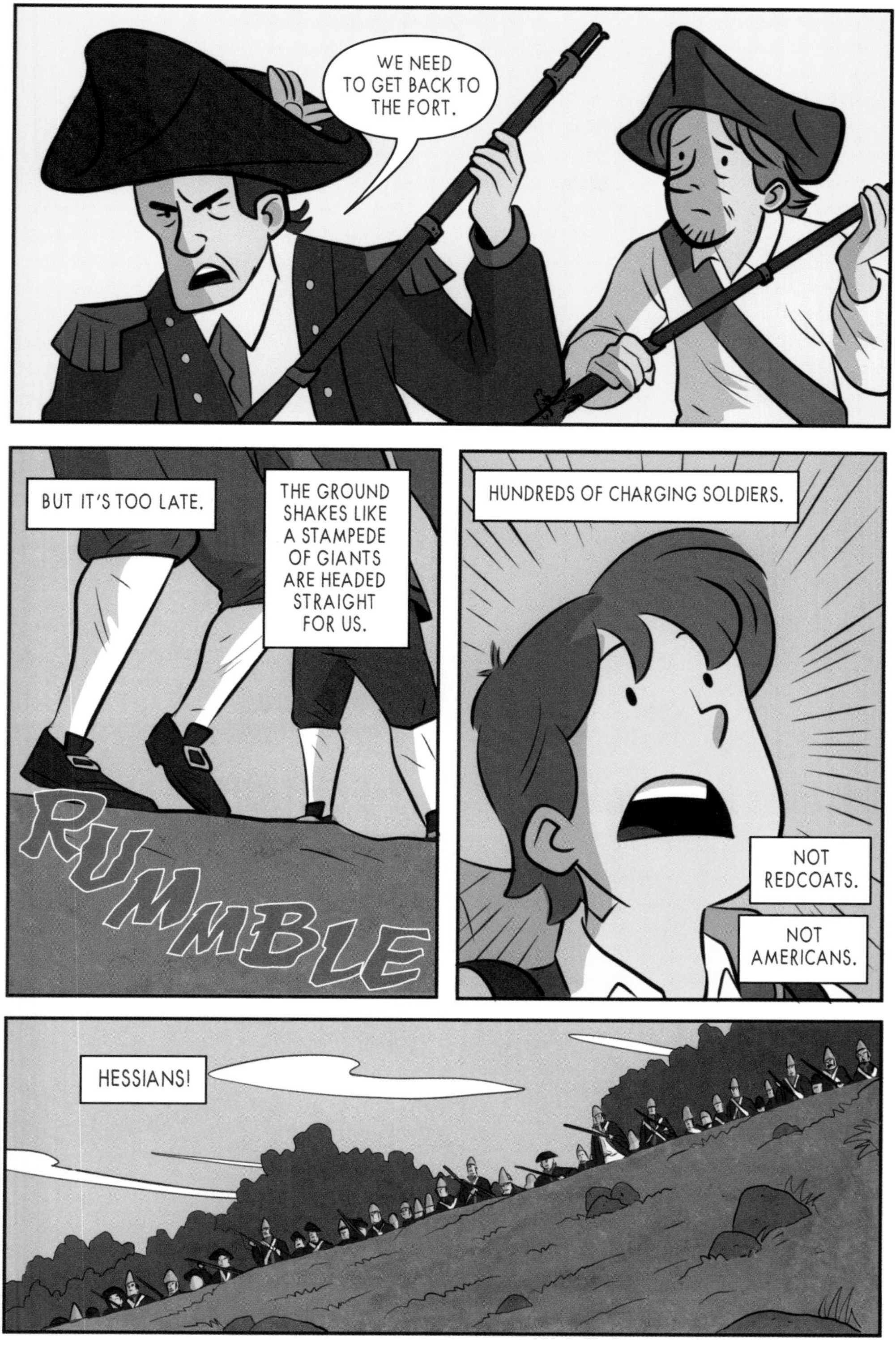
WE NEED TO GET BACK TO THE FORT.
BUT IT'S TOO LATE.
THE GROUND SHAKES LIKE A STAMPEDE OF GIANTS ARE HEADED STRAIGHT FOR US.
RUMMBLE
HUNDREDS OF CHARGING SOLDIERS.
NOT REDCOATS.
NOT AMERICANS.
HESSIANS!

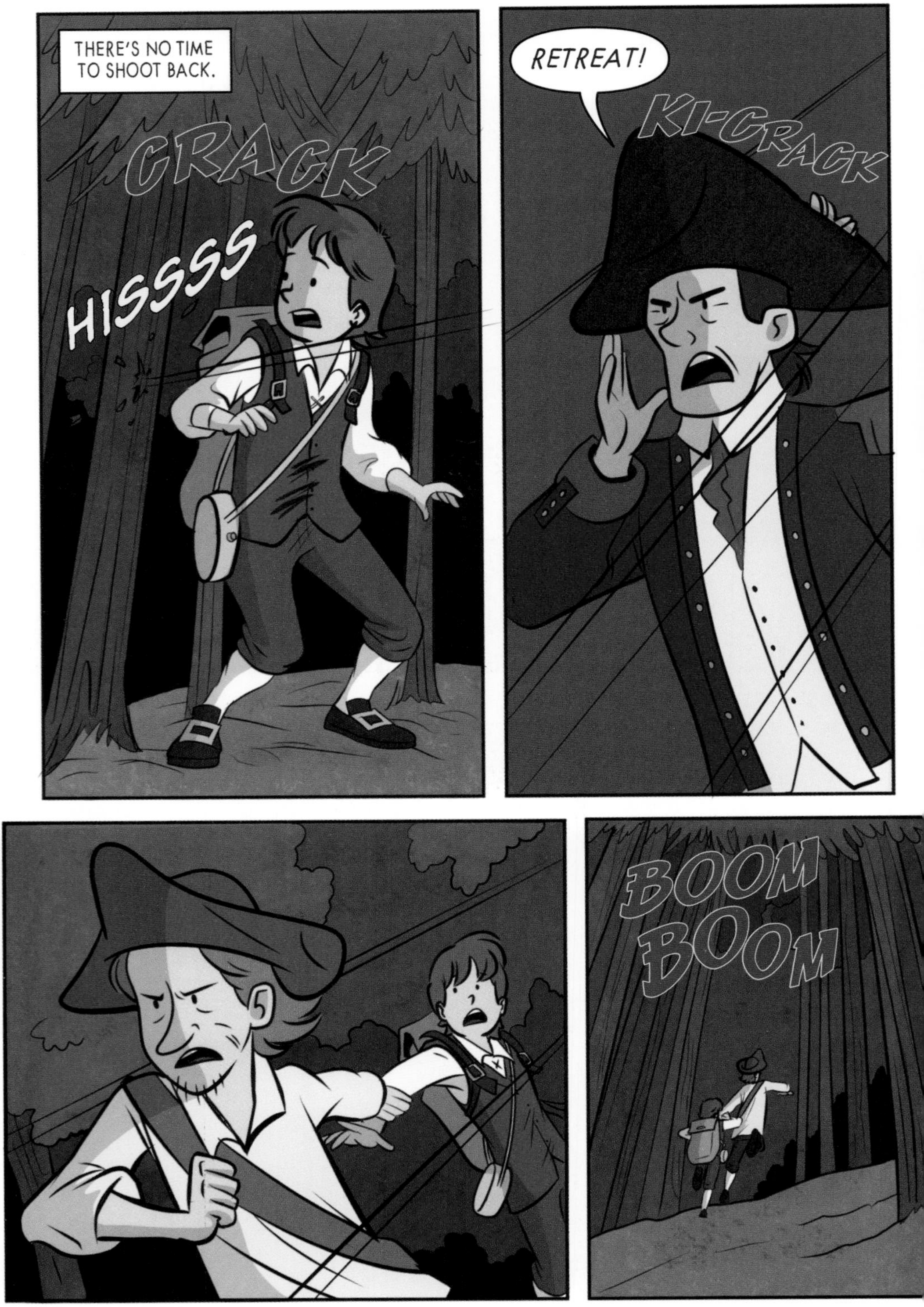
THERE'S NO TIME TO SHOOT BACK.
CRACK
HISSSS
RETREAT!
KI-CRACK
BOOM
BOOM

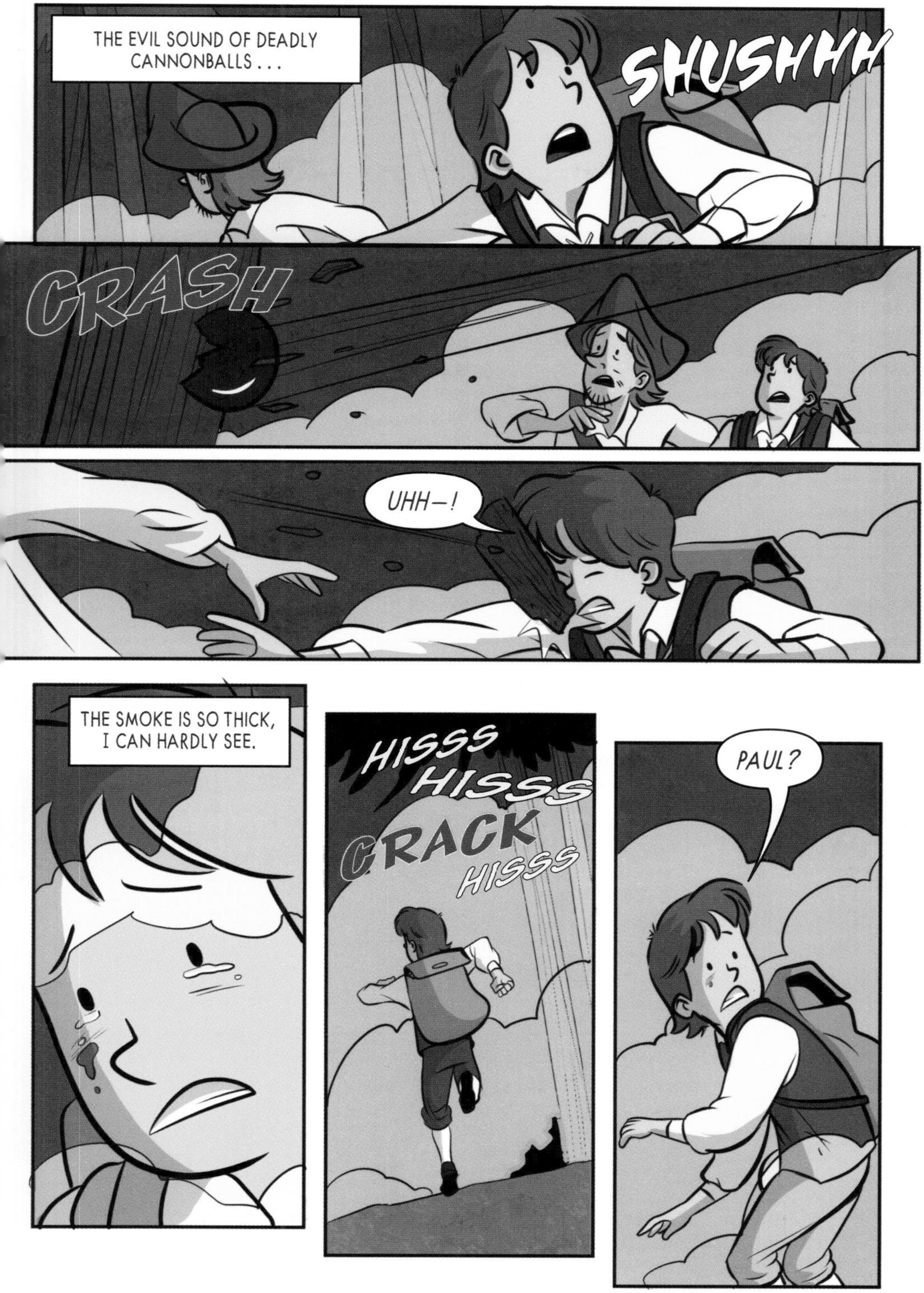
THE EVIL SOUND OF DEADLY CANNONBALLS . . .
SHUSHHH
CRASH
UHH—!
THE SMOKE IS SO THICK, I CAN HARDLY SEE.
HISSS
HISSS
CRACK
HISSS
PAUL?

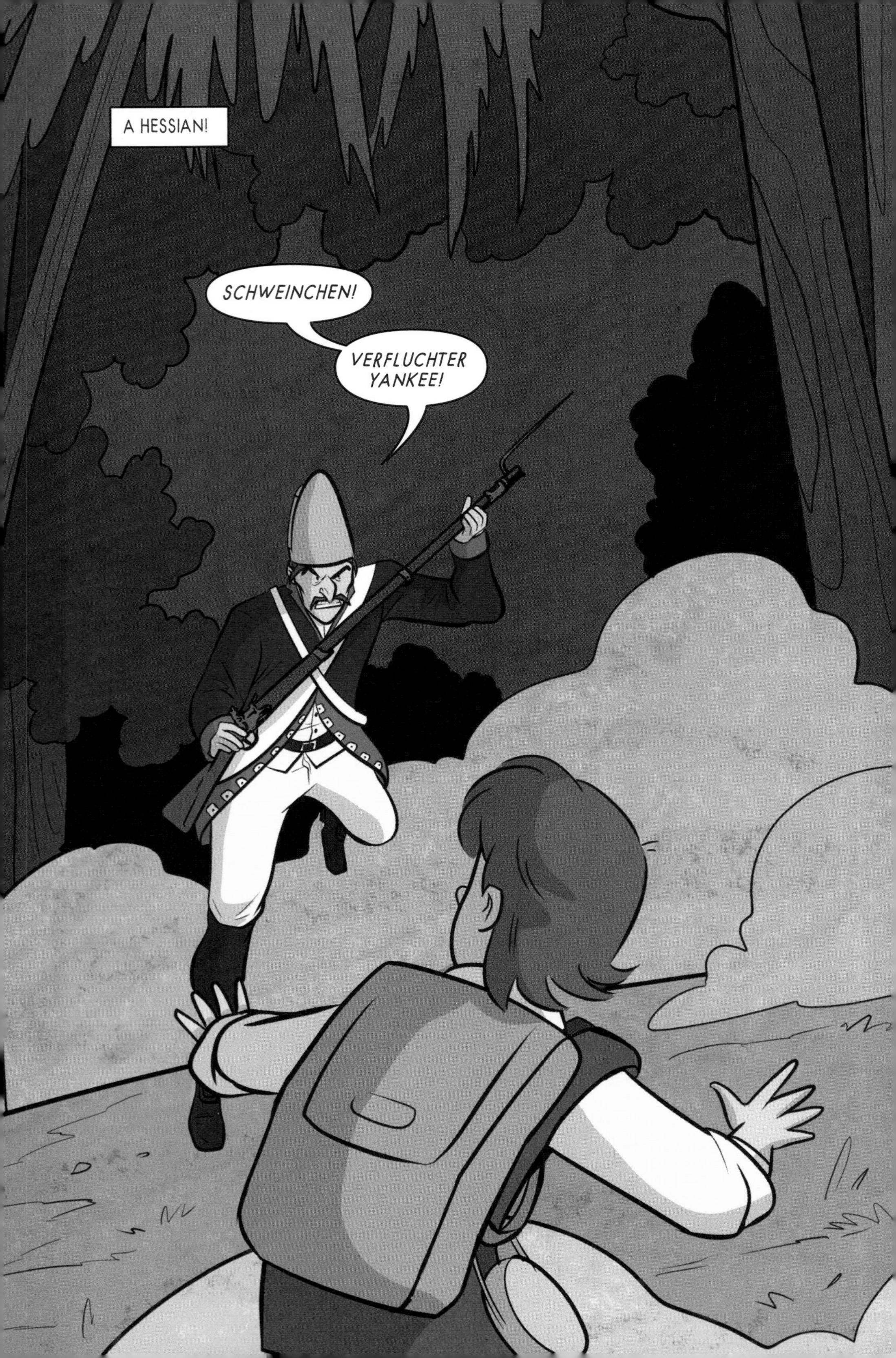
A HESSIAN!
SCHWEINCHEN!
VERFLUCHTER YANKEE!

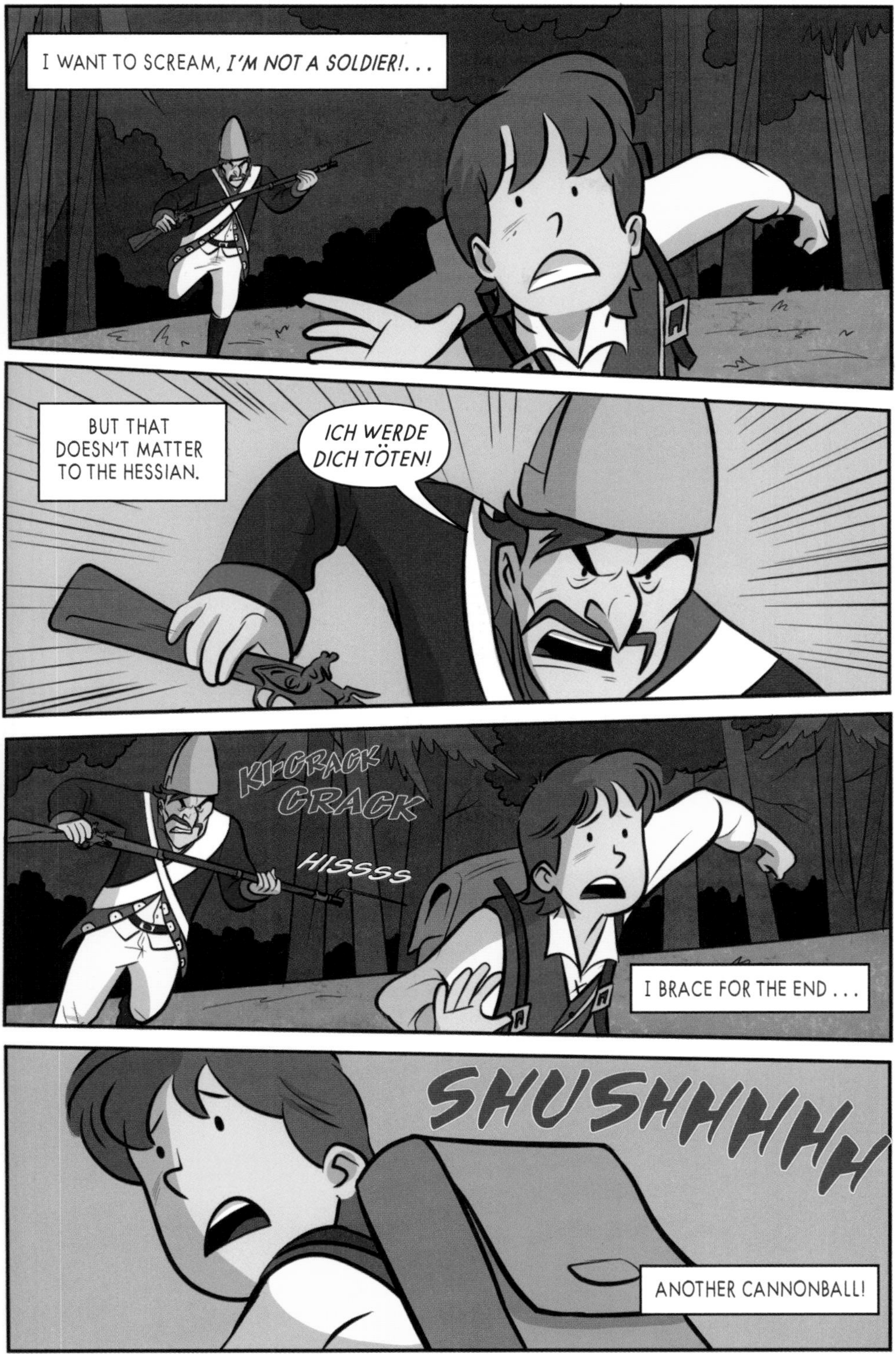
I WANT TO SCREAM, *I'M NOT A SOLDIER!*. . .
BUT THAT DOESN'T MATTER TO THE HESSIAN.
ICH WERDE DICH TÖTEN!
KI-CRACK CRACK
HISSSS
I BRACE FOR THE END . . .
SHUSHHHHH
ANOTHER CANNONBALL!

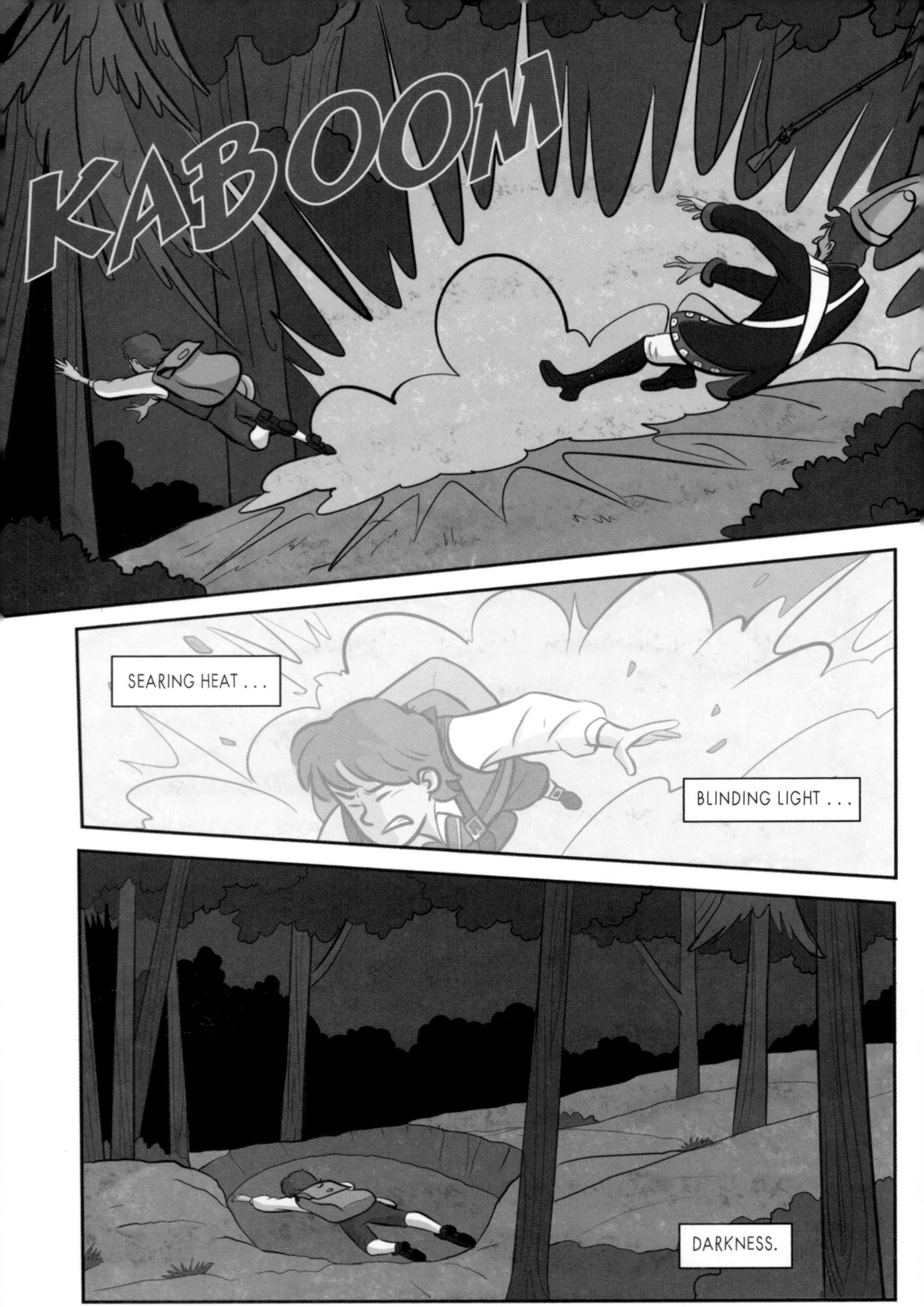
KABOOM
SEARING HEAT . . .
BLINDING LIGHT . . .
DARKNESS.

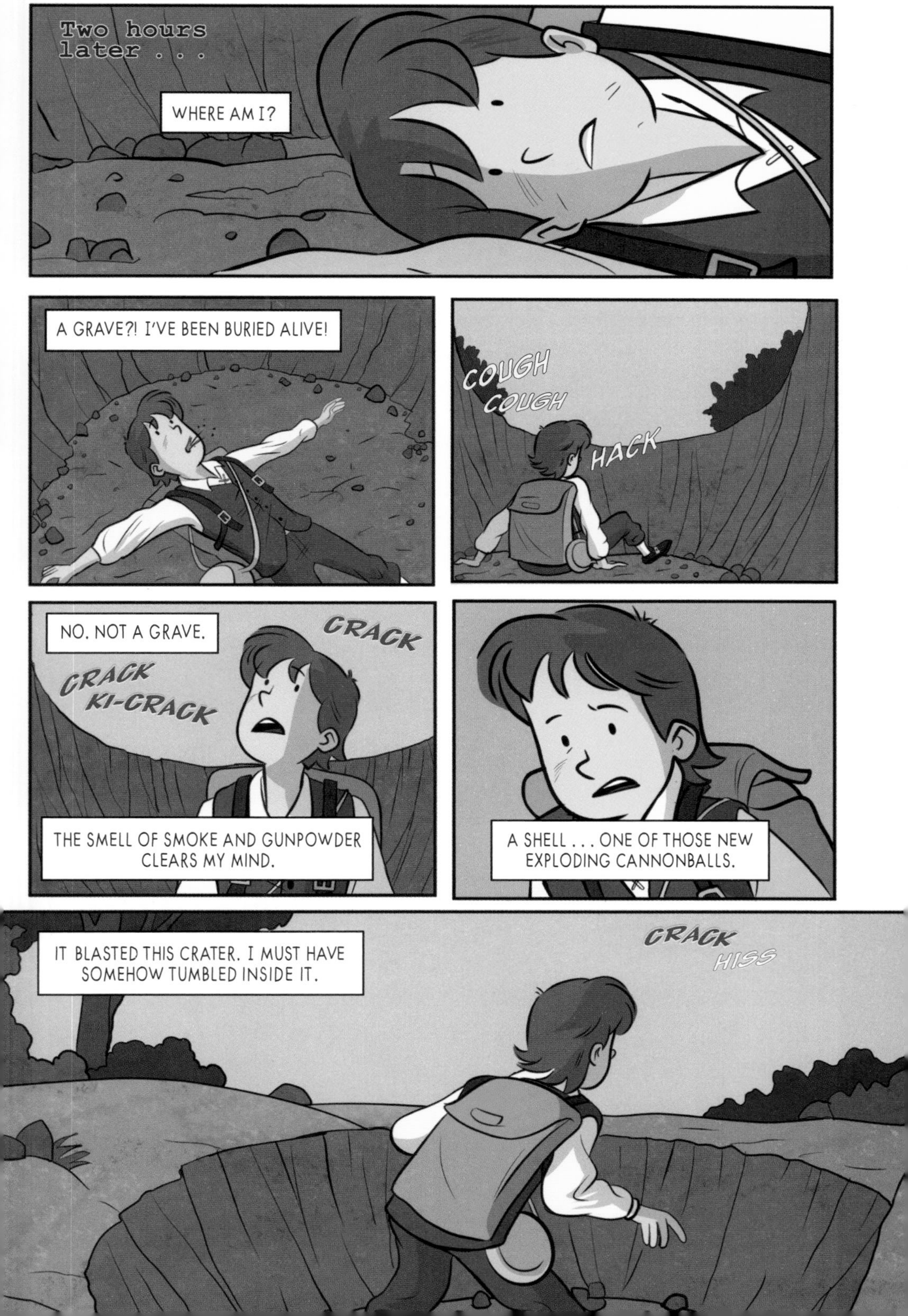
Two hours later . . .
WHERE AM I?
A GRAVE?! I'VE BEEN BURIED ALIVE!
COUGH
COUGH
HACK
NO. NOT A GRAVE.
CRACK
CRACK
KI-CRACK
THE SMELL OF SMOKE AND GUNPOWDER CLEARS MY MIND.
A SHELL . . . ONE OF THOSE NEW EXPLODING CANNONBALLS.
IT BLASTED THIS CRATER. I MUST HAVE SOMEHOW TUMBLED INSIDE IT.
CRACK
HISS

THE CUT ON MY FACE IS OOZING BLOOD.

CRACK

I FEEL LIKE I'VE BEEN RUN OVER BY A HORSE WAGON.

STILL, I'M ALIVE.

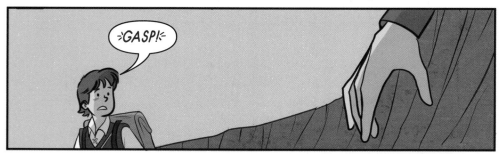

~GASP!~

I CAN'T SAY THE SAME FOR THE HESSIAN.

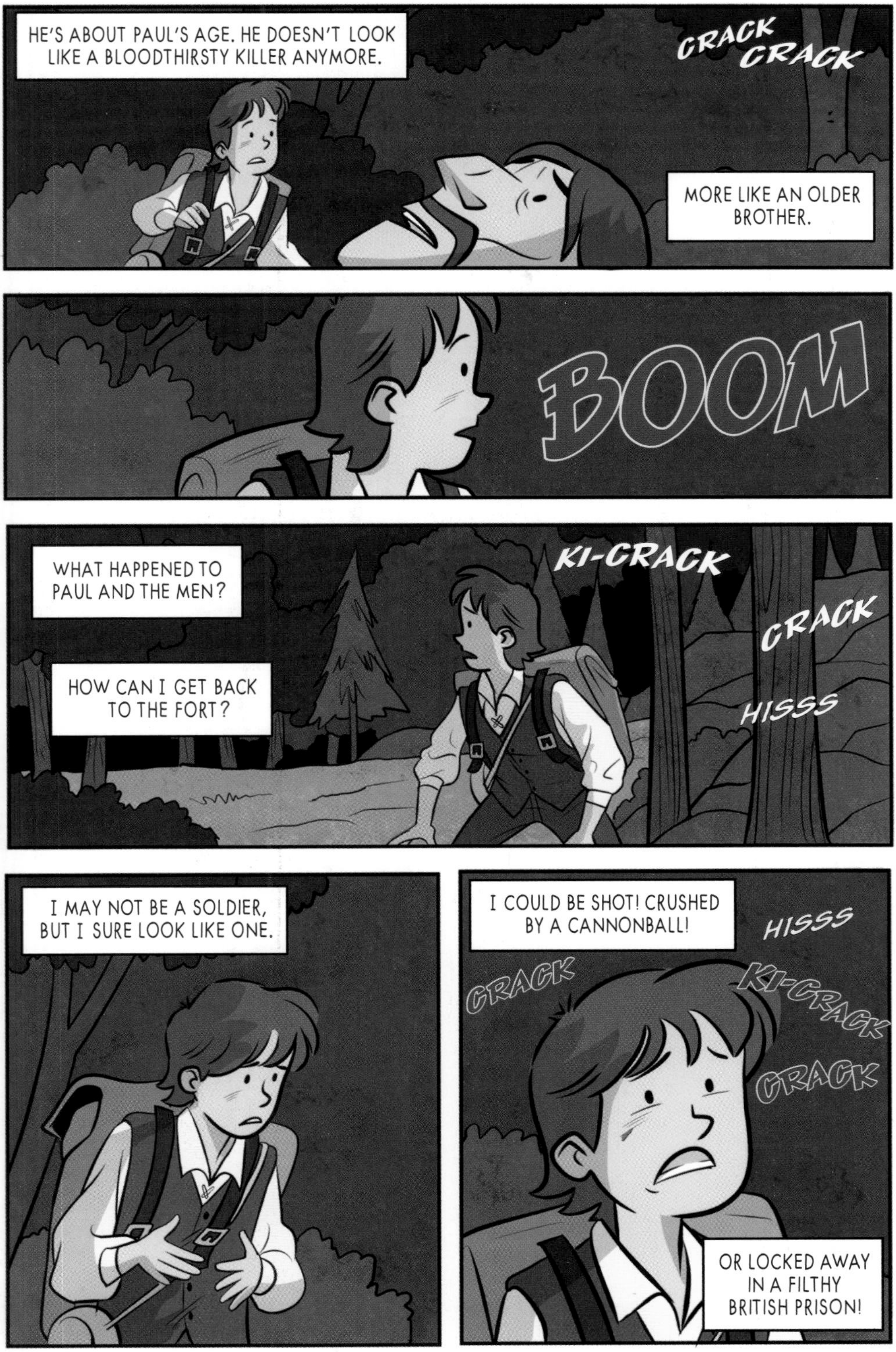
HE'S ABOUT PAUL'S AGE. HE DOESN'T LOOK LIKE A BLOODTHIRSTY KILLER ANYMORE.
CRACK CRACK
MORE LIKE AN OLDER BROTHER.
BOOM
WHAT HAPPENED TO PAUL AND THE MEN?
KI-CRACK
CRACK
HOW CAN I GET BACK TO THE FORT?
HISSS
I MAY NOT BE A SOLDIER, BUT I SURE LOOK LIKE ONE.
I COULD BE SHOT! CRUSHED BY A CANNONBALL!
HISSS
CRACK
KI-CRACK
CRACK
OR LOCKED AWAY IN A FILTHY BRITISH PRISON!

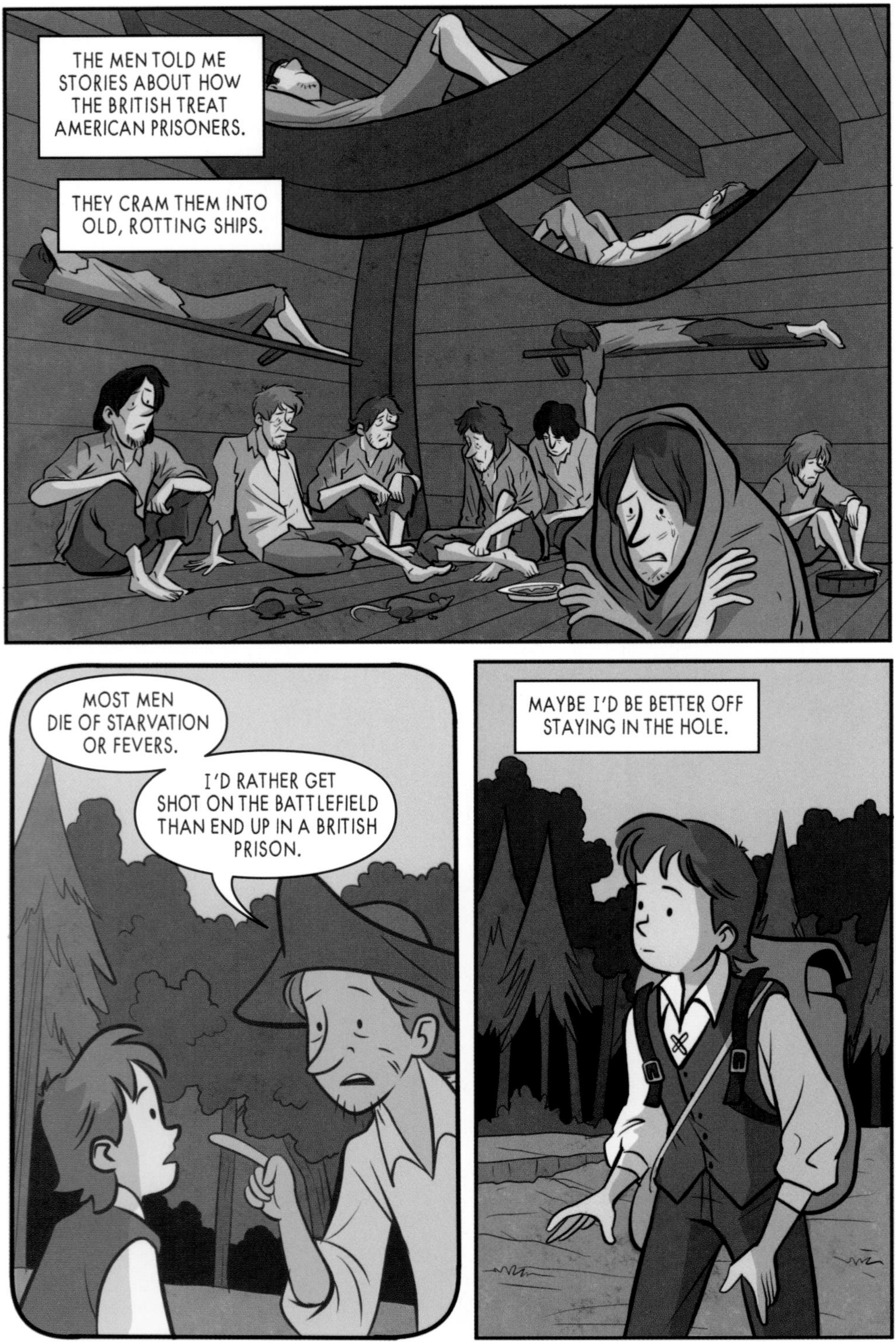
THE MEN TOLD ME STORIES ABOUT HOW THE BRITISH TREAT AMERICAN PRISONERS.
THEY CRAM THEM INTO OLD, ROTTING SHIPS.
MOST MEN DIE OF STARVATION OR FEVERS.
I'D RATHER GET SHOT ON THE BATTLEFIELD THAN END UP IN A BRITISH PRISON.
MAYBE I'D BE BETTER OFF STAYING IN THE HOLE.

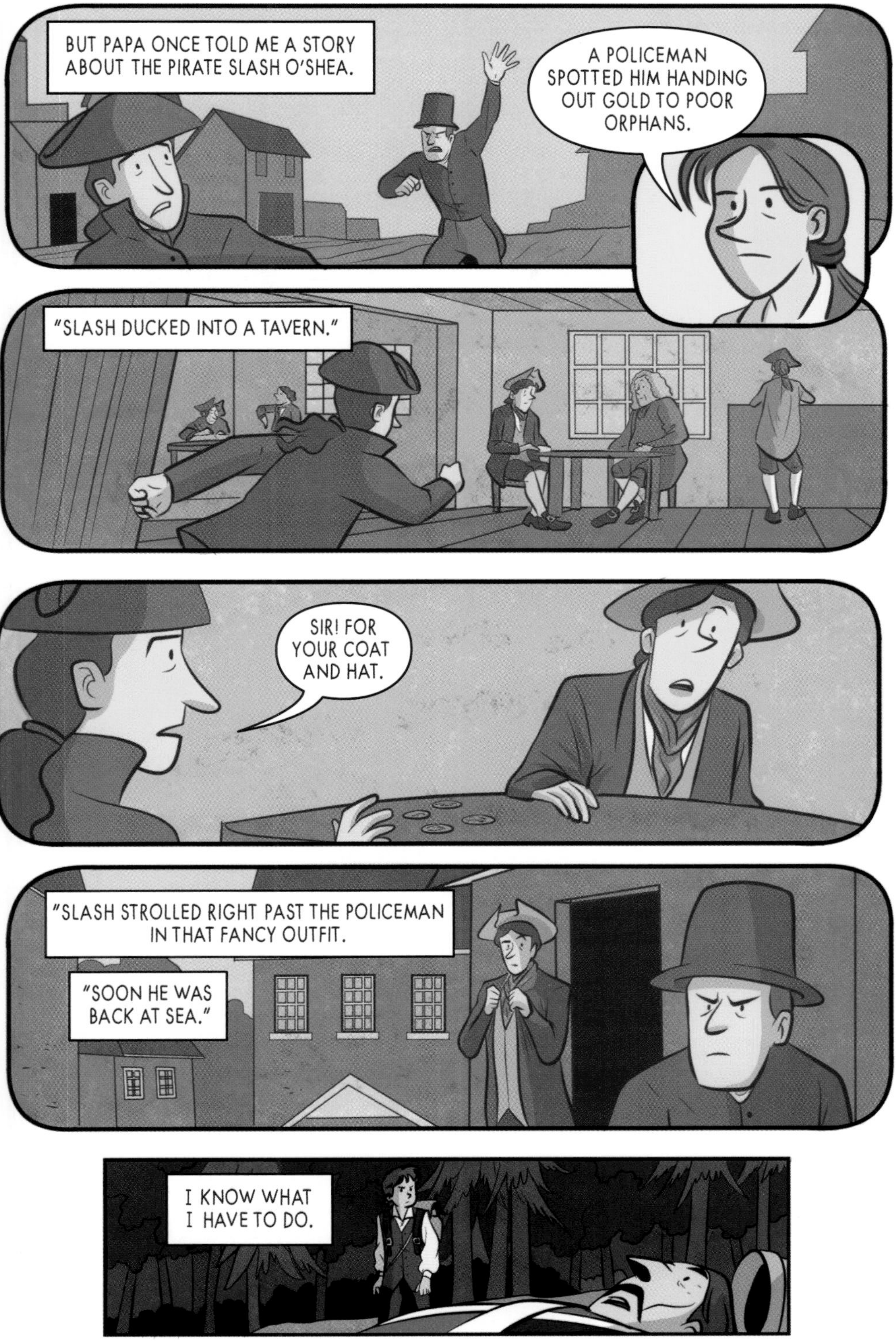
BUT PAPA ONCE TOLD ME A STORY ABOUT THE PIRATE SLASH O'SHEA.
A POLICEMAN SPOTTED HIM HANDING OUT GOLD TO POOR ORPHANS.
"SLASH DUCKED INTO A TAVERN."
SIR! FOR YOUR COAT AND HAT.
"SLASH STROLLED RIGHT PAST THE POLICEMAN IN THAT FANCY OUTFIT.
"SOON HE WAS BACK AT SEA."
I KNOW WHAT I HAVE TO DO.

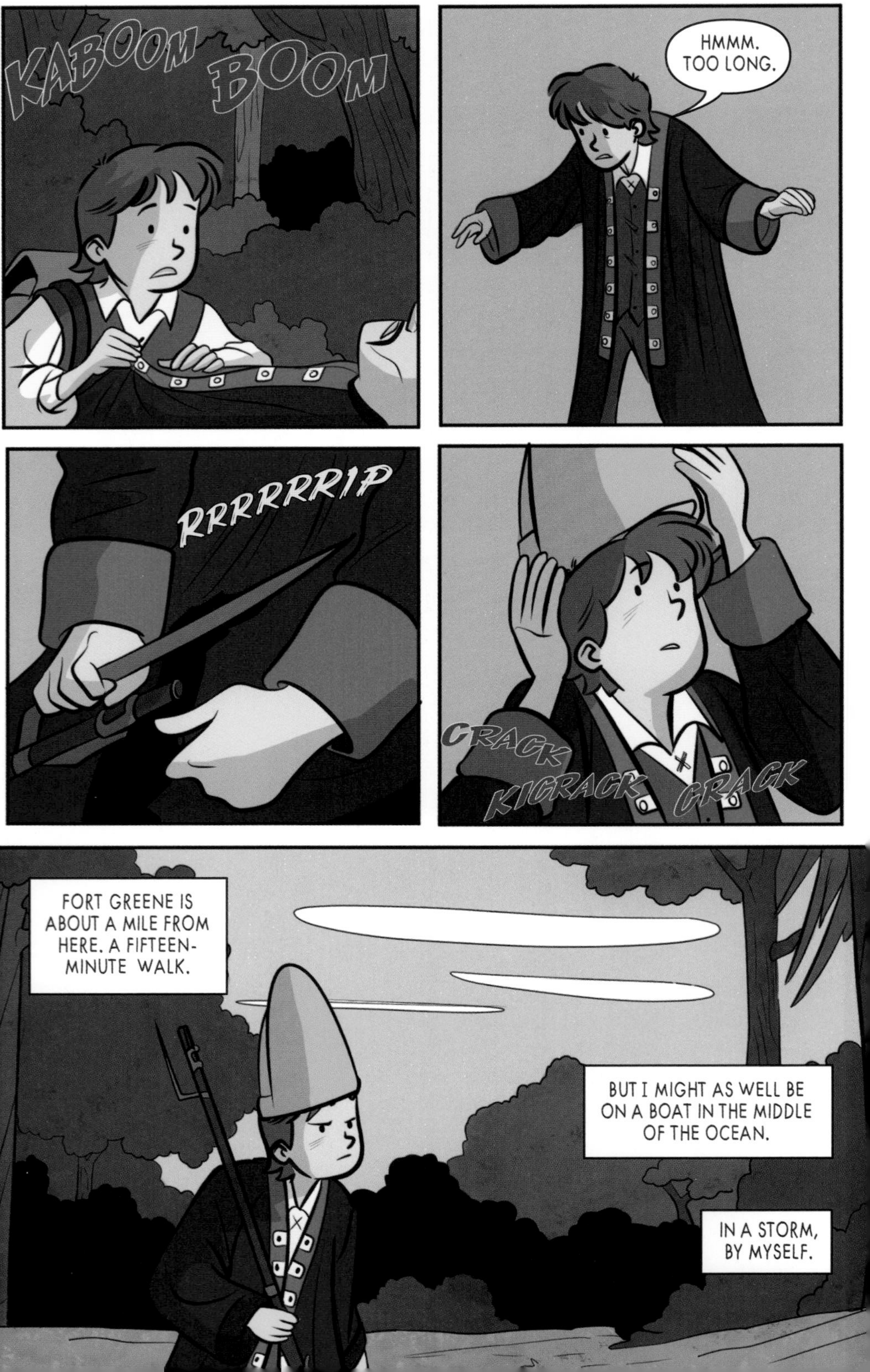
KABOOM
BOOM
HMMM. TOO LONG.
RRRRRRIP
CRACK
KICRACK
CRACK
FORT GREENE IS ABOUT A MILE FROM HERE. A FIFTEEN-MINUTE WALK.
BUT I MIGHT AS WELL BE ON A BOAT IN THE MIDDLE OF THE OCEAN.
IN A STORM, BY MYSELF.

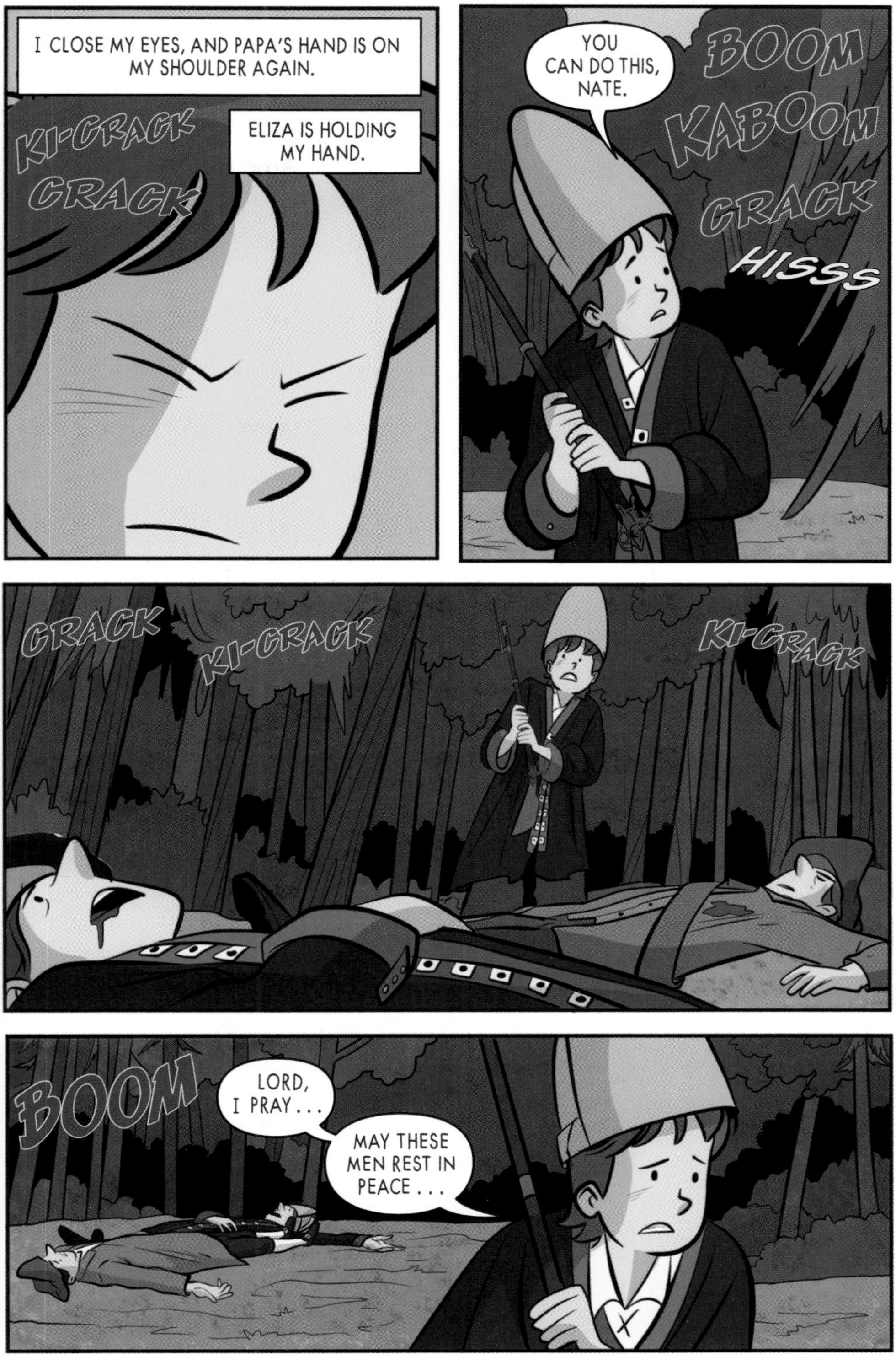

I CLOSE MY EYES, AND PAPA'S HAND IS ON MY SHOULDER AGAIN.
ELIZA IS HOLDING MY HAND.
KI-CRACK
CRACK
YOU CAN DO THIS, NATE.
BOOM
KABOOM
CRACK
HISSS
CRACK
KI-CRACK
KI-CRACK
BOOM
LORD, I PRAY . . .
MAY THESE MEN REST IN PEACE . . .

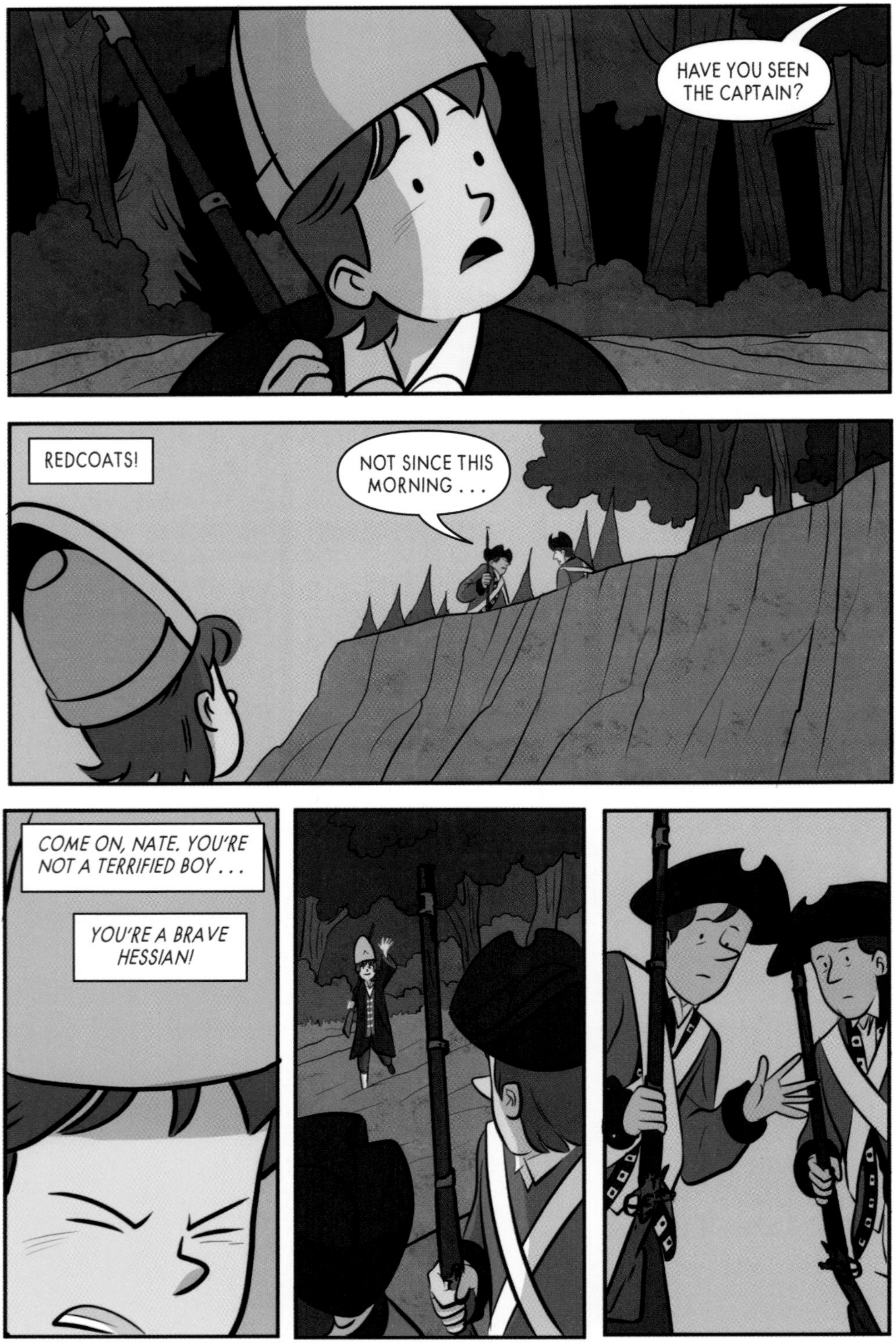
HAVE YOU SEEN THE CAPTAIN?
REDCOATS!
NOT SINCE THIS MORNING . . .
COME ON, NATE. YOU'RE NOT A TERRIFIED BOY . . .
YOU'RE A BRAVE HESSIAN!

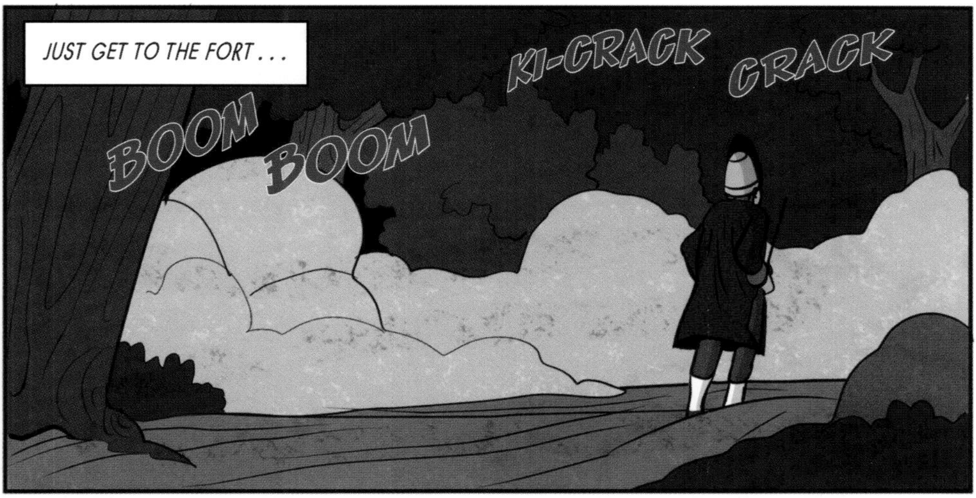
JUST GET TO THE FORT . . .
BOOM
BOOM
KI-CRACK
CRACK

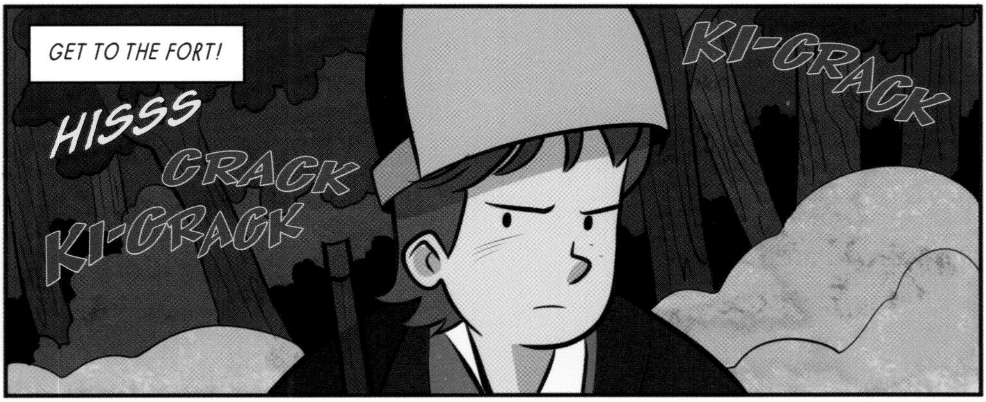
GET TO THE FORT!
HISSS
CRACK
KI-CRACK
KI-CRACK

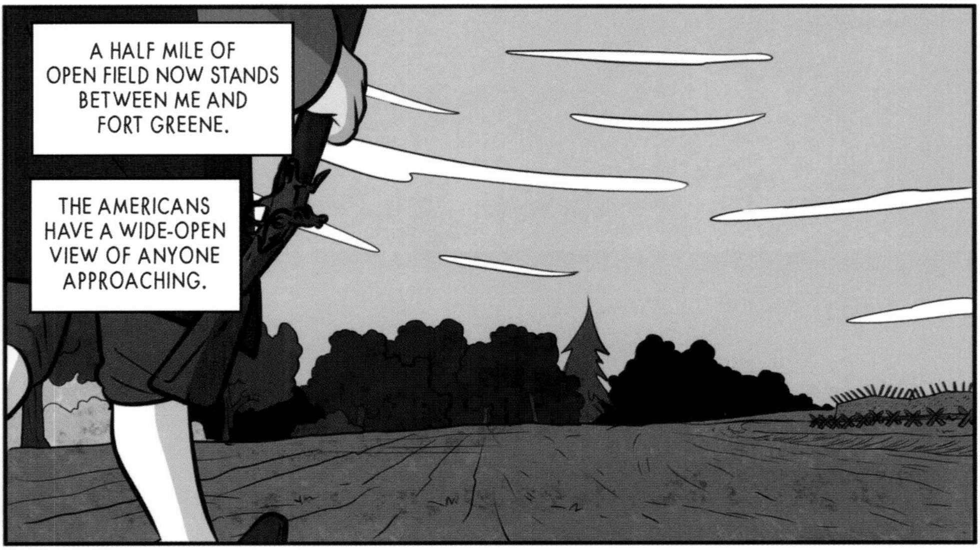
A HALF MILE OF OPEN FIELD NOW STANDS BETWEEN ME AND FORT GREENE.
THE AMERICANS HAVE A WIDE-OPEN VIEW OF ANYONE APPROACHING.

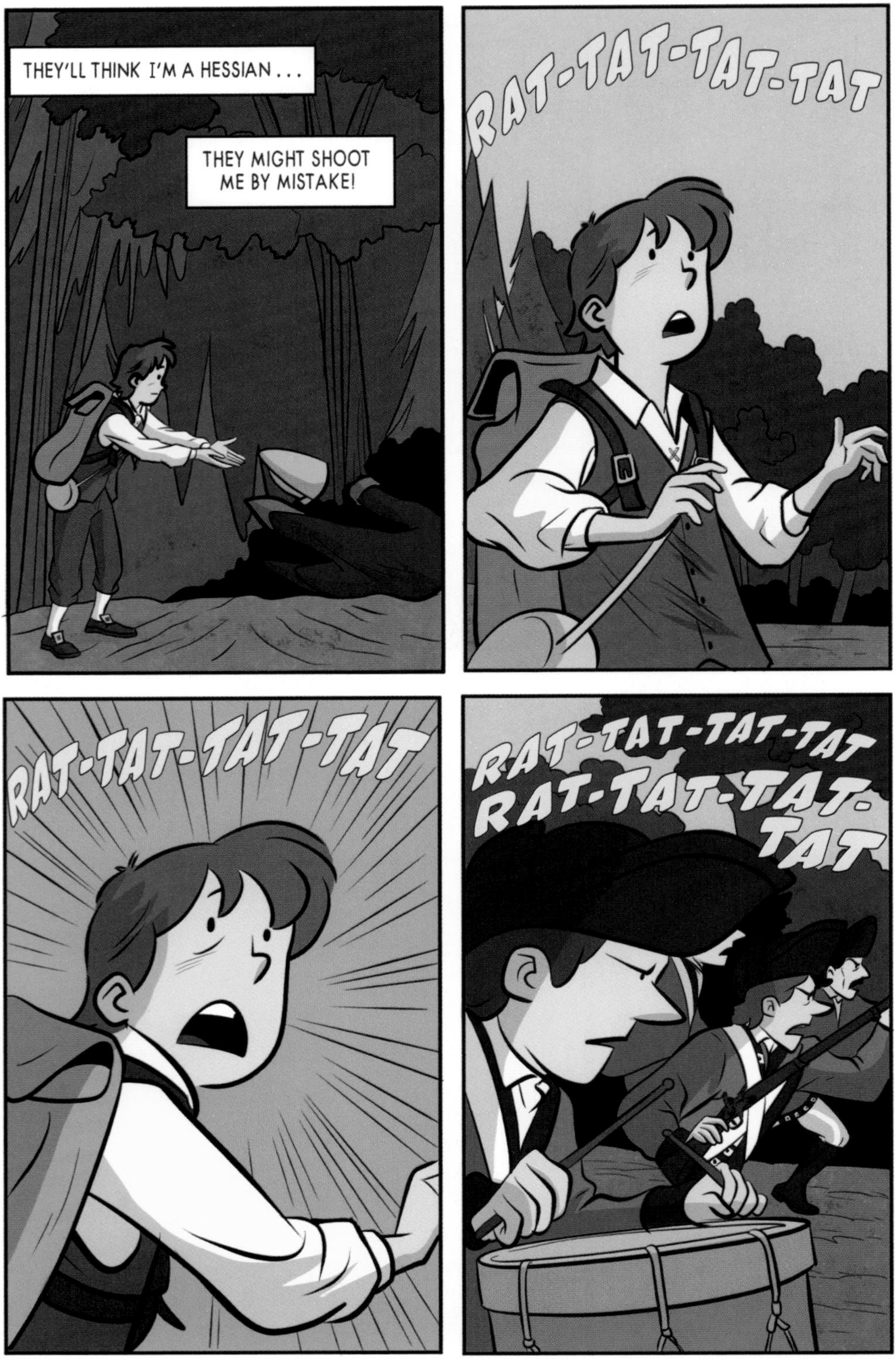
THEY'LL THINK I'M A HESSIAN . . .
THEY MIGHT SHOOT ME BY MISTAKE!
RAT-TAT-TAT-TAT
RAT-TAT-TAT-TAT
RAT-TAT-TAT-TAT
RAT-TAT-TAT-TAT-TAT

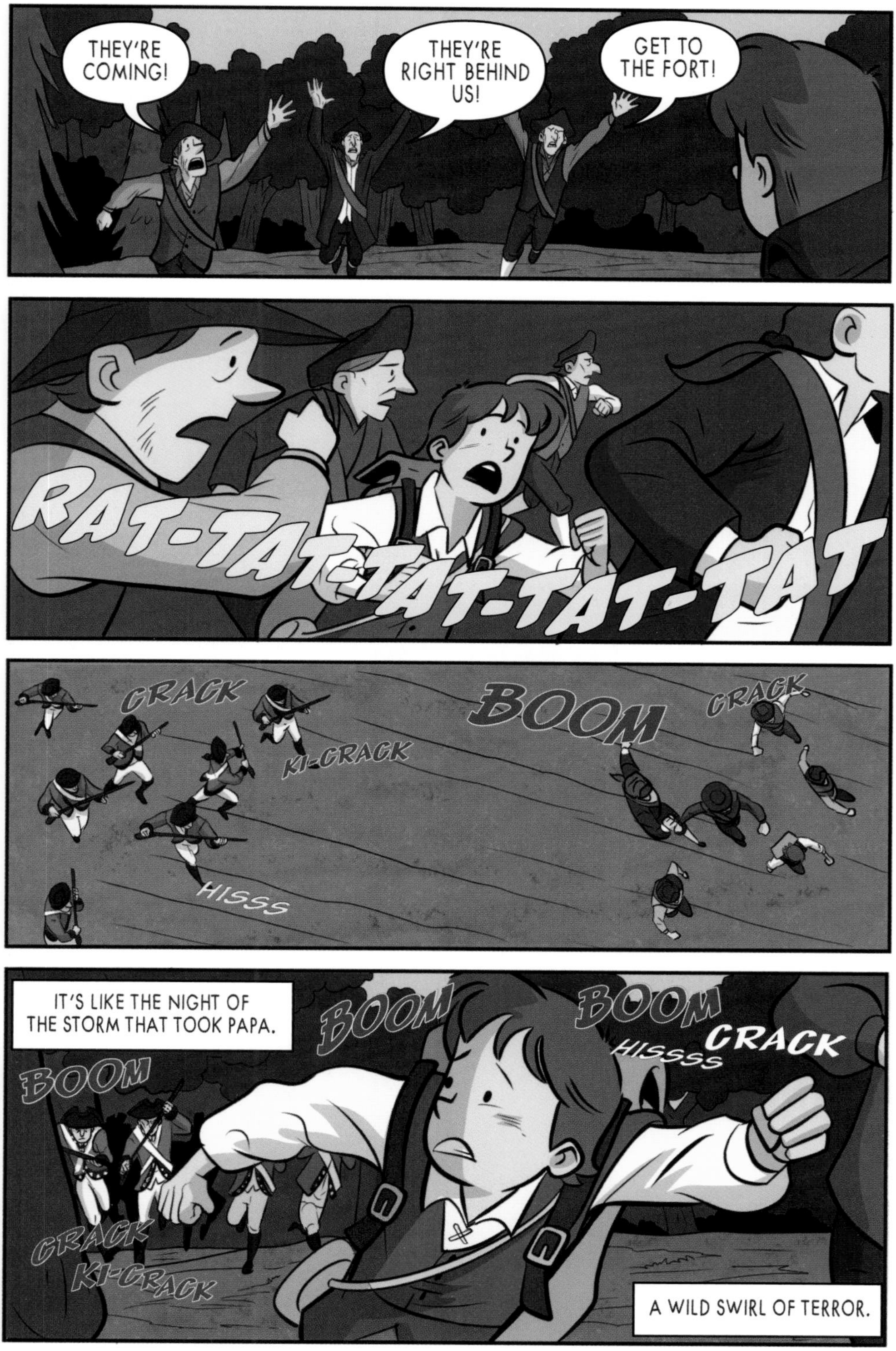
THEY'RE COMING!
THEY'RE RIGHT BEHIND US!
GET TO THE FORT!
RAT-TAT-TAT-TAT-TAT-TAT
CRACK
KI-CRACK
BOOM
CRACK
HISSS
IT'S LIKE THE NIGHT OF THE STORM THAT TOOK PAPA.
BOOM
BOOM
BOOM
HISSSS
CRACK
CRACK
KI-CRACK
A WILD SWIRL OF TERROR.

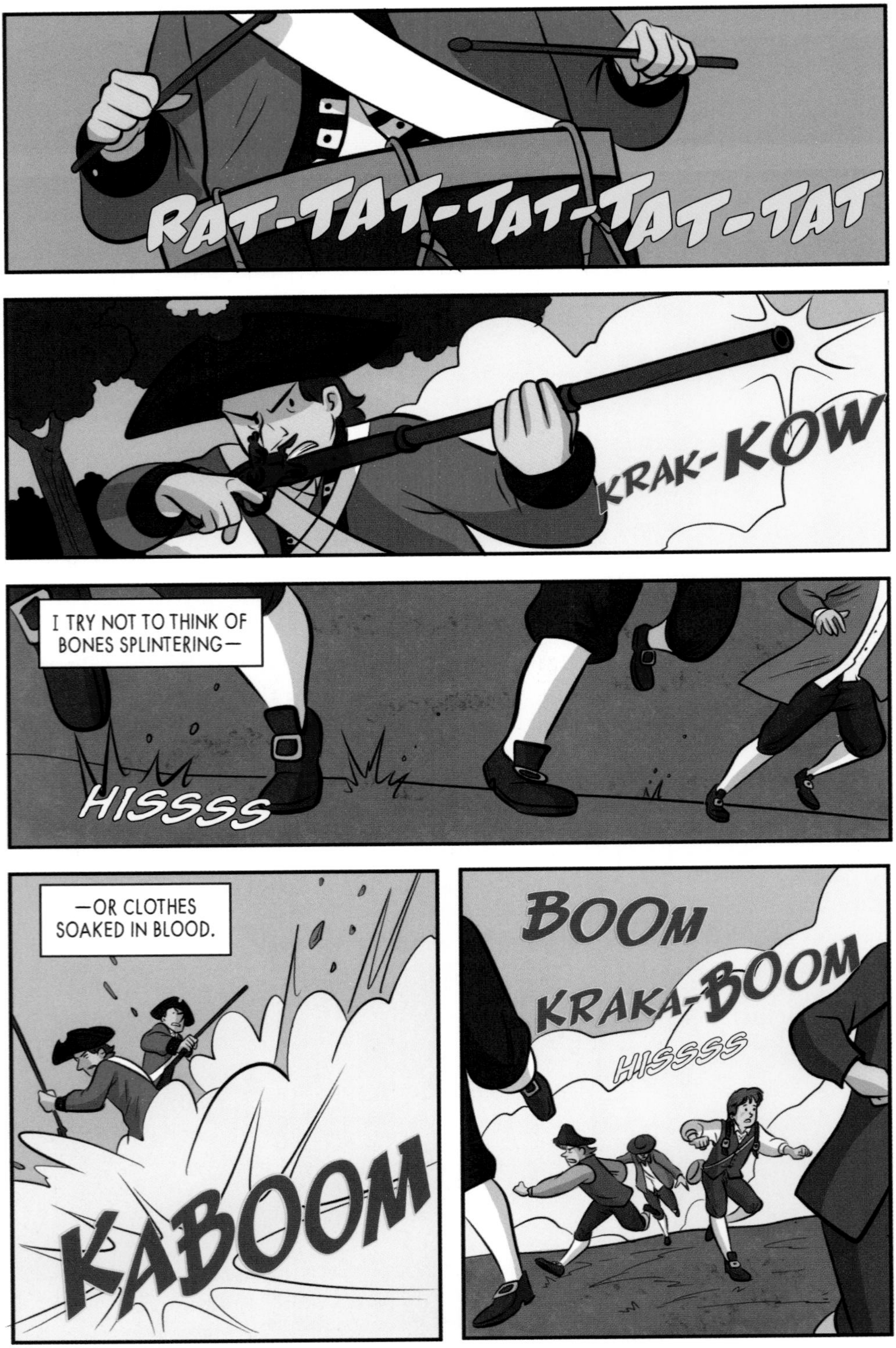
RAT-TAT-TAT-TAT-TAT-TAT
KRAK-KOW
I TRY NOT TO THINK OF BONES SPLINTERING—
HISSSS
—OR CLOTHES SOAKED IN BLOOD.
KABOOM
BOOM
KRAKA-BOOM
HISSSS

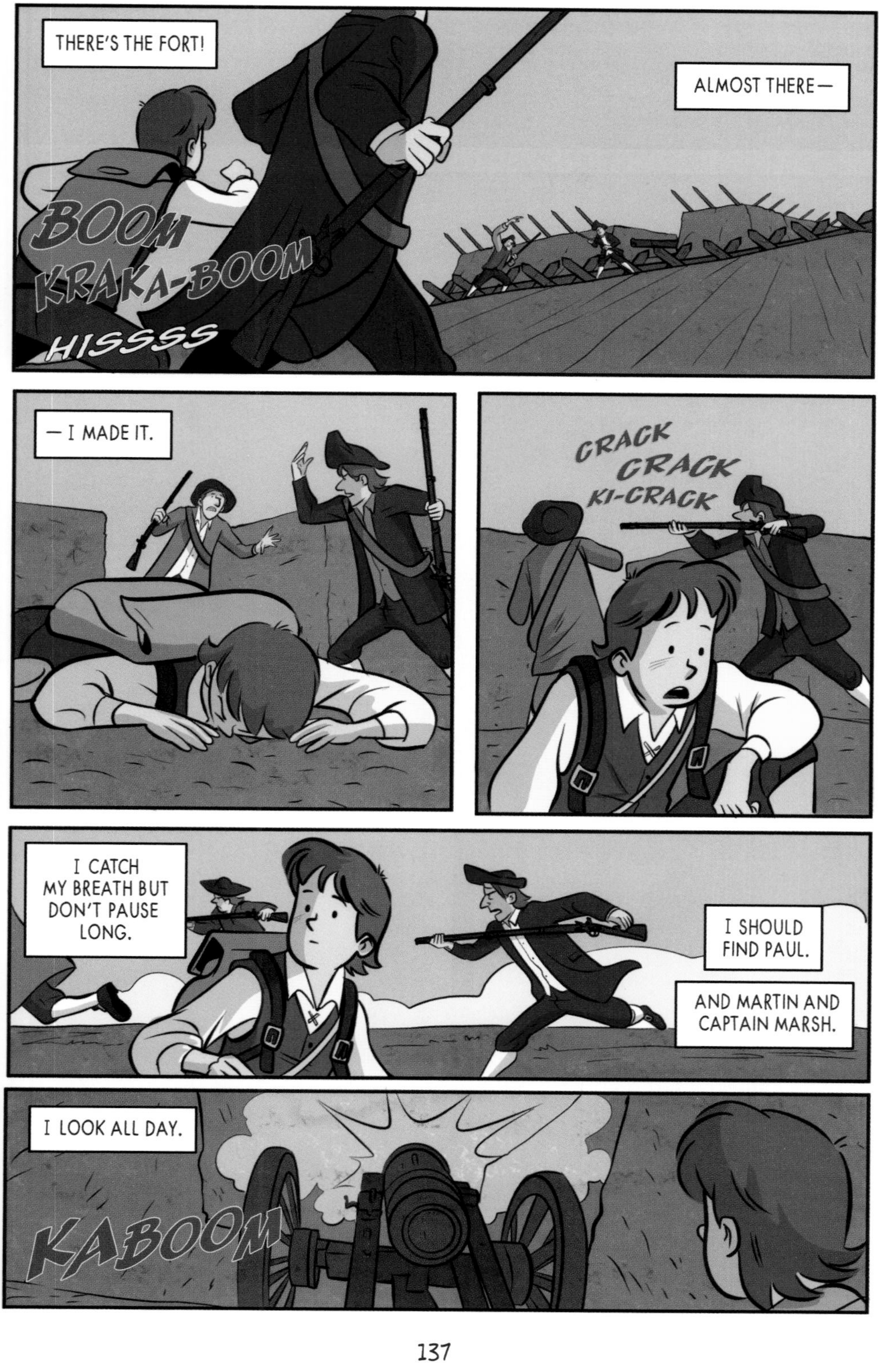
THERE'S THE FORT!
ALMOST THERE—
BOOM
KRAKA-BOOM
HISSSS
— I MADE IT.
CRACK
CRACK
KI-CRACK
I CATCH MY BREATH BUT DON'T PAUSE LONG.
I SHOULD FIND PAUL.
AND MARTIN AND CAPTAIN MARSH.
I LOOK ALL DAY.
KABOOM

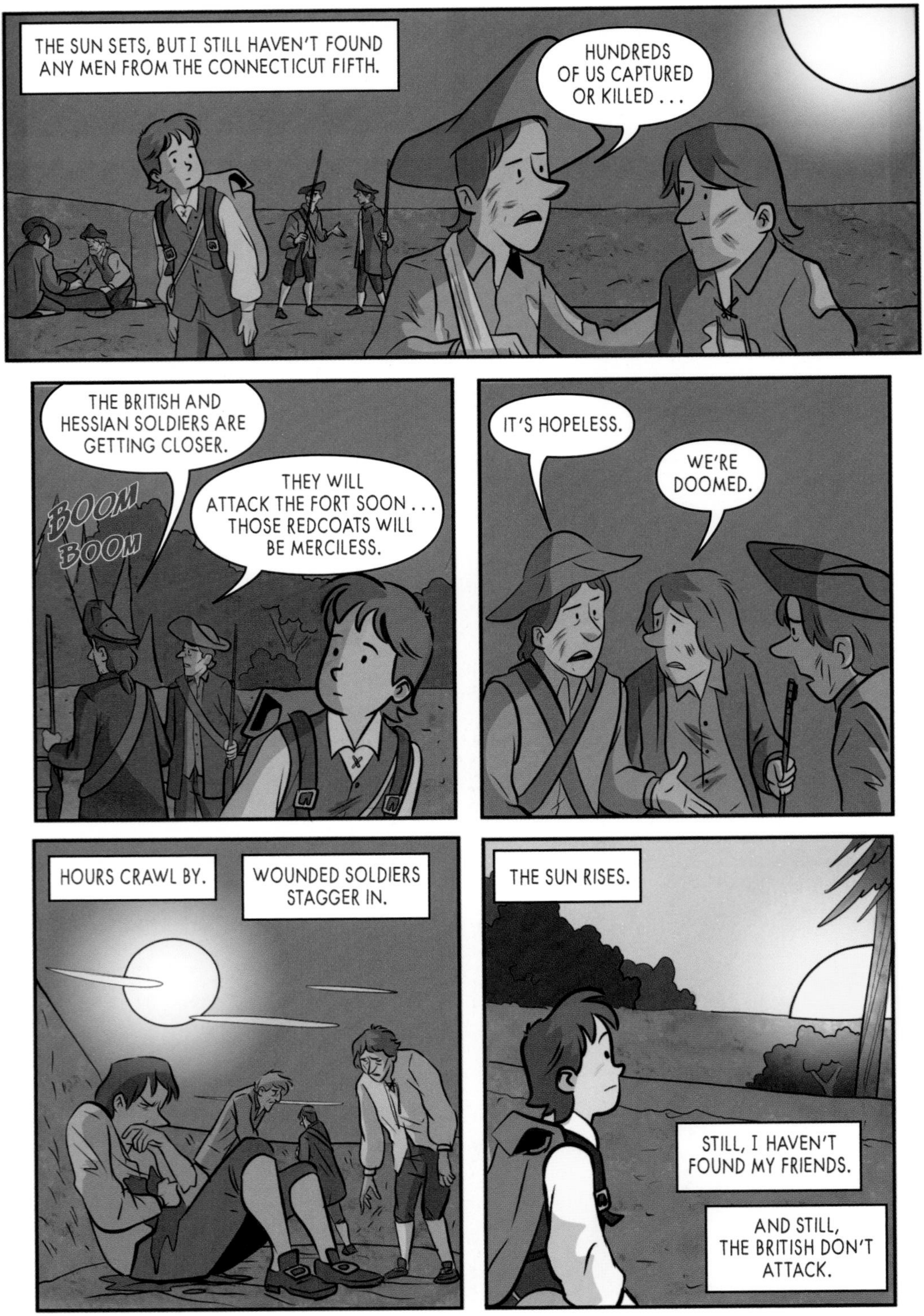
THE SUN SETS, BUT I STILL HAVEN'T FOUND ANY MEN FROM THE CONNECTICUT FIFTH.
HUNDREDS OF US CAPTURED OR KILLED . . .
THE BRITISH AND HESSIAN SOLDIERS ARE GETTING CLOSER.
BOOM
BOOM
THEY WILL ATTACK THE FORT SOON . . . THOSE REDCOATS WILL BE MERCILESS.
IT'S HOPELESS.
WE'RE DOOMED.
HOURS CRAWL BY.
WOUNDED SOLDIERS STAGGER IN.
THE SUN RISES.
STILL, I HAVEN'T FOUND MY FRIENDS.
AND STILL, THE BRITISH DON'T ATTACK.

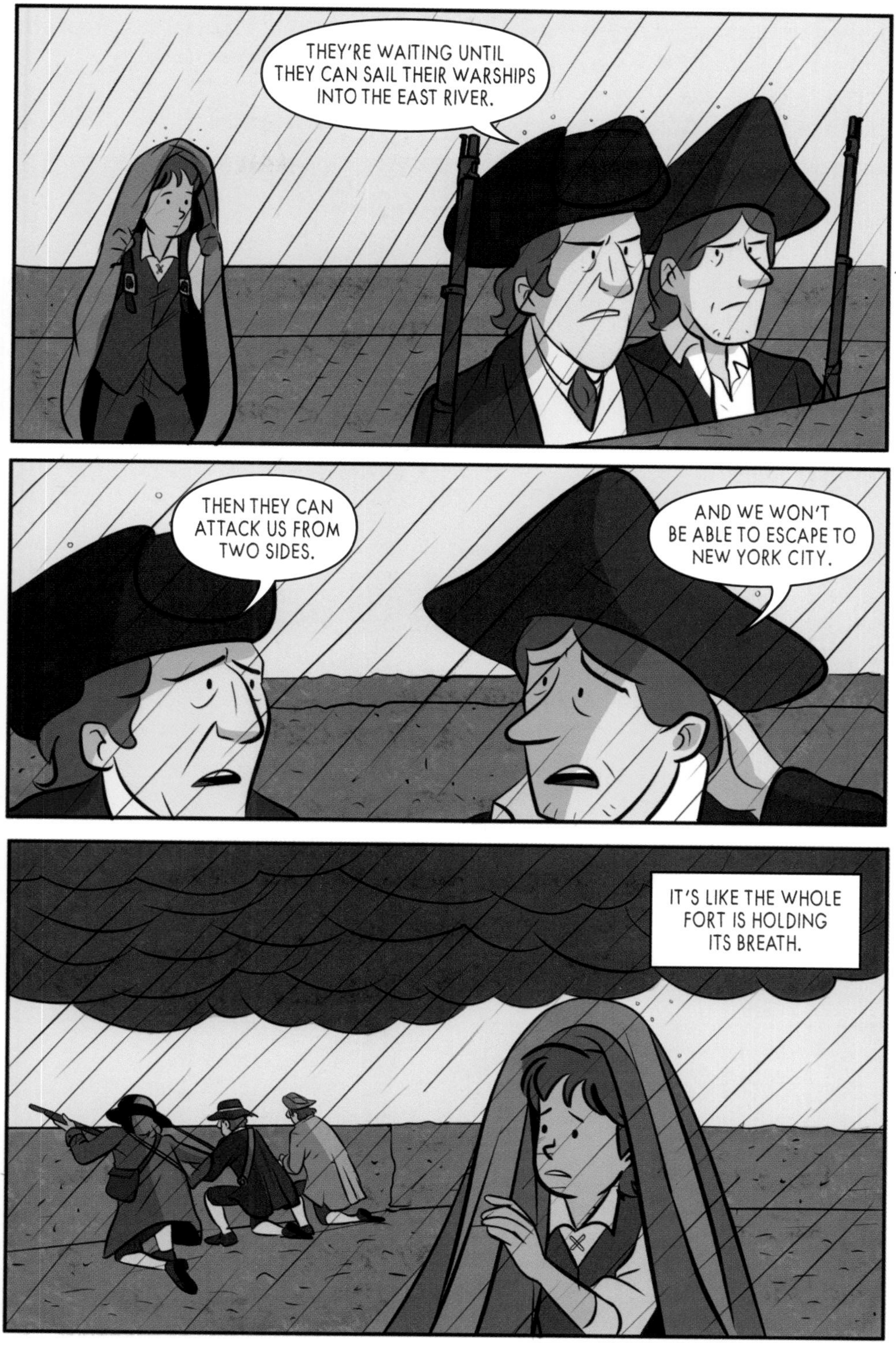
THEY'RE WAITING UNTIL THEY CAN SAIL THEIR WARSHIPS INTO THE EAST RIVER.
THEN THEY CAN ATTACK US FROM TWO SIDES.
AND WE WON'T BE ABLE TO ESCAPE TO NEW YORK CITY.
IT'S LIKE THE WHOLE FORT IS HOLDING ITS BREATH.

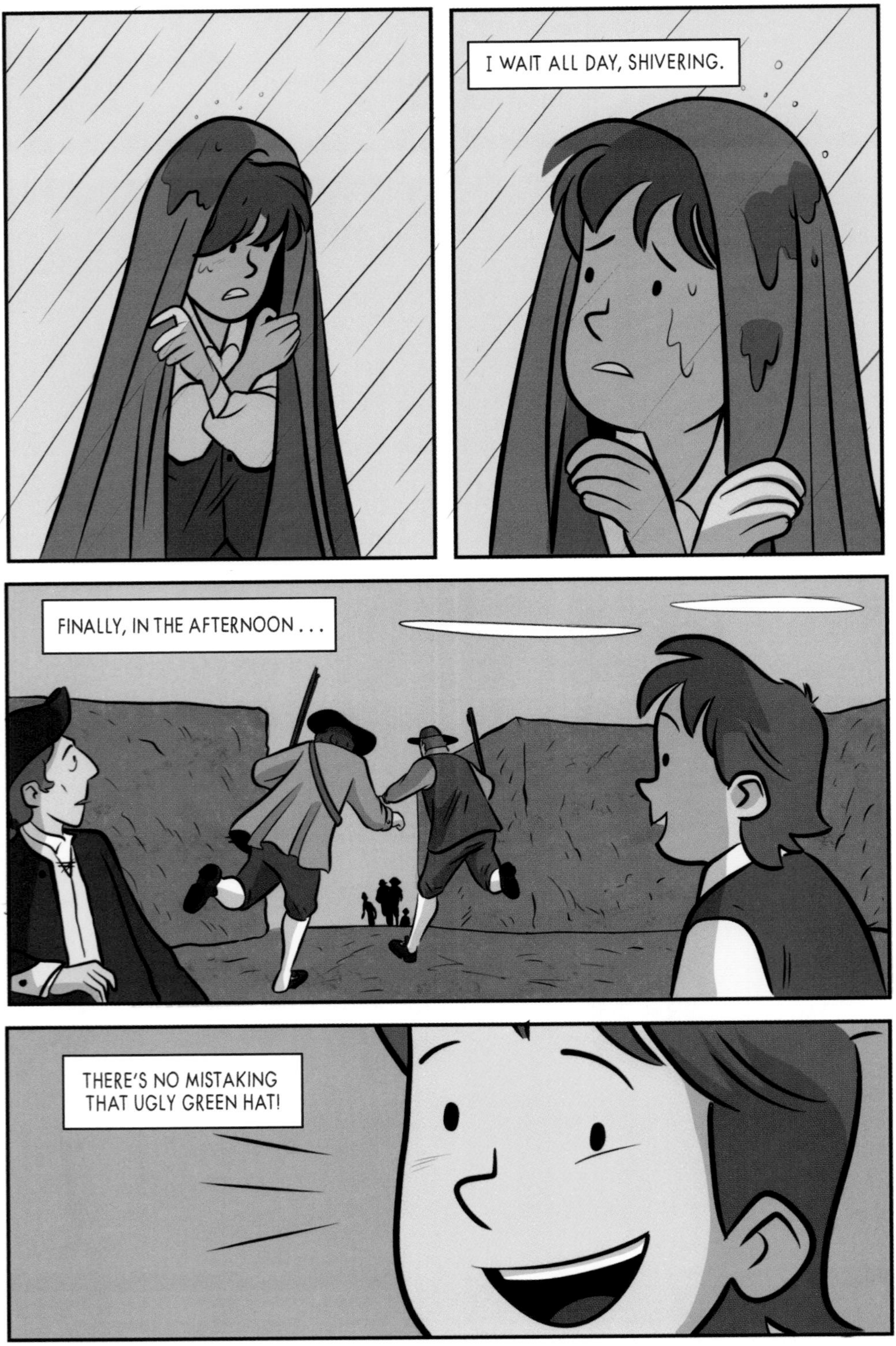
I WAIT ALL DAY, SHIVERING.
FINALLY, IN THE AFTERNOON . . .
THERE'S NO MISTAKING THAT UGLY GREEN HAT!

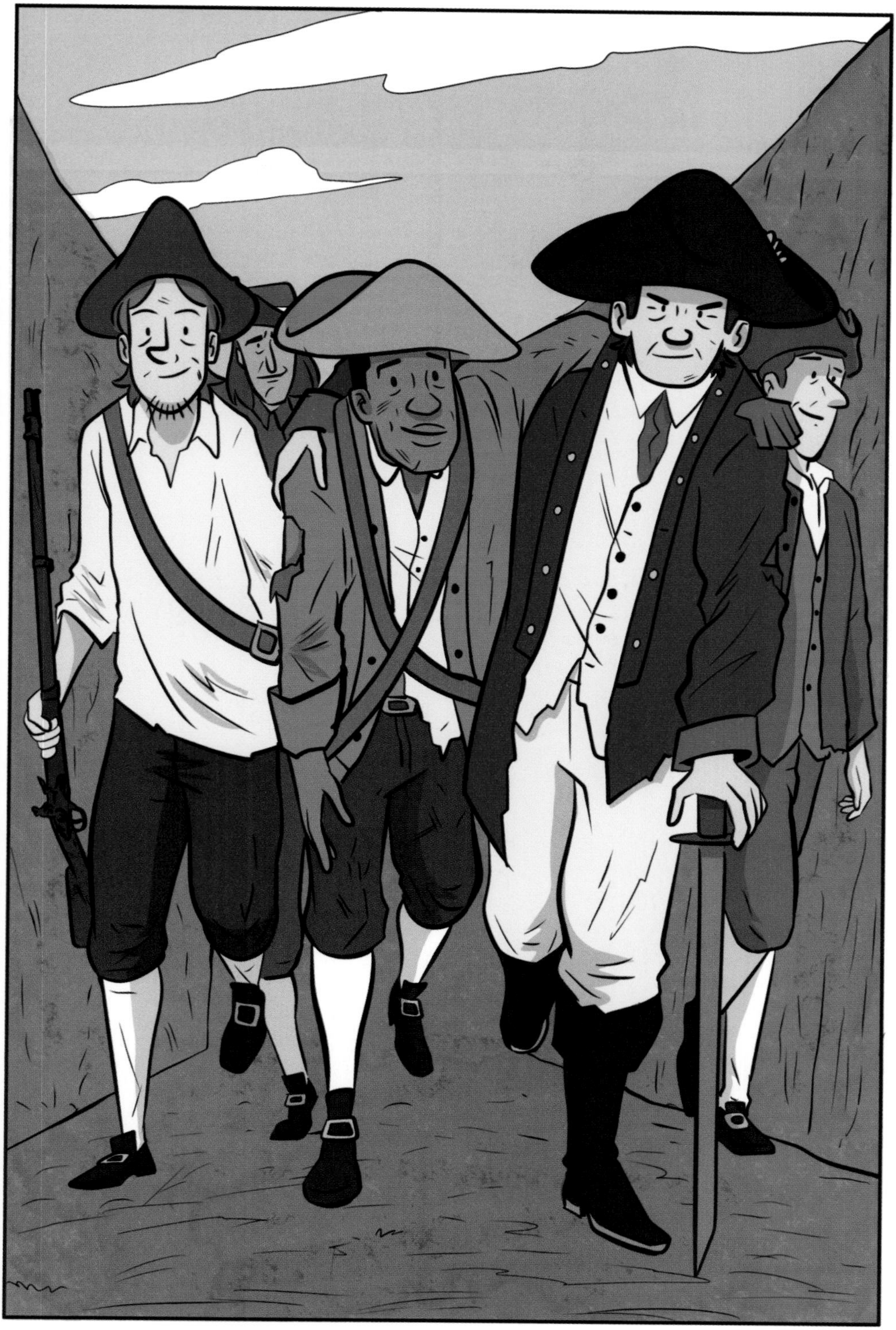

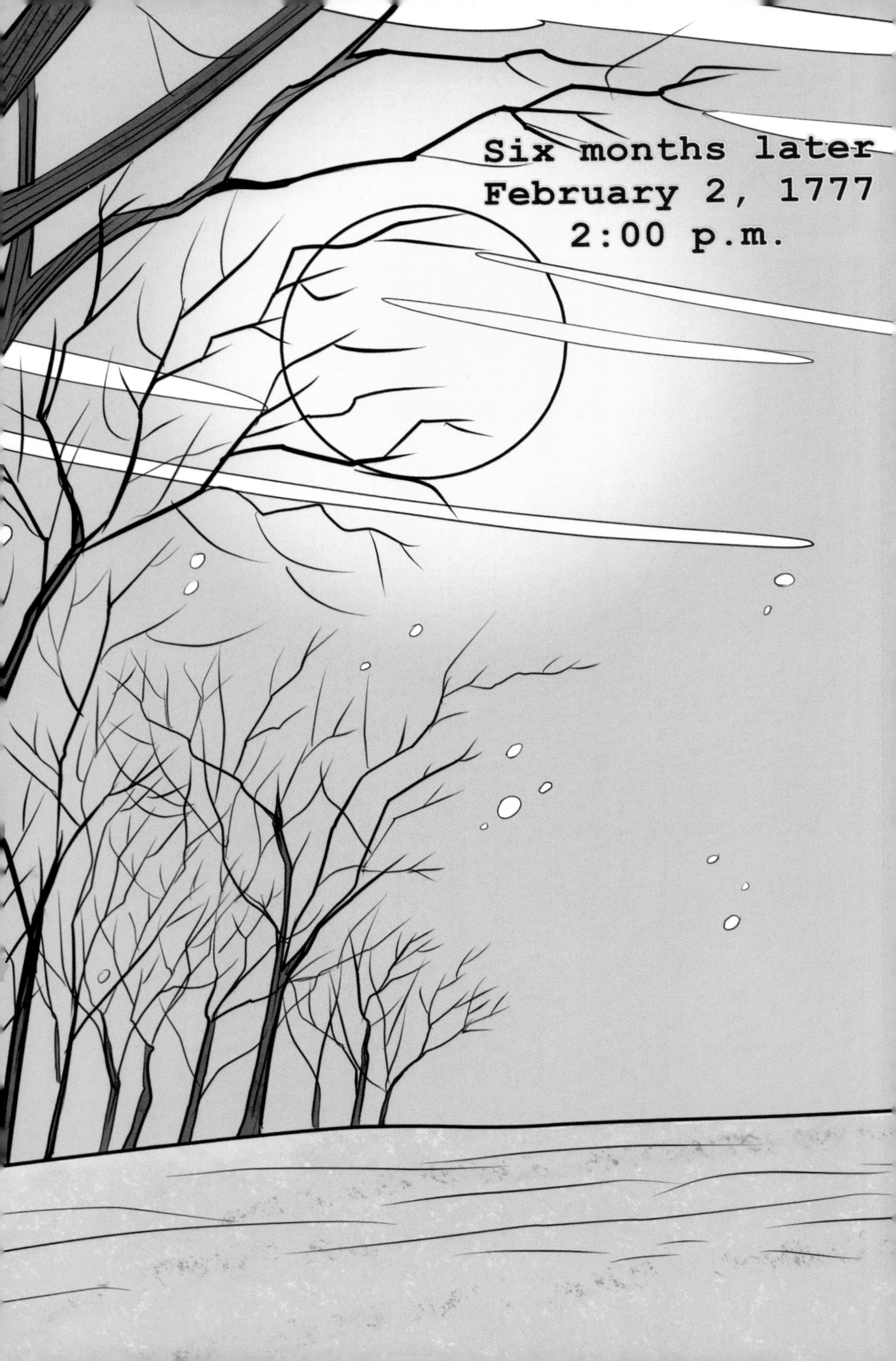
Six months later
February 2, 1777
2:00 p.m.

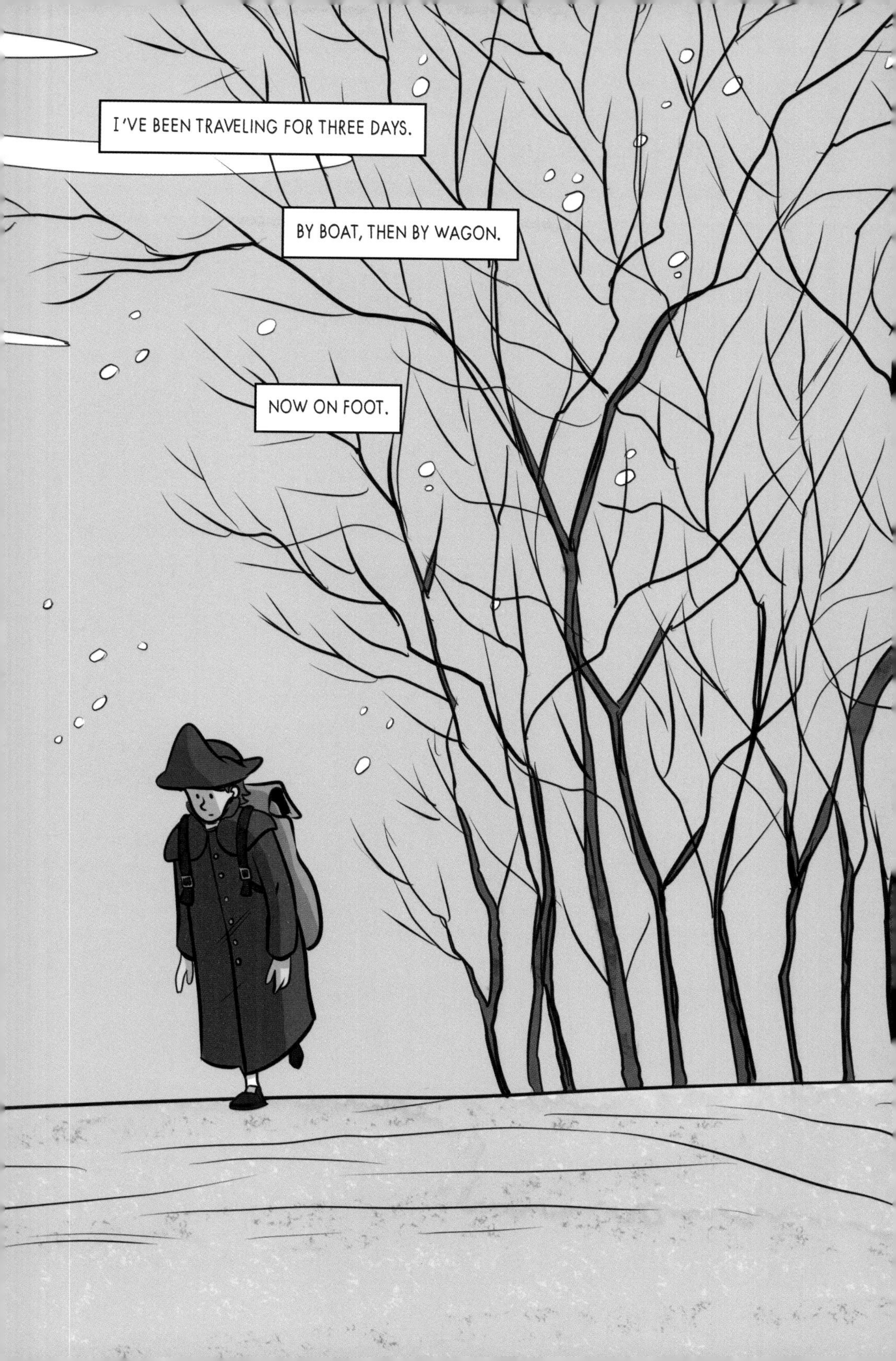
I'VE BEEN TRAVELING FOR THREE DAYS.
BY BOAT, THEN BY WAGON.
NOW ON FOOT.

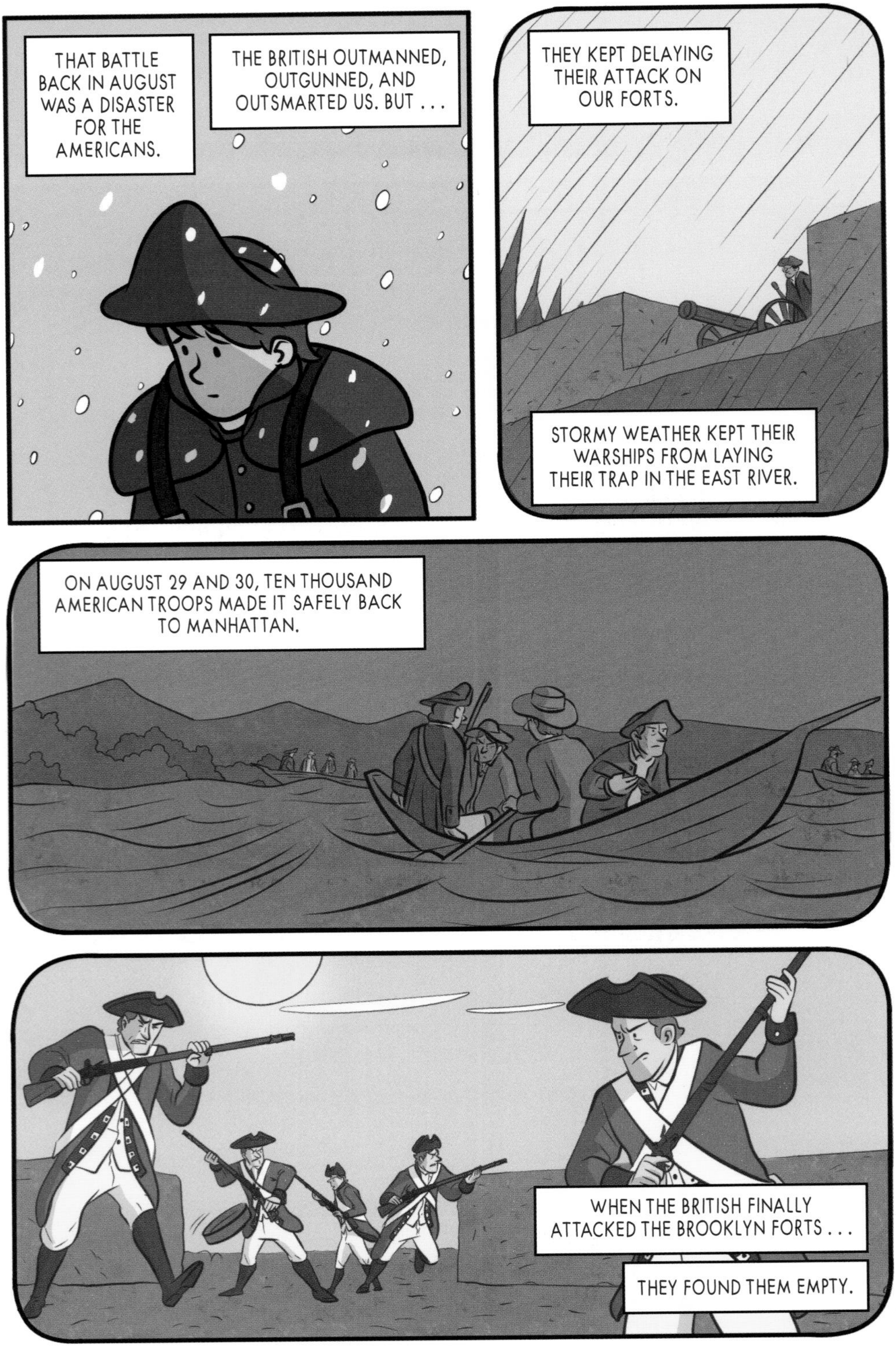
THAT BATTLE BACK IN AUGUST WAS A DISASTER FOR THE AMERICANS.
THE BRITISH OUTMANNED, OUTGUNNED, AND OUTSMARTED US. BUT . . .
THEY KEPT DELAYING THEIR ATTACK ON OUR FORTS.
STORMY WEATHER KEPT THEIR WARSHIPS FROM LAYING THEIR TRAP IN THE EAST RIVER.
ON AUGUST 29 AND 30, TEN THOUSAND AMERICAN TROOPS MADE IT SAFELY BACK TO MANHATTAN.
WHEN THE BRITISH FINALLY ATTACKED THE BROOKLYN FORTS . . .
THEY FOUND THEM EMPTY.

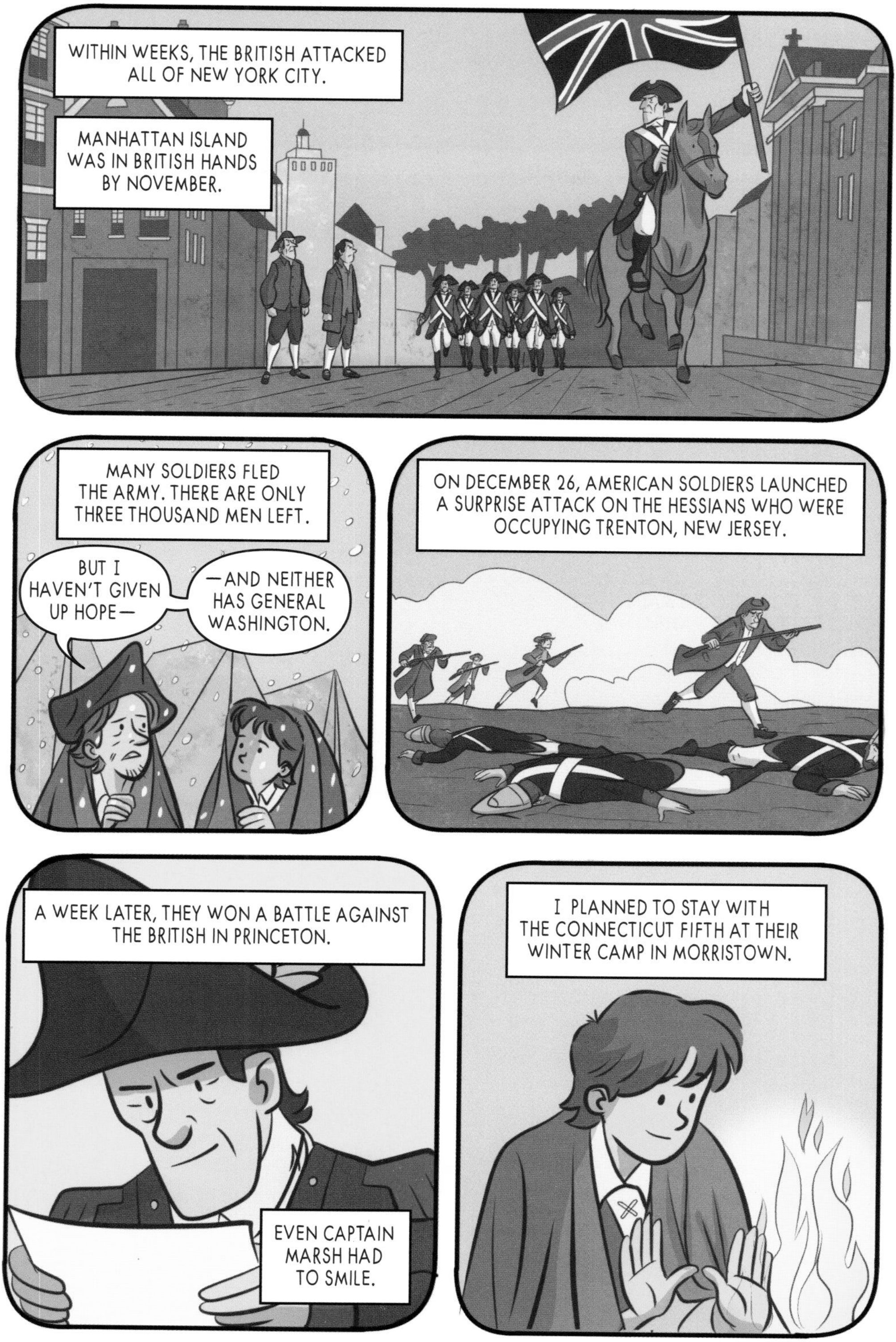
WITHIN WEEKS, THE BRITISH ATTACKED ALL OF NEW YORK CITY.
MANHATTAN ISLAND WAS IN BRITISH HANDS BY NOVEMBER.
MANY SOLDIERS FLED THE ARMY. THERE ARE ONLY THREE THOUSAND MEN LEFT.
BUT I HAVEN'T GIVEN UP HOPE—
—AND NEITHER HAS GENERAL WASHINGTON.
ON DECEMBER 26, AMERICAN SOLDIERS LAUNCHED A SURPRISE ATTACK ON THE HESSIANS WHO WERE OCCUPYING TRENTON, NEW JERSEY.
A WEEK LATER, THEY WON A BATTLE AGAINST THE BRITISH IN PRINCETON.
EVEN CAPTAIN MARSH HAD TO SMILE.
I PLANNED TO STAY WITH THE CONNECTICUT FIFTH AT THEIR WINTER CAMP IN MORRISTOWN.

BUT SEVEN DAYS AGO, I RECEIVED A LETTER.

"YOUR UNCLE HAS DIED OF SMALLPOX.

"I'M AFRAID THE RETURNING AMERICAN SOLDIERS BROUGHT THE DISEASE TO NORWALK.

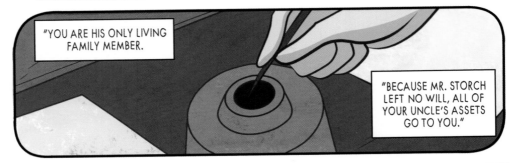

"YOU ARE HIS ONLY LIVING FAMILY MEMBER.

"BECAUSE MR. STORCH LEFT NO WILL, ALL OF YOUR UNCLE'S ASSETS GO TO YOU."

I READ THAT LETTER TWENTY TIMES BEFORE I UNDERSTOOD WHAT IT MEANT.

I GET THE HOUSE AND THE LAND—

—AND I ALSO GET TO SET THEO AND ELIZA FREE.

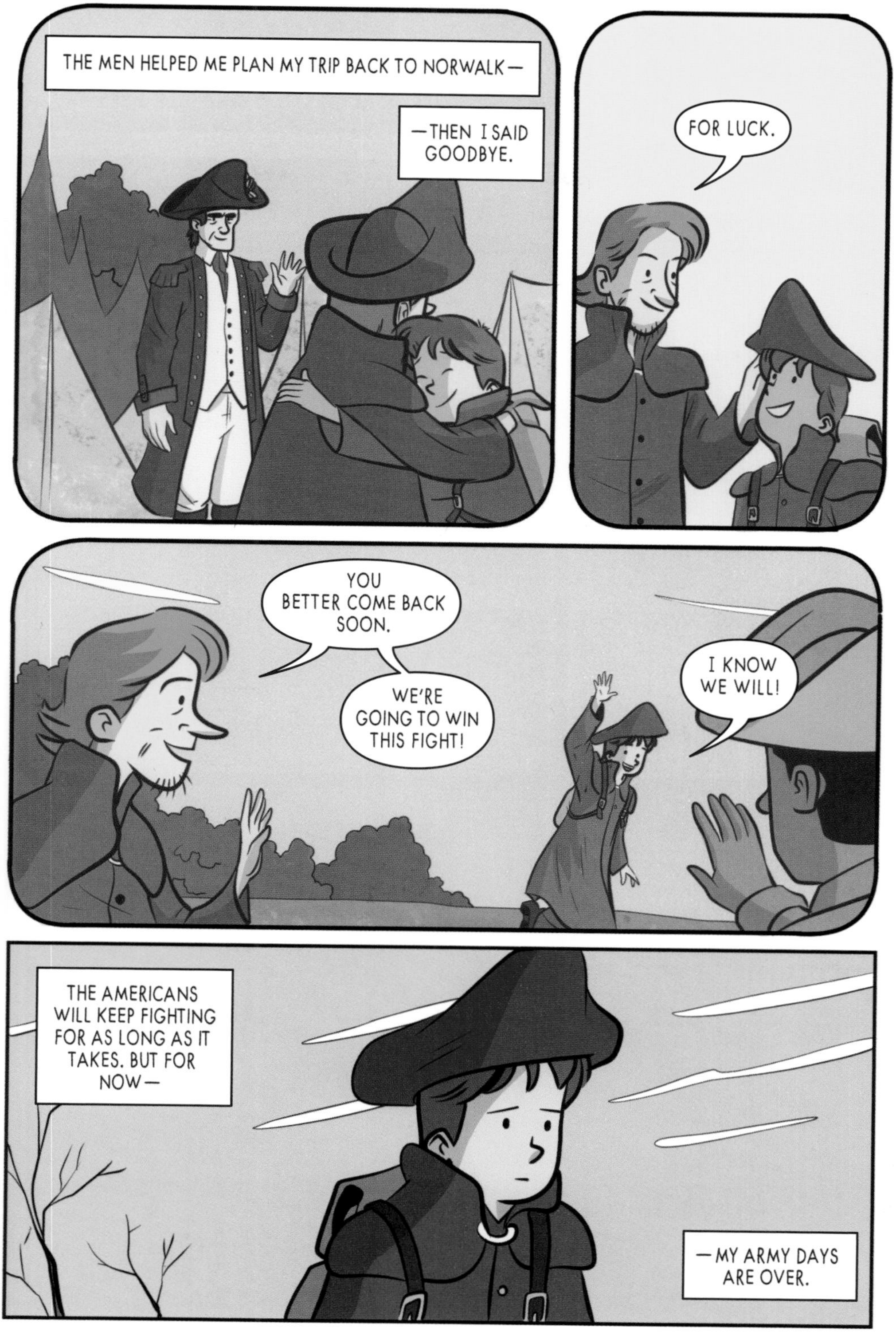
THE MEN HELPED ME PLAN MY TRIP BACK TO NORWALK—
—THEN I SAID GOODBYE.
FOR LUCK.
YOU BETTER COME BACK SOON.
WE'RE GOING TO WIN THIS FIGHT!
I KNOW WE WILL!
THE AMERICANS WILL KEEP FIGHTING FOR AS LONG AS IT TAKES. BUT FOR NOW—
—MY ARMY DAYS ARE OVER.

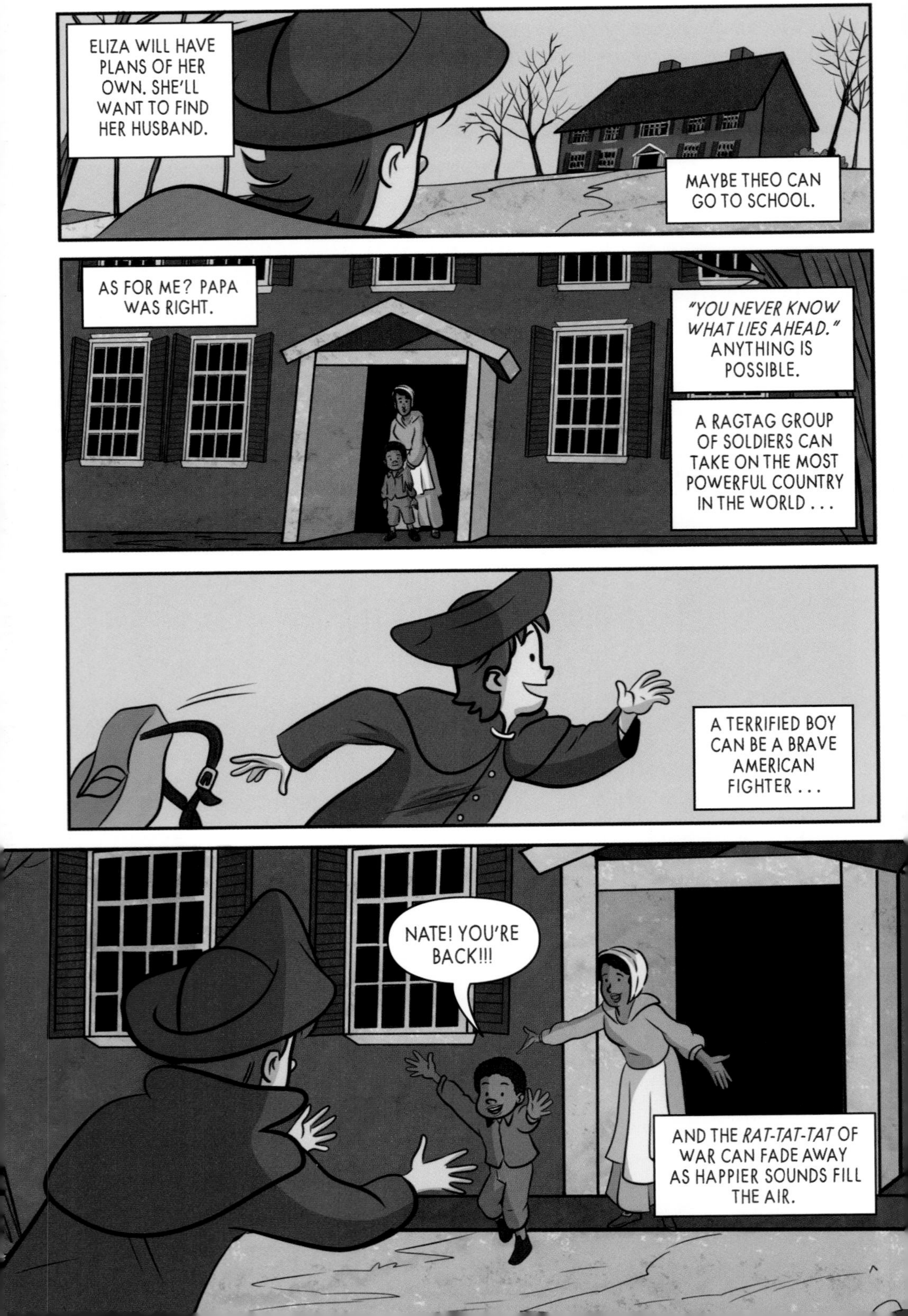
ELIZA WILL HAVE PLANS OF HER OWN. SHE'LL WANT TO FIND HER HUSBAND.
MAYBE THEO CAN GO TO SCHOOL.
AS FOR ME? PAPA WAS RIGHT.
"YOU NEVER KNOW WHAT LIES AHEAD." ANYTHING IS POSSIBLE.
A RAGTAG GROUP OF SOLDIERS CAN TAKE ON THE MOST POWERFUL COUNTRY IN THE WORLD . . .
A TERRIFIED BOY CAN BE A BRAVE AMERICAN FIGHTER . . .
NATE! YOU'RE BACK!!!
AND THE *RAT-TAT-TAT* OF WAR CAN FADE AWAY AS HAPPIER SOUNDS FILL THE AIR.

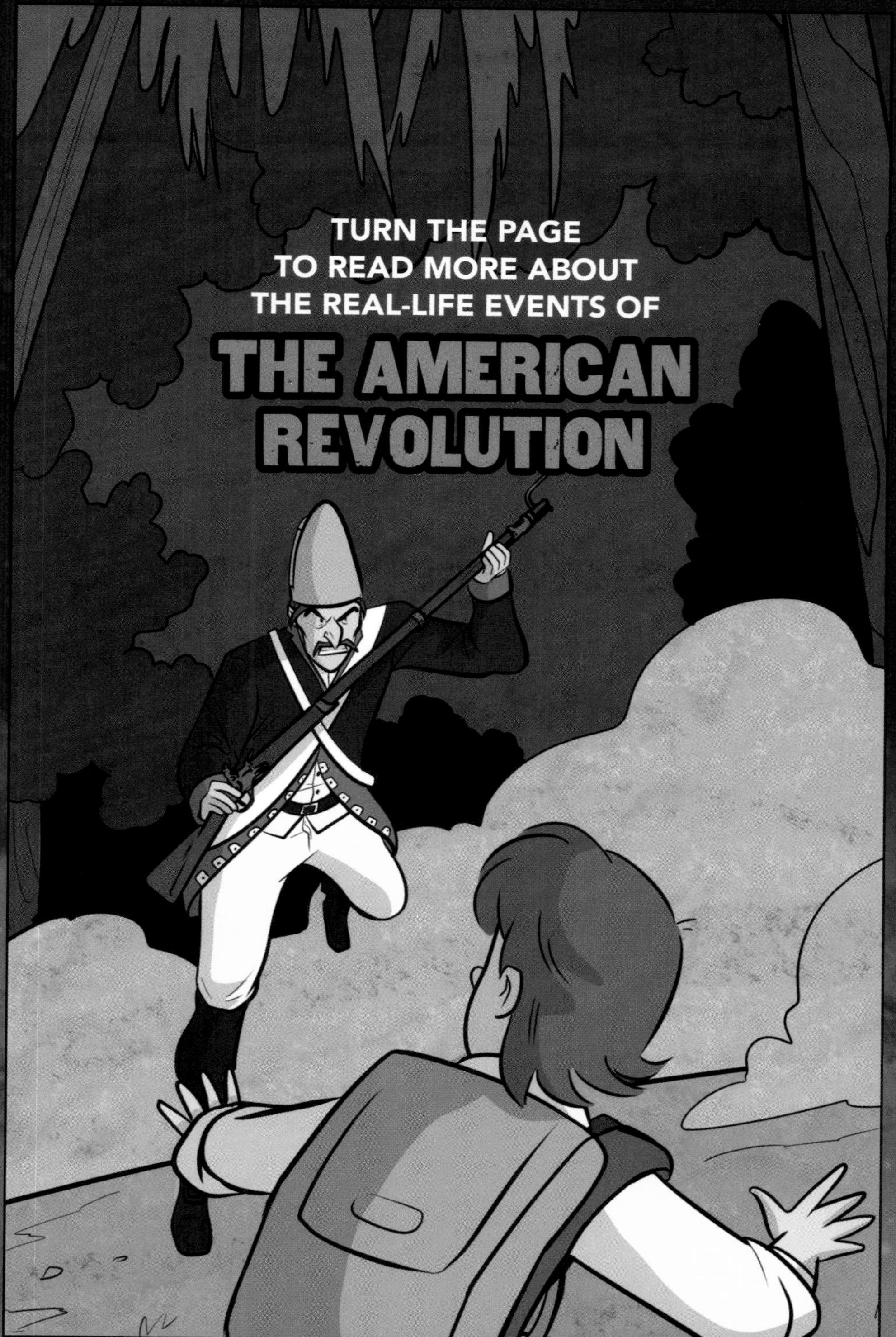

TURN THE PAGE
TO READ MORE ABOUT
THE REAL-LIFE EVENTS OF
THE AMERICAN
REVOLUTION

Hello readers!

I live in Connecticut, in a town where a big American Revolution battle was fought.

When I first started thinking about writing an I Survived book about the American Revolution, I had no idea what I would focus on. The war was very long—it lasted more than eight years, from 1775–1783. There was no way all of that would fit into one I Survived book.

Then one day I was at a park in Fort Greene, Brooklyn, in New York City. There's a huge monument there. Reading the plaque, I learned it was created in honor of 11,500 American soldiers who died on British prison ships. Many of them were captured during the Battle of Brooklyn.

I had never heard of this battle. And I was shocked to learn it was the biggest battle of the Revolutionary War. As I learned more, I decided that this would be the topic for my I Survived book.

That trip to that Brooklyn park began a research project that included reading about thirty books plus dozens of letters, diary entries, and battle reports written in 1776. I visited battlefields and museums and talked to historians. I learned that the Revolutionary War was far more terrifying, complicated, messy, and miraculous than I'd ever imagined.

I hope my story inspires you to take your own journey into this fascinating time. Keep reading to learn more about it with Nate, Paul, Eliza, Captain Marsh, Storch, Samuel, and Martin to guide you.

Huzzah! (That's a word from the days of the American Revolution. It means "hooray!")

Lauren Tarshis

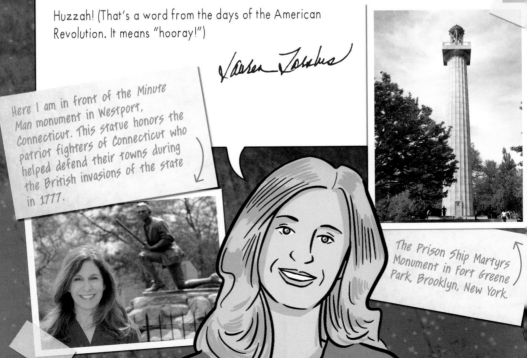

Here I am in front of the *Minute Man* monument in Westport, Connecticut. This statue honors the patriot fighters of Connecticut who helped defend their towns during the British invasions of the state in 1777.

The Prison Ship Martyrs Monument in Fort Greene Park, Brooklyn, New York.

THE FIRST AMERICANS

FOR THOUSANDS OF YEARS BEFORE EUROPEANS ARRIVED, PEOPLE LIVED IN THE LAND WE NOW CALL THE UNITED STATES. THEY BELONGED TO HUNDREDS OF DIFFERENT **NATIVE NATIONS** AND TRIBES, EACH WITH A DIFFERENT CULTURE, LANGUAGE, AND WAY OF LIFE.

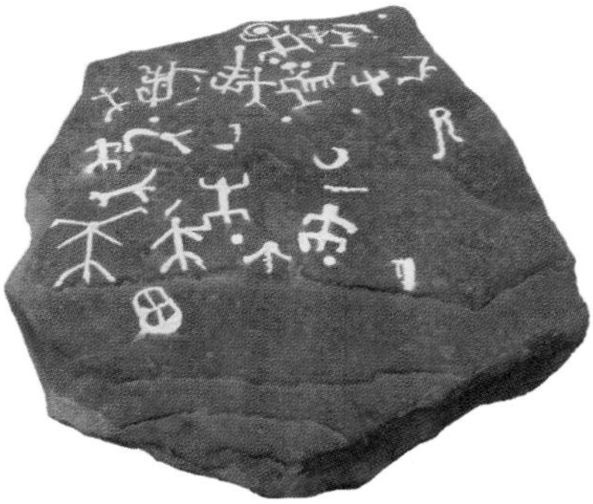

This petroglyph is estimated to have been created by native people 3,000–5,000 years ago in what is now New Jersey.

THOSE PEOPLE WERE THE **ANCESTORS** OF PEOPLE OF NATIVE AMERICAN HERITAGE LIVING ACROSS THE UNITED STATES TODAY.

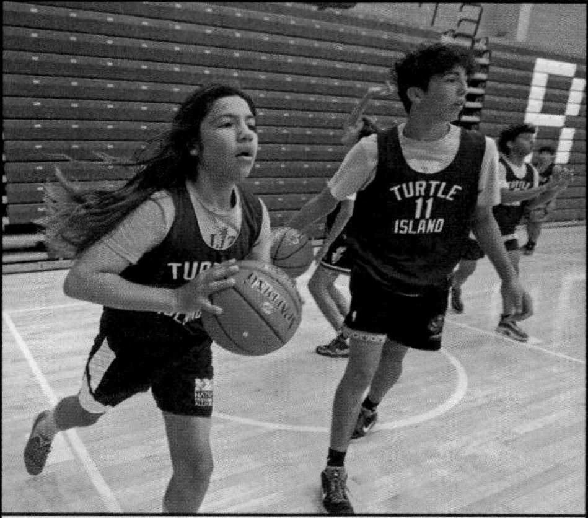

TURTLE
11
ISLAND

Native American high schoolers run drills at a Scholar-Athlete basketball program in Boston.

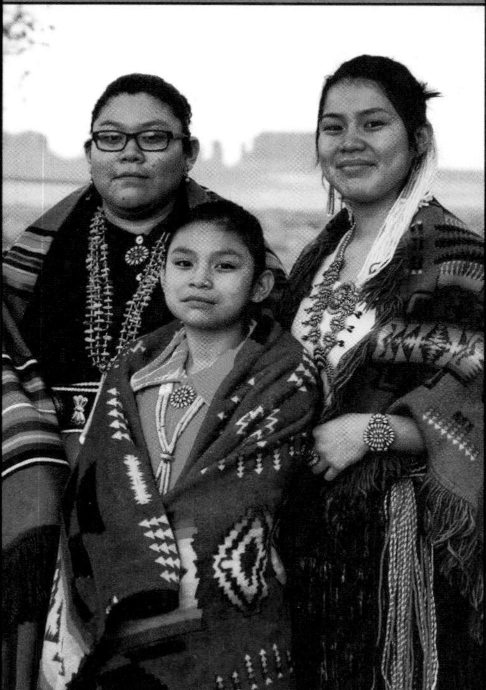

Three sisters, members of the Navajo Nation, pose in Arizona.

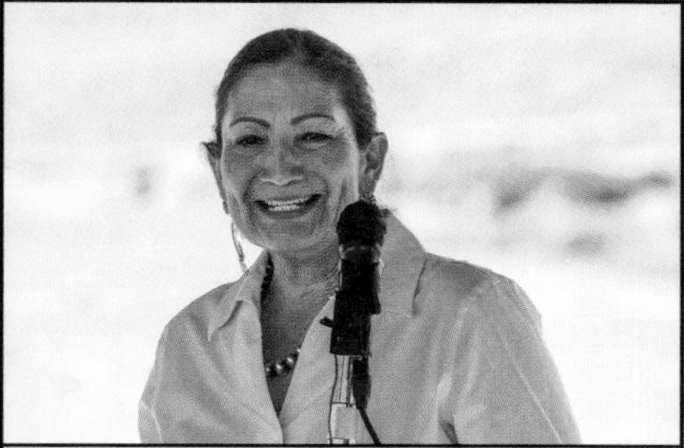

Deb Haaland, a member of the Pueblo of Laguna tribe, from New Mexico, is serving as the US secretary of the interior for President Joseph R. Biden.

A MORE CROWDED LAND

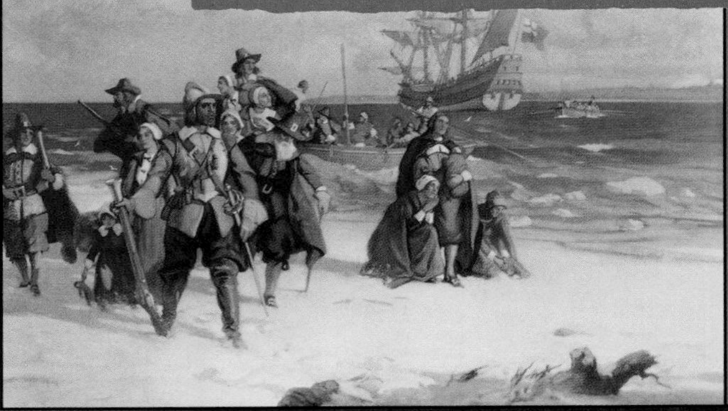

BEGINNING IN THE LATE 1500S, NEWCOMERS FROM ENGLAND, HOLLAND, FRANCE, AND OTHER COUNTRIES BEGAN ARRIVING IN AMERICA. THESE PEOPLE BECAME KNOWN AS **COLONISTS** OR SETTLERS.

BY THE 1770S, THERE WERE MORE THAN 2.5 MILLION PEOPLE LIVING IN WHAT WOULD BECOME THE UNITED STATES. ABOUT 500,000 OF THESE MEN, WOMEN, AND CHILDREN WERE BLACK PEOPLE FROM AFRICA. MOST OF THESE PEOPLE HAD BEEN KIDNAPPED FROM AFRICA AND FORCED TO COME TO AMERICA AGAINST THEIR WILL. THEY WERE MADE TO WORK AS **SLAVES**.

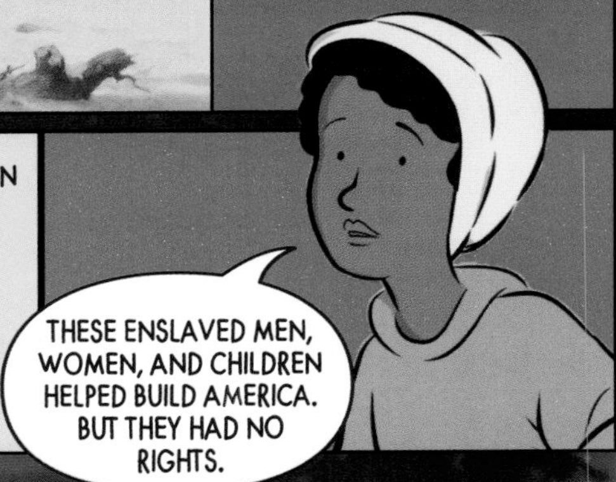
THESE ENSLAVED MEN, WOMEN, AND CHILDREN HELPED BUILD AMERICA. BUT THEY HAD NO RIGHTS.

THE THIRTEEN COLONIES

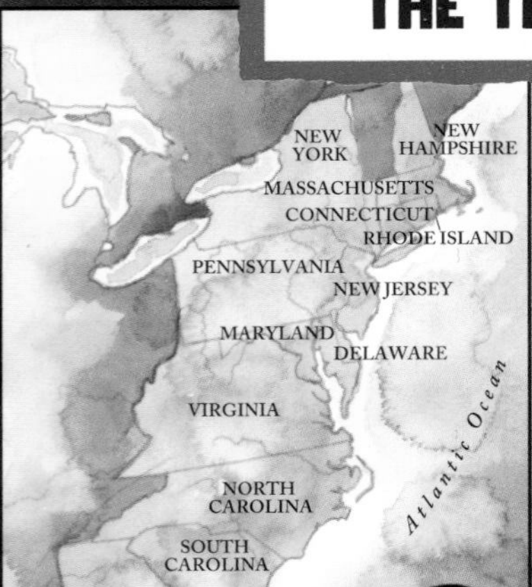
NEW YORK
NEW HAMPSHIRE
MASSACHUSETTS
CONNECTICUT
RHODE ISLAND
PENNSYLVANIA
NEW JERSEY
MARYLAND
DELAWARE
VIRGINIA
Atlantic Ocean
NORTH CAROLINA
SOUTH CAROLINA
GEORGIA

MOST OF THE NEWCOMERS LIVED IN THE AREA CLOSEST TO THE ATLANTIC OCEAN. OVER TIME, THIS AREA WAS DIVIDED UP INTO DIFFERENT PARTS, WHICH BECAME KNOWN AS THE **THIRTEEN COLONIES**.

IF YOU LIVED IN A BRITISH COLONY, YOU HAD TO **OBEY BRITISH LAWS**. KING GEORGE, ENGLAND'S RULER, WAS YOUR RULER. MOST COLONISTS WERE PERFECTLY HAPPY WITH THIS. ENGLAND WAS ONE OF THE MOST POWERFUL COUNTRIES IN THE WORLD.

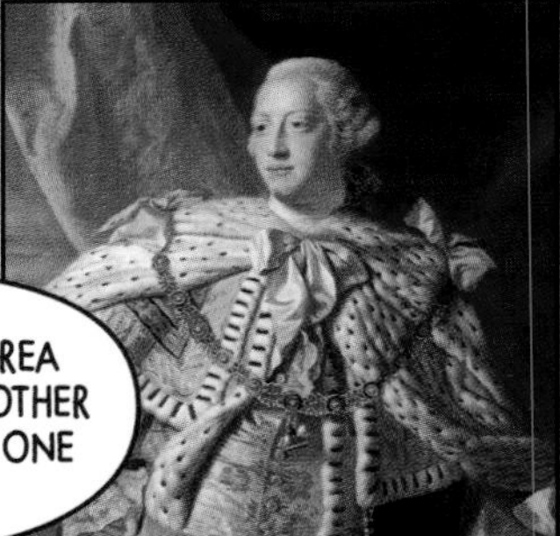
King George III

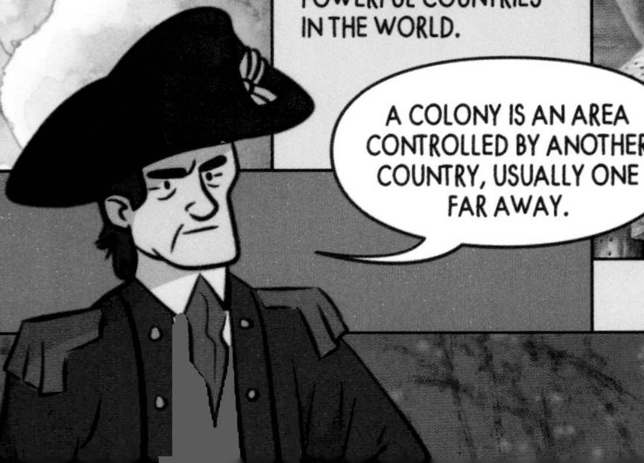
A COLONY IS AN AREA CONTROLLED BY ANOTHER COUNTRY, USUALLY ONE FAR AWAY.

GROWING ANGER

BUT BY THE MIDDLE OF THE 1700S, MANY AMERICAN COLONISTS WERE GETTING **FRUSTRATED WITH BRITAIN** AND KING GEORGE. THEY WANTED MORE CONTROL OVER LAWS IN THE COLONIES.

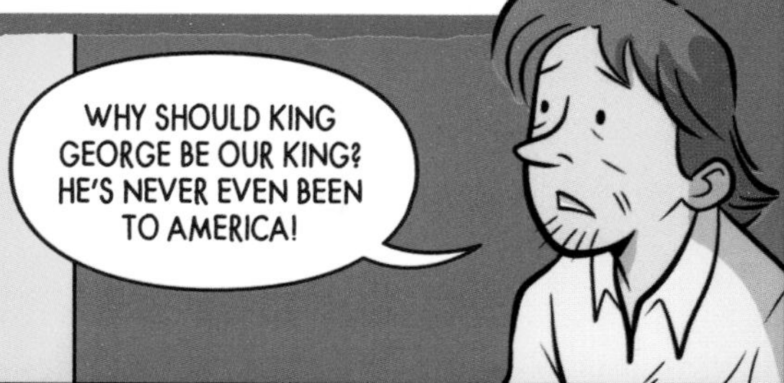
WHY SHOULD KING GEORGE BE OUR KING? HE'S NEVER EVEN BEEN TO AMERICA!

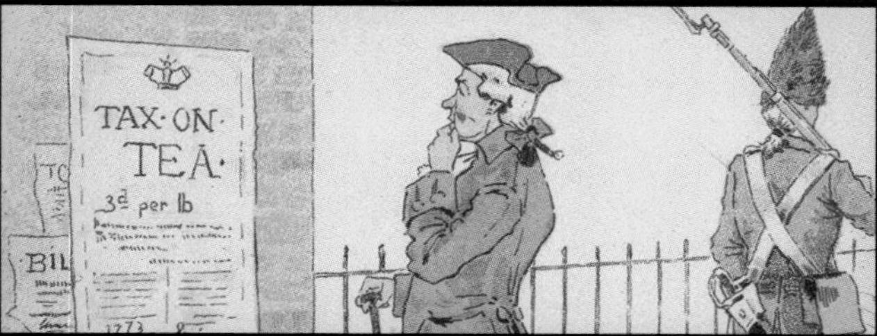
TAX·ON·
TEA·
3d per lb
1773

MANY COLONISTS ESPECIALLY HATED PAYING SO MANY **TAXES** TO BRITAIN—EXTRA MONEY ADDED ON TOP OF THE PRICES OF TEA, PAPER, STAMPS, AND OTHER IMPORTANT THINGS THAT THEY BOUGHT.

MANY AMERICANS WANTED THE COLONIES TO TEAR AWAY FROM ENGLAND AND BECOME A NEW, INDEPENDENT COUNTRY. THESE PEOPLE BECAME KNOWN AS **PATRIOTS**.

BUT MANY COLONISTS THOUGHT BREAKING AWAY WAS A BAD IDEA. BRITAIN HAD PROTECTED THE COLONIES AND HELPED THEM GROW. WHY GO TO WAR?

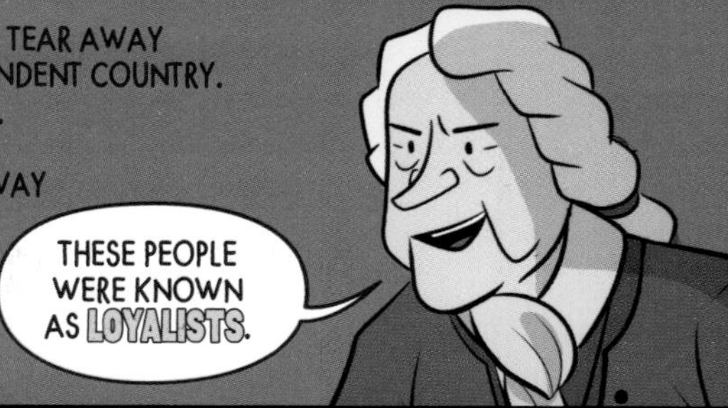
THESE PEOPLE WERE KNOWN AS LOYALISTS.

WAR ERUPTS

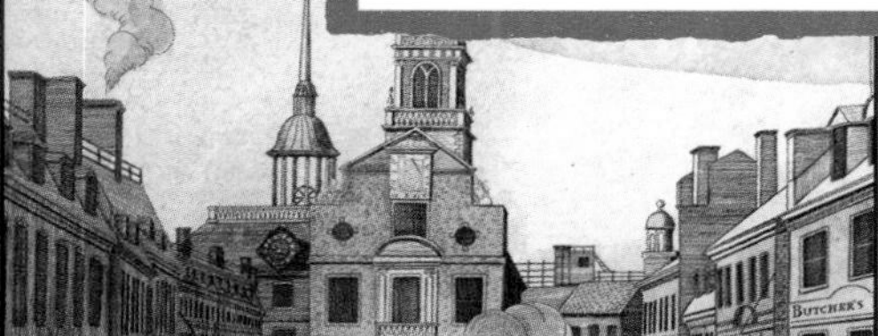
BUTCHER'S

IN 1770, A GROUP OF COLONISTS CONFRONTED SOME BRITISH SOLDIERS IN BOSTON AND BEGAN PELTING THEM WITH ROCKS AND SNOWBALLS. BRITISH SOLDIERS FIRED THEIR GUNS. FIVE COLONISTS WERE KILLED. THIS BECAME KNOWN AS THE **BOSTON MASSACRE**.

OVER THE NEXT FIVE YEARS, MORE AND MORE PEOPLE CAME TO BELIEVE THAT AMERICA SHOULD BE ITS OWN COUNTRY.

IN THE SPRING AND EARLY SUMMER OF 1775, THE FIRST **BATTLES** BETWEEN BRITISH TROOPS AND AMERICAN FIGHTERS BROKE OUT NEAR BOSTON: THE BATTLE OF LEXINGTON AND CONCORD AND THE BATTLE OF BUNKER HILL.

A LONG AND BLOODY WAR

GEORGE WASHINGTON BECAME COMMANDER OF THE NEW AMERICAN ARMY, WHICH WAS CALLED THE **CONTINENTAL ARMY**. HE HAD NEVER LED SUCH A LARGE ARMY BEFORE.

AMERICA'S FIRST SOLDIERS WERE FARMERS, SHOPKEEPERS, AND TEENAGE BOYS. FEW HAD ANY FIGHTING EXPERIENCE. THEY WORE THEIR OWN CLOTHES AND FOUGHT WITH WEAPONS THEY BROUGHT FROM HOME.

BRITAIN'S ARMY WAS ONE OF THE BIGGEST AND MOST MODERN IN THE WORLD. ITS SOLDIERS WERE KNOWN AS **REDCOATS**.

British soldiers in a Revolutionary War reenactment in Mount Vernon, Virginia, in 2017.

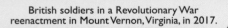

TO HELP THE BRITISH SOLDIERS, KING GEORGE BROUGHT IN THOUSANDS OF GERMAN FIGHTERS CALLED **HESSIANS**. THEY WERE KNOWN FOR THEIR STRENGTH, COURAGE, AND FEROCIOUS FIGHTING.

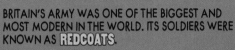

THE MOST COMMON WEAPON DURING THE REVOLUTIONARY WAR WAS A **MUSKET**. FOR EXTRA DEADLY FORCE, SOLDIERS CARRIED A LONG KNIFE CALLED A **BAYONET**, WHICH COULD BE ATTACHED TO THE END OF THE MUSKET.

NO WONDER THE AMERICANS LOST THE BATTLE OF BROOKLYN!

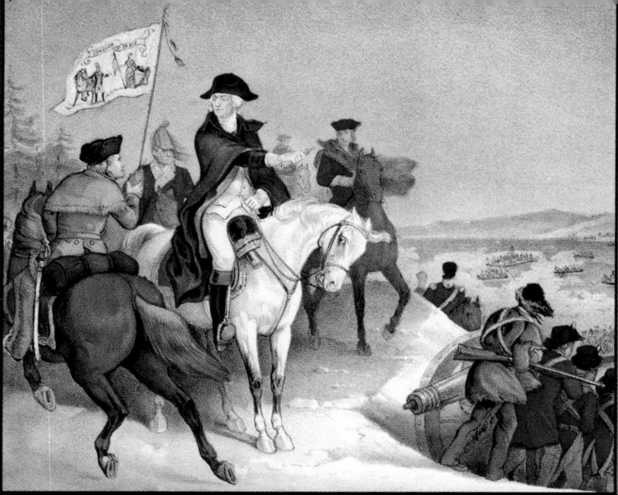

THE AMERICAN ARMY STRUGGLED AT FIRST. SOME PEOPLE BELIEVED GENERAL WASHINGTON SHOULD BE FIRED. BUT HE **DIDN'T QUIT**. HE LEARNED FROM HIS MISTAKES.

OVER THE NEXT EIGHT YEARS, THE AMERICAN REVOLUTION DRAGGED ON. THERE WERE HUNDREDS OF BATTLES, FROM THE SNOWY WOODS OF UPSTATE NEW YORK TO THE SWAMPS OF GEORGIA.

THERE WERE WINS AND LOSSES ON BOTH SIDES.

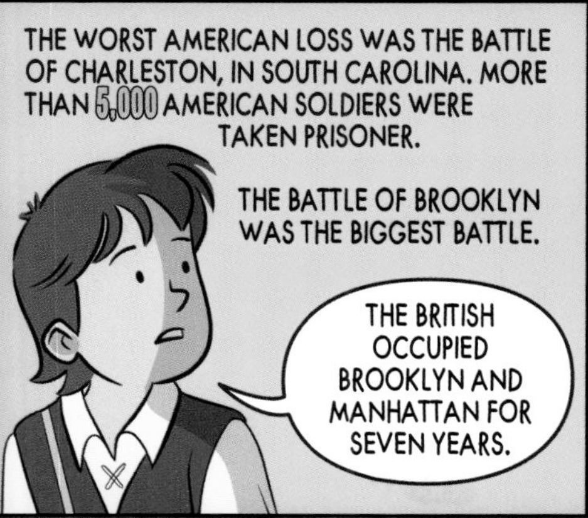
THE WORST AMERICAN LOSS WAS THE BATTLE OF CHARLESTON, IN SOUTH CAROLINA. MORE THAN 5,000 AMERICAN SOLDIERS WERE TAKEN PRISONER.
THE BATTLE OF BROOKLYN WAS THE BIGGEST BATTLE.
THE BRITISH OCCUPIED BROOKLYN AND MANHATTAN FOR SEVEN YEARS.

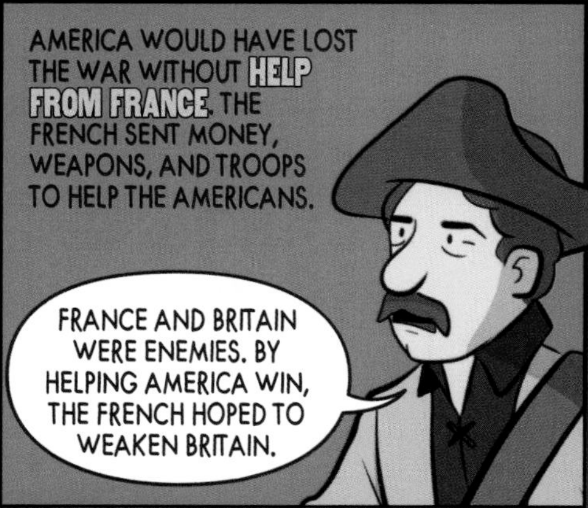
AMERICA WOULD HAVE LOST THE WAR WITHOUT HELP FROM FRANCE. THE FRENCH SENT MONEY, WEAPONS, AND TROOPS TO HELP THE AMERICANS.
FRANCE AND BRITAIN WERE ENEMIES. BY HELPING AMERICA WIN, THE FRENCH HOPED TO WEAKEN BRITAIN.

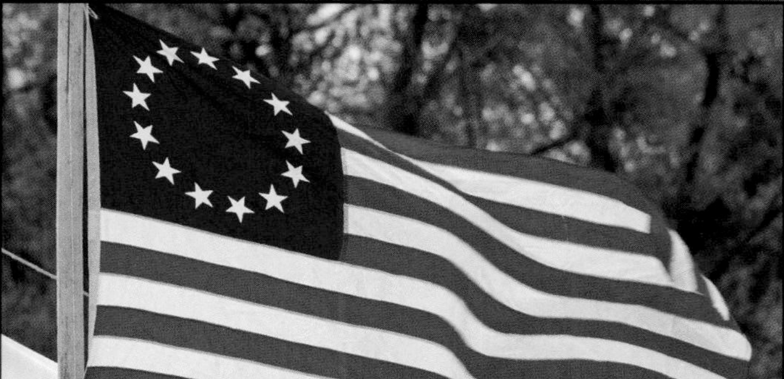

The first official American flag had thirteen stars to represent the thirteen colonies.

THE LAST BIG BATTLE OF THE WAR WAS THE **BATTLE OF YORKTOWN**, IN VIRGINIA, IN 1781. BUT IT TOOK TWO MORE YEARS BEFORE THE WAR ENDED.

THE AMERICANS WON THE WAR, AND THE NEW COUNTRY GREW AND THRIVED.

EQUALITY FOR ALL?

EVERY JULY 4, AMERICANS CELEBRATE INDEPENDENCE DAY. THIS HOLIDAY HONORS THE TIME IN 1776 WHEN LEADERS FROM THE THIRTEEN COLONIES SIGNED A DOCUMENT CALLED THE **DECLARATION OF INDEPENDENCE**.

IN CONGRESS. JULY 4, 1776.
The unanimous Declaration of the thirteen united States of America.

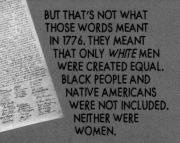

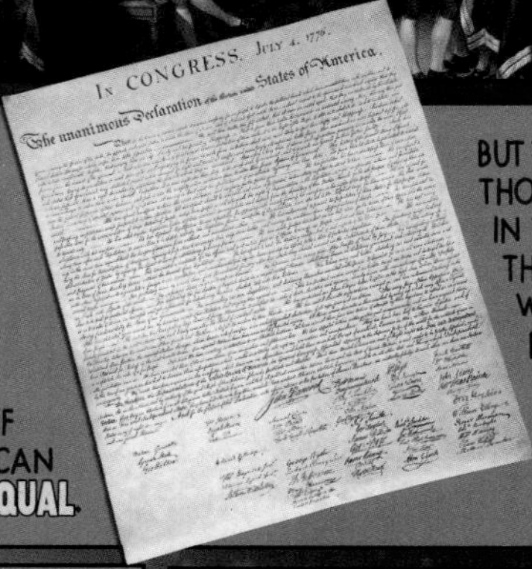

IT INFORMED KING GEORGE—AND THE WORLD—THAT THE THIRTEEN COLONIES WERE BECOMING AN INDEPENDENT NATION CALLED THE **UNITED STATES OF AMERICA**.

THE FIRST LINE OF THE DECLARATION OF INDEPENDENCE INCLUDES SOME OF THE MOST FAMOUS WORDS IN AMERICAN HISTORY: **ALL MEN ARE CREATED EQUAL**.

BUT THAT'S NOT WHAT THOSE WORDS MEANT IN 1776. THEY MEANT THAT ONLY *WHITE* MEN WERE CREATED EQUAL. BLACK PEOPLE AND NATIVE AMERICANS WERE NOT INCLUDED. NEITHER WERE WOMEN.

FROM AMERICA'S START AS A NEW NATION, THE **STRUGGLE FOR EQUAL RIGHTS** FOR ALL PEOPLE HAS CONTINUED.

BLACK MEN TECHNICALLY GAINED THE RIGHT TO VOTE IN 1870, THOUGH IN REALITY MANY WERE STILL DENIED ACCESS UNTIL THE 1960S.

WOMEN DIDN'T WIN THE RIGHT TO VOTE UNTIL 1920.

NATIVE AMERICANS WERE NOT GRANTED LEGAL CITIZENSHIP IN THE UNITED STATES UNTIL 1924.

Dr. Martin Luther King Jr. is a hero for leading the fight for equal rights for Black people.

US president Calvin Coolidge is photographed with members of Native tribes in 1925.

I WISH MA COULD VOTE

These women's suffrage activists are on a protest march, circa 1913.

AMERICAN HISTORY IS COMPLICATED. BUT TALKING HONESTLY ABOUT THE PAST IS IMPORTANT!